EARLY PRAISE FOR

THE AGE OF HEROES I: FIRST BORN

"Stueve delivers with a quick paced, character centered novel that will leave sci-fi readers begging for just one more page!"
    —*Caleb Narva, ELA teacher & writer*

***

"This visceral tale takes the reader on an absolute roller coaster and offers an ending with hope for humanity."
    —*Kitty Bardot, author of the* Burlesque River *series*

***

*"*First Born *weds the earth we know with a world we don't, and AE Stueve does so in a way that even a fantasy-averse reader like myself couldn't stop turning the pages to discover the connections between the two worlds. His ability to create relatable characters is a mainstay in his body of work and does not disappoint in this latest epic.*
    —*Julie Rowse, author of* Lies Jane Austen Told Me

***

"First Born *defies easy genre categorizing. Instead, Stueve has written a thrilling story that also serves as a field guide to all things radical and terrifying from our pre-internet childhoods."*
—*Carl Smith, author of* Cycle of a Rat

***

"A dark and action-packed send up to classic pulp fiction and pre-code comics with an 80's aesthetic. Murder! Aliens! Conspiracy! I had an excellent time from start to finish."
—*Jason Bustard, author of* Mira

First Born

The Age of Heroes #1
AE Stueve

Midnight Tide Publishing

Publishing by Midnight Tide Publishing

www.midnighttidepublishing.com

Cover illustrations, design, and interior formatting by Vanae Uteros

Author photo by Bryce Wetzler

1st edition 2025

Paperback ISBN: 978-1-964655-90-1

Harback ISBN: 978-1-964655-91-8

Midnight Tide
PUBLISHING

Contents

This book is dedicated to everyone who ever read a comic book
and thought, "This is awesome."

Chapter 1
Paperboy

IF RICKY COMPLAINED ABOUT the weather in the early springtime, he had no business calling himself a paperboy. Besides, despite the chill, it was beautiful. The red sun climbing over the horizon caused the temperature to grow more spring-like with each paper delivered. Also, this was fun.

All he could hear was Blondie's "Rapture" playing over his headphones and the joker card flipping through his bicycle tire spokes. He liked to pretend it made his hand-me-down Schwinn roar like his dad's motorcycle. It didn't. But he liked to pretend. Like the proverbial cherry on a delicious sundae, a slight breeze brought with it the fishy smell of the Missouri River, only about a mile or so away. It was a scent Ricky loved. It reminded him of sitting on the bank with his dad and his older brother, poles in the water and nothing on their minds. When Ricky thought about it, he realized this was the kind of morning you didn't think existed until you lived it.

It was a perfect jewel of a morning.

He would have laughed if he wasn't afraid of disturbing the balance. Instead, he only peddled on and smiled while Debbie Harry explained what rapture was all about.

At every trailer he had a newspaper for, he slowed down, grabbed a tightly rolled *Oakview Courier* from his bag, and whipped it at the front door. The fall before, Tucker, the slovenly paperboy manager, had told Ricky he no longer had to get the paper squarely on the front step.

"We don't care if the trailer park trash has to walk out to their yard to pick it up," he had said.

Ricky disagreed, partly because he was "trailer park trash" and partly because his dad had said that everyone loved having their newspaper right outside their door and that Tucker was only the paperboy manager because his uncle owned the paper. But there was more. Ricky prided himself on his arm. He knew he was going to be a varsity pitcher for West Oakview High by the time he was a sophomore. Eventually, he'd get a scholarship to Mizzou and hopefully play pro one day. He loved ball so much that he didn't even mind if he'd never make it out of the minors. With any luck and a lot of practice, though, he would.

With that thought, he tossed a copy of *Oakview Courier* on Mr. and Mrs. Welker's porch. That smack as it landed right on the cement step outside their front door was music, like a baseball hitting a catcher's mitt. Ricky's pride grew to bursting when he spied the front-page headline practically shouting upward: OAKVIEW METEOR CELEBRATION TONIGHT WILL BE LARGER THAN LAST SUMMER'S FAIR.

"Yes," he whispered as he peddled on to the faint musical yapping of Frick, Frack, and Freak, the Welkers' rat terriers. The front-page headline pointing upward where everyone could read made Ricky feel like more of a success. To his ears, those dogs were a cheering crowd. He pretended to be the no-hit pitcher he one day would be and waved his cap at an imaginary crowd.

His arm was growing weary, though. He shoved his cap back over his mess of a dishwater blond mullet and peddled forward. His route was long because no one wanted to deliver papers to Oakview Lanes. To be fair, Ricky knew that in many ways, the trailer park had earned a bad reputation. There were some unsavory folks about. But his dad often said, "There are folks like that everywhere, and most of them aren't bad just to be bad but are bad because society gave them no other choice."

Ricky had never really been sure what that meant, but he did know that everyone he delivered papers to paid their bill on time and was nice to him. He thought it was because their newspapers were always close enough to their front door so that they didn't have to leave their trailer to pick them up. Good or bad, people who subscribed to *Oakview Courier* enjoyed having their news right there at their door waiting for them every morning. They didn't want to traipse across their dew-soaked lawns to pick it up and find that it was as wet as the grass it had bedded down in for hours. Or, even worse, they didn't want to discover that their newspaper was lost in a sea of unseasonable snow. They didn't want to go on a scavenger hunt to find today's news, and the paperboy should care about that, no matter what Tucker said.

Ricky checked his red Snoopy watch. It was almost six. He had about ten minutes to finish before the sun came up. He was going to make it, even if it killed him. Ricky always began his route with the Normans' trailer right next door to his, which was at the far southeast corner of the park, near the massive empty field the city owned but did nothing with, the field that everyone knew was a five-mile-wide barrier between the town proper and the dirty trailer park. East of that was the river and west of the park was the highway. It was like a weird little kingdom of freaks that Ricky was, on some level, proud to be a part of. He made his way up and down the through roads as he headed for the street closest to the highway that led to Oakview. After that, he would sometimes pedal past the laundromat at the entrance and chat with groundskeepers Linc and Buster if they were awake. Maybe eat one of their donuts. Then he'd head home.

In a place like Oakview Lanes, routine was a gift.

As he approached the street closest to the highway, the breeze grew angrier. Winter was giving its last best effort to stay alive. Ricky shivered beneath the baggy West Oakview High sweatshirt that his older brother, Ronny, had gifted him for Christmas years ago, before he had graduated high school, before he had run off to fight in a jungle half a world away, and before he had disappeared and been presumed dead. Had Ricky been more concerned with his surroundings instead of thinking about his brother's dog tags that his mom wore around her neck, he would have known that his shiver hadn't been caused by the breeze alone. It was also his own animalistic sense of danger warning him that he was being watched.

***

It was the baseball cap that did it.

The Lonely One had intended to wait for nightfall. The meteor shower was going to be such an amazing show for the stagnants that everyone would be preoccupied with what they saw in the sky. If that wasn't enough to take their attention away from what was happening right here on Earth, the extravagant celebration the city was throwing would do it. The morning DJ droned on about the festival from The Lonely One's station wagon speakers. The mayor of Oakview had scheduled a fair in the town park with a band, food trucks, vendors, games, rides—the whole, as they say, enchilada. It was spring break after all and the children were out of school and the children were antsy and the children needed a distraction.

But they weren't the only ones who'd be distracted. Not really. It would be their cornhusking hick parents with their heads craned back like they were made of rubber and their slack jaws opened in awe at the meteors. As though falling rocks were anything to be excited over.

The children would be running around like unleashed dogs. And The Lonely One knew he'd have his pick of the litter. All of those pathetic little stagnants with their pathetic little lives would be entranced with the light show and the festivities. If he was patient, he would wait and use the festivities as cover to slither and shift around until he found what he needed: a child. There were certain parts that only a child could provide.

That baseball cap though. He saw it and knew he couldn't wait for the night to hide his kidnapping. He couldn't wait for the meteors. He couldn't wait for the celebration. He had to have this child and he had to have this child now.

Still, it would have been fun to do it during the celebration that his taxes had helped pay for.

The prospect of stealing a child from a crowded event full of adults looking at the sky when they should have been looking after their children was so enticing it left the phantom taste of sweet saltwater taffy in his mouth, his favorite. Taking a child from that facetiously named celebration of nothing more than overheated rocks burning away in the atmosphere was so ironic that he would have driven right past that dirty little trailer park without a second thought to the paperboy, something he had done more times than he could count.

If it hadn't been for that baseball cap.

It cut through the Nebraska morning like a beacon.

It was perfect.

When he saw the cherub-face under the cap, the bag of newspapers over his shoulder, the way he pedaled madly on his bicycle, and the ear-to-ear smile, The Lonely One had to have him. Ignorant little animal. Ignorant little prey. Those giant black headphones over his ears only added to his charm.

The Lonely One had to have him and his cap and his hoodie and his blue jeans and his black high tops. The boy was like something out of a Norman Rockwell painting, magically slipped into 1981 as a gift to him. Damn his plan.

He had to have the boy.

He had to.

Now.

Normally he was not this impulsive. He coordinated his efforts. He calculated all possible outcomes. He made it impossible to be caught during the act. He made it impossible to be caught after the act. His work with the stagnants was just that important. How many years had he spent in the shadows the stagnants were terrified of? How many unsolved abductions, murders, and rapes had he committed in his time on this rock out here on the edge of space? He had lost count. But he knew he was legendary and the only way to remain so was to remain secret. He had to remain secret if he wanted to continue his studies. The only way to remain secret was to plan, plot, and dissect every possible outcome before he took action.

But that cap on that boy was something special. How had he never noticed him? He'd been driving from his house a few miles away to his daily life in Oakview for years. He shrugged, turning into the trailer park. It didn't really matter that the boy had never caught his eye before, because today he definitely had.

And today he would have him.

He pulled into the trailer park and cut the inane morning DJ off in mid-sentence as he said something about the upcoming meteor shower that Oakview was strategically placed to enjoy. He rolled down his window as he let up on the gas, creeping toward the paperboy. There was nothing now. Only him. Only the boy.

It was nothing special, just a simple red and white Nebraska Cornhuskers baseball cap. Banged up and faded, it had some personality, but nothing The Lonely One hadn't seen before. The way it sat on the boy's head, like a battered old crown—it was like something out of a comic book or movie. Did this small, poor child from the trailer park have a personal assistant and design team who made him perfect for the day? The Lonely One laughed at the thought and turned his radio back on. "Come Sail Away" played softly from the speakers.

The Lonely One loved Styx.

Not as much as the cap though.

Not as much as the boy.

Stars twinkled out in the dark blue sky above them. The card stuck in the bicycle's rear tire spokes clicked and clacked so loudly that The Lonely One was able to drive right up to him, slow down, auto lock his doors, reach out through his open window, and with a hand like a bear claw, grab the child by his arm, and pull.

The bike fell with an unfortunate clatter and the boy's headphones toppled off his head. A scuffed joker card fluttered away in the wind.

A look of recognition flashed across the boy's face and his lips parted, ready to scream.

A quick hand over the boy's mouth and a point to the sparkling black ax in the backseat made him as silent as the grave.

"Take off the bag and throw it out the window," The Lonely One said softly before he hit the gas.

"But—"

A fist to the cheek shut down the boy's defiance.

He screamed.

Another fist.

He whimpered.

A third fist.

He sniffled and reached for his face. An obnoxious red watch caught the sun's glare and hurt The Lonely One's eyes.

The Lonely One drew back his hand again.

The boy flinched.

Somewhere nearby tiny dogs yipped.

"The bag," The Lonely One repeated.

With tears, snot, and blood trying their best to ruin what the fresh bruises could not, the boy removed the bag and moved to throw it out the window.

"Wait," The Lonely One said. "I'd like a copy."

The boy pulled a paper from the bag and, with a shaky hand, offered it to The Lonely One.

"Thank you," The Lonely One said, and meant it. "I'll pay you when we get home," he added, taking it from him and placing it on his lap.

The boy nodded, all sense gone, replaced, it seemed, by a wall of fear.

"I am called The Lonely One and I am going to kill you," The Lonely One said, smiling wide at the boy to show him rows of teeth that grew sharper as his mouth grew wider and wider until it was no longer anything resembling human.

Faced with an actual monster, the boy was struck silent.

The Lonely One pressed the buttons on his door to roll the windows back up. Beside him, the boy sat dazed. In the battle of flight, fight, or freeze, or fawn, freeze had won out completely. The Lonely One was used to that sort of thing. What he wasn't used to was seeing it in daylight. He usually did this at night. He had to admit, this made him a little nervous. But when he looked at that cap, still somehow balanced on the boy's implausible little head, he knew he had done the right thing.

He turned right on the highway and headed back home without incident. Unfortunately, this had changed things. He was going to be a little late to work today. After his shift, he was going to have to come home and figure out the best way to kill the boy and get the body off his property. Or maybe he'd get the boy off his property and then kill him. Or maybe he'd kill him and then go about his business of killing another child later tonight. It would take some serious thinking to figure out just what to do.

But it would be worth it.

***

OAKVIEW METEOR CELEBRATION TONIGHT WILL BE LARGER THAN LAST SUMMER'S FAIR

Oakview's Meteor Fair looks to be largest public gathering in local area.

By Charlie McKinstrey, staff writer

MAYOR GREYSON ROSE and the Oakview City Council decided to have a party to kick off spring. They came to this decision months ago when the University of Nebraska at Lincoln announced that between 8 p.m. and 2 a.m. tonight, the ten-mile radius around Oakview would be the "perfect place" to sky watch an unprecedented meteor shower. The shower, known to astronomers as the Northern Ignotus, is made up of meteors that appear to have broken off from the asteroid belt 111.5 million miles from Earth. Though that is quite the trip, Rose and the city council believe the meteors' destination will be worth it, at least for Oakview.

Willa Cather Park is lined with pavilions and trailers selling everything from homemade tchotchkes to corn dogs and funnel cakes. There is also a Ferris wheel, bumper cars, and a slew of other fair games for the young and young at heart. Local musicians will be performing throughout the day and evening in the park's center pavilion. But perhaps the most interesting aspect of Oakview's Meteor Fair is the placement of the portable, coin operated viewer binoculars all over the park. For a single quarter, fair goers will get a minute to look through the devices for a close-up view of the meteor shower. These viewers will be monitored by Oakview's own police force to ensure that everyone with a quarter and the desire to do so, gets their chance to see the meteors close-up as they fall from the heavens.

But that does not begin until the meteor shower begins. At 9 a.m. The fair will officially open to the public with all of the above activities up and running. The mayor, for one, hopes to see people there as soon as possible.

"Everyone from Omaha to Lincoln and beyond is invited when the gates open," said Rose. "We have a lot to do even before the meteor shower starts!"

He believes this fair will kick start the city's plans to revitalize the outdoors.

"With this festival, we look to bring the love of community and nature back to our town and surrounding areas," Rose said. "With video games and TV keeping our children inside no matter the weather, we wanted to do something that could pull them away from their screens."

It is not only the children that Rose and the city council are concerned about though, for it is the parents who will bring the revenue.

"We aren't a ghost town, we aren't a dying city, or anything like that," said Councilwoman Erica Straithaven. "We want to make sure that doesn't happen to Oakview either, which is why we are having this big push for more outdoor events. This is only the beginning."

For a full list of prices and festivities around the Meteor Fair, see page E3.

Chapter 2
The Fall of Essa

"TAKE SOLACE IN THE fact that the Essan people will never be able to repay you, Aur,"Jon'Oh said. His voice quivered. Sweat dripped from his matted peppery hair.

"This is the fault of the Essan people," Aurora huffed.

"*I* will never be able to repay you then," Jon'Oh said softly.

He looked away from the woman he loved and hung his head before a glowing Technoid screen. It bulged like a tumor from a tubal, rotting podium in the center of his lab. Though yellowish and porous with infection, the screen stood defiant against its inevitable end. Putrefied viridescent nectar bled from a crack in its rotted exoskeleton. Jon'Oh touched the screen and noticed the Technoid's blood clinging to his fingers like a disease. He wiped it on his tattered lab coat and gagged on its stench.

Like the lab around it, the podium had once been beautiful, a masterwork of pure Essan biological technology, a Technoid whose only purpose was to obey, elaborate, and assist—a symbol of all that Essan science could create. Now this Technoid, like most other Technoids created by Essans and like the planet of Essa itself, was a pathetic, dying thing, a symbol of his people's arrogance. The Technoid whined like a wounded animal, its rotting rigid flesh dripping from beneath its exoskeleton. It was once a gleaming, fluid silver lined with the brightest blue veins. Now it was a pain-ridden monstrosity. Particles of ruin crumbled from it like dandruff—from the Technoid walls, from the Technoid building, from everything.

Without warning, all structures in the lab save one shimmering platinum wall grumbled as they fought to survive, reminding Jon'Oh of the urgency of their situation.

"All the Technoids will be gone soon," Jon'Oh said. "The buildings will start to fall." He shot nervous glances around the room as cracks ripped through three of the four walls, the ceiling, and the floor. As the Technoid building heaved its last sigh of life around them, Jon'Oh stumbled. "We have to make the final preparations now, Aurora," he said as he balanced on wobbly legs, waiting for more cracks to appear. He gulped. "Now."

"Please stop." Aurora hugged herself tightly. Her back was to a floor-to-ceiling window that pulsed with feverish heat. She stared at Jon'Oh. Tears welled in the almond shaped eyes that covered half her face, and her dual eyelids fluttered. "Come with me," she said. Her words shattered into cries of shock as the ceiling sagged above her and several floating orb lights popped. Their iridescent guts splashed at Aurora's feet.

"Aurora, I—"

"No!" Aurora's nasal slits quivered as she failed to suppress a sob. "Come with me!" She sniffled and wiped tears from her sharp cheeks and snot from her smooth upper lip, hating herself for how pathetic she felt, how helpless. This was no way for an Ascendant to act, to feel. She was a decorated peace officer, not some broken-hearted podling. But this hurt, this hurt so much.

She ran her hands over the sleek gray skin on her hairless head, trying to think of something—anything—to make Jon'Oh change his mind and throw this plan to the wind where it belonged. Now that the end was here, now that they had to actually do what they had been planning for so long, she didn't think she could go through with it. Not without him. She couldn't leave Jon'Oh to die, no matter the reason. The almost imperceptible narrow gills on her long neck flitted as she suppressed another sob.

Sky and land burned outside the window, demanding that she go through with it, screaming that she needed to. She refused to look, keeping her eyes locked on Jon'Oh.

"I'm sorry, Aur. You know I wish I could." Jon'Oh crossed the room to her with sudden purpose, as though the world was not ending around them. "I wish we all could, but it's too late." One hand reached up to each of her shoulders and he gently turned her so that she faced the terror with him. They were two-hundred sixty stories up in a Technoid science spire over the Essan capital city of Chall. "Look. Please."

The towering, glimmering structures of ancient Essa were nightmare memories of what they once had been. Technoid buildings of shattered bone and charred cartilage clawed toward the sky, broken fingers desperately reaching for a life that was already gone.

"It's like this everywhere," he said.

The people of Essa, with their mad race for perfection, had invited Death to this planet and she was an angry, red god. The rotting, burning smell of her leaked into everything they had created, leaked into them.

"Jon'Oh, I can't." She spun away from what she saw as if turning from Death could solve anything.

He forced her around so he could look up at her. She was so tall and thin that she seemed almost fragile. Jon'Oh knew she was far from it. Her gray skin sparkled like platinum, and it was just as strong. But it had always been her black eyes that captured him. Slightly slanted and able to see through to his soul, it was her eyes he had fallen in love with before he had fallen in love with any other part of her. He could lose himself in their infinite dark depths and be at peace. They were as eternal as the cosmos and held all the secrets he wanted to know.

More tears dripped down Aurora's cheeks, and she found comfort in the contrast of her four smooth fingers laced within his five rough ones, his slightly warmer skin, the almost imperceptible layer of hair covering most of it—his touch magic, always magic, even now at the end of all things.

"Stop," he whispered. "Please, Aurora."

"Come with me," she pleaded, letting go of his hands and reaching for his face. Despair barreled over her as she ran her thin fingers through his wiry beard. "We can hide. We can plant all the DNA somewhere else. The cosmos is vast!"

"A Whitley and an Essan together, hiding from your fellow Ascendants? From the entire UCA? Even in the NetNeg we'd stick out." He laughed but it was elusive, vague. "It wouldn't work. You know Earth is the only viable candidate for the Helix Needles. We've studied it for ages. It's not part of the UCA but it's not in the NetNeg either. And the people there are close enough to Essan. It's perfect. Or as perfect as we'll get, Aur—"

"I know all that!" she shouted. "But there has to be another—"

"There's not!" he matched her pitch, his words somehow both firm and afraid. Lips trembling, his chin fell to his chest. "There's not," he whispered. "I'm sorry."

"Please, Jon'Oh, please . . ." Aurora trailed off, grasping for words as she felt the warmth of his skin on her fingertips, the edge of the cheekbones below his beard, and the subtle arch of his nose. "Please look at me."

When Jon'Oh spoke again, his voice had thinned into a hard scientific line. "I can't," he said and pulled himself from her to look out the window. It was as though he had forced himself away and observed from afar; this was only an experiment, nothing more. "Someone has to manually input the coordinates for the HyperRift from here so you can escape without the Ascendancy tracing you. You know all of this, Aur. You just said so—"

"Peel could—"

"If we have Peel do it, the ExoNet will sense it and you'll be followed." His voice was a muted monotone. His back was still to her.

Aurora's replied with silence.

Jon'Oh's shoulders slumped. "I'm sorry," he said. "We've gone over it a thousand times."

"No. No!" She pushed back at his stoicism, reaching for him. "Make DC do it!"

He took her hands once more. "DC can't," he explained with a patience reserved only for her. "If he knew the coordinates, the Ascendancy could trace them through the ExoNet faster than Peel. Even after we're gone, they could find it in whatever tendrils remain. Techs are monitoring Essa right now! Aurora, you know this. You know all of this! Please stop making me say it again!"

"I've talked with Peel." Aurora's desperation forced her to ignore Jon'Oh. Plans spat out that could never work. "She can reproduce if we go to her home world. She can birth you a Correlative that can hide you and we can find another planet somewhere, please—"

"Aurora." Jon'Oh leaned in, locking his eyes to hers.

"Jon'Oh, I—" Her words broke like the world around them. She leaned in as well, bending slightly so that their foreheads touched. When she felt his skin on hers, she couldn't suppress a shudder. He placed one hand on her chest, over Peel, the Correlative that acted as

Aurora's second skin and silent sister. He slid his fingers across the bright white starburst over Aurora's left breast. His fingers were so warm, so comforting.

Knowing how much Aurora enjoyed this, Peel spread away from Jon'Oh's hand so that there was nothing between it and her body. The Correlative would not interfere with this moment. Jon'Oh's touch was soft, but his hands were those of a man who had worked with them most of his life.

Aurora sobbed once more and Peel slid back into place as Jon'Oh let his hand fall.

"This Correlative you wear is the symbol of a protector. The star says it all," Jon'Oh said. "You cannot wear it and run and hide. I cannot wear it at all." He found her hands again. "Even if I could, we both know your plan wouldn't work. Pelora is the most highly protected planet in the cosmos . . . and for good reason," he added.

"There has to be another way," Aurora begged. "There has to be."

An explosion outside rumbled through the lab. Tables fell, delicate instruments crumbled, the floor cracked. Walls groaned. Dust rained. Technoids melted away, whining and wailing as they died. Somewhere outside a shriek broke through the sounds of barely living buildings falling apart, and the sky rumbled its death tolls. Instinctively Aurora and Jon'Oh pulled each other closer, waiting for another shriek. Jon'Oh felt Peel reach out herself, tiny black tentacles of her powerful flesh touching the fine hairs standing in fear on his forearms.

"You know there isn't." Jon'Oh pulled away, steadying himself. He pointed out the window. "Look at the sky, Aurora, it burns my eyes. It's happening as I predicted, as my mother predicted . . . only sooner. We do not have time for this. Earth is the only hope for saving my people."

Aurora closed her clear secondary protective eyelids and studied the burning horizon. Its violence was almost beautiful.

"Why save them?" Aurora asked. "This is their fault." Her cheeks darkened and her eyes became slits.

Jon'Oh took a deep breath. "You know as well as I do that it's more complicated than that." He motioned out the window. "The people didn't want this; it was the leaders." His hand fell, defeated. "But if you're there on Earth, if you're monitoring the new Essans, you will be able to prevent anything like this from happening again and maybe, just maybe you'll be able to change inter-rim laws, Aurora."

"This can't be happening. I didn't think it would be so soon."

"If only the Essan High Council would've listened to me, to my mother. To those who came before her." Jon'Oh turned to the only unscathed wall in the room. Forcing his regret away, he cleared his throat. "DC, is the new 'Cyclo almost ready?"

A large masculine face emerged from the untouched wall. Fluid yet statuesque, it spoke with a humming, electric, monotone. "It is Friend-Jon'Oh, but I must once again protest. According to the records in Talmund's Legal Library of Annam, if this plan were to be discovered, punishment for you alone could be a triple postponed life sentence in the gas quarries of Nadar. And Ascendant Friend-Aurora," DC's clear eyes turned to Aurora, "could lose more than her freedom. Though the SoloPen that could become her new home would be bad enough, there would be so much more. Her position as an officer in the Ascendancy, her inter-rim passport and exploration visa, all records of her true name could be eradicated from cosmotic history, and any hope of ever—"

"It's a good thing I'll be dead soon, then," Jon'Oh interrupted. "And Aurora won't be caught."

DC frowned. "Very well, Friend-Jon'Oh," he said as, from the wall next to his face emerged a small, platinum twenty-sided DieCyclo. Each side held between one and twenty blue hued indents. A translucent liquid coated it so that it gleamed with newborn freshness. "It is calibrated to open only when one of Essan DNA touches it."

"Blue circles inside a sea of platinum, DC? The Twenty Chances. Nice touch."

"The Essan symbols and history will live, not only inside this DieCyclo, but upon it as well."

A hidden love quivered below DC's robotic Technoid voice and it broke Aurora's heart. The few Technoids who could speak, rarely did because they knew how unnerving their strange, robotic words sounded to biological ears. But DC, like his creator Jon'Oh, did what he had to. Even as his family was dying around him, he helped Essa survive.

"Thank you, old friend," Jon'Oh said, and motioned for Aurora to take the DieCyclo from the wall. "You have the Helix Needles?"

Aurora nodded, placing the DieCyclo in a pouch on her belt with a collection of Helix Needles. "All of them. Jon'Oh, you—"

"I wish we could've saved more." He wiped a hand across his eyes. "And the coordinates above Essa?"

Aurora placed a finger on her temple. "All here." Tears streamed down her cheeks like rain. "Locked from Peel."

Something boomed in the sky; a wave of destruction followed. It gouged the distant terrain like a monstrous shovel and forced the scent of burnt plant and animal flesh through the crumbling building. On the edge of the city, more structures collapsed. The lab creaked as if on a weak hinge, lights shattered, DC faded back into the wall as voices throughout Chall cried out in unison. It was a hopeless sound, loud but fearful in the face of imminent death. It was the strange sound of panic and resignation, a weak thing hiding behind a mask of noise.

"Jon'Oh," Aurora cried softly.

"Stop, please," Jon'Oh said. "I can't—"

"Come with me!" she demanded. "Come with me!"

"You know I can't," Jon'Oh said. "I have no choice."

"You do!" she shouted, her voice cracking with a petulant sound she abhorred hearing from her own mouth.

"Shhh." Jon'Oh took her into his arms. "We are doing something great, Aurora. We are saving my people. Not even the Alliance could do that."

"They could," she said angrily. "They won't."

He pulled her face down to his and kissed her. "This is the only way." Another explosion splashed a burning light across the sky.

The world rumbled. Death let loose a glutton's laugh as it ate Essa.

"Jon'Oh—"

"Go! Now!" Jon'Oh said, pulling away from her and backing toward DC's wall. "I will send you Earth's coordinates from inside DC. The signal will be protected but only for a few seconds. I should be safe there . . . until it's done."

"Jon'Oh, please, no!" She struggled to hold him. Peel stretched as Jon'Oh pulled from her. But even the Correlative could not penetrate DC's wall so easily. As Jon'Oh sank into it, disappearing behind the liquid-like substance, it hardened against any invading force.

"I'm sorry, my love," Jon'Oh said. "DC, keep her away," he added as he disappeared from Aurora's life forever. "The timing has to be perfect."

"I am also sorry," DC's voice sounded throughout the room, that quiver of sorrow in his otherwise robotic tone returned, crumbling the pieces of Aurora's already broken heart. "I find this plan foolish but cannot betray Friend-Jon'Oh. You must leave, Friend-Aurora. The HyperRift will be small and if you do not reach Earth during the scheduled meteor shower, your presence could be known despite all of our precautions, not only by the Ascendancy Technicians observing Essa's Fall, but by the primitive inhabitants of Earth itself or even the Gray Star Ascendancy of the Outer Rim. None of this can happen if you are to have the time to do this correctly."

"No," Aurora said, charging the wall.

A laser blasted, barely missing Aurora. A CorreBlade grew like a sharpened tentacle on the end of Aurora's right hand. She swung.

"You cannot penetrate my wall in the time you have left before Essa is gone. We have used all remaining Technoid power to build it, Friend-Aurora."

"I can try!" Aurora's anger and sadness found a unified front on the end of the CorreBlade as it scraped against the wall. Sparks flew through the collapsing room.

DC fired again, this shot glanced Aurora's shoulder. Peel rippled around the wound, healing it as quickly as she could.

Aurora ignored the pain and sliced again.

Peel sent painkilling nanites to eat up any discomfort Aurora felt.

"I will do my best not to hurt you," DC said, another, stronger blast, fired at the floor where Aurora stood. It crumbled below her and she stumbled away.

"Jon'Oh!" Her cry carried on the wings of pain.

"But I will force you to leave. You do not have much time to escape. You do not have much time before Essa is gone. If you are anywhere near the planet when it ends, you will be gone with her, with us. But you are not going to die with us, correct Friend-Aurora? You are going to escape and see this foolish plan to its end."

"But . . . Jon'Oh . . ." she whispered, hanging her head. Peel absorbed the CorreBlade as Aurora's hands touched the wall. It was cold. Lifeless.

"Friend-Aurora, there is no other way," DC said, not unkindly.

Crying, Aurora nodded.

Her arms hung limply at her side as her nearly invisible lips trembled and her nasal slits flared, suppressing another sob.

Peel flowed like living liquid, covering every bit of Aurora's exposed skin, her hands and feet, and finally her face. All of her features now hidden behind the black Correlative, Aurora clenched her fists and struck a frightening image in the crumbling room, a living shadow, or a chunk of space, molded into the form of a slender Whitley. The only bright spots on her were her two white eye lenses, the shining white starburst on her chest, and the matching belt at her waist. Running from her own sadness, Aurora charged the window and smashed through, sending a great explosion of shards into the sky. The stench of a world dying rushed at her on a fiery wind as she flew up and up and up.

In a matter of moments, the Correlative powered Aurora through the raging red sky, over the broiling black clouds, and beyond every Essan sphere past the welkin into the vastness of space. She was a black blur that any who saw knew signified the end.

Jon'Oh's voice sounded in Aurora's ear through her Correlative communicator Peel had embedded there long ago, "I've done it. The 'Rift will shimmer any second, if you flew straight and true, you should see it soon. All you have to do is open it. I'm sending Earth's coordinates now." He cleared his throat. "This is my last communication. I love you, Aur."

"I love you too," Aurora replied softly.

She saw the familiar flutter in the dark matter of space that indicated a HyperRift. It shimmered as Aurora reached out, ignoring her own tears while the Correlative stretched from her fingertips to form micro thin blades. She swung her arms, slicing an "X" before her, creating a small HyperRift Window. She felt the vacuum as a great white light spilled forth.

"Stop!" another voice sounded through her Correlative communicator.

Shocked, Aurora spun away from the window to face a small contingent of Ascendant Officers. Though their bodies were almost hidden in the darkness of their Correlatives, their white lenses, and matching starbursts and belts all shone brightly. She could not tell who they were but knew some of them must have been friends. Peel shivered, causing her to do the same.

The HyperRift yanked at her.

"How?" Aurora said. "How did you—"

An Ascendant sent a frigid, silent CorreBeam blasting through the darkness. The pouch on Aurora's belt where the Helix Needles were stored exploded. Countless needles sprayed into the darkness. No longer protected by her Correlative, they burst in the cold vacuum of space. Aurora reached out for whatever she could grab as another beam fired toward her and the light pulled her into the HyperRift window.

"Follow her!" she heard through the communicator. "We need—" The voice died as the window slammed shut around Aurora.

She found herself tumbling through the blinding whiteness, desperate and afraid, her hands clenched around two small Helix Needles and a DieCyclo, her heart seated on the hope that Earth was the perfect untouched jewel Jon'Oh thought it to be.

***

TALMUND'S SCIENTIFIC ADVANCEMENT INDEX
BRIEF ENTRY: EXONET

- The ExoNet is the cosmos wide communication device used to send and receive information planet-to-planet, system-to-system, and galaxy-to-galaxy.

- Additionally, on all UCA planets, it is the primary form of communication from lifeform-to-lifeform there.

- In the NetNeg (those habited planets outside of the Rim system), there is no connection to the ExoNet, making the planets there essentially cut off from the wider cosmos.

- The ExoNet uses a system of interconnected energy nodes that act as a net around the cosmos keeping information available. Without it, all communication signals (audio, video, or otherwise) would eventually find their way to the end of the cosmos.

- Invented by Leerodite Dr. Therumomium in 1.23776.4AST, the ExoNet has been programmed to grow with the Rims. When new planets are added to the UCA, a team of Leerodite engineers arrives planet-side and brings the ExoNet connection to the people.

Status

- Official Creation Date: 1.23776.4AST

- Inventor: Doctor   Therumomium
  (1.23742.4-1.23800.4AST)

- Leerodite Accessibility Status: Common

- UCA Accessibility Status: Common

- UCA Patent Registration: 87462.90l-1.42/Leerodite/

Top Factual Documentation

- ExoNet: Travel The Stars From Home

- ExoNet: Sleeping On The Net

- ExoNet: Behind The Scenes In A Leerodite Net Factory

- ExoNet: No Net In The NetNeg

- ExoNet: Turn It Off Then Turn It On Again: The Mysteries
  Of The ExoNet

Top Opinions/Entertainment

- ExoNet: Music For The UCA

- ExoNet: Hope Signals

- ExoNet: Vee Wired Plus

- ExoNet: Sleeping Showman

- ExoNet: Jump Time X

For more information and for answers to specific questions, please see **"Talmund's Scientific Advancement Index Complete Entry: ExoNet."**

***

TALMUND'S LEGAL LIBRARY BRIEF ENTRY: SOLOPEN

- A classified group of scientists, architects, and artists created the SoloPen as a form of punishment for criminals who commit only the most serious inter-rim crimes.

- Situated in isolated locations throughout the cosmos, SoloPens are impenetrable, self-sustaining, solitary confinement satellites.

- Powered by the prisoner through a series of menial labors, SoloPens are completely cut off from the ExoNet and have no form of outgoing communication.

- Incoming communication can only be done through waves scheduled and approved by the Ascendancy.

- Each SoloPen has a series of rotating Red Star guards who

monitor the prisoner residing within for signs of mental fatigue, suicidal ideation, physical illness, and/or attempted escape.

- The use of SoloPens, particularly in life sentences or deferred life sentences, has been highly contested for countless Annam Standard Years.

Top Factual Documentation

- SoloPen: A History

- SoloPen: One Man's Immobile Journey

- SoloPen: The Construction and Distribution of SoloPens Throughout the Cosmos

- SoloPen: Under Construction: The Ultimate Punishment for 99.99% of Lifeforms

- SoloPen: Punishment in the Pen: A Life Inside Alone

Top Opinions/Entertainment

- SoloPen: Barbarity in Practice

- SoloPen: Keep it Quiet: The True Effects of SoloPens

- SoloPen: Arguing Against Eternity

- SoloPen: How Did I Get Pregnant in a SoloPen?

- SoloPen: Unseen Torture is Still Torture

For more information and for answers to specific questions, please see **"Talmund's Legal Library Complete Entry: SoloPen."**

***

TALMUND'S SYSTEM LIBRARY BRIEF ENTRY: NADAR

UCA Designation: Nadar System-Incorporated

- The Nadar system in the Mid Rim consists of countless energy-rich, gaseous planets in 3,271 galaxies that are inhospitable to most known lifeforms.

- Nadarites, one of only two-hundred intelligent lifeforms known to be able to withstand the harsh, gaseous conditions of the planets, are a peaceful, private, solitary people who keep their social, political, religious, and community practices and beliefs to themselves. However, thanks to the Treaty of Nadar, they have offered up much of their technology and many of their planets, in exchange for unhindered passage throughout the UCA.

- Easily spotted, Nadarites are long, skinny creatures with bulbous heads and countless tendrils that communicate through visual sound wave manipulation, making them at home on the UCA capitol planet of Annam.

- Though inhospitable, Nadar gas quarries naturally reproduce a seemingly endless supply of "gas" used to power 99% of all vehicles with cosmos traveling capabilities and 100% of all vehicles with HyperRift traveling capabilities. Due to its high demand, the power source is traditionally mined by prisoners who are watched over by Red Star Ascendants.

Status

- Planetary Status: Incorporated

- System Status: UCA Mid Rim

- Cosmotic Status: UCA Member Mid Rim Prime Standing

Top Factual Documentation

- Nadar: Unearth the Mid Rim: A History

- Nadar: The Quiet Culture

- Nadar: Gas Quarries and Their Reproduction Possibilities

- Nadar: Nadarites: An Eternal Peace and a Permanent Piece

- Nadar: Nadar and the HyperRift Highway

Top Opinions/Entertainment

- Nadar: We Need To Leave

- Nadar: Who Runs the Cosmos? Nadarites

- Nadar: Just Keep Mining: Lucrative Career Paths in Nadar

- Nadar: Nadarites on Nantuk: A Comedy of Errors

- Nadar: Sleeping with the Slims

For more information and for answers to specific questions, please see **"Talmund's Planetary Library Primary Entry: TinNadar-Incorporated"** (extended and brief entries), **"Talmund's Planetary Library: Nadar Prime"** (extended and brief entries), and **"Talmund's Bestiary: Nadarites"** (extended and brief entries).

***

TALMUND'S BESTIARY BRIEF ENTRY: CORRELATIVE

UCA Designation: CorrePelorinian-Prime

- A culture adjacent, emotional communicating, omni dwelling, ignometamorphic psychrolosymbiote that is distinct in the cosmos, as Pelora is the only known celestial body in which any lifeform such as this has evolved. They are distinguishable by their flat black color that mimics the dark matter of space as well as their shapelessness, like a sheet without form. They possess metamorphic talents that, when paired in a symbiotic relationship with a host of any known classification, seem limitless. Their stingers, known as CorreBeams, shoot cold energy to varying degrees and their "shell phase" can withstand the vacuum of space and has been known to survive the destruction of planets. With effort and time, when hardened into a blade, or CorreBlade, they can slice through the strongest metal in the known cosmos, Tungstonadamite, as well as the space barrier or "Reality Wall" to create a HyperRift in order to traverse HyperLanes. Additionally, they are one of only two known lifeforms able to survive the rigors of space travel without requiring a suit and/or ship. Their ability to psychologically connect with the ExoNet as well as with their host, who they support in all things, creates the symbiotic relationship developed in a joining. This is why The Ascendancy partnered with them eons ago in order to establish a superior police and military force throughout the three Rims.

Status

- Average Height: N/A

- Average Weight: N/A

- Average Lifespan: Classified

- Home Planet: Pelora/Corre System/Inner Rim

- Planetary Status: Sole Lifeform

- System Status: UCA Superiority Inner Rim

- Cosmotic Status: UCA Member Inner Rim (Prime Standing)

Classification

- **RIM**: **Inner**

- **SYSTEM**: **Corre**

- **PLANET**: **Pelora**

- **DOMAIN**: **CLASSIFIED**

- **KINGDOM**: **CLASSIFIED**

- **PHYLUM**: **CLASSIFIED**

- **CLASS**: **CLASSIFIED**

- **ORDER**: **CLASSIFIED**

- **FAMILY**: **CLASSIFIED**

- **TRIBE**: **CLASSIFIED**

- **GENUS**: **CLASSIFIED**

- **SPECIES**: **Peloran**

Top Factual Documentation

- CLASSIFIED

Top Opinions/Entertainment

- Correlative: Secret Savior or Subtle Spy?

- Correlative: God's Body

- Correlative: The Ascendancy's Weapon of Mass Destruction

- Correlative: Symbiotic Peace Blob

- Correlative: Kill Trigger Switch Code Vol. #1

For more information and for answers to specific questions, please see **Talmund's Bestiary Primary Entry: Correlative**. Accessing this file requires unwritable hyper-classified codes.

***

TALMUND'S BESTIARY BRIEF ENTRY: ESSAN

UCA Designation: ZraEssaninian-Prime

- A culture bearing, verbal communicating, land dwelling, bipedal evolutionary mammalian primaticus that presents itself as, overall, average in that class and order. They possess social and political structures based on "the will of the people" of their planet. Religious and spiritual matters have been of little to no concern to most Essans for millennia. They reproduce through sexual contact and have a gestation period of approximately forty Annam Standard Weeks.

- Most significantly, however, Essans are distinguished by a more highly developed brain than most of their counterparts in the genus homo and are known to have a unique "battery" quality to their cells that absorbs the energy of the nearest star and translates it to abilities uncommon in similar lifeforms such as flight, laser vision, impenetrable skin, etc. (for a complete list see "Understanding Essan Physiology: A Working Theory"). Curiously, this trait seems to be irrevocably connected to the star nearest them in their youth. So that, as adults, Essan "battery" qualities only operate at full power when they are near that star. Some hypothetical proposals have been brought to light to indicate that there are materials throughout the cosmos that can cancel and/or alter these abilities, though, as of this date, there is no tangible evidence to support this theory.

- As of the writing of this entry, scientists are still studying Essans to determine the cause of this unique mutation with only one breakthrough. It has been discovered that the strength/age of the star as well as the mindset of the individual Essan helps establish the unique abilities. As they are the dominant species on Essa, they are classified by

Talmund as homo essanian. Essans are anatomically similar to others in the primaticus order in evolutionary traits. Like many in the primaticus order, Essans display an erectness of body carriage that frees their dual hands of five digits each (four fingers and one thumb per hand) for use as manipulative members.

Status

- Average Height: 1.70 meters

- Average Weight: 70 kilograms

- Average Lifespan: 130 Annam Standard Years

- Home Planet: Essa/Zra System/Inner Rim

- Planetary Status: Dominant Lifeform

- System Status: UCA Equality Inner Rim

- Cosmotic Status: UCA Member Inner Rim (Weak Standing)

Classification

- **RIM: Inner**

- **SYSTEM: Zra**

- **PLANET: Essa**

- **DOMAIN: Eukarya**

- **KINGDOM: Animalia**

- **PHYLUM: Chordata**

- **CLASS: Evolutionary Mammalian**

- **ORDER:Primaticus**

- **FAMILY: Hominidae**

- **TRIBE: Homini**

- **GENUS: Homo**

- **SPECIES: Essanian**

Factual Documentation

- Essan: Planet Politics and Wars

- Essan: Religion

- Essan: Art

- Essan: Famed Essans Throughout the Rims

- Essan: Understanding Essan Physiology: A Working Theory

Top Opinions/Entertainment

- Essan: What Went Wrong

- Essan: Mammalian Emotional Insecurity

- Essan: The Hubris of the Essan Civilization

- Essan: The Problem With Prime Planets

- Essan: Inner Rim Hierarchy and Its Hypocrisy

For more information and for answers to specific questions, please see **Talmund's Bestiary Primary Entry: Essan.**

***

TALMUND'S BESTIARY BRIEF ENTRY: TECHNOID

USA Designation: ZraEssanian-Subprime

- A biological techno-organic lifeform created and grown on Essa by the Essans as everything from towering skyscrapers to handheld communication devices, little is known of the Technoids. Though considered a sentient lifeform within the UCA, that designation has been debated by Essans as well as scholars in other systems.

- Essan science is highly guarded and secretive so any data on classification, behaviors, appearances, etc, is minimal at best. Though a sentient lifeform, it appears that Technoids live to serve their creators, the Essans, and have no ambition to leave their home planet without an Essan present, which is why Essa is the only place in the known cosmos where one might come into contact with a Technoid regularly.

Status

- Home Planet: Essa/Zra System/Inner Rim

- Planetary Status: Submissive Lifeform

- System Status: UCA Equality Inner Rim

- Cosmotic Status: N/A

- **Classification**

- Unknown

Top Factual Documentation

- Technoid: The Essan Secret

- Technoid: Failed Attempts at Replication

- Technoid: Essan Science and Its Achievements

- Technoid: Hypothesis: Their Life is Connected to Essa's

- Technoid: A Deep Understanding of Theologies In Essan Culture

Top Opinions/Entertainment

- Technoid: The Essan Failure

- Technoid: What to Avoid

- Technoid: Subservient Slave of a Dying People

- Technoid: My Weekend with a Technoid Lover

- Technoid: Technoids Are Destroying Essa From Within

For more information and for answers to specific questions, please see **Talmund's Bestiary Primary Entry: Technoid.**

***

TALMUND'S BESTIARY BRIEF ENTRY: WHITLEY

USA Designation: BelWhitlian-Prime

- A culture bearing, verbal communicating, amphibian dwelling, bipedal evolutionary amphibialopsidia anuriticus that presents itself as, overall, exemplary in that class and order. Whitley are possessed of smooth skin in various shades of green and gray. They are, comparatively, taller and thinner than others in their class and order. Possessed of bones whose density shifts depending on their location (water or land), they are an agile and swift lifeform. Traditionally, they are rural, farming lifeforms who build their homes in the giant Welvon Trees that grow both on land and in the water of their lush, green planet of Whit. Whitley social structures are loose and based on a hierarchical matriarchy that has been seen to grow at a natural and even pace with the evolution, both physically and culturally, of the species.

• Their primary religious beliefs refer to a Great Podmother who created the universe and all who inhabit it. Those Whitley who are believers claim that she will one day return and turn the entire cosmos into a paradise on par with Whit. Unique amongst most religions throughout the cosmos, proselytizing is strictly forbidden so the religion has stayed almost entirely confined to certain more conservative societies on Whit.

• Unique amongst most of the lifeforms in Talmund's Bestiary, the Whitley reproduces through a combination of plant-like pollination and lizard-like egg insemination that does not require a traditional male. Instead, certain females are "gifted" with the ability to produce spermatozoa in order to pollinate the egg-bearing Whitley Blossom that all females develop upon pubescence. Like many in the anuriticus order, Whitley display an erectness of body carriage that frees their dual hands of four digits each (three fingers and one thumb per hand) for use as manipulative members while their four elongated webbed toes on each foot (two in the front and two in the back) provide them with superior climbing and swimming abilities. It is theorized that this evolutionary trait is directly linked to the Welvon Trees they inhabit.

- It is relevant to note, though this is a brief entry, that Whit was the last planet to fall victim to the Draconian Reign and, as a testament to Whitley strength and endurance, it was a Whitley contingent of The Ascendancy that ultimately ended the Draconian Reign that nearly destroyed the UCA.

Status

- Average Height: 2.1 meters

- Average Weight: 60 kilograms

- Average Lifespan: 150 Annam Standard Years

- Home Planet: Whit/Bel System/Inner Rim

- Planetary Status: Dominant Lifeform

- System Status: UCA Equality Inner Rim

- Cosmotic Status: UCA Member Inner Rim (Strong Standing)

Classification

- **RIM: Inner**

- **SYSTEM: Bel**

- **PLANET: Whit**

- **DOMAIN: Eukarya**

- **KINGDOM: Animalia**

- **PHYLUM: Chordata**

- **CLASS: Evolutionary Amphibialopsidia**

- **ORDER: Anuriticus**

- **FAMILY: Ranidae**

- **TRIBE: Holarctic**

- **GENUS: Rana**

- **SPECIES: Whitlian**

Top Factual Documentation

- Whitley: The Draconian Reign: A Complete History

- Whitley: A Complete History

- Whitley: Planet Politics and Wars

- Whitley: Interplanetary Politics and Wars

- Whitley: Geography and Countries

Top Opinions/Entertainment

- Whitley: How Peace Ended War

- Whitley: Running With the Whitley: The Wonderful World of Whit

- Whitley: Whiticisms: An Off Worlder's Understanding of Whitley Wisdom

- Whitley: Draconian Fangs and Whitley Wonders

- Whitley: When Faced With Destruction, True Whitley Revealed Itself And We Should All Be Scared

For more information and for answers to specific questions, please see **Talmund's Bestiary Primary Entry: Whitley**.

Chapter 3
Fire In The Sky

"YOU KNOW, THERE ARE families who would kill for that baby inside of you," Dr. Broyles said through a cigar shoved between his thick lips. "That little mulatto could have a great life." He sniffed and leaned back in his chair, enormous, calloused hands resting on his desk. His eyes were black slits cut into his round face.

May wasn't sure what was hiding in that blackness, but she knew she didn't like it.

"Mulatto?" she asked.

Sitting across the desk from Dr. Broyles, she cocked her head to the side, locking eyes with the man. In her crisp, mint dress with her legs crossed and her back straight, she seemed out of place in this smoky old office on the first floor of Draco General Hospital. Outside the open window behind the doctor, she could hear children playing down the street somewhere, laughing and yelling.

"I didn't mean anything by it, you understand," Dr. Broyles said, a false sincerity dripping from his words like thick vomit.

"We understand exactly what you mean, Doctor."

May's husband, Jackson, wore a flannel and a pair of bell bottom blue jeans, one leg of which covered the titanium prosthetic strapped just below his right knee. He also looked out of place. It was as though someone had plucked him from the garage where he worked and dropped him in a strange new scientific world filled with medical books, deep, rich mahogany shelves, and terms he couldn't hope to understand. In many ways, this was true, and his only lifeline here was his wife's warm hand in his own. His wary blue eyes pivoted from Dr. Broyles to May, his frustration growing like a well-watered seed.

"Now Jackson, I come from a different time," Dr. Broyles said. Though he meant to sound placating, the heavy growl below his words seemed predatory.

"He could have a great life?" Jack repeated Dr. Broyles' words. In the cage of his psyche, fight had made out over flight. Forget freeze. "His life will be just fine with us." His face was a woodcarving of anger heated to a ruddy red. His left hand sweated in May's grip; his right hand clenched an armrest.

"You misunderstand me, Jackson, my boy. I don't mean to disrespect one of our brave veterans." Dr. Broyles pointed his cigar at him, its trail of smoke struggling up from its burning ember as though trying to escape. "You were a late entry into the war, weren't you, son?"

"Y-Yes, I—"

"You couldn't have been more than eighteen in '73, correct?"

"Look, that isn't what this—"

"Never mind all that. You're a hero." Dr. Broyles spread his arms out, showing his hardened palms to the couple. "We got off on the wrong foot when I was late this morning. Allow me to apologize."

"Apologize? You need more—"

"I'm sure the two of you are full of love for this baby." Dr. Broyles' words steamrolled right over Jack's. He looked down at the paperwork on his desk. "But I can help get you—"

"We're not having this discussion, Doctor," Jack interrupted, giving as good as he got. Both hands now on his forehead, he struggled to massage away the headache suddenly chiseling at his skull. "You may be the best, you may be a big shot, you may be a saint for opening this hospital in our lick-spittle little town, but we do not have to suffer this from anyone. If you can't see that, we'll head to Omaha." Bright tomatoes bloomed on his cheeks. His blond hair started to slick with sweat. Rage stretched out at the edge of his words. He could feel his nerves fray, flashes of bloody jungles forced themselves to the front of his mind. Explosions. Gunshots. The smell of smoke and blood.

Children crying.

Always children crying.

Closing his eyes, he told himself, *This is not the war. All will be well*, the mantra May had taught him to use during times of high stress, the one her grandmother had taught her, the one that had helped her survive her own pieces of hell.

May pulled one of his hands away from his forehead and placed one of her own on his cheek. "Shhhh," she whispered, leaning toward him, suppressing her own frustration at the doctor as their foreheads met. "All will be well."

Dr. Broyles pursed his lips and cleared his throat. "I," he said, focusing on May, who now refused to look back, "am just trying to help. You're only a month along. Now is the time to think about things like adoption. Imagine, with the money you could make, you could go back to college, May." He turned to Jack. "And you could too, boy! College! You have money from the military, correct? How about some more? You could get out of this town, out of that damnable trailer park at least."

May held her hand to Jack's cheek, feeling the subtle shudder of his skin. Her knuckles were soft against the scruff there. "Jack," she whispered, "stay with me."

Broyles shrugged, spinning slowly in his creaking chair so he could ash his cigar out the window behind his desk. The sunlight hit his massive frame as he leaned over the sill, causing his shadow to fall upon the young couple, a skyscraper crumbling down upon them. "All right then, I'll leave it for now." He bit down on his cigar as he swiveled to face them again. "But this discussion is far from over, you two. Understand?"

"Thank you," May said, holding Jack's eyes with her own.

Dr. Broyles exhaled, causing his cigar tip to glow stronger. "I want you to know that I have no prejudice against your relationship." An uncomfortable cough escaped his chest. "A white man and a black woman together are fine by me; it's the '80s after all and your baby will be beautiful. But dear God, you're children yourselves and you have no money. I'm just trying to help." Shoulders falling, Dr. Broyles showed his exasperation as he breathed out their ages, "Twenty-six and twenty-two, no college education between the two of you, your house is on wheels, you have no idea what you're getting into."

May faced the doctor, letting her hand fall from Jack's face. "We know exactly what we're getting into," she said.

"Look on the bright side," Dr. Broyles smiled wryly, reaching out a hand that Jack did not shake. "You're both obviously very fertile." He winked at May.

A chill traced her spine as she turned away. At first, she wasn't sure what she was feeling because it was a sensation that had been foreign to her for some time, at least since Jack had come into her life or she had come into his or they had come into each other's. Both of them had been broken in their own ways, both of them running from their own demons, they had saved each other. They had stopped being prey for the world's predators.

But that wink from that man had brought those feelings of helplessness, fear, and even shame back and for a skittering moment May found herself alone, a rabbit in a hungry snake's eyes. She could already feel his fangs digging into her flesh. She wanted to squirm away, to run, to hide.

"No," she whispered.

Dr. Broyles ignored her. "We'll get you another appointment in a couple weeks so we can keep an eye on that baby."

"Thank you, Dr. Broyles, but I think we'll be finding a new doctor," Jack said. He picked up his cane and headed for the door.

"Now Jack, don't be ridiculous. You're not going to find an obstetrician as good as me."

"I'm only looking for one who isn't you," Jack replied as he opened the office door.

May followed him out and slammed the door behind her.

They made their way silently through the waiting room and into the hospital's main hall. May's shoes clicked and Jack's cane clacked speedily over the speckled blue tile. As they reached the exit, May huffed, "This place is ridiculous. I knew we shouldn't have come here."

The hospital, for its part, ignored the jab. It rested comfortably on the southern end of Main Street like a dignified castle that did not have to pay attention to the pitiful cries of local trailer park trash. Its rounded red brick entrance surrounded by a spiral of circular windows had always reminded May of the castles scattered across the French countryside she saw in books her grandmother had given her. But there was something wrong with this building, something somehow off. She could never put her finger on her exact issue with Draco General. In a way, it was beautiful, even fantastical. Conical and turret-like, the entrance was connected to a long, rectangular five story brick building that was so majestic, it really had no place in Oakview, NE. It ended in a giant smokestack that gave off the subtle appearance of a freshly awakened dragon. It was a mystery why Dr. Broyles, an

OB/GYN to the rich and famous of the East Coast, had come to Oakview of all places and built this monstrous testament to his power and altruism on half a town block.

"Someone needs to help the small-town folk, the farmers, factory workers, mechanics, and their families," was all Dr. Broyles had ever answered when asked why by sycophantic reporters.

May ran a hand over her face. "How can one of the best baby doctors in the world be so . . . awful?"

Jack, of the same mind as May, growled his response.

They approached the statue of the ancient Greek lawgiver Draco, the hospital's namesake. It stood on a pedestal in the middle of an elaborate fountain in the hospital's open atrium. Water trickled from a pen in one hand onto a book in another, then it slid down in rivulets to the fountain where it was recycled back up through the pen again. The sound tried its best to pull Jack away, back to Vietnam, back to the battle in which he had lost his leg.

May stopped and looked up at the grim stone face. "Why did he name a hospital after this man?" she asked, her voice alone pulling Jack to now, to her.

"Who knows?" Jack said, raising his arms in exasperation. "Broyles probably worships him or something."

"Oh, that old smokestack only worships himself, honey," May said.

"We really do need to find another doctor. Maybe there is one in Omaha as good as him?"

She placed her hands on his shoulders and smiled up at him, noticing the way the twinkling coins at the bottom of the fountain reflected in his light eyes. "Let's not worry about it now, okay? Let's go home and eat lunch and relax. Tonight, we'll watch the meteor shower and tomorrow we can figure out what to do next."

"May, I—"

"Jackie," May interrupted, her voice all silk, light and strong, "please, for me."

He relented and took her in his arms. "For you."

"All will be well," she whispered in his ear and kissed him.

As she pulled away a pickup truck screeched to a halt near them, and Linc, the old man who maintained Oakview Lanes, hopped out of the bed like an elderly bullfrog.

"Jack!" he shouted, eyes bulging. "We need you to come right away!"

"What? What is it?"

"It's Del's boy! He's missing!"

***

Hours later, the Nebraska evening sky lit up with fiery meteors, sparks of orange fury that faded as they fell. The way they sped over the backdrop of the black night reminded Jack of a work of art he had seen in Vietnam. It was a simple thing, painted on a scrap piece of crumpled kraft paper probably by a child, but he had nonetheless been awed by it. Left in the middle of a dirt road, there had been something pure in the heavy lines and mix of bright colors on a scribbled black background that showed nothing and everything at once. Looking at the simple childish art, what anyone else may have called trash, had calmed Jack that day, even as he could hear gunfire and screams in the distance. That art was in his wallet even now, folded and faded, and creased and crumpled, but still there, struggling to bring him peace whenever he thought of it. Tonight was the same. Like the painting had, like the painting did, the bright streaks cutting through the sky made Jack appreciate rare moments of calm. It was as though everything dangerous was far away, someone else's problem.

It was a glorious lie.

"It is amazing," May said, following Jack's gaze to the heavens.

She squeezed his hand a little tighter. The two of them were alone, standing on the edge of the empty field north of the trailer park, near the small forest that separated the field from the Missouri River. Oakview Lanes was off in the distance, the town hidden somewhere in the other direction, and the highway offered only the occasional faint cry of a truck zooming past out there in the darkness. They were more alone than they had been in a long, long while. They could see streaks of flashlight panning back and forth in the woods and hear men and women holler for Ricky.

Jack clicked the walkie-talkie and listened to the static for a moment, lost in it. He sat it down in the back of his Jeep. "I can't believe this is happening. Ricky."

"We will find him. Someone will."

Jack's chest rose and fell. "I know. It's just . . . I don't know. I guess it scares me." He ran his flashlight's glow idly over the ground before them.

"Jackie," May nuzzled into his neck, "how many of us are out right now looking?"

"I don't know. A lot."

"We'll find him."

"I don't know how much we're going to be able to do tonight with just our flashlights."

May pointed to the trees. "Look at all those lights crisscrossing through the woods. If he's out there—"

"We were out there all day. He's not. I don't see how he could be. I don't know why we're doing this!" He threw his flashlight. "I don't know why the police haven't . . ." He trailed off, not wanting to say what he was thinking. Why hadn't the police started dragging the river?

His frustration had been a formless thing all day, flowing around him as he limped through the trailer park, peeking in every nook and cranny he could find. That same frustration had grown dark and swollen as the police refused to help in the search. They had said it was because the boy hadn't been gone long enough. But Jack knew, just like everyone else in the trailer park, it was because of where Ricky lived that they weren't looking. That had only added to his aggravation at everything. By the time the sun set and he had to leave the woods for fear that he'd fall and hurt himself, become more of a burden than he already thought he was, Jack's frustration had turned green like a three day old bruise.

"Jack, I—"

"And I can't believe Wilton didn't spare a single officer! Not fucking one."

May offered him a sad, defeated grin. "Did you really expect him to?"

"I'm sorry, baby," Jack said. He walked over to where his flashlight had landed and picked it up then pointed it out toward the trees. "Ricky's not out there, though. Hell, he's just as likely to be up there." He looked to the sky again and raised his hand to shade his eyes as some of the meteors flying overhead gave off an increasingly bright light. "I don't know if that is a good thing or a bad thing." During his time in Vietnam, he had spent his nights knee deep in blood, shit, and mud. He had witnessed jungles, villages, and even cities become graves. For the last eight years, death wails and gunfire had torn through his dreams and chased him into his waking life, the stench of war lingering after he woke up every morning.

It was a toxic mix of burnt earth and vomit, a sour chemical odor that lodged itself in his nasal cavity and tainted everything. Many nights since he had come home, waking up, gagging on nightmare, and scratching at the acid scars on his neck and shoulder, he saw phantom clouds of Agent Orange sinking into his carpet and leaving blood-colored stains. Those were the times he wondered if his mind would ever actually leave that pointless war. Officially, it had ended in 1973 but Jack knew that was a lie.

May rested her head on his chest, listening to his heartbeat speedup. "Still," she paused, the sound of her voice acting as a brake, "still," she repeated.

Her black hair smelled of strawberries and its thick curls danced upon Jack's chin, tickling him as he momentarily exhaled away his anxiety.

Tendrils of fog climbed up through the forest. She knew they were growing from the Missouri River and that they were at least a mile away, but just seeing them made her colder.

"Take my jacket," Jack said, handing her his insulated flannel before she had time to decline. "It'll keep you—"

As she was putting it on, a whistling from above, louder than either of them had ever heard, drowned out his words.

As one, Jack and May looked up to see a meteor in the sky much closer than it was supposed to be. Less than a second later, the ground quaked and the world exploded as somewhere not too far away in the empty field, that meteor became a meteorite.

Chapter 4
The Beach

THE LONELY ONE CAME home from work, made a light supper of steak and eggs, ate it, did the dishes, and sat on his front porch swing with a cup of coffee. Breathing deeply the air out here in the middle of nowhere, he polished his ax and admired his new baseball cap. It did look better when it sat jauntily on the boy's head but seeing it there on the other end of his swing gave him small goosebumps. It was beautiful no matter what.

According to the radio sitting on a table next to him, back in Oakview "nearly the whole dang town" was attending the meteor festival. If the DJ could be believed, the crowd was growing larger and larger by the minute, even if the weather was a bit chilly. All on duty police officers were there, acting as crowd control and calming presence. Not that those folks had anything to worry about. It was a beautiful night in March in Nebraska, the sky was giving them a free show, and for just a quarter they could get an even better show. All was right with the world.

What the DJ didn't mention, however, was that the people who lived in Oakview Lanes were madly searching for the little boy he had kidnapped earlier that morning. Last he heard, some of them were going door-to-door asking if anyone had seen or heard anything. Others were combing through the woods near the Missouri River. A few, if water cooler gossip could be believed, were even diving into the murky shallows of the river, clawing through the mud, and screaming for the little boy he had locked away safely in his basement.

He clicked off the radio and laughed at the lie by omission.

No one was safe.

And no one came here looking in The Lonely One's basement for the boy. No one came here seeking justice. No one suspected a thing. Still, his plans had been thrown asunder. All because of that baseball cap, that beautiful, beautiful baseball cap.

He finished his coffee and smacked his lips, thankful that it was still chilly enough that he could sit out here in peace. No pesky mosquitoes buzzing around in search of blood. No moths darting toward his porch light and slamming into the screen with dull, ignorant thuds, or even worse, June bugs. He hated June bugs. Thankfully, it was too early in the season for those wretched things.

He could have stayed here all night, just enjoying this.

But as the town and all of its citizens had been madly discussing the missing boy or the meteor shower, he had been busy concocting a plan. And he had to stick to it if he wanted to maintain his situation.

"It is time," he said, loving the sound of his own voice. It was deep and reverberated from his chest out to the world. It was the kind of voice that people listened to even if they didn't want to. It was the kind of voice it had taken years to perfect.

His original plan had been simple: grab a child at the festival, take him to an empty beach, kill him, take what he needed, and wait for his body's eventual discovery. The chaos and fear that such a discovery created would have been delicious. More importantly, it would have taken little effort. Normally, it was easy to fool and frighten the stagnants of this world. Now, because of that cap, he had to be careful. He had to be quick.

"No time like the present," The Lonely One said, clapping once more before he went back inside and made his way to his basement. He paused for a moment, enjoying the damp smell of this dark, terrifying place. He had designed it after watching the slasher flick, *The Texas Chainsaw Massacre*. The film had been inspiring and he had to admit there was something amazing at how these stagnants could capture their own fears so well. Listening, he noticed there was no noise coming from the chest where he had placed Ricky earlier that day. It was shoved into a dark corner with no chance of light from the small windows reaching it. He hoped the boy wasn't dead in there but if he was, he'd still cut him for parts and bleed him. No matter. Then he'd maybe even find time to get another one from the festival. A "twofer" as they called it.

He checked his watch. He'd never have time to get the parts to his lab, but they would be fine overnight in his refrigerator.

He pulled the chest out of the corner and up the stairs, wondering how much it hurt the boy, hoping it hurt him as much as possible. When he scooted it to a stop in his living room, he grabbed a syringe full of a special concoction that made certain he slept and he unlocked the chest. The lid sprung open.

The boy's chest moved lightly up and down. Good. All was as it should be.

No. It was more than that. There was a purity to the boy that spoke volumes. "You are perfect," The Lonely One whispered. He clasped the boy's arm with an iron-like grip, injected him with the concoction, hefted him out of the chest, and threw him on the floor. "I wish I had kept count though," The Lonely One lamented. "How many has it been?" He lifted Ricky's head and gingerly placed the cap back on it, admiring that face one more time. Bruised, it was still beautiful.

Though Ricky had not been awake when The Lonely One had opened the chest, he was more than asleep now. He was in that place between life and death where the concoction took stagnants. He was what The Lonely One liked to call "hovering."

Now The Lonely One had to get ready. He took off his clothes and inhaled the crisp spring air, pausing to look at the child. *So perfect*, he thought as he took Ricky by his shoe and pulled him toward the front door. When The Lonely One was outside, he sheathed his ax and hung it over his naked back then wrenched the cap from Ricky's head and gripped it with his teeth.

He rolled his shoulders and cleared his throat before morphing into the largest bird that Nebraska had seen in millions of years. It was a seamless, painless shift, as though his body had turned into warm clay and easily reformed itself into a massive hawk. Feathers unfolded from his skin like flower petals in the sun. His bones, thick and human, hollowed themselves out. Eyes shifted; human feet washed away revealing talons. There was no pain, only a tingling from the inside out as his cells did what needed to be done. Tonight, he needed them to fly so he could carry the boy quickly to where he needed to be.

He knew he should have killed the boy at home. His basement had seen its fair share of murders already, so one more wouldn't have mattered. It would have been easier, safer. He could have thrown the body on the roadside the next morning. Everything would still have gone as planned. He would have been satiated for a time. He would have the parts for his experiments. He would have put another marker out there in the universe to prove this meager little mud ball was his.

The town would have been afraid.

But for some reason, The Lonely One needed the danger. He had to admit it after this morning. He had pulled that boy into his car at the break of day when anyone could have caught him. It was a taste of danger like he hadn't had for a long, long time.

And he liked it.

Tonight, he'd feel it again.

People weren't supposed to trespass on the beach where he wanted to do the killing, so naturally, people trespassed all the time. Tonight, he knew, it would be even worse. Those people who lived in the trailer park would be out there in the woods hollering for this little boy, each one hoping in the back of their pathetic little minds that they would be the one to find him. No one, he thought, really cared whether he was found.

They just wanted the glory. Stagnants. So predictable.

The Lonely One would have laughed at their idiocy, their concerns, their desires. Beaks, however, were not designed for laughter and he was, after all, holding onto that beautiful, beautiful cap.

No matter. This new plan was going to work. He flew up, the boy in his talons, and headed toward the woods, free. It was an easy flight that ended as quickly as it started. No one had seen his massive frame flying through the skies since all eyes were on the meteor shower, which, thankfully, was in the other direction. At the southern edge of the woods, he swooped down and made his way into the forest, well away from the searching masses for now, making sure to shift his legs so that deer hooves clomped along the muddy forest paths instead of stagnant feet. Even if a good tracker discovered that a body had been pulled through the woods, the hoof prints would throw them off his trail. Deer, especially two-legged ones, didn't tend to pull bodies behind them.

"Never going to catch me," he whispered gleefully.

The little boy seemed heavier than he had in the morning when The Lonely One had hefted him off his bike and into his passenger seat and then again when he had pulled him, kicking and screaming, from his car to his cellar. It also didn't help right now that The Lonely One was carrying his ax in a sheath on his back and had just flown. Flapping wings was no joke.

"I just flew in from the country and boy are my arms tired." He giggled to himself.

For every give, The Lonely One supposed, there was a take.

In any case, dragging a boy through the woods was hard work for someone his age, especially for someone his age who was going out of his way to be as careful as he could. What had to be done, had to be done though. To pass the time and try to forget how difficult his work was, he told the boy a joke.

"A man and a boy walk hand in hand into the woods," The Lonely One said.

The boy did not respond beyond a few soft, mostly nonsensical mumbles. The concoction was still working.

"'It's scary here,' the boy says." The Lonely One laughed through labored breaths, as though he was so funny he couldn't help but take a break to let the comedy wash over him. "'You're scared?' the man says. 'I have to walk out of these woods alone.'" He guffawed at that, releasing his laughter into the night like an uncaged beast.

The uncaged beasts who already inhabited the forest were not happy with this.

"Do you get it?" The Lonely One asked. "It's because the man is going to kill the boy."

"The Lonely One," the boy said.

Though his words were as mushy as a cookie taken out of the oven too soon, The Lonely One knew his name when he heard it. "Strong," he said. "You remember who I am." He chuckled until his throat became phlegmy and he coughed until he almost choked. "That means you know what's coming. It's always good to have an idea of your own future."

After a few minutes to gather his strength, The Lonely One continued on, huffing through the growth, batting budding branches away from his face, wondering if maybe he should morph completely into a deer instead of just partially, and occasionally looking up through the trees to enjoy the light show. The meteors were beautiful, heavenly even out here a few miles from town. But also, with their bright burning tails, hellish. They were the perfect mix of beauty and horror for what he had to do. Maybe he had been a bit harsh when thinking of the parents whose attention he knew was taken by these things. There was something about space and what the stagnants could see of it, something simply entrancing, even for someone like him, someone who had lived longer and seen more than most.

But he could not stare for long. Not when he had a child to kill.

Somewhere, not too far away, there were people looking for the boy. He could hear them shouting his name. "Ricky!" He could even see, if he focused his eyes toward the distant north, the faint glow from their flashlights waving across the woods out that way.

Dangerous, he thought, just how he wanted it. But maybe he shouldn't have been laughing so loud a moment ago.

The Lonely One let his eyes fall to the boy. His hands were tied together with manila rope, the end of which The Lonely One held. His face was pale and covered in scratches. Dried blood caked around his nose and mouth. One eye was swollen.

Studying the boy's closed eyes, The Lonely One wondered what he was dreaming in that strange in-between place where the concoction took him. Were there pirates in his dreams? Monsters? Toys like GI Joe come to life? Or was he old enough for a disco party? Did the boy have simpler fantasies? Did he see himself running through a field with a trusted dog at his side on a bright afternoon? Playing hide and seek with a few friends right after sunset? *Pong* in his living room? Was the boy dreaming about a time before The Lonely One? Or was he dreaming about delivering newspapers? Was he going about his day in dreamland as though he had never met The Lonely One? In dreamland, had he finished his work? Was he hanging out with his friends, and even attending the Meteor Festival as The Lonely One picked off another child? What was little Ricky's alternate reality?

Ricky mumbled something that brought The Lonely One's thoughts out of dreamland. He grinned, pulling the boy closer so that he could feel his warmth. It was getting chilly out here in the woods. And with the Missouri River not far away, the cool watery air surrounding it was growing wispy fingers of fog that would only make things colder. He hefted the boy over his shoulder and marched on. He would be at the beach soon, the forbidden one where he'd do the killing.

The only spectators to The Lonely One's crime were owls and mice and crickets and lightning bugs. Those creatures, he knew, were preoccupied with one another. All the people searching for poor Ricky were far enough away and the fog was growing heavier. They would be stopping their search for the night soon. As he approached the beach, the river's musky scents and repetitive sounds grew stronger. It felt like the boy was gaining weight by the minute. The Lonely One knew he would be awake again soon, and his own adrenaline that had kept him so charged earlier that day was quickly fading. It would grow again but not until he began the kill. That was just the way of it.

Fog was everywhere now. It hid amongst the trees and muffled the night sounds as though it was his true enemy. It held secrets. It was against him. The Lonely One, only for a moment, became lost in his own fear. There were monsters out here, he knew, monsters who wanted to stop him, monsters from his past, those who had destroyed what he had worked for here and everywhere else, those who did not understand what it was he was trying to do, what it was his people had tried to do throughout the cosmos.

"No," he grumbled, holding a stop sign up to his negative thoughts again. None of that was true. No one with any real power even knew that he had come here, not just to this out of the way town in Nebraska, but to this planet. He would not be interrupted. He stopped himself from dropping the boy to the ground and running for his life. The Lonely One was brave. He could still spy the meteors through the fog, still see them shining down their bright light. This was a message for him to keep working. He knew it.

He plodded on.

The hard dirt floor of the forest grew softer. Trees grew skinnier. The beach was near. He paused for a moment, set the boy down once again and squinted through the darkness at his face. Still beautiful. Still pure, even with its injuries. He placed one calloused hand on the boy's warm cheek. There was so much life there, growing from his insides, pulsing, pounding even. He almost felt bad about what he had to do.

Almost.

He was so happy he had brought the baseball cap. To see the little boy—to see Ricky—once more in it was grand.

The Lonely One gaped in awe.

"Yes," he said. All the night sounds stopped at the echoing of his voice, as if shocked into silence by this quavering, quivering thing. "Yes," he repeated and, shaking his desire away, trudged on.

He was on sand now. The trees were behind him. It wasn't much farther. There was a small stone wall in the way. Placed here years ago for a reason he would never know, he used it as a marker. He had arrived. He hefted the unconscious boy over it and climbed. A moment later, sinking into the sand, he grinned.

Far above him the meteors flew by, dim streaks in the distance. Next to him the boy lay still, his breathing shallow but steady. He shifted his eyes into those of a cat's so he could see him better.

He pulled his ax from the sheath on his back. Its handle was long and black and the matching blade shimmered with the fog's moisture. He knew it wouldn't rust though. This metal was special. This metal was from another place and possessed power like no metal on Earth.

He was going to use it to hack away this boy's useless insides, to create a show. He was also going to use it to gently slice out the pieces he needed.

"But first," he said as he let the ax rest on his shoulder and stared down at the child, "a moment."

The boy's hair was dirty with fear sweat and his pale cheeks were blushing somewhat from blood rushing to his face to help keep him warm as the night crept on, getting colder and colder the way nights did in early spring in Nebraska.

He cleared his throat and shrugged.

"No time like the present," he whispered to himself and lifted the ax over his head. He brought it down on the child's chest. The loud crack of the boy's sternum shattered against the ax's weight. The boy's eyes shot open for a fleeting moment. Less than a second after the bone cracked, the blade found its way to the heart and blood gushed from the wound, soaking his West Oakview High sweatshirt in black ichor.

The little boy was dead before he knew he had been killed.

The brightness in his eyes faded. The Lonely One enjoyed every aspect of the killing, but the dimming of the eyes had always been his favorite. He was taken back to moments on the battlefields of his youth in which he had stopped to watch that dimming, to drink it in, to revel in it.

His mouth watered.

Though there was some sputtering as blood flew forth from the boy's throat and out his mouth, The Lonely One knew this had nothing to do with his fight for life. It was over. This was more like the boy's body accepting that fact.

The Lonely One dropped the ax and knelt over the boy's prostrate form. Blood flowed from the wound and trickled from the mouth, feeding the sand beneath him. The Lonely One sniffed the coppery scented air and ripped at the new hole in the sweatshirt so that it was large enough to accommodate both of his hands. Then, taking another deep breath to get as much of that smell as he possibly could, he reached into the open wound on Ricky's chest with one hand and reached for the ax with the other. Using a combination of his strength and the ax's blade, he tore. The squelching, cracking sounds that forced themselves into the night competed with no other noise. All of the things that made noise had left, fear and revulsion at what was occurring pushing them away. Or perhaps they had simply been silenced, stuck in terrified awe, gaping at what they were witnessing. In moments, the body was splayed open from neck to crotch, and The Lonely One had both hands tucked deep into the body cavity, searching.

He wrapped fingers around an organ, felt it, thought, yanked it free. Sometimes a dampened snap accompanied the yanking, sometimes it was more of a slow tear. Occasionally he had to use the ax. But the parts always came free. He studied the gray, pink things for a moment and determined their value. If the organ was useless, it was thrown in a slimy pile at The Lonely One's feet. If he thought he could use it, he placed it in a sack that had been stuffed into the ax's sheath.

The Lonely One could not say how long this went on. Hours maybe because it was meticulous work that required every bit of his attention. Bathed in the hazy glow of the meteors shooting above the fog, he lost himself. Naked body, half man, half deer, covered in the boy's blood and flesh, ax at his side, he felt safe. He hadn't heard a shout in ages. He knew the search must have been called off, or at least moved closer to the field and out of the woods, away from the riverbank.

He reveled.

***

Until.

A large crash sounded somewhere nearby and the ground rumbled. Trees fell in a massive gust of wind, a few trunks shattered. Sand flew into the air, scratching at The Lonely One's skin.

Panic.

Fear.

It had finally happened. He had been caught not by the local authorities but by those far more powerful than any stagnant police officer or military agent. He lay on his chest and covered his head. It was all he could do. He was caught. There was no denying it.

Minutes crept by. He stayed hidden under the weak cover of his arms, meekly pondering what was to come next before he realized he had not been caught.

One of the meteors, it seemed, had become a meteorite.

And it had made earthfall nearby.

People would be coming for that.

New panic took The Lonely One like a demon in the night.

He leapt to his hooves. Looking down, he realized he was covered in blood. He charged into the river. After he was sure everything had been swept away, he climbed back onto the beach, and, in a swift motion, he grabbed the ax and flung it into the river, knowing it would come back to him. It always had.

He had to leave.

Should he take the organs with him? The body? A meteorite so close to this beach would bring emergency vehicles and visitors, visitors who would not like what they saw.

Should he throw the body in the river? The air was thick and dry. He coughed, his lungs aching. He stumbled. The fog that had been almost pleasant, was now gone, replaced by a heavy dust, mud in the air. He couldn't breathe well. He couldn't do anything to the body now even if he wanted to.

Panicked, The Lonely One changed into a deer and ran on four nimble legs as fast as he could.

Chapter 5
Impact Event

MAY LAY ON HER belly tasting dirt and copper.Coughing, she rolled onto her back. A high-pitched alarm blasted through her ears. Everything ached. An angry river of blood flowed from a gash on her right cheek into her mouth.

She lifted her head and tried to focus through a dusty haze biting at her eyes like an army of gnats. Sparse fires danced across the landscape, blurry and weak in the angry dust. Their hot voices were dulled by the ringing of the loudest bell May had ever heard. A ripped newspaper fluttered eerily by May's face. She read half a headline, "OAKVIEW METEOR CELEBRATION TONI—" before it floated away.

Destruction.

Everywhere.

The golden-brown field was now blackened and ruinous. Piles of burning earth crumbled. Flecks of charred grass floated on an ashen breeze. Jack's Jeep looked as though it had been flung with the force of a tornado's fierce winds. Jagged pieces of the machine his father had gifted him before he died littered the ground around the chassis, which lay flipped and dented in the dirt. Barbed wire from the fence surrounding the field was twisted and mangled in the upturned earth. Where moments ago the air had smelled of spring weeds and grass, now it stank of smoke. It had been damp with fresh dew and a slight fog had been climbing from the river a few miles away. Now it was all ash. Now it was all dead. May's eyes itched. A sadistic ringing cacophony pounded through her head.

Breathing quick and deep, she coughed, choking on dirt. She convulsed and crumbled. She could not tell whether it was from the cold or her nerves. Time trundled through the destruction. She waited for another explosion.

None came.

"Jack," she whimpered as she climbed to her feet and ran shaking hands over her tattered dress. Her legs wobbled. The world jumbled, falling in on itself and bringing her down with it. She vomited. The ringing refused to die. Her eyes refused to focus. Her head bellowed. Her cheek burned and bled.

"Jackie!" she cried out, but the word sounded far away and warbled. Her head lolled from side to side. Bubbly, pink spittle ran from her lips. She forced herself up on her elbows and knees and tried batting at the dusty air as though she could clear it away. "I need help," her words fell in dry clumps from her lips. "Jackie."

She touched the cut on her cheek and her legs went to water beneath her. She fought to stay upright, moved her head from side to side; it was heavy and unbalanced.

Her face fell in the dirt.

Looking up, she saw a dark shape come into focus ahead of her. Black from head to toe, the thing was so thin it looked fragile, but it stood tall and strong in the sea of destruction.

Death? May thought. She tried backing away but couldn't find her strength. Hyperventilating in fear, she felt herself crumble as her eyes rolled to the back of her head.

***

Static shot through ringing.

Ringing slipped away.

Static stung.

Strange words.

Garbled language.

"Hello?" a feminine voice broke through.

"Who," May asked, "who is there?"

She opened her eyes and saw above her what she thought was an oddly elongated oval head covered in a featureless black mask. The head, cocked to the side, sat atop a neck that seemed a little too long. May's emotions battled one another. Fear wanted to control everything. But a sluggish calm fought it off with a slow-moving arm, batting it away like a loathsome fly.

"Where is Jack?" she asked.

"I know no Jack." Now the voice seemed nervous, jittery. Large, almond shaped all white lenses spread over the mask.

"Who are you?" May asked. She was floating, her eyelids were fluttering wings. She reached for the face. "Death?"

"I am life." The face pulled away and May's hands fell to her own cheek.

"My face . . ." May said, "What . . . what happened?"

"I administered a minor sedative while my Correlative made sure your body was viable. Then I healed your major wounds as best I could. You'll need a medical professional to finish up though. Chances are there will be a slight scar on your face at least. Also, Peel is certain your brain suffered a severe concussion. Other than that, you should be fine and thankfully your fetus should be fine as well." She paused; her head tilted once more. This time it seemed as though she listened to a voice only she could hear. "I believe we are being followed. Watched? No. It's not possible. Still. Time is of the essence. I must ask you to be still."

"What? Why . . . ?" May whispered, darkness taking her once more.

***

"You will feel a slight sting," the same voice pulled May from the darkness. It was still on edge, still nervous.

"This isn't real," May said. Her lips felt heavy. Speaking was a chore. Opening her eyes was an impossibility.

"If that is what you need to believe," the voice said while a hand touched May's forehead. "Don't try to open your eyes. You can't. I gave you another sedative."

May reached up sluggishly to grab the hand on her forehead. "You have four fingers," she said, her words like a ball of dough in her mouth. "They're so . . . thin."

"I am not like you."

The hand pulled away, leaving May's own hands to slide across her face where they found a small mask covering her nose and mouth. "What . . . ?"

"An air purifier. You were coughing heavily due to the rubble and detritus in the air from my . . . unfortunate landing."

"What . . . are you?" May's words were strewn across a windy cavern. They formed in the air before her, just out of reach.

"We do not have time for questions." Staccato, fierce, this thing's words were urgent. "I was supposed to have time, I was supposed to be able to tell you everything, to teach you."

"I can't . . . I can't . . . focus."

"The sedative."

"How can I understand you?"

A sigh, heavy, tragic, final.

"It's my Correlative. She understands languages and translates my words to you and your words to me." The head shook, the four fingered hands ran over the face. "No. We don't have time for these questions, Peel."

"Who is following—"

Before May could finish, she felt a needle pierce her abdomen. Though small, it was sharp and cool and deep. She wriggled to stop it, to pull it out, but before she could grasp the invasive thing, it had vanished into her, silencing the pain.

"What did you do?" she asked, fear fired through the sedative and exploded. "My baby!"

"This is not as we planned. No, no, no, no. So many needles lost. No time to study, to teach."

"What did you do?" May's voice quivered with rage.

"I am sorry. Please believe me. It wasn't supposed to be like this."

"What have you done to my baby?" May sat up and shook her head violently to free herself of the fog. It was too thick. Her brain felt like a heavy fruit bouncing around her skull. Her arms felt foreign. Her legs. Her body.

"Thank you for helping me," the thing before her said.

"Helping you?"

"I do not have the time for this!"

"You're not making sense."

The creature stood swiftly and wiped a hand across her chest, revealing a white starburst that had been hidden by dirt.

"I apologize for what this may do to your life. The fact that you were here when I crashed and that your DNA matched one of my remaining needles is a stroke of luck I do not deserve. I cannot expect more. I must leave or they will find me here and if they do—"

"Who will find you?"

"There are laws, do you understand?" the creature shouted, looking down on May. "Unjust laws! I broke them! We broke them!"

May nodded. Trying to fend off the drowsy calm from the sedative, she leaned forward, clasping anger and holding on tight.

"If a planet murders itself through its own foolishness, The Ascendancy is not to get involved. It is against the Code of the Cosmic Tribunal. It's one of the Sacred Six! The Alliance does not allow it!"

"What did you do to my baby?" May shouted.

"I had to!" She grabbed May's upper arms, lifting her to her feet, panic rising in her voice. "I had to for Jon'Oh! I could not let his people die! Damn the law!"

"What did you do to my baby?"

Her chin tilted up as though she studied the sky for a moment before returning her attention to May. "No," she said, placing May back on the ground.

"No?"

"Peel, you can't be right. There are no—"

"What did you do to my baby?" May struggled against the black clad creature's grip. She batted at those arms and watched, shocked, as what she thought was its skin, bubbled up and hardened at her touch.

May tried to scream but her shock would not allow it.

"I injected you with Essan DNA that will latch on to your developing fetus. Are you evolved enough to understand that?" Its hands squeezed May's arms tighter.

"My baby?" May said, blinking constantly, eyes dry and unable to focus through the dust and concussion. "You said you—"

"A baby in the works then," Aurora said, "you and your sperm donor are very viable. It's the only good thing that's happened this day."

"What? My what?"

"You are going to save the Essan race, or come as close to it as possible."

"I don't think—"

"There is no thinking. This has been done." She looked toward the trees. "Do you know what is over there?"

"Over where? I can't—"

"Those small Welvons—trees. Peel senses something."

"I don't know. It's just the woods. We were looking—"

"I am sorry."

"You need to explain—"

"You have helped do a great thing, regardless of the law." She pulled herself from May's grip and from a pouch on her belt found a small, metallic die with blue circles on each of its twenty sides. "Take this," she said, placing it in May's hand. "There is much information on this DieCyclo. Only someone with Essan DNA will be able to open it. There was supposed to be more planning. It wasn't supposed to be this way. I was supposed to have more time with you to study, to learn, to teach."

"Yes, but—"

She wrapped her hands around May's. "Do you feel the 'Cyclo trembling? It senses Essan in you already, but it isn't strong enough for you to open. Not yet. Not until the baby has grown more. When the baby is born, he will open it, you will learn much. Don't let it out of your sight." Her urgency was terrible. "There is something . . ." She trailed off, eyeing the woods once more. "What lives in that forest? What is beyond it?"

May backed away. "Nothing! The river!"

"If I am discovered here on Earth with you . . ." She shuttered. "I must leave." She pulled a tiny tube from a pouch on her belt and handed it to May as well. "Hide this with the 'Cyclo. It is my last Helix Needle. It is very important. Do not use it. I will be back for it."

"You can't just leave!" May shouted.

"I am sorry," she said before reaching over and pulling the air mask from May's face.

"But I—"

Ignoring May, she crouched and leapt into the air, breaking through the dust and leading a black streak into the hazy night sky.

May fell back as the creature's propulsion sent a shock wave outward. She looked up after her, once again hearing nothing but ringing.

"What about Jack?" she asked.

A bent playing card skittered by her feet; a burnt Joker stared up at her.

***

TALMUND'S SCIENTIFIC ADVANCEMENT INDEX BRIEF ENTRY: ESSAN DIECYCLO

- The DieCyclo was invented by Essan Professor Sher'Dee Lox in 1.94515.1AST. Essan historical documents of the period are incomplete and convoluted as it was a time of great social and political upheaval on Essa; however, the invention of the DieCyclo was one of the major catalysts for the UCA's eventual First Contact.

- In a nod to the nearly dead Essan theology, every DieCyclo is a twenty-sided infocube shaped and sized to its maker's convenience and formed of microcached platinum, a rare cosmotic metal, with each side representing a different branch of study. The branches of study are determined by the maker. Diecyclos can remotely connect to the ExoNet to both send and receive information in digital bytes. When it was first invented, it could only connect to the Essan specific neuronet. Modifications were made to increase its strength and reach when Essa was admitted to the UCA.

- Using highly advanced techno-organic mechanizations, the DieCyclo can convert information to a semi-physical holographic form to replicate a traditional teacher/student relationship between the DieCyclo and its maker. Or, if the maker would prefer, the DieCyclo can connect to a diescreen, dietab, diewall, or dieboard and relay information to its maker that way. In rare cases, a DieCyclo can connect directly to its maker and mimic the relationship a host has with a Correlative, thereby receiving and transmitting information through a psychic link of sorts. It is not as strong, fast, or convenient as the Correlative/host relationship.

- Creating a DieCyclo is both an intimate and arduous process for each maker. Though there are similar design elements to all of them, such as the twenty sides, microcached platinum surface and core, and certain conduit elements, each DieCyclo is distinct to its maker.

- Though it is considered antiquated by many throughout Essa and the UCA, the complete art and science of creating a DieCyclo is the planet's second most highly regarded secret (to Technoid creation) and thus very little is written about it in Essan or any other known language in the Cosmos.

- Only fifty-two non-Essans in recorded history have successfully made one.

Status

- Official Creation Date: 1.94515.1AST

- Inventor: Professor   Sher'Dee   Lox (1.92534.1-1.97563.1AST)

- Essan Accessibility Status: Uncommon

- UCA Accessibility Status: Rare

- UCA Patent Registration: 21994.56e-1.376/Essan/

Top Factual Documentation

- Diecyclo: The Science and The Art

- Diecyclo: Ten Sides Twice

- Diecyclo: An Ancient Artform for the Modern Age

- Diecyclo: Opening Doors for Essans

- Diecyclo: Essan Ingenuity Under the Microscope

Top Opinions/Entertainment

- Diecyclo: Secrets and Lies

- Diecyclo: Rare Adventures in Living Under the Yoke of a Robot

- Diecyclo: Essan Ingenuity Under the Microscope (opinion piece)

- Diecyclo: What Lies Beyond the Facts?

- Diecyclo: Cursed From Creation

For more information and for answers to specific questions, please see **Talmund's Scientific Advancement Index Complete Entry: Diecyclo.**

***

TALMUND'S SCIENTIFIC ADVANCEMENT INDEX BRIEF ENTRY: HELIX NEEDLE

- The helix needle was invented by Cromlonican Dr. Hrrks Lrfgth a Crnths in 1.70008.1AST. There is no Evolutionary Historical Reckoning for the creation of the helix needle because Dr. Hrrks died without revealing it. Dr. Hrrks's helix needle is most significant for its purpose: methodical gene therapy that targets one species and slowly manipulates it to eventually become another.

- The helix needle is a small device that can be made of various hardened chemical compounds that can safely inject themselves and dissolve into a lifeform's system creating a chemical change on the molecular level without causing serious injury. The type of compound is determined by the species it is being used upon. Once fully dissolved into the system, the helix needle manipulates the lifeform's DNA until, over time, the original lifeform is now something different. The younger the lifeform, the quicker the change.

- The UCA outlawed the use of the helix needle sixty-three years (UCACTR) after its creation, when it was discovered that Dr. Hrrks and those associated with him were using the needles to create a mythical "pure race" that could survive in any environment and spread across the cosmos, thusly eradicating what Dr. Hrrks perceived as the cosmos's first and most egregious failure: diversity.

- Two-thousand systems with a total of eighty-nine hundred planets were infected with helix needles before the process was reversed through further manipulation and UCA approved helix needles.

- Since the reversal and Dr. Hrrks's execution twenty-three years later (UCACTR), they have been outlawed.

- Outlawed though they may be, some scientists throughout the cosmos have petitioned the Cosmic Tribunal to legalize their use in dire situations in which entire races of people would perish without DNA assistance of certain similar lifeforms. These petitions have never been successful.

Status

- Official Creation Date: 1.70008.1AST

- Inventor: Dr.   Hrrks   Lrfgth   a   Crnths Unknown-1.77777.2AST

- Cromlonican Accessibility Status: Forbidden/Outlawed

- UCA Accessibility Status: Forbidden/Outlawed

- UCA Patent Registration: None

Top Factual Documentation

- Helix Needle: Savior of Menace?

- Helix Needle: An (In) Complete Understanding

- Helix Needle: What We Know

- Helix Needle: Dr. Hrrk's Biography

- Helix Needle: Scientific Soliloquies

Top Opinions/Entertainment

- Helix Needle: A Special Report

- Helix Needle: When Science Goes Too Far

- Helix Needle: The Point of Destruction

- Helix Needle: A Necessary Evil

- Helix Needle: Not on My Block

For more information and for answers to specific questions, please see **Talmund's Scientific Advancement Index Complete Entry: Helix Needle**.

***

TALMUND'S SCIENTIFIC ADVANCEMENT INDEX BRIEF ENTRY: COSMIC TRIBUNAL

- The Cosmic Tribunal's true origins were taken from the cosmos when the original Annalang left.

- It is forbidden to study the origins or inner workings of the Cosmic Tribunal.

- The Cosmic Tribunal is a collective melding of the minds and thoughts of all citizens of the UCA. When activated, the Cosmic Tribunal stands in judgment of whatever case is presented before it. Its judgment stems from the collective emotional and intellectual bases of all sentient members of the UCA who are in direct and regular contact with the ExoNet.

- Essentially, an amalgamation of minds, when the Cosmic Tribunal passes judgment, it is final because its judgment literally is the will of the people.

- On rare occasions, the Cosmic Tribunal will make an edict or announce its desire to oversee a legal hearing.

Status

- Official Creation Date: Unknown

- Inventor: Unknown

- Annalang Accessibility Status: Forbidden

- UCA Accessibility Status: Forbidden

- UCA Patent Registration: N/A

Top Factual Documentation

- Cosmic Tribunal: This Is Known

- Cosmic Tribunal: This Is Unknown

- Cosmic Tribunal: All Are One

- Cosmic Tribunal: A Physical Explanation for a Metaphysical Being

- Cosmic Tribunal: The Dark and The Light: My Diary Beyond the Connection

Top Opinions/Entertainment

- Cosmic Tribunal: What If?

- Cosmic Tribunal: A Song For Us

- Cosmic Tribunal: Judgment Stands

- Cosmic Tribunal: Finding Life

- Cosmic Tribunal: Subconscious Overseer

For more information and for answers to specific questions, please see **Talmund's Scientific Advancement Index Complete Entry: Cosmic Tribunal**.

Chapter 6
Eye Witness

THE LONELY ONE EMBRACED the skin of the deer like an old friend. This creature's ability to weave and maneuver through a heavily wooded area and still maintain speeds the stagnants couldn't hope to match was always invigorating. Or, it had always been invigorating until this moment, until he found himself running for his life, for he had to be as far away from here as possible.

His thoughts raced, fear pumping through his blood as quickly as his hooves moved. He knew that it was not just a meteorite that had crashed in that field. It was something worse. Some hunter from the Draconian Diaspora had finally tracked him down. There were those who sought Draconians like him, the unrepentant ones, the proud ones, the ones who knew that someday the Draconian Reign would return to power. A rogue Ascendant could have sniffed him out and gone off book to murder him. No. That couldn't happen under The Alliance's watchful eye. Could it?

That's why they're rogue, he chastised himself.

He would not face them on their terms. He would run. He should have run when this little part of the cosmos had been allowed into the Outer Rim. He should have made his way to the NetNeg as many of his brethren had done, as those fools in the Diaspora had, those fools who thought they could one day rejoin the UCA, those fools who had thrown away their pride to wander as a helpless and hapless people, as a people without a home, as a people who he would no longer claim, as a people who would no longer claim him. They were fools and they had always been fools. He could remember their banal bantering and pathetic pleading for the Reign to end, for the wars to stop. But they had lost their debates on the senate floor, hadn't they? They had been reduced to something less than Draconian.

No matter. He had made a life of survival on this and other planets in the past and he would make another life of survival on still another planet until the Reign was ready to begin anew. He would not let those who refused to understand stop him, he would not—

Wait.

Beyond the trees. In that field that acted as a border between the trailer park and Oakview. Was that an Ascendant speaking with May Norman?

Why? he thought, slowing. *Why?*

He moved as close as he deemed safe, remembering how acute Correlative hearing could be, especially when combined with that of a trained Ascendant Officer. But his Draconian eyes were better, some of the best in the known cosmos. He could keep his distance and find out what was going on.

The Ascendant appeared to be helping heal May. But there was more. He squinted at them, watching as May passed out and the Ascendant went to work. It was almost like a field operation. A Correlative ball formed in her hand and rolled to the end of the pointer finger. She touched May's cheek and the ball fell from the finger, spreading like black slime over the woman's injury. A few moments later, the Ascendant placed a mask over May's mouth and felt her belly as if looking for something.

"The baby," The Lonely One said aloud, unable to control himself.

The Ascendant looked up and around at those words. The Lonely One silently cursed himself for a fool. He thought he was caught for sure, but in a moment that was far quicker than it felt, the Ascendant was back to work.

He took a closer look.

A Whitley! he thought, remembering what the Whitley had done, how many of his brethren they had taken. Whit was the planet where the end for the Draconian Reign had begun. Whit was the planet that had caused the Diaspora. Whit was the planet that had left his people without a home, without safety, and without a seat at the UCA. On that planet his people had fractured. Some had given into the whims of the UCA while others, like him, had gone into hiding.

But the Whitley had thrived. Their planet, almost burned to nothing, had risen from the ashes and sent its daughters across the cosmos to every rim. It took all of The Lonely One's self control to not shift into an Earthling beast and charge the thing while it helped May. If May fell victim to his rage too, so be it. He thought of a rhinoceros and felt his body changing, thick fur seeping back into skin, the hide hardening and—

He steadied himself, forcing the shift away. Though he imagined the Whitley's fragile body shattering under a massive rhinoceros horn, though he tasted her light blue blood, though he heard her bones crack and shivered at the thought of her death, he stopped himself. There would be no rampaging rhinoceros on a Nebraskan field tonight. This Ascendant, this vile Whitely, was not here for him.

But why was she here? And what was she doing to May Norman's baby? That baby, after all, was his business.

He shot away, knowing he had much, much to do. The boy's body all but forgotten on the beach, The Lonely One made his way toward the highway. Reaching it, he leapt over the pavement and was nearly hit by a sleek black Cadillac Coupe de Ville speeding toward the impact event.

The car screeched and spun on the pavement only to land in the ditch with a solid crunch.

The Lonely One, now safely off the road, turned to take a look at the car. If he knew the person who emerged from that mess in the ditch, he'd kill them right now, damn the consequences. People needed to respect the deer crossing signs in Nebraska.

A moment later, the Cadillac's passenger side window came down automatically. A woman with bright red hair leaned out. She held a pair of glowing green binoculars over her eyes. The mechanical monstrosity whirred in her hands as metal accouterments slid up and down its barrels. She adjusted the settings and zeroed the collecting lens in on the creature they had almost hit.

"A deer," she said.

"I hate the Midwest," a man in the driver's seat replied.

"Could be worse. We could have hit it," she said, turning back into her seat. "I'm checking the suitcase."

"I'm sure it's fine," the man in the driver's seat replied.

"Yeah, well," the woman said as she opened her door. "Still checking."

She stepped out into the night and The Lonely One saw it. A fine black suit.

No, he thought.

The man opened his door to join her. His suit matched hers perfectly. All black, save for the white button up shirts they both wore. The man had an added fedora for a touch of the classic.

Not them, The Lonely One thought.

"I guess we wait until someone comes along to help us. Betty ain't getting out of this ditch no matter how many knobs and whistles the white coats put on her." The man's voice cracked when he said the car's name and The Lonely One let himself laugh a little.

"Yep," the woman said, stretching the word and hitting the "p" sound hard so that it snapped in the now silent night. She stood at the back of the car where she opened the trunk. "Suitcase is fine," she said.

"Small victories," the man said. "Local is going to love this."

In the distance, closer to Oakview, sirens blared.

***

TALMUND'S COLLECTION OF SIGNIFICANT HISTORICAL EVENTS BRIEF ENTRY: DRACONIAN DIASPORA

- 3.98654.9AST-current.

- At the end of the conflict known throughout the UCA by many names, but prominently the Draconian Reign, those Draconians who were not supportive of the Reign and whose planets were laid to waste during the conflict, took it upon themselves to leave the UCA, becoming the Draconian Diaspora.

- Those Draconians who supported the Reign or were directly involved in its expansion were imprisoned, executed, exiled, or escaped. None, save the repentant, were accepted into the Draconian Diaspora.

- Various tribes of the Draconian Diaspora settled throughout the NetNeg in self-imposed exile. The Cosmic Tribunal quickly decided to endorse this exile and decree that, "There may come a day when the UCA welcomes our Draconian brethren back into the fold with open arms. But that day is not today, nor will it be tomorrow or tomorrow or tomorrow onwards."

Top Factual Documentation

- Draconian Diaspora: Separating Fact From Fiction

- Draconian Diaspora: A Proud People

- Draconian Diaspora: From Humble Beginnings to Humble Endings

- Draconian Diaspora: Life in the NetNeg

- Draconian Diaspora: Traumatic Guilt Through Generations

Top Opinions/Entertainment

- Draconian Diaspora: Keep Them

- Draconian Diaspora: The Great Rejoining: A Future to Celebrate

- Draconian Diaspora: Empathy Aligned in the NetNeg

- Draconian Diaspora: Keeping Up With The J'Onezz Clan

- Draconian Diaspora: Brother Gelding's Wanderings

For more information and for answers to specific questions, please see **Talmund's Collection of Significant Historical Events Complete Entry: Draconian Diaspora**.

***

TALMUND'S COLLECTION OF SIGNIFICANT HISTORICAL EVENTS BRIEF ENTRY: DRACONIAN REIGN

- 3.97432.9-3.98654.9AST

- The Draconian Reign came about when the Draconians from a collection of Draconian planets in the Flak and Sim Systems joined forces to declare war on the UCA in order to, as their writing tells it, "Bring peace through uniform destruction."

- With advanced technology, uncommon longevity (some are recorded to have lived over a millennium), years of preparation and training, and the element of surprise, the Draconians succeeded in taking over countless planets and entire systems until their forces invaded the small water/jungle Inner Rim planet of Whit.

- The Whitley won the first small victory against the Draconians and created a wave of support from systems throughout all three Rims.

- Eventually, under the command of Ascendant Pinnacle Romulus Vulcan, the Reign was ended and the Draconian ruled systems were destroyed.

- When the Draconians were officially defeated and peace declared, the Draconian Diaspora began.

Top Factual Documentation

- Draconian Reign: Papers On War

- Draconian Reign: The Rim Theaters and How The War Was Won

- Draconian Reign: Whitley and Draconian: A Balance

- Draconian Reign: The Autobiography of Ascendant Pinnacle Romulus Vulcan

- Draconian Reign: A Collection of Draconian Writings With Annotations By Doctor Prk'0'j0ck981

Top Opinions/Entertainment

- Draconian Reign: The Beginning of the End

- Draconian Reign: Siege: Whit

- Draconian Reign: How Did This Happen?

- Draconian Reign: How Did This Happen? II: How Can This Happen Again?

- Draconian Reign: Temple Time

For more information and for answers to specific questions, please see **Talmund's Collection of Significant Historical Events Complete Entry: Draconian Reign.**

***

TALMUND'S LEGAL LIBRARY BRIEF ENTRY: UNITED COSMIC ALLIANCE (UCA)

- At the beginning of time, The Cosmic Tribunal was formed when the First People of Annam joined minds and sent a psychic signal out to all who could hear.

- It took millions of Annam Standard Years for societies throughout the rims to evolve to a level that was able to connect with The Cosmic Tribunal.

- Once First Contact was made with the dominant species on the Nif System planet of Tyros, the Alliance was born.

- Throughout the centuries, the United Cosmic Alliance has grown and evolved, engulfing three cosmotic rims known as the Inner Rim, Mid Rim, and Outer Rim. Outside of the Outer Rim is the NetNeg, which is not part of the UCA, though explorers and settlers have mapped out settlements and mining, exploration, and science operations throughout.

- Every planet and system within the UCA has their own form of government that obeys its own laws. However, the systems are expected to abide by UCA Common Law as well.

- There is no Common Law in the NetNeg though Ascendant patrols are regularly scheduled.

Top Factual Documentation

- UCA: A Complete History

- UCA: An Incomplete History

- UCA: Operations and Procedures

- UCA: Connections Through HyperRifts

- UCA: In Our Time: The Past, Present, and Future of the UCA

Top Opinions/Entertainment

- UCA: What Works and What Does Not

- UCA: Complete Guide to the Dismantling of Government

- UCA: Annam Inside and Out

- UCA: Structural Plays That Are Played Out

- UCA: Keep It Coming

For more information and for answers to specific questions, please see **Talmund's Legal Library Complete Entry: United Cosmic Alliance,** and **Talmund's Collection of Significant Historical Events Complete Entry: Formation of the United Cosmic Alliance**.

***

TALMUND'S LEGAL LIBRARY BRIEF ENTRY: THE ASCENDANCY

- The Ascendancy is the United Cosmic Alliance's police and military force.

- Made up of lifeforms from across all three rims, The Ascendancy's primary duty is to enforce cosmotic law and protect UCA citizenry from inter-rim assaults.

- Legally bound against interference in self-contained planet-side legal matters, The Ascendancy is an inter-rim organization that no single planet or system can weaponize, including Annam.

- Every Ascendant Officer joins in a symbiotic relationship with a Correlative that acts as their partner for life (commonly).

- To join The Ascendancy a prospective officer must attend rigorous training for a minimum of five Annam Standard Years.

- Being an Ascendant Officer is a lifetime post because even when the officer is past standard working age for their lifeform to continue regular patrol, investigation, and battle duties, they are "retired" on Pelora where they take up posts as internal investigators, ExoNet researchers, and Correlative Caretakers.

- Once a Correlative bonds with its host, it grows a star and belt of the appropriate color of its host's rank (white, blue, gray, or red). These colors can be changed if an Ascendant changes position.

- There are no official NetNeg Ascendant Officers, but each rim has its own branch of The Ascendancy and there is a fourth branch whose primary duty is that of prison guard:

  - Inner Rim: White Stars

  - Mid Rim: Blue Stars

  - Outer Rim: Gray Stars

  - Prison Guards: Red Stars

- Within each branch, Ascendant Officers can hold various

positions ranging from Ascendant Tech (those who monitor and report crimes for others to investigate), Ascendant Officer (those who investigate crimes), Ascendant Galaxy Captain (those who run the operations of the galaxy where they are stationed. For a complete list see the complete entry.

- Though there are four different branches of The Ascendancy, each follows a series of six directives, known as the Sacred Six. They are:

  - Serve and Protect the Innocent

  - Protect the Correlative

  - Detect the Criminal

  - Subdue the Criminal

  - Know Thy Jurisdiction

  - Obey the Law

- Additionally, all members of The Ascendancy are required (as is every citizen of the UCA) to obey The Code of the Cosmic Tribunal, also referred to as UCA Common Law, the official laws set forth when the UCA was created and updated regularly when determined by the Cosmic Tribunal.

Top Factual Documentation

- The Ascendancy: A Day In The Life Of An Officer

- The Ascendancy: The Pinnacle Journals

- The Ascendancy: The Draconian Reign

- The Ascendancy: Operational Guide (Unclassified)

- The Ascendancy: Reporting For Duty: A Guide For The Prospective Ascendant

Top Opinions/Entertainment

- The Ascendancy: Police State at the Cosmotic Level

- The Ascendancy: Two Officers For The Price Of One: The Raping of Pelora

- The Ascendancy: Policing The Police

- The Ascendancy: Truth Hurts: A Journal of Injustices

- The Ascendancy: Truth Hurts II: A Journal of Justices

For more information and for answers to specific questions, please see **Talmund's Legal Library Complete Entry: The Ascendancy**.

***

TALMUND'S COSMOTIC LIBRARY BRIEF ENTRY: THE RIMS

- There are three known rims throughout the cosmos. Though referred to as Inner, Mid, and Outer, it must be understood that these designations have more to do with chronological association with the UCA than cosmotic location. The cosmos is far too vast and shapeless to be successfully separated by arbitrary borders to indicate location. Though within each individual rim approximations as to edges and centers can be made.

- That said, all Inner Rim systems are in relatively close proximity to one another, as are all Mid Rim, Outer Rim, and NetNeg systems. Each rim is separated by great expanses of dead space of few planetary systems that can be cut through using HyperRifts

  - Inner Rim: Home of Annam, capital planet of the UCA, located in the Ann System. The birthplace of the UCA that expands across several million star systems. The oldest and most highly advanced systems in the cosmos are found in the Inner Rim

  - Mid Rim: Home of the Nadar System where much of the material used to bring energy and inter-rim travel to the masses is mined. The largest of the three official rims, the Mid Rim holds the most lifeforms and the most interplanetary travel, commerce, and co-species mingling.

  - Outer Rim: This rim houses the newest members of the UCA. This is where the youngest cosmotic societies can be found. It is the only rim in which entire systems are not integrated, rather individual planets such as in the Sol System.

- ○ NetNeg: Outside of the last region of "dead space" is this relatively lawless area. Known as the NetNeg because the ExoNet is not linked there, each planet in this rim obeys its own sets of rules that the UCA does not interfere with. Some planets are too primitive while others have simply not been deemed worthy of joining the UCA for one reason or another.

Top Factual Documentation

- The Rims: Outer Rim Exploration

- The Rims: Solitude in the NetNeg

- The Rims: Mining For a Home: One Nadarite's Reclamation Of His Homeland

- The Rims: Running Through the Rifts: A Guide To Your Greatest HyperRift Vacation Through All Three Rims

- The Rims: Joining the UCA: A Step-By-Step Explanation

Top Opinions/Entertainment

- The Rims: Division Creates Suspicion

- The Rims: Open The Gates

- The Rims: Hopping I: The Inner Rim

- The Rims: Hopping IV: The NetNeg

- The Rims: Lord of the Outer Rim

For more information and for answers to specific questions, please see **Talmund's Cosmotic Library Complete Entries: Inner Rim, Mid Rim, Outer Rim, NetNeg**.

Chapter 7
Gray Stars

AURORA DODGED METEORS OF all shapes and sizes as she rocketed away from Earth. If The Ascendancy had known their plans, if they had known the coordinates for the HyperRift near Essa, anything was possible. They had been right there waiting, watching her when the rift had swallowed her up. If one of them was a tech, they could have easily duplicated her window, no matter how rough her trip through had been. If, as she suspected, she had somehow been followed, she needed to create a trail that would lead her pursuers as far from Earth as possible. The CorreBeam one of them had fired was too perfect a shot to be accidental. They had known she carried Helix Needles and they had even known where on her belt she had carried them. They had known at least some aspect of their plan, probably all of it.

And now, if Peel was right, there was a CorreAxe on Earth. Where there was a CorreAxe, there was a Draconian.

How could they have studied Earth and not discovered that?

She couldn't think about that now.

She had to escape.

The Ascendancy could not find evidence that Aurora had made it planet-side. They could not find evidence that any Helix Needles had survived and she had used one. If the Zenith discovered that Aurora had used a Helix Needle, the results for Earth could be disastrous in the most literal sense. Aurora could remember reading the court cases about their usage during her studies at Ascendancy Academy. She imagined hearing The Cosmic Tribunal utter it as the law was ordained, its voice profound and deep, resonating from the depths of Annam. One phrase stuck out to her:

"Lumbering Genocide."

The theory was that Helix Needles destroyed one race at the benefit of another. But on Earth, she was not destroying a race, she was saving one and making the other one *better*. She had used the Earthling's fertilized embryo to help keep an entire race alive. And Earthling DNA was so close to Essan DNA that there would be no significant change and surely no negative one. Aurora was not destroying a people, she was raising a people up.

Wasn't she?

Questions like this raced through her mind as she darted up through the Earth's spheres and into the blackness of space. Meteoroids that had split from the asteroid field some 400 million miles away zoomed close enough to the planet to be sucked into its orbit. Rocks spun so fast and were of so many sizes that avoiding them required the most difficult maneuvering she'd ever accomplished.

Yet while doing so, she still pondered what had gone wrong and more importantly, if she had been right to do what she had done. The idea that there was a Draconian on Earth hovered behind all of her thoughts as well, forcing more worry like water through leaks in a dam. Peel had sensed a CorreAxe. There was no record of a CorreAxe on Earth. Nothing was right. Was the plan right? Had she made a terrible mistake? She wished Jon'Oh was with her now, comforting her, telling her things would be fine.

But Jon'Oh was dead.

Their plan was in ruins.

This is not how it was supposed to happen! she thought. How had The Ascendancy found them out? Jon'Oh had planned this so precisely. Nothing had gone unchecked, unchallenged. It had been the perfect plan, hadn't it?

The silence of space answered her. It pushed against her chest as she sped through a sea of flying stones, all of which rushed at speeds so fast even Peel had trouble calculating them. Through their psycho-emotive connection, she helped Aurora dodge what she could, and even blasted a few meteoroids away with CorreBeams of her own making.

For years, Aurora's comrades had made light of her relationship with Peel, telling her that an Ascendant imparted directives to a Correlative, not the other way around. And she could tell most Correlatives, including Peel when they had first bonded, felt that way too. But her connection with Peel was stronger because they were equal, not because she was the Correlative's commander and the Correlative her silent "Yes Man." In her mind, seeing Peel's CorreBeams destroy incoming meteoroids proved it.

As shattered stone spun around her, Aurora let herself cast one quick glance at the planet she had escaped. It was a magnificent blue and green marble resting on the black tabletop of space. Wispy white clouds encircled it. And far in the distance, the star, Sol, powered the lifeforms there and, she knew, would have given the new lifeforms she was sent to create greater power. It seemed to glow with life. But their plan had not worked. Jon'Oh was dead, his planet destroyed, his people gone, and the Helix Needles she was supposed to have used to bring them back shattered into millions of pieces frozen in some void where Essa used to be.

Now only one remained and it was in an Earthling's possession.

It wasn't supposed to be this way! she thought again as she looked away and allowed herself a moment of rage. A meteoroid careened toward her. It was a massive, jagged thing, dense to its core. She screamed, soundless in the vacuum of space, and formed eight CorreBlades, one from each finger and thumb. The tingling sensation that coursed through her when her blades bit into the rock was invigorating. When the great craggy thing crumbled around her, she let Peel take over completely and floated there inside the Correlative like a podling, momentarily unburdened.

There was supposed to have been a process.

She was supposed to have had enough Helix Needles to change all the Earthling DNA to Essan. She was supposed to have enough time to find the perfect specimens, to approach them as friend, instructor, and bearer of a great gift. She was supposed to have been able to teach them about Essa, Whit, and all of the UCA before using the Helix Needles. Nothing was to have been forced the way it had been with that poor creature on Earth.

Done right, many Earthling lifeforms would've slowly, over four generations, maybe five or six, become Essan. It would have been harmless to them. Jon'Oh's people would have survived and thanks to Earth's yellow sun, the Earthlings with Essan DNA coursing through their veins would have been made better, stronger, smarter. They would have all been gifted abilities beyond their primitive dreams. Their lives would have been longer. When the Earthlings were finally able to join the Alliance, Jon'Oh's plan may have been discovered. But by then, Aurora would have been long dead of old age herself, Jon'Oh's people would have still been alive, and the Earthlings would have been better because of it. It would have been a new Essa, a second chance, a second chance Jon'Oh deserved.

Of course, The Alliance, The Cosmic Tribunal itself, didn't consider this moral. It wasn't legal at all. "Lumbering Genocide," echoed in her mind once more, The Tribunal's great voice sounding into even the deepest crevices of her thoughts. But after The Tribunal had prevented her and Jon'Oh from saving the Essans with the help of the UCA, using the Helix Needles had been their only option. Was The Tribunal right? Was The Tribunal moral? Why was it legal for them to allow one race to die? Why was it illegal for Aurora to help one Non-Alliance planet better itself?

Jon'Oh had called Earth a jewel, had named it Et'a in his language, "hope." Essa had once been that beautiful. Essa had once been like a shining symbol of societal harmony in the Inner Rim. It had been a beacon. Lessons were taught in classrooms in all three rims about the symbiotic relationship between the planet Essa and its dominant species who fancied themselves caretakers of the higher lifeform. The Essan people and their home had been compared to Ascendant Officers and their Correlatives.

But that had been ages ago, long before Aurora's planet had survived the Draconian Reign. Long before Aurora had been born, enlisted in The Ascendancy to honor those who had lost their lives when the Draconians had invaded Whit. Long before she had met Jon'Oh Lox and fallen in love with him as his planet died, and long before she had learned of the twisted morality of the establishment she protected.

Today Essa was no longer thought of as a beacon, but a cautionary tale. They had grown arrogant in their knowledge. They had brought about their own demise when their leaders had somehow collectively decided that Essa was not a living thing to be cared for, but a resource to be exhausted. Not Jon'Oh though. He had known for so long what was happening. He had tried to warn everyone.

Few had listened. And those who had were powerless.

No! Aurora screamed to herself as she shot a CorreBeam at a large incoming meteoroid. When it shattered before her, it revealed Earth's moon hiding behind it in the distance. Aurora had become so spun around in space that she wasn't sure which direction she was flying anymore, but seeing the pale, pockmarked surface caused images of the Correlative home world of Pelora to swim through Aurora's thoughts.

The rocky, nameless moon reminded her of Peel's birthplace. Only Pelora did not rotate the way Earth's nameless moon clearly did. Though Pelora circled around its sun, it did not spin. The permanently dark side where Correlatives went to die was so cool and somber that Ascendancy Officers used it as a place of meditation and learned from those who came before them. It held a massive burial volcano for Correlatives and any Ascendant who so chose to be put to rest there. It was heavily guarded so as to keep those like the Draconians away, those who would use the carcasses of deceased Correlatives to make weapons like CorreAxes.

There was also a record of retired Ascendant journals for study. There were retirement grounds, soft and, if somewhat eerie, also somewhat pleasant. The warm bright side where Correlatives lived was covered in black rocks that sparkled like dark diamonds. Their beauty was as alluring as it was terrifying—their beauty was alive. The fire dens where Correlatives were born and bred bled enticing effervescent liquid that fueled Ascendant connection to Correlatives. Aurora tasted the sweetness, felt the warmth. Absorbed in her memory of the connection ceremony, she cried. It had been an honor to be allowed there, on the bright side of Pelora, to be made one with Peel under the orange sun and multi-colored sky. It had been an honor to go forth and guard the cosmos.

"On my honor," she began The Ascendancy Oath for reasons she couldn't entirely understand, "I will defend—" She stopped.

Was she even an Ascendant anymore?

She could see the loose sprinklings of space dust signifying the end of the storm of rocks. Somehow she had managed to fly out of the asteroid belt offshoot. But what was she to do now that all of their plans had been laid to waste?

Before she had time to figure this out, a force flying like one of the meteors, hit Aurora in the back and latched on.

"Going somewhere?" The words sounded as though they had been raked through a field of gravel.

"Blast," Aurora said under her breath as she struggled to face what she knew was another Ascendant. No one else could have caught her off guard.

"They told me you were dangerous," the voice said through their Correlative connection, smug even through the watery veil encircling its rough words. "They told me I wouldn't be able to sneak up on you, that your senses were some of the sharpest in the cosmos. And yet here I am. You must have been deep in conversation with your Correlative. Were you?"

Whatever it was, its strong arms squeezed around Aurora so tightly she knew escape wasn't possible. Their trajectory changed, and Aurora found herself heading straight for the moon circling Earth.

"No!" Aurora shouted as they sped closer. Her fruitless struggles grew more intense until it was clear they were going to slam into the moon's surface at full speed. At the last second, Aurora went limp. The moon's rocky surface dug at her but failed to penetrate her Correlative which expanded and hardened like a stretching net of thick wire. Within seconds Aurora found herself lying in the second small crater she had created that evening. Only this time, instead of stumbling out and finding a scared Earthling, she leapt to her feet and found herself looking up at the large frame of a Tholin Ascendant.

The Tholin, a hulking cloud-like creature, the dominant species from the Saturnian moon, Tho, stared down at her. Tholin had soft outer shells made of a wispy, amorphous flesh, but beneath that, their bones and organs were as hard as stone. Tholin manipulated these bones and organs with ease, shifting their size, shape, and density at will. Their eyes were bulbous, golden things that could see farther, faster, and more than any creature in Talmund's Bestiary except for Draconians. As the realization of this officer's species hit Aurora, Peel, whose connection to the ExoNet was permanent and perpetual outside of the NetNeg, accompanied it with biological information and historical data.

Tho was the only Alliance member in this system, and one of only four celestial objects with intelligent life out here on the edge of the Outer Rim. Some in the Inner Rim found the Tholin ways barbaric and obtuse, but they were part of the UCA, and thus, obeyed cosmotic law, held space in the collective psyche of The Cosmic Tribunal and could become members of The Ascendancy.

Aurora blinked. *Thanks for the download, Peel.*

The Tholin towered above Aurora, shimmering in the darkness like a mirage come to life. He wore the same uniform as Aurora, save where her starburst and belt were white, his were gray. Aurora knew Tholin to be some of the fiercest creatures in the Outer Rim. As she ran through the records on Tholin that Peel could serve her without overloading her brain, Aurora observed this one grow larger. Though encased in his own Correlative, his liquid outer shell expanded to what Aurora hoped was his full size. She heard the bones of his legs stiffen through the Correlative connection and watched his feet dig into the moon's blue dirt while his hands formed fists she knew were growing much harder as they spoke.

"How did you find me?" Aurora demanded.

"I'm afraid that's above my pay grade, honey," the Tholin said from behind his mask. "Someone from the Inner Rim gave my captain a list of your crimes and the coordinates where we could find you and since I was closest, he sent me here first. Told me you'd be hard to catch. He was wrong. Why?"

Aurora clenched her fists at her side. "You're going to try to take me in, then?"

"'Try'?" The Tholin laughed. "I am Outer Rim Ascendant Nash, and I've seen shit you Inner Rim bitches can't even begin to imagine," he said. "It don't sparkle out here in the dust." He laughed. "Aurora Vega, I hereby arrest you for high crimes against the United Cosmic Alliance. You may speak your dissent but you may not refuse to comply with your arrest."

With a swiftness Nash could not hope to emulate, Aurora's right hand grew into a thick CorreBlade. Charging toward him, she swung.

Shocked at the speed of Aurora's instinctual movements, Ascendant Nash pulled his feet free and dodged, nearly missing a full blade to the face. He responded in kind, his hand becoming not one but dual blades. Nash and Aurora clashed there, on the rocky dark surface of Earth's moon, their blades angry at the lack of sound in this vacuum. One a giant rock of a thing and the other a thin knife of a Whitley spun and swung in a kind of dance while their blades scraped soundlessly against one another. The black clad figures parried and sliced, both highly trained in the workings of CorreBlades. The boulders and rocks served as high points and walls they weaved around and over. Though, from a distance, their dance appeared silent, inside each Correlative, their voices could be heard.

"You're outmatched, Nash," Aurora said as she twisted, bringing her blade down again. This time, Nash was not fast enough. It hit his shoulder. His own Correlative quickly hardened to meet it. It grew tentacles to pry Peel away and shove Aurora back.

Nash fought her off with his preternatural strength, forcing her on her back. "Am I?" he grunted.

Aurora was up before Nash's blade came down.

"I don't want to hurt you." Aurora's own blade now fought its way against a second, smaller blade Nash grew from his free hand. Peel fed her as much information on Nash as she could. The Tholin was newer to the force and had risen in the Outer Rim ranks based on his strength and, if Aurora's estimation was correct, the sheer lack of numbers out here on the edge of civilized society.

"Could've fooled me," he said through clenched teeth.

"You think multiple blades can match my speed?" Aurora said, unable to hide the shock in her voice.

"Impressed? Didn't think some Outer Rim Podunk had it in him to grow more than a single CorreBlade at a time did you?"

"You talk too much," Aurora replied, growing her own second blade, not from her free hand, but from a foot, sending it crashing against the Tholin's ankle.

He fell, a cloud of dust exploded around him.

"I'll say again, I don't want to hurt you." Aurora held her hand blade at his throat as secondary ones emerged from it and the lonely foot blade slipped silently back into Peel.

"Then surrender," Nash replied, kicking Aurora in the gut and flipping to his feet.

Aurora landed on her own feet, sliding through the loose gravel. She flicked out her free hand and formed four smaller CorreBlades from her fingers before charging and screaming a Whitley curse.

The Tholin, like any good Ascendant, had been studying his enemy through their battle and dodged her charge with a laugh. "I'm a quick learn, Vega," Nash said. "I know your tricks now."

In response, she released a CorreBlade like a projectile at him.

The blade crashed upon his hardened Correlative and he stumbled to his knees, still laughing. "What are you doing out here anyway?" he asked as he climbed back to his feet.

Aurora spun back around and swung a regrown blade at him. He brought his own up to block and forced her back. "Does it have anything to do with Earth? Have you seen the Earthlings? They are dumb. Let me tell you. My people have been watching them for centuries and they're still bickering about imaginary lines in the ground and such nonsense. They don't even have a planet wide governing system, or a single dominant language, can you believe that?"

"Earth? The Ascendancy monitors Earth?"

"Did I say The Ascendancy?"

Aurora swung again.

Nash dodged again.

Using all her strength, Aurora spun her CorreBlades around Nash. She vaulted to his side and smashed him in the back of his head with a hardened, jagged elbow. As he stumbled forward, she sheathed her weapons and blasted away from the moon.

It did not feel good to run from a fight she knew she could win, but Nash's words scared her. Not only had Peel sensed a CorreAxe but this Tholin had been monitoring Earth. How had Jon'Oh not known that? How had she? Unsure of what to do, she began to grow the thin blades she could use to cut a HyperRift Window to anywhere far away from here, when four more Ascendants appeared out of the blackness of space. They approached her as one rapid unit.

A particularly large officer landed a blow to Aurora's head that sent her careening back down to the moon's surface as Nash stood, laughing and dusting pebbles from his Correlative.

"How did you not notice them? Aren't Correlatives supposed to be able to spot their own?"

Aurora looked up to see Nash once again. Only now there were four other Ascendants at his side. Based on their shapes and sizes, Peel knew what sort of lifeforms they were and uploaded basic knowledge to Aurora's brain. When Peel tried to force specific information about each individual Ascendant, she turned her down.

"I don't need to know more about them," she said. She felt it and decided the humanoid one with a pink mohawk jutting from her head was the most dangerous. The other ones, though, one with several tentacles, another with four legs, fours arms on a stretched torso with an accompanying long face ending in a wide muzzle, and one more with six arms and an elongated, if humanoid, head who floated in what appeared to be a sea of his own making, were all dangerous in their own rights.

Still, Aurora thought she might be better. A CorreBlade grew from her right hand and a CorreBeam from her left. "It won't happen again."

"Not playing around anymore, are we?" Nash huffed.

"Why do you ask so many questions?"

Nash shrugged, circling Aurora like a predator. "You fascinate me I suppose."

"Leave. You don't want to fight me again."

Nash laughed. "There are five of us, now, little girl."

"Podmother save me," Aurora mumbled.

"Why did you run? Why did you stop? How are you so good?" The questions came rapid fire and Aurora felt herself wondering what it was like to teach podlings.

She let a CorreBeam blast at her nearest enemy, the tentacled officer. They only barely dodged the cool beam of energy breaking through the darkness between them.

Nash put his hands on his hips and guffawed. "You are amazing."

"Thank you," Aurora replied, swinging her blade at him while simultaneously firing a round from her CorreBeam at the others.

"Warning shots, at best," Nash said. "Why not just do us in? The list of crimes you're being accused of is so large, what's murdering a few Ascendants?"

"I haven't murdered anyone."

"No," he said, "I suppose not. You've only broken some of the Sacred Six. You're a traitor, a deserter." He raised his hands. "I'm not fool enough to fight you anymore, Whitley. I just want to know what is going on."

"That's enough, Nash," the one who had punched Aurora back to the moon finally spoke.

Aurora let a second CorreBlade slip from her foot and moved to kick Nash so swiftly that the Tholin lost his balance.

Aurora was on top of him in an instant. A blade at his throat and a beam in his face. "This will hurt," she said, "and for that I apologize."

He started to say something but the beam went off in his face. The only thing that saved him was his own Correlative's quick reflexes.

"You . . . are . . . cold," he said, struggling to his feet while his Correlative's skin softened around the blast area, doing its best to make sure its host would not be seriously harmed.

Aurora backed off and circled them all, the prey becoming the predator. Her CorreBlade and CorreBeam moved around her, aiming at all five officers. Peel's skin hardened into the strongest shell she could manage.

Aurora was silent as she prowled.

"So, you're going to tell me nothing, no matter how nicely I ask?"

"I said enough, Nash."

"Captain," Nash said, "she's not going to cooperate."

"You remember your time working the SoloPens, Aurora?" the other large Ascendant asked.

She didn't speak, but sadness or madness, Aurora knew, were the only two ways for any sentient being in the vastness of the cosmos to deal with SoloPens. It was the one thing everyone everywhere had in common.

She had seen it time and again in the SoloPens that The Ascendancy had scattered throughout countless galaxies, and had even lived it for thirty terrible rotations above a nameless moon of Avgar in another Outer Rim system. Every Ascendant had to do their time in one of those places, both as a prisoner and a guard. The philosophy was sound. If your job would involve sending citizens of the rims to one of these places, you had to know what it was like, really know. Of course, the reason was two-fold. Having spent a small amount of time as a prisoner, even knowing full-well that it was temporary, that you had committed no crime, and that on the other side of this ordeal was the career, no, *the life*, that you had struggled and fought for years to obtain, you knew what it would be like on the inside if you ever committed a serious offense.

You knew.

She knew.

Yet . . .

Peel rippled around her, trying hard to pull Aurora away from memories of the SoloPens, of the fear of them.

If I'm taken in, I'd probably spend most of my time in the quarries anyway, she thought sarcastically.

Peel, who could feel the sarcasm, did not respond.

"Well," she said, "I guess you Gray Stars are going to have to take me in and remind me."

"You've slowed down," a familiar voice sounded in her ear.

Aurora spun around and noticed a seventh officer, a Whitley. She laughed wickedly. "Hello Mia," Aurora said, her CorreBlades sinking back into her hands. "I shouldn't be surprised they'd send you."

"Sister," the other Whitley replied. Her Correlative held the same gray starburst and belt as the others. "If our Podmother could see you now."

"It's about time you showed up, Nova," Nash grunted. "Wasn't supposed to have to take her without you."

"Stop," the large captain said. "There is no need for this We're doing this by the book."

"Captain, I just—"

The captain raised his hand and Nash's words faltered and fell. Aurora had to admit she liked that.

"Ascendant Aurora Vega, my name is System Captain Flux," he said, his voice taking on the official cadence that Aurora knew she had used more times than she could count. "Accompanying me are Ascendants Mia Nova," he motioned toward Aurora's sister, "Nalumbaum Black," he pointed at the four legged Ascendant with the long face, "our tech, Cheer Slum, Dawlish Coldbloom Redcoarath," he nodded toward the tentacled Ascendant and the one who floated nearest her, "and Neo." He placed one large hand on the Ascendant with the mohawk's shoulder. "You've already met Nash," he added and cleared his throat. "I hereby arrest you for high crimes against the United Cosmic Alliance. You may speak your dissent but you may not refuse to comply with your arrest."

"I'll speak my dissent," Aurora growled. She crossed her arms and created two more CorreBlades. "And I'll refuse to comply."

Captain Flux looked skyward, clasping his hands together as though praying. "I'm too old for this," he muttered before returning his gaze to Aurora.

Aurora, for her part, hadn't moved. She now appeared rock-like herself and the CorreBlades shimmered with what looked like a million microscopic stars. "So quit while you're ahead," she said.

"Aurora, don't," Mia said. She stepped forward. "There are six of us. We only need three with Bracing ability. Did you think we would come without that? You can't beat us."

"I can try." She swung one blade at Captain Flux, who raised his own CorreBlade so swiftly that it caught Aurora in mid swipe.

"If you try, you will fail and your list of crimes will only grow longer," Captain Flux said, shoving Aurora down. "Now I am willing to let that go, but if it happens again—"

"What about what she did to me?" Nash put in, urgently.

Flux laughed. "Anytime someone can put a beat down on you, I'm happy. So, we're going to let that go too."

"Seriously?" Nash asked, seemingly genuinely hurt. The other officers laughed. Two of them held their own CorreBlades at their sides while Mia and another pointed CorreBeams at Aurora's face.

"Nash, stop."

Peel sent shockwaves of anxiety through Aurora.

"Peel, no. We'll never get away from them."

"Peel?" Flux asked.

"She named her Correlative," Mia said.

"Hmmmm," Flux said. "Interesting."

"How is that interesting?" Aurora shot.

Mia placed a hand on Aurora's shoulder. "Your crimes, Aurora, they're—"

"Don't worry about it," Flux said. "Are you coming quietly?"

Aurora turned from her sister and shrugged her hand off her shoulder.

"I asked you a question. Are you going to come quietly?" Flux said. "Or do we need to Brace your Correlative? I don't want to do it, but I will."

Aurora inhaled sharply, ready to strike, the thought of Peel getting Braced hurt her almost physically. "You can't—"

"Aurora!" Mia shouted, looking down at her sister. Her Correlative gave the impression that it was sliding off her face, but really, it was shifting to clear mode, revealing a face almost identical to Aurora's save for one small scar under her left eye. On Whitley, their faces were called "treasure" because they were considered perfect. Their pointed chins and ovoid heads were the features most Whitley wanted. Their large, slanted eyes were like black jewels on their pale skin. With thin lips and an almost imperceptible stub of a nose containing symmetrical nasal slits, on Whit, their beauty was second to none.

Seeing her sister now with a look of pain, of confusion, and of hurt etched into her beautiful features, was too much. Aurora turned from her. "You shouldn't force your Correlative to do that, you know it's painful."

"Look at me!" Mia shouted.

"This is stupid," Nash said. "Just Brace her!"

Aurora took a breath and turned back around to face her sister.

"Take off the mask," Mia said.

Aurora stared up at her sister, unmoving.

"Aurora, I want to talk to you as a sister not as an Ascendant."

Aurora's mask shimmered and went invisible. "Peel did that," she said. Her voice was cold.

"It doesn't work like that, Ascendant Vega," Captain Flux said. "We may be bumpkins out here in the boondocks but we have our own Correlatives, you know. We understand they only work on their own in matters of life and death." There was a certain indignation in his grizzled voice. "Don't try to pull a fast one on us. We know you did the crimes, not some overzealous Correlative."

"It doesn't work like that with Aurora. Her Correlative has a certain amount of anonymity," Mia said.

"What?" Nash asked, shocked.

"How did you become an Inner Rim Ascendant?" Captain Flux asked, authentic shock in his voice.

"Graduated at the top of her class, collared a few big names as a rookie, and generally dedicated her life to it," Mia said.

Nash chuckled. "Look at her now."

"Why am I looking at your face, Mia?" Aurora asked. "Why are you looking at mine?"

Mia exhaled her frustration. "I want you to know that I understand. I get it. Hell," she motioned to Flux, "Flux already told me he gets it."

"What do you mean?"

"Love is a many-splendored thing, Vega."

"I don't—"

"Flux is a student of Earth."

"I still don't—"

"Flux and I read the report about your crimes," Mia said. "Now, can you talk to us?"

"Ascendant Vega, your record speaks for itself," Flux said. "You can beat all of this, even the Helix Needles. Yes, we know about the Helix Needles, we know about everything. We have—"

"Helix Needles? I didn't read about Helix Needles!"

The shock and disgust in Mia's voice made Aurora tremble. She wasn't sure if it was with fear or anger. "Let me explain. I just—"

"You didn't—"

"Ascendant Nova," Captain Flux said calmly. "Do not interrupt me."

"Sorry sir," Mia said and hung her head, whether it was shame at her outburst or disgust at what her sister had done, Aurora couldn't tell. Her Correlative's color faded to black.

Flux cleared his throat. "We have reason to believe you managed to get to Earth before Nash found you. There are investigators covering the most likely places you could have landed. It's over. If you come with us now, chances are you will get off lightly. Your Correlative will be spared."

"There's something you don't know!" Aurora shouted, backing away from them, arms up, Correblades forming, ready to fight once more.

"Aurora, you're my podsister. Please," Mia begged, looking back up at her.

"Mia, you don't understand, on Earth, there's—"

"Aurora," Mia said, "please."

"No. My Correlative felt a—"

"This is getting us nowhere," Flux said. "Brace the Correlative." He waved a hand and Nash and two of the officers spread their fingers and fired a series of thin CorreBeams at Aurora. They came together quickly and encircled her like a net.

Though she jumped to avoid them, there were too many and moved too swiftly. The first one that hit held her in place. When the others followed, the space around Aurora split as though opening a HyperRift Window but stopped just short of doing so, offering only enough pull to immobilize Aurora and shock Peel. The sensation was paralyzing for both of them

Within moments, Peel went limp and Aurora blacked out.

***

TALMUND'S LEGAL LIBRARY BRIEF ENTRY: ZENITH

- The Zenith is made up of a rotating group of inter-rim rulers.

- Though it is made up of a single ruler from all three rims, the Zenith's roster changes every ten Annam Standard Years.

- The standing Ascendant Pinnacle is also a member, though their term only ends when their term as a Pinnacle ends.

- The Zenith sit with The Cosmic Tribunal on all legal cases brought to it.

- Collectively, along with The Cosmic Tribunal, they are responsible for making sure law and order is sustained throughout the cosmos.

Top Factual Documentation

- Zenith: An Exploration

- Zenith: A Complete Living History

- Zenith: The Misadventures of King Orreloneous Monk Ack

- Zenith: The Unauthorized Biography of King Orreloneous Monk Ack

- Zenith: Most Famous Tribunal Cases

Top Opinions/Entertainment

- Zenith: Bless Them Father, For They Know Not What They Do

- Zenith: Ten Years Too Long

- Zenith: Annam's Secret Shame

- Zenith: The Battle of Neverworld

- Zenith: Peace Through Power: Can the Zenith's Hands Reach the NetNeg?

For more information and for answers to specific questions, please see **Talmund's Legal Library Complete Entry: Zenith**.

***

TALMUND'S BESTIARY—ABOVE HYPER-CLASSIFIED—BRIEF ENTRY: DRACONIAN

UCA Designation: No designation

Information on Draconians is above hyper-classified. All declassified information on Draconians can be found in **Talmund's Collection of Significant Historical Events Complete Entry: Draconian Diaspora** or **Talmund's Collection of Significant Historical Events Complete Entry: Draconian Reign**.

Much like this file, accessing any files regarding Draconians requires an unwritable, above hyper-classified, secure clearance code. If you do not possess a clearance code, or if you obtained one through illegal means, Ascendant Officers will be on their way to your location before you finish reading this entry.

***

TALMUND'S BESTIARY BRIEF ENTRY: THOLIN

USA Designation: Sol Tholinian-Prime

- A culture bearing, verbal communicating, ammonia-amphibian dwelling, bipedal evolutionary aquaelasticorundum anuriticus that presents itself as, overall, average in that class and order. Possessed of bones and internal organs whose size and density Tholins can shift at will, they are one of the sturdiest lifeforms in the Outer Rim. With a complicated social structure that is a mixture of densely populated urban areas and sparsely populated rural ones, the Tholins live below the surface of their home world of Tho (Earthlings refer to this cosmic body as "Titan") in ammonia rich ice structures and bodies of water. Their evolution is recorded to have occurred at a much faster rate than comparable lifeforms throughout the cosmos as well as completely different ones nearer their home. Tholins are primarily divided into two sexes: male and female, though they do not join together in pairs to raise their children. Tholin reproduction is ritualistic in nature and never leads to partnership (as in many lifeforms). Rather, Tholins have mating and birthing ceremonies twice yearly (Tholin reckoning) in which entire communities come together to reproduce and assist in birthing. Children are then, in turn, raised by their communities. Since their outer shell is cloud-like and weak, the children are jealously protected from their many predators until they learn to control their bones and internal organs. With exceptional eyesight, Tholins often operate Rift Trains through HyperRifts. Like many in the anuriticus order, Tholins display an erectness of body carriage that frees their dual hands of three digits each (two fingers and one thumb per hand) for use as manipulative members. Their three toes on each foot are buried inside their wispy flesh. When walking, they use the tips of these toes, making them digitigrades.

Status

- Average Height: 3.5 meters

- Average Weight: 900 kilograms

- Average Lifespan: 300 Annam Standard Years

- Home Moon: Tho/Sol System/Outer Rim

- Planetary Status: Dominant Lifeform

- System Status: UCA Equality Outer Rim

- Cosmotic Status: UCA Member Outer Rim (Experimental Standing)

Classification

- **RIM: Outer**

- **SYSTEM: Sol**

- **PLANET: Tho**

- **DOMAIN: Eukarya**

- **KINGDOM: Animalia**

- **PHYLUM: Chordata**

- **CLASS: Evolutionary Aquelasticorundum**

- **ORDER: Nephdecapoda**

- **FAMILY: Nephcancridae**

- **TRIBE: Neph**

- **GENUS: Cancer**

- **SPECIES: Tholinian**

Top Factual Documentation

- Tholin: A Cultural Review

- Tholin: The Outer Rim's Socio and Economic Impact on the Cosmos

- Tholin: A Complete History of the Ammonia Ice Cloud Arts

- Tholin: Clouds: A People Whose God Weeps

- Tholin: The Structural Steps of Sol's Integration Into the UCA

Top Opinions/Entertainment

- Tholin: Newest UCA Member Brings Unique Perspective to Cosmos

- Tholin: High-Low Duality and the Detriment of the Outer Rim

- Tholin: Culture Wars in the Outer Rim

- Tholin: Level-Up With Mank, the Greatest Gamer in the

Cosmos

- Tholin: Enraged Rock Monsters or Complex Cloud Men?

For more information and for answers to specific questions, please see **Talmund's Bestiary Primary Entry: Tholin**.

***

TALMUND'S LEGAL LIBRARY BRIEF ENTRY: CORREAXE

- Formed from a desecrated Correlative corpse, a CorreAxe is the most dangerous weapon in the universe. There are no known metals, materials, or biological lifeforms that can withstand a CorreAxe's blade.

- There are only twelve known to exist, nine of which are guarded in hyper-classified locations.

- The location of the other three CorreAxes is unknown.

- CorreAxe creation is forbidden/outlawed in all three rims.

- The science behind CorreAxe creation was founded by a Draconian whose name, science, discoveries, and life have been wiped from every Talmund collection.

- The science behind CorreAxe creation has been lost to time.

Top Factual Documentation

- CorreAxe: A Study

- CorreAxe: The Art of Death

- CorreAxe: In Search Of (S12): CorreAxe-The Missing Three

- CorreAxe: On The Use of CorreAxes During the Draconian Reign

- CorreAxe: So It Goes: A CorreAxe Summary

Top Opinions/Entertainment

- CorreAxe: Keeping It Real With Mickey Dawls R2

- CorreAxe: The Weapon We Need

- CorreAxe: Gone But Not Forgotten

- CorreAxe: Forget History And The CorreAxe Will Return

- CorreAxe: An Ax To Grind

For more information and for answers to specific questions, please see **Talmund's Legal Library Complete Entry: CorreAxe.**

***

TALMUND'S LEGAL LIBRARY BRIEF ENTRY: CORRELATIVE/ASCENDANT WEAPONRY

- •Correlative/Ascendant weaponry can be divided into five main categories

    - Defensive: CorreBlade, CorreBeam

    - Offensive: Shelled Skin, Bracing Needles, Bonding

    - Subjective: Electro-fiber Cuffs

    - HyperRift: HyperNeedles

    - Forbidden: CorreAxe

- **Defensive**

    - All Ascendant Officers are adept at CorreBlade and CorreBeam usage to varying skill levels.

    - CorreBlade: Sword like growths of various sizes that can admit and retract at Ascendant's will.

    - CorreBeam: Concussive energy beams the Correlative produces that can be fired at will when the Ascendant forms a canon commonly at the end of an appendage.

- **Offensive**

    - All Ascendant Officers are adept at Shelled Skin and Bracing Needle usage to varying skill levels.

- ○ Shelled Skin: Correlatives naturally have a harder shell form that they can access when needed, however, combined with the will of the Ascendant, this shelled skin ability increases to offer varying degrees of protection even during space and HyperRift travel.

- ○ Bracing Needles: A variation of the HyperNeedles all Correlatives can create, a Correlative's Bracing Needles, when combined with two other Correlatives' Bracing Needles can temporarily incapacitate a rogue Correlative/Ascendant. Though it is known they work through a sound wave alteration, all other information regarding Bracing Needles is hyper-classified.

- ○Bonding: While not technically considered a weapon, the Bonding process is what brings a Correlative and Ascendant together as one. It is an intimate process that can only be initially performed on Pelora or, on rare occasions, during the heat of battle. Once a Correlative and lifeform Bond, only a Severing or death can break it.

- **Subjective**

  - ○ All Ascendant Officers are adept at creating Electro-fiber Cuffs from their Correlative. These cuffs are not physically connected to the Correlatives however they are psychically, so that arresting officers and/or their Correlatives will be aware of their prisoner's location (as long as they are wearing the cuffs).

- **HyperRift**

- HyperRift Needles: Appear to cut holes in the fabric of space, but in actuality, they are bending the sound waves in space in order to alter the time structure of the dark matter and allow Ascendant to slip onto Hyper Highways for speedy travel.

- **Forbidden**

  - CorreAxe: The CorreAxe can only be created from a Correlative's dead and dried out husk. It is forbidden. As the protection and defense of Correlatives both alive and deceased is one of the Sacred Six Laws, there are only twelve known CorreAxes in existence.

Top Factual Documentation

- Correlative/Ascendant Weaponry: All Available Information

- Correlative/Ascendant Weaponry: What We Know

- Correlative/Ascendant Weaponry: Purposes

- Correlative/Ascendant Weaponry: Breaking Barriers

- Correlative/Ascendant Weaponry: Power

Top Opinions/Entertainment

- Correlative/Ascendant Weaponry: The Inevitable Demise of All of Us

- Correlative/Ascendant Weaponry: Keep It Simple, Sama

- Correlative/Ascendant Weaponry: On The Other End of a CorreBlade

- Correlative/Ascendant Weaponry: You Are The Ascendancy Series

- Correlative/Ascendant Weaponry: Open Season

For more information and for answers to specific questions, please see **Talmund's Legal Library Complete Entry: Correlative/Ascendant Weaponry**.

***

TALMUND'S SCIENTIFIC ADVANCEMENT INDEX BRIEF ENTRY: HYPERRIFT

- The HyperRift, sometimes referred to as "the space behind space" or HyperRift Highway is a cosmos behind this one in which time and space have different properties that allow lifeforms to traverse billions and trillions of miles in little time.

- The other properties within the HyperRift are similar enough to this one that ships, when built properly and reinforced with precise metals, can sail through it as they can in this cosmos, only much faster. Due to some of the unique properties of the HyperRift, the speed with which ships travel has no lasting detrimental effect on any known lifeform as long as they are wearing the proper gear.

- In order to reach the HyperRift, one must use a HyperRift Window, invented by Eloi-Magman Dr. Sigmund Rolhfs in 1.85634.6AST.

- To create a HyperRift Window, one must know the exact coordinates of a "bump" or weak fold in the fabric of the cosmos which can only be done in two ways: using an Eloi-Magman HyperRift Locator and Cosmic Blade or using a Correlative.

- On his deathbed, Rohlfs granted the instructions to build an Eloi-Magman HyperRift Locator and Cosmic Blade to the UCA. The UCA then granted it to the public so that all could have access.

Status

- Official Creation Date (of HyperRift Locator): 1.85633.6AST

- Official Discovery (of HyperRift): 1.85634.6AST

- Inventor/Discoverer: Dr. Sigmund Rohlfs 1.54851.6-1.86635.6AST

- Eloi-Magnan Accessibility Status: Common

- UCA Accessibility Status: Common

- UCA Patent Registration: None

Top Factual Documentation

- HyperRift: HyperRift For Dummies

- HyperRift: Behind the Universe

- HyperRift: Biological, Economical, and Environmental Benefits of HyperRift Travel

- HyperRift: Biological, Economical, and Environmental Detriments of HyperRift Travel

- HyperRift: HyperRift Windows Explained

Top Opinions/Entertainment

- HyperRift: And Hell Follows

- HyperRift: Lurking In The White

- HyperRift: My Time Alone

- HyperRift: Train Days Gone

- HyperRift: On Successful Integration Into The Unreality of the Whiteness

For more information and for answers to specific questions, please see **Talmund's Scientific Advancement Index Complete Entry: HyperRift.**

Chapter 8
Shell Shock

JACK WOKE UP ON his back screaming into the void. He tried sitting but bashed his forehead on what felt like a wooden board. Ringing bounced around his brain as he groaned. Explosions sounded somewhere in the distance and he found himself in the jungle once again, the past six years nothing but a dream.

Blood dripped over his brow, out his ears. Sweat streamed down his skin. A phantom rifle appeared in his hands and the chemical stench of Agent Orange invaded his nose. Contrary to popular belief, it didn't end in 1971. Jack knew that.

Brothers in arms screamed for their mothers, whimpered for death. Nearby, a child yelled in a language he didn't understand. But he could feel the intent. Murder was on their mind. It was a violent, animalistic sound. It was an attack.

No.

"No," Jack put a stern voice to his thought, though it was difficult to hear over the ringing and screaming. "I'm home. I made it out of Saigon. The war is over. All will be well." He reached out a shaking hand to discover what felt like wooden planks above him. "What?" he whispered, panic edging its way into his words, sneaking the war with it like a Vietcong in the night. His other hand shot up. "Wood?" He looked from side to side and saw only darkness. He reached out.

It wasn't wood, but some sort of metal all around him, dirt below, crumbling, hard.

I'm buried? Dread overcame him. And anger. Am I dead? he thought. In a coffin? He punched at the metal. "I am not dead!" he shouted even as images of his body, riddled with bullets, falling on a battlefield of rice paddies, did a twisted waltz through his mind. "No!" He punched again. His skin split. His bones cracked. His blood spattered. "No!" he screamed, defiant against his own certainty that he had died somewhere in the middle of a humid Vietnamese jungle. Had a pack of guerrilla fighters run him down then buried him in some kind of strange metallic coffin? Had a grenade blown him into an early grave? Or had he, like so many of his brothers in arms, killed himself out of a fear too great for the fragile human mind to comprehend? Like them, had he finally succumbed to his own guilt over what he had been forced to do in that God awful jungle? Had he simply forgotten those last few moments sequestered in some out of the way mud-pit, gun to his head while warm rain fell like piss through his hair?

Was this his eternal penance for suicide?

Was he in hell?

No.

None of that felt true.

None of that felt right.

Only May felt right.

"May!" he finally cried, a pleading sound, full of sadness and fury. Blood dripped from the shattered skin on his hands, sliding through the dirt and drowning metallic slivers.

His arms grew weak.

His eyes fluttered.

He smelled smoke, tasted burnt earth on his tongue. His breathing stuttered. His sides ached. His fists were nothing more than twisted, broken bundles of flesh and bone. May's name burned through his throat. He longed for stars, meteors, wheat, the cool spring air of Nebraska, any sign he wasn't somehow still in Vietnam buried under an assault, any sign that the last eight years since he had returned from that hot green hellhole hadn't been a dream, any sign that he wasn't beyond rescue, beyond life.

Croaks and whistles, the night sounds of the jungle creatures, echoed through his thoughts and he cried, trembling, afraid.

"I'm back," he muttered, his words stilting and weak. "I never left."

Someone shouted an order.

He reached for a rifle. His rifle wasn't where it was supposed to be. His rifle was always where it was supposed to be. He never lost it. Never misplaced it. Somewhere a child laughed playfully, another squealed. He thought of the art folded up in his wallet.

Someone slashed at his belly.

Ghosts flew through his thoughts, memories that became now.

The jungle was dark and damp and so hot. Enemies crept everywhere, whispering in their foreign tongue, daring him to step forward where he knew there was a hole filled with punji sticks. It felt like even the trees didn't want him here, the way they pressed on him, the way their leaves slapped his face like offended women.

And his presence was offensive, wasn't it? He didn't belong halfway around the world from home in this oppressive wild. There were no trails here, no destinations even. He marched through the darkness, fear coating him as much as sweat. When the enemy appeared, as it always did, as it always would, the explosion of gunfire lit up the night, ripping through branches and bodies alike.

Panic.

Grunting, mindless, darkness took him.

* * *

Something popped. Something shattered.

A Vietnamese voice called out as a subdued light forced his eyes open.

Jack tried to raise his arms to fight but there was no strength left in them, in him.

The Vietcong had him. Finally. He had no idea how they had gotten him, where he was, or what was going to happen next, but he knew he was their prisoner and he had torture to look forward to, torture that he deserved. Everything else had been a fever dream, probably brought on by one too many mosquito bites. Malaria. This was malaria. There was no May. There was no baby. There was no life back home in Oakview, NE.

Hazy light flooded his eyes. Shapes. Men. More voices.

Someone pulled him up. Jagged metal scraped his belly. Blood oozed over his belt.

Madness.

Madness everywhere.

Small, searing flames sprinkled the landscape alongside chunks of broken rock and piles of upended dirt. Thick dust filled the air, choked him. Floating red lights fought against the dust, swirling, taking him away. Lanterns bobbed around, giant confused fireflies in the night, searching for some little safety, for a partner.

"May . . ." he muttered his wife's name, wondering if she was real or if he would be like those bugs, always looking, never finding. Eventually trapped in some child's glass jar, an oddity, a prisoner.

Hands on his sides.

Single foot on the ground.

"I lost my leg," Jack whispered. "I lost my leg."

Voices.

Shouting.

Above, meteors yowled through the sky, trying to hide behind a thick haze of ash. Ringing. Burning. Jack's mouth tasted of copper. His stomach ached like he had been shot. A pulse pounded in his ears, shrieking in an anomalous mixture of fear and relief to battle the constant ring. It fought through it all to live. His breaths climbed their way out of his body in giant waves. He coughed up blood. He had no balance.

"Small breaths!" a man shouted nearby.

He pushed the man away but the pain in his hands caused him to fall back. Wavering on one foot, he fell.

"May!" he called out and gagged on the blood that shot up his throat. Something stabbed his hands when he tried to force himself up. There was a terror in his voice he had only ever heard during the war. And even then, he had not been this afraid.

But he was in the war.

Wasn't he?

Where was his sergeant? Where were his brothers?

This was war. This was the war. He needed a rifle. He needed a mask. Next to the Agent Orange and the rain, the smoke and dust were his worst enemies, far more dangerous than the Vietcong. Gunshots blasted around him. He felt the earth crumble. Someone helped him up.

Where was his gun?

Words came to him as if from behind a thick door.

"Jack," he heard. "Calm down!"

"We can't find his leg!"

"She's fine," another voice. "May's fine!"

Who was speaking? They were blurry, hunched over, almost monstrous things. They moved, their flashlights like beacons for the enemy. He wanted to yell at them to turn them off, to hide. But these men were his enemies. Weren't they?

"May?" he asked.

More lights, these red and orange, screamed away to his left while bodies like shadows emerged from the dust and haze. They weren't men though. They were monsters. He must have died.

This must be hell.

He was in hell.

Jack staggered on his single leg like a drunk, pulled along, a prisoner, his sides and belly stinging. He vomited black blood down his chin and struggled to force strength to his legs.

"May!" he repeated, his throat aflame.

Why couldn't he feel his right foot?

Hollow and cold, tears came and brought with them an army of sobs that morphed into more wild coughs. Hope faded and Jack's voice grew weak. His chest tightened. He hung his head and heard only ringing. "May," he whispered. "I'm sorry May . . . I'm so sorry. I didn't mean to. I didn't—"

Darkness.

Cold.

Pulling hands on his wrists, his waist, his foot forced across broken earth. Lolling side to side, his head weightless.

"Get him up and on!" someone shouted.

Lifting.

Lying.

Hands.

Warm.

Soft.

On his face. Holding.

May's breath in his ear like summer.

"I'm here Jack," she said. "Listen to me. Please." Her voice cracked. She had been crying. "All will be well."

"May." He tried to touch her face but could not lift his arms. "May." The word was a whimper.

"They're taking us to a hospital, Jack." May was calm, deliberate, her lips brushing against his cheek, the music of her voice sounded softly through the ringing. "We're going to be fine. All will be well."

Chapter 9
The Reporter

CHARLIE MCKINSTREY WAS NOBODY'S favorite. But Chief Ben Wilton considered himself to be at the top of the list of people who did not like her. She reminded him of a rabbit. Cute enough, but annoying as all hell.

"What the hell happened out here, Chief?" she asked. Her eyes were watering thanks to the dust in the air. Her cheeks were flushed red because she'd been running around the field, looking for answers she wasn't going to find, but more because she was struggling against the grip of two of Ben's younger officers who also were not her biggest fans.

"McKinstrey, wasn't your editor-in-chief supposed to put a muzzle on you after that bullshit with the Satanists?" Ben asked. He held a handkerchief over his mouth and was still unable to suppress a cough as he spoke.

She only grimaced by way of reply and struggled free of the officers' tight grips. Her ability to do so was, of course, predicated on the fact that Ben nodded to his officers to back away.

"See if there is anybody alive out here," Ben said, motioning them away. He saw Charlie and rolled his eyes. "What can I do for you, McKinstrey?"

"You can tell me what your plan of action is here."

"Plan of action?" Ben asked.

"What are you going to do?"

"Well," he said, holding the handkerchief over his mouth once again, "I think I'm doing it."

Charlie coughed. The lights from an ambulance and three police cars brightened her already rosy cheeks. She would have been cute in this light if it wasn't for the snarl on her lips.

"Wandering around a burning field?" she asked.

"I'm hardly wandering and this field is hardly burning."

Charlie pointed at a patch of burning rubble about twenty feet from them. Ben followed her finger as it moved from that patch to another and another. By the time it hit the third one, a firefighter was standing over it with a bucket.

"What about all of this?" Charlie demanded.

The firefighter dumped a bucket of water on the burning rubble.

"I think that firefighter is taking care of it."

Charlie rolled her eyes. "Why weren't there any officers out here to begin with?" she asked. "Wasn't there a search party for a missing boy?"

Ben opened his mouth to answer but as he did so, Charlie dug into the jean jacket buttoned halfway up and pulled out a small notebook and pen.

With one hand she clicked the pen to life and with the other she flipped the notebook to a blank page. "This is all on the record, by the way," she insisted.

Ben grunted. "I'm getting some oxygen. You should too," he said, turning from her and heading toward the ambulance.

Ben's long legs moved quickly across the charred ground toward the ambulance. Charlie ran to keep up.

"Chief Wilton!" she called after him. "Chief Wilton!"

"Can't you give an old man some peace, McKinstrey?" he asked as he sidled up to the ambulance where an EMT was offering hits of oxygen.

"No," she said as if the very thought of offering him peace was the most shocking thing she had ever heard. "Why would I—No, Chief, no."

He sighed from inside the cool safety of the oxygen mask. "Turn it up, can you?" he asked the EMT.

"That's not how it works, Chief," the EMT said awkwardly.

"Is it true that the mayor wouldn't let you send any officers out here to help in the search?"

"I thought you'd want to know more about the meteorite," Ben said. "Shouldn't you be harassing some scientists about this? It was those guys who said nothing like this could happen with this meteor shower."

"Oh, don't worry," Charlie said as the EMT offered her an oxygen mask. "I'm heading over to Lincoln tomorrow to talk with those guys." She took the mask and inhaled dramatically once before giving it back to the EMT.

"Thank God," Ben said.

"What's that supposed to mean?" Charlie asked.

"You're a little much, Miss McKinstrey," Ben said.

"Maybe if you'd just answer my questions."

Ben wiped his brow and noticed that the dirt had turned into mud on his forehead. "Maybe if I knew any of the answers, I could."

"You know what the mayor told you."

Ben closed his eyes and prayed for patience. "The mayor was very concerned about the festival, Miss McKinstrey."

"But not about the missing boy?" She flipped through her notebook. "Ricky Sims is his name. His older brother is MIA in

Vietnam and considered dead." She flipped through the notebook again, almost frantically, until she came to the page she needed. "When the casualty assistance officer visited the Sims household and news broke that Ronald Sims was considered officially missing in action and presumed dead Mayor Rose said, and I quote, 'No one in our society is of more value right now than the family members of a soldier lost in the line of duty.'"

Ben's countenance darkened.

"He did say this, correct?" Charlie asked, as sweet as Grandma's pecan pie. "It was a long time ago, but—"

"You know damn well he said that, Charlie," Ben replied, ripping the mask from his face and stepping toward her.

"And wouldn't it have been prudent to have a law enforcement officer or two on site in case Ronald Sims' little brother was discovered alive or dead?" She blinked those big brown eyes of hers and the idea that she was a rabbit once again raced through Ben's mind. "I mean, think about it," she continued, unnerved by Ben's approach, "these civilians could taint a crime scene. Furthermore," she added for emphasis, "if your officers were here when the meteorite hit there wouldn't have been nearly as long a time before the assists came."

Ben gritted his teeth and spoke through lips that barely moved. "The mayor is my boss, McKinstrey."

"So, this is the mayor's fault?" she asked, finally stepping back. But Ben could tell it had less to do with fear of him and more to do with the fact that she needed space to write in her notebook. "Would you say?"

Ben spread his arms. "This is an act of God, McKinstrey."

"Is that your official statement?"

"Official?" Ben asked, his eyebrow raising enough to lift his duty cap up so that a stray strand of silver hair fell out. "Weren't you supposed to be *Oakview Courier's* official reporter at the festival tonight? Why aren't you there right now?"

Twitching a little, Charlie once more reminded Ben of a rabbit. And he was beginning to feel a little bit like an owl.

"That's right," he said. "Ernest told me that you were covering the festivities tonight. What are you doing out here?"

Charlie gulped, panic flitted across her round features and Ben thought that maybe, just maybe, he'd be rid of her right now. But just as the panic sat in, it slipped away. She grew stern, her hands fell to her hips and she looked up at him, her normally plump lips set in a thin line. "Don't try to intimidate me, old man," she said.

"You listen here, girl—"

"Don't you tell me what to do!"

Ben's finger was in Charlie's face. Charlie was shoving her notebook and pen back in her jacket pocket with a force that could have ripped the fabric.

"I have too much going on at the moment to—"

"I'm just trying to do my job!"

"I am too!"

"Jesus," the EMT put in over both of their screaming voices. "Take this somewhere else," he said. "I could have seriously injured people over here in a minute and I do not need this mess." He waved around the two of them like an angry parent. "Is this really what you two should be doing right now?"

"Sorry," Charlie muttered and took a step back from Ben.

Ben coughed again. "Me too," he said. Gulping, he looked at Charlie and reached out a hand. "I'm sorry to you too, Charlie."

She took it begrudgingly. "Thanks Chief," she said. "Maybe I came on a little too strong."

"That happens sometimes with you," Ben said.

She rolled her eyes. "So, what *is* the plan?"

"Honestly, kid, all we're doing right now is looking for survivors and bodies." Ben took his cap off and wiped his forehead. "We're doing everything we can."

"There were only two people known to be out in the field when the meteor hit," Charlie said.

"How do you know before me?" Ben asked, unable to hide his shock.

"Linc told me."

"Linc? That old man who manages the trailer park?"

"Who else?"

"He talks to you?"

"He likes me."

"Do you live there?"

"No. He read a story I did about the trailer park about a year ago and thought that I was fair and balanced in my reporting."

"Was that the hit piece on Mayor Rose's proposal to sell this land to that department store chain?" He smiled.

"I wouldn't call it a hit piece," Charlie said.

"Who were the two?"

Charlie looked at her notes once more. "The Normans, May and Jackson."

"Shit," Ben said. "That's another vet."

"I know," Charlie said.

"Well, what else do you want to know?"

"Can you tell me why the mayor didn't have anyone out here?"

"You'd have to ask the mayor that."

"He won't talk to me."

"Can't imagine why."

"Well, it's not—"

"Chief!" someone yelled from out there in the dirt filled air. "Chief, we found someone!"

Running toward the sound of the voice, Ben held his handkerchief over his mouth. By the time he reached one of his officers and a couple EMTs hovering over a slight Black woman sprawled in the dirt, he was coughing and wheezing. Charlie, right behind him, wasn't doing much better.

"Is she alive?" Ben asked between coughs.

"Looks like she's fine aside from a few bumps and bruises," one of the EMTs said.

"What about Jackson?" Charlie asked.

"Who?" the police officer replied.

"Her husband," Charlie said, exasperated. "He was with her."

"She's the only person we've found."

"Dr. Broyles found her," one of the EMTs said.

"Broyles?" Charlie asked. "He's here?"

"He beat us here!" the police officer said.

"How the hell—"

"He said he was at home and came running as soon as he saw the explosion. Said it blew out a few of his windows and shook his whole house."

"Happened in the trailer park too."

"Some in town too."

"Well damn, hopefully he can help Jackson if we find him," Ben said. He knelt down and studied May's face. Her lips parted slightly and her eyes fluttered. "May?" he said softly. "May Norman?"

"What are you?" May asked. Her words were slow, encumbered with sleep.

"I'm the chief of police in Oakview," Ben said. "How are you?"

May's eyes shot open. "Where's Jackie?" she asked urgently.

"Mrs. Norman, Mrs. Norman," Ben said, gently touching her shoulders as she struggled to sit up, "you've been in a terrible accident." He shot a hard look at an EMT. "Get her some oxygen!"

The EMT sprang into action and offered May a mask quickly.

"Is that better?" Ben asked.

May nodded. She removed the mask. "Where's Jackie?"

"We don't know where your husband is," Ben said.

"Has anybody looked through that?" Charlie asked, pointing a finger toward the twisted Jeep that lay about fifty feet from where they were.

Ben looked to his officer. "Well?" he asked.

"I, uh, I haven't," he stuttered.

"I guess you better get on it then," Ben said.

The officer shot off toward it and gathered a few others to his side. They approached the Jeep cautiously; the smell of gasoline was overpowering. The jagged pieces of metal scattered across the rubble strewn ground made maneuvering closer to it all the more dangerous.

"Oh my God," the officer said. "There's someone under there!"

"Someone find Broyles!" Ben yelled into the night as he ran toward the Jeep.

Charlie, standing over May and the EMT, took out her notebook. "This is going to make one hell of a story."

"It's more than a story," May said softly. "It's my life."

"I'm sorry, I just—"

"Don't worry about it," May said. "Help me up." She reached for Charlie.

"Ma'am, that is not a good idea, you're—"

"Listen here, young man," May interrupted the EMT who could not have been more than two years her junior, "my husband is under that Jeep and I am going to go over there and help him."

Charlie admired this woman's tenacity and helped her up. As she did so, she noticed two small objects tumble from her lap.

"Can I have those, please?" May asked the EMT.

He nodded, shocked, and picked them up.

May quickly shoved them in her jacket pocket as Charlie helped her forward.

"What were those?" Charlie asked, trying her best at a friendly tone.

"None of your business," May said, not unkindly.

***

OAKVIEW METEOR CELEBRATION INTERRUPTED BY IMPACT EVENT

Meteorite strikes field outside of Oakview, two injured.

By Charlie McKinstrey, staff writer

During last night's meteor shower an unexpected event occurred on the outskirts of Oakview. While local citizens, Jackson and May Norman were assisting in a search for missing local boy, Ricky Sims, a meteorite landed in Five Mile Field situated between the Oakview Lanes Trailer Park and Oakview.

At the time, the Normans were acting as lookouts for the group of good Samaritans who were combing the woods nearby in search of the missing child. The full scale of the damages this meteorite wrought are yet to be determined; however, it has been confirmed that Jackson

Norman sustained serious injuries while May Norman walked away with little more than bumps and bruises.

As most Oakview citizens were busy at Mayor Greyson Rose's Meteor Fair, including Oakview's entire police force, the Normans, and several other residents of the Oakview Lanes Trailer Park, were searching for any sign of Ricky Sims. According to Harold Lincoln, caretaker of Oakview Lanes Trailer Park, Jackson Norman and his wife had taken it upon themselves to maintain a base of operations of sorts when the sun set.

"Jackie, you know, doesn't walk as well with the fake leg, so when it got dark, he thought he'd be a better use to us in the field, kind of running things," Lincoln said.

A veteran of the Vietnam War who lost his right leg from the knee down in the jungle, Jackson Norman received a Purple Heart Medal as a result of his injury. Other than his time in Vietnam, Jackson has lived in Oakview his entire life. His wife, May Norman, is a relatively new resident who grew up in Omaha and only moved here in the late 1970s to be with her husband (Jackson).

The two have been staples of the Oakview Lanes Trailer Park, helping out with social activities, and at times assisting Lincoln with his caretaker duties. Well loved by their neighbors, there was an outpouring of concern for the Normans' wellbeing.

"I just don't know why they were even out there," neighbor Francine Welker said.

Though both Normans were taken to Draco General with injuries, Jackson's were far more severe than May's. Currently, he is said to be in critical condition. Meanwhile, Ricky Sims, son of Del and Jenny Sims, is still missing. An official search is said to be starting today.

"We're doing everything we can," Police Chief Ben Wilton said.

Chapter 10
Nowhere Agents

A FULL BLACK CADILLAC Coupe de Ville pulled slowly into Oakview Lanes. There was a large dent in its passenger front side fender and some scratches on the otherwise spotless car. As it moved, a low muffled growl sounded from under its hood. It made the contraption seem like a predatory animal staking out its new hunting grounds. Heavy fog lay thick upon the ground, a cold, wet blanket that mingled with the leaden dust in the air, making the world muddy.

Linc, the trailer park caretaker who'd been at the job longer than anyone could remember, didn't like the look of the thing. He knew it was a 1977 model. He knew it had all the bells and whistles anyone could possibly need, and, chances were, a few more that no one could possibly need but everyone would want. The windows were so dark that even when Linc squinted, he could not see inside as the elegant beast crept by. He'd seen tints like that on cars like that before, and every time he had, the person driving had been bad news. The people who drove cars like that had been the kind of people he left Detroit to get away from, the kind of people that did not find themselves in Oakview Lanes in Oakview, NE, of all places, by accident.

He spat as it crawled by. His eyes moved from the trailer park's entrance to the car's trailing rear lights. "This is why we need a locked gate right here," he muttered to himself as the Cadillac disappeared into the fog.

Bucky, Linc's big, red-headed assistant who was about as useful as cat piss in a carriage, walked out of the laundromat near the trailer park's entrance and waved at Linc with his free hand. In his other hand he held a jelly donut.

"Who was that?" he asked, his voice so full of idiocy and donut that he came off as a big orange cartoon character.

Linc tolerated him because the boy was strong and compliant but he would be damned if he ever admitted he liked him. Hiring Bucky on as an assistant the summer after he had graduated high school had been nothing more than a moment of weakness. A favor to his mama. Now, there was a saint of a woman. How could she have birthed this moronic behemoth?

"How the hell should I know, boy?" Linc snapped.

Bucky flinched at the edge in Linc's words, donut crumbs trickling down his chin.

Linc immediately felt guilty. "Ah," he groaned. "I'm sorry. It's been a long night what with," he ran his twiggy arms in circles, opening his large hands like dead leaves, "everything."

"It's okay," Bucky said as he rubbed the donut crumbs from his chin.

"Well," Linc said, trying to be cheery for the big galoot he knew was broken up about Ricky's disappearance and scared about everything that had happened with the Normans and the meteorite, "best go get the golf cart so we can follow 'em."

***

The two Nowhere Agents inside the Cadillac paid Linc and Bucky no mind as they cruised on by. Agent Mary Jones, driving, was small with a serious face, blaze of red hair, and bright bottle green eyes that took in everything.

"This place makes me sad," she said, silently thanking a god she didn't believe in for the fact that her special binoculars were safely stowed in the trunk. She'd hate to be able to see this dirty little locale any better. "At least I have Journey."

Her partner, Agent Eugene Ha, nodded. A little taller than Jones, but wearing an identical black suit, his grimace said everything. "It makes me angry." He folded up the newspaper he was reading—this morning's issue of *Oakview Courier*—and turned off the radio, silencing Journey just before Steve Perry told them about all the ways he wanted it. Everyone said Steve Perry's voice was like butter (everyone meaning his partner, mostly). But he found the man's keening whine more like margarine.

Fake.

Agent Eugene Ha took Led Zeppelin or AC/DC over Journey any day of the week. "I cannot believe this is already news," he said. "Shouldn't we have put a stop to this?"

"You're just angry because you think this is another wild goose chase." Mary turned the car slowly around the corner of Shady Lane and onto Wisconsin Drive where the skeleton of a deserted playground stood. In air still heavy with detritus from last night's meteorite and dense with morning fog steaming off the Missouri River, it was difficult to see more than jagged dark shapes. Mary could make out what she knew was a rusty swing set, some rusty monkey bars, and a rusty merry-go-round. All of them rested in what might have been a giant sandbox but was probably little more than a litter box for feral cats. Spring riders surrounding the sand had probably once looked like friendly cartoon animals. Now, if Mary squinted, she could tell that they appeared to have been shot up with buckshot. Cracks over their faded pastel animal faces made them broken Easter Eggs out of which could pour nightmare monsters in place of chocolates and candy. Mary couldn't help but wonder if they still did their job, if kids could still have fun riding on them. "And because you don't like Journey," she said, while turning the radio back on.

"Oh Jesus," Eugene said, exasperated.

It wasn't always the appearance of a thing that mattered, and if anyone knew that, it was a Nowhere Agent. But at Oakview Lanes, maybe appearances did matter. What looked like a murder shed stood on the edge of the playground near the road. A crudely painted sign next to it announced that it was, in fact, a far cry from a place where people went to die. It was, instead, a bus stop for Oakview Public 42. Then again, maybe those two concepts were not mutually exclusive here in this shady looking little trailer park in Southeastern Nebraska.

"You know, it's been scientifically proven that people who like Journey are happier than people who do not."

"What?"

"You're angry because you don't like Journey. Journey makes you angry. Don't think I haven't noticed that. If you'd just like them, like me, like millions of others, then you'd be happy."

"You're being ridiculous, you know that, right?"

Mary only laughed as Steve Perry's dulcet tones faded away with Neal Schon's guitars only to be replaced by The Who's "You Better You Bet."

"Hey! This is better! You like The Who!" Mary's excitement over the new song was tiptoeing close to contagious.

Eugene would not catch it. "You really are a strange girl," he said, turning the radio down and hoping it would be an acceptable compromise. It wasn't that he disliked Mary. She was a good partner, and had been since his old one, Mike, had advanced up the ladder and left him here in a perpetual limbo of assignment work.

In their unique field it was always a toss-up on who you'd get stuck with if a partner retired, transferred, or worse. And you'd have to be stuck with them for the duration. Eugene had heard of other agents demanding to have their partner changed but the last thing he wanted to do was make waves. He had joined the Nowhere Agency because if he wanted to remain who he was after what he had seen, he had no other options. Testing reverse engineered spy planes for the South Korean government hadn't been easy. But hot damn had it been fun . . . until it hadn't been fun anymore. He thought about the newspaper article he had just read and wondered if that missing boy would be found alive or, like most other test pilots he had worked with, dead.

Some people were not as lucky as Eugene. "You know, you should be angry too," he said.

"Oh yeah, why?" Mary asked. She maneuvered the Cadillac around the corner of Wisconsin Drive and Raindrop Road.

"I'm angry because a deer ran us off the road last night, hurting Betty by the way," he added, patting the dashboard, "and because of that, the impact event has been severely compromised, and we have no idea what we're walking into. And we already know Mike is pissed at us for something that isn't even our fault. I mean, we didn't write this article!" He slapped the newspaper. "We didn't skid off the road on purpose!" He threw his hands up. "We didn't—"

"You know, chances are pretty high, Local is recording this," Mary said, putting extra emphasis on Mike's official title. She smiled and winked at Eugene.

Eugene's head fell back and he blinked up at the ceiling of thin black fabric. If he let his eyes wander across it, he could almost pretend he was in space, flying. Almost. "I kind of actually do hope this is another wild goose chase. If it's not, what are we going to have to do to all of the people who were wandering around the field last night? What are we going to have to do to all of the people that live in this place?" He let his head fall back down and shot a sidelong glance out his window so he could only slightly see the dirty, gray environment he was going to be wandering around in soon.

"Chances are it is a wild goose chase, so no worries. I mean, what's the likelihood really that there was some kind of event here last night? When was the last actual event?"

"Nineteen-forty-seven," Eugene said stoically.

"Right? I know that isn't long in the cosmic scheme of things, but over thirty years is a pretty long time in the human scheme."

"Human scheme," he muttered. "Funny." He turned to face her now, studying her profile as she concentrated on the pothole ridden roads in this rotten old place full of what he was sure were miserable people. "You know, even if there is something here, I don't like the idea of having to deal with trailer park trash to get to it."

"You literally just said you were worried about what we'd have to do to all of these people."

"That doesn't mean I want to interact with them."

"Don't be so prejudiced. I'm sure they're fine. Better than those swamp folk from a few years back. If we never go to Florida again, I'll die a happy woman."

"Yeah," Eugene had to agree. "Everything with that stupid sphere and that family was pretty terrible."

"And we couldn't keep a lid on that."

"We manipulated the information fine, which is better than a Croatoa."

"I suppose."

"But that's not what I meant. We shouldn't be here right now, at daybreak the day after the meteor shower. We should have been notified by the lab coats as soon as the meteor shower registered as something possibly important so we could've been here *before* it even started."

"Come on, Ha, don't blame the scientists. They can only do so much."

A door creaked open on a rusty trailer house to their right and an angry older woman stuck her head out. Three little dogs surrounded her, growling. The woman looked down at her crumbling cement stoop, then she looked up, eyeing the Cadillac for what it was: out of place. Her lips were sunk like the muddy rim of a fresh hole. She hadn't put her false teeth in yet. The three tiny dogs yipped behind her. Eugene leaned over and pressed a button on the console between them. A swishing sound announced itself in the small space and a moment later the agents were engulfed in silence.

"That's better," Mary said, smiling at her partner. "It was getting kind of loud."

"Still," Eugene said, wondering if that woman had any false teeth to put in.

"It looks like that old lady is as angry at us being here as you are. Maybe you should go speak with her. You already have something in common."

"Shut up and get us where we're going."

Mary grimaced as she pulled the Cadillac to the only lane without a street sign on its corner. There were a handful of trailer houses scattered up and down its dirt shoulders. Unlike the others, they were not formed in straight, symmetrical lines, but seemed scattered, like a small crowd of people waiting for something. A bus maybe? A way out? They looked worse than the others, somehow sadder than their already sad surroundings. This was where the forgotten and the hated of a community of forgotten and hated went to die.

Mary pointed to the end of the lane. "That's the gate for the field. And it's destroyed, just like Local said it would be since we're so late."

"And guarded." Eugene pointed at the two police officers standing near the shredded gate.

"They shouldn't be too much trouble. Local has already spoken to the chief or sheriff or whatever he is. Wanted us in last night, you know?"

"He mentioned that this morning when he called and berated me for forty-five minutes."

"I'm glad he likes redheads."

"I bet."

"Anyway," Mary rolled her eyes, "with the missing kid and all of the people about, we wouldn't have been able to do much last night."

"Well, I would've rather been doing that than walking to the nearest garage and dealing with that tow truck driver."

Mary nodded. "He was . . . less than pleasant."

"Not going to be any issues with the National Guard either?"

"Local says everyone has been contacted. This is all ours now until he says otherwise."

"Not that it'll be anything significant."

"We are in the Midwest, Ha. Anything can happen."

"Jesus," Eugene whispered, "this is the asshole's asshole isn't it?" As Mary let the Cadillac creep toward the broken gate, Eugene caught the sight of a dead cat in one of the gravel driveways. It looked as though it had been freshly run over, splattered blood and fresh innards lay all around it in the mud like discarded confetti covered in New Year's Day mud. He thought for sure he could see steam rising from its gaping belly wound as well. He patted his partner's shoulder and pointed toward it.

"Well that's a bad omen," Mary said. She pulled the Cadillac to a stop at the broken gate and looked to her partner. "Ready?" she asked.

"As I'll ever be," he said.

The two stepped out into a foggy spring morning, Eugene putting his hat on. Though the sun was rising over the horizon, a thin dust hung in the air, covering everything in a strange, smoky haze.

Eugene rubbed his hands together. "Cold." He screwed his eyes, scanning the land. "Can't see shit through the dust and fog."

"Lots of dust in the air."

"Regular, everyday, run of the mill meteorites do that. I'm sure it's nothing . . . again."

"Pessimist." Mary approached the gate, waving at the uniformed police officers standing there. "Hello," she said through a wide, friendly grin. Her eyes seemed to sparkle even in the grimy air and Eugene could've sworn the dimples an inch or so away from the edges of her lips grew as she headed toward the slack jawed yokels that passed for police officers here in the middle of nowhere.

They nodded and waved back at Mary.

"Are you from the FBI?" one asked.

"That's what they tell us," Mary said as she pulled a badge from her jacket pocket and flipped it at him so quickly he couldn't see the strange triangle symbol emblazoned into the golden badge.

"Thank God," he said. "You're our relief."

"Where's your car?" Eugene asked.

"We're parked down by the Sims trailer. The chief is there."

"The missing kid?" Mary looked from the police officers to Eugene. "The one that went missing yesterday, right?"

"How did you know about that?"

"We're the FBI, it's our business to know everything."

"And you didn't start the investigation right away? That's why the woods over there were full of regular folk but no police?" Mary asked.

"Ma'am, we had a lot on our plate yesterday."

"Interesting."

"Uh-huh," one of the police officers said. "Well, we'll be on our way then." They nodded once more to the Nowhere Agents and walked down the road and around a corner as quickly as they could.

"That was . . . weird," Eugene said. "Why were those two cops acting like . . ." He trailed off.

"Like what?"

"Weird?"

Mary shrugged. "Missing kid in a small town like this is going to mess lots of people up. Also, that festival here last night kept most of the cops busy. And there were some fights when the cops finally did show up. It was a mess. That's why no one came out to help us when we had our unfortunate accident with the deer."

"I'm sure, I—"

"Excuse me!" a phlegmy scream sounded from behind them. It was accompanied by the buzzing sound of a small, weak engine.

As both agents turned, an overworked, dingy camouflage golf cart zipped around the corner toward them. A large red-haired white boy drove and a Black man who looked to be as old and broken as the trailer park, hung out of the side, screaming something about laws.

"This will be fun," Mary whispered. She pulled the badge from her coat pocket as Eugene did the same. Together, they approached the golf cart. Mary smiled; Eugene grimaced.

Before either of them could take the upper hand in the coming conversation, Linc stepped off the still moving golf cart and approached them in a half-walk/half-run gait that he should not have been able to pull off without falling on his wizened face. The dirty overalls he wore made him seem more official in this trailer park than Mary or Eugene in their pressed black suits could have hoped to be.

"Can I help you two?" he asked as he slowed down and stopped before them. Hands on his hips, his tone indicated that he did not want to help them one bit.

"Mr . . . ?" Mary asked.

"Mr. Mind Your Business," Linc said. "Can I help you two?" His eyes darted from one agent to the other. They were strong and bright. They were quick and shrewd and mean and if Eugene was being honest with himself, kind of scary.

After more than a decade in the Nowhere Agency, Eugene didn't scare easily.

Mary kept her smile but put her badge away. Eugene followed suit.

"I am Agent Mary Jones and this is my partner Agent Eugene Ha of the Federal Bureau of Investigation, we're here to investigate the—"

"Missing boy?" Bucky announced, excitedly interrupting the agent. The golf cart skidded to a halt in front of them sending a splatter of mud against the Cadillac with a flat finality.

Eugene cringed at the brown stains on Betty.

Bucky hopped off the golf cart and jogged over to the agents. As he nearly fell from his excitement, the golf cart breathed an audible sigh of relief. "You're here to find Ricky?"

The agents looked from Bucky to one another.

Linc let a mirthless laugh escape the jagged prison bars of his teeth. "Ain't no government agency here to find Ricky, Bucky. The cops haven't even started looking for him yet. These government folks sure as shit aren't about to."

"Oh." Bucky hung his head, dejected.

"They're here because of the meteorite and the Normans."

"That was fast," Bucky said. He wasn't impressed with their speed. He wasn't angered by it either. Bucky's entire demeanor had folded in on itself. Curiosity and excitement had been replaced by a sadness that threatened to swallow all of them.

"It's okay, Bucky." Linc patted the boy's back. "If Ricky were a space rock maybe then they'd be here to help find him." His tone was wet with derision.

"I'm sorry," Mary said. "But you're right. We are here to investigate the meteorite. But that doesn't mean we can't help with a missing person, does it? He's been missing since yesterday?"

"Since yesterday morning," Bucky said, his voice a soft, sad thing. "Linc never even got the paper," he added, pointing at Linc.

"He never finished delivering his newspapers. No one did Ricky's route today either," Linc added. "His parents called the police but they were busy getting things ready for the festival. Del told me they said Ricky probably ran away and that they'd look into it today." Every word was laced with anger.

"Then the meteorite hit," Eugene said. "Right—Linc, was it?"

"Yeah," Linc huffed, throwing angry side-eye at Bucky. "That's what got the cops out here last night, you better believe it. It might have been the entire force for all we know. They shoved everyone off the field. Then they stayed at the border between the field and the park, keeping us out. Did any of them look for the boy though? Only guarded the gate. Shouldn't be surprised, they treat us like we don't matter."

"That was our fault. We needed the scene as clean as they could get it," Eugene said.

"Well, you should be happy then, because these stormtroopers did their job."

"They said something about their chief speaking with the Sims just now though."

"Did they now?" Linc said. He spat. "That chief is as useless as tits on a bull."

"How many people do you think have been through this area?" Eugene pointed behind his back, wanting to change the subject. The field behind him was filled with chunks of mud and debris that appeared to have fallen from the heavens.

"Lots of people, some cops, some trailer folk."

"Just wandering around the crash site?"

"The police and doctors helped the Normans!" Bucky said, a bit of excitement breaking through the sadness in his voice.

"The couple in the field, right?"

"They were in the field!" Bucky agreed, eager to help. "They were looking for Ricky!"

"Yeah. They were out here—" Linc stopped himself and raised an eyebrow at Mary. "What did you say your names were?" he asked shrewdly.

"I'm Agent Jones and this is Agent Ha, we're—"

"Ha and Jones, is it?" Linc asked.

Jones nodded. "It is."

"Uh-huh." Linc nodded right along with Jones. "And what agency did you all say you worked for?"

"We're with the FBI," Eugene said. Where Mary's words had been filled with saccharin sweetness, Eugene's were sharp and bitter. In this game of good cop/bad cop, he was bad.

"I didn't think—"

Eugene raised his hand. "We're from a specific branch of the FBI." He pulled his badge out of his jacket again and flashed it. "But trust me, we're official. Now we're going to go into that field and conduct our investigation. We've already spoken with the authorities." He placed his badge back in his jacket, sure to reveal the butt of his revolver. "Are you going to try to stop us?"

"Nope," Linc said.

"Nope?" Eugene asked.

"We're going to go find out what's going on at the Sims' trailer I think."

Eugene closed his eyes and nodded. "Thank you for your time," he said as he walked toward the field. "Please don't touch the car," he yelled over his shoulder.

Mary followed, stopping at the Cadillac to retrieve a large black suitcase from the trunk.

"Bye-bye, now," Linc said, suspicion holding his words together.

Once the agents were disappearing into the haze, Bucky looked down and noticed the dead cat.

"A dead cat." He pointed to it.

"That's a bad omen," Linc said. "Clean it up. I'll start the burning drum so we can treat it properly. Then we'll get to work on the fence. Can't have it looking like that, can we?"

"What about going to the see what the police are doing with Ricky's parents?" Bucky asked.

"We'll get there when we get there," Linc said. He rubbed his chin and watched the agents as the fog swirled around them and they vanished like ghosts.

***

"So, there is a missing kid and there was a couple at the impact event and so far, there hasn't been any news about what happened other than that little piece in the local paper?" Mary said. She huffed along next to Eugene over the field. "That is amazing."

"Well, even though he had trouble admitting it to me, it's Local's job to control shit like that. How long did you talk to him last night?"

Mary shrugged. "Long enough to calm his ass down."

"It didn't work too well. The man literally only yelled this morning."

"You know Mike. He worries. But look, kids go missing all the time and if no one milling around last night found any weird alien shit, then there is no news. This probably is nothing. I mean, we're on the outskirts of Po-Dunk Nebraska looking at mud and dealing with crazy people." She stopped, an idea hitting her hard. "We should just drive back into town, hit up that bar, and drink for the next two days. We'll tell Local there was nothing and move on with our lives."

"We have to follow protocol, Jones," Eugene said, the exasperation in his voice hard to hide.

"Are you pissed about protocol or me?"

"Both."

"What?"

"I'm just pissed."

"Hey, maybe it's connected? I have a feeling Linc could be helpful." Mary looked back toward the trailer park.

"I have a feeling that old man will be a pain in our ass no matter what we do," Eugene said. "We should have wiped their minds right there."

"If we wiped their minds, they'd be the only two in town that didn't know about the meteor. Bad idea."

Eugene rolled his eyes.

"Even if it is nothing, I'd rather have that than whatever that mess was in Florida," Mary said.

"Fair," Eugene replied.

***

TALMUND'S LEGAL LIBRARY—ABOVE HYPER-CLASSIFIED—BRIEF ENTRY: NOWHERE AGENCY (EARTH)

- The Nowhere Agency is an organization made up of lifeforms who have had and/or investigate close encounters with extraterrestrial lifeforms.

- Most information on the Nowhere Agency is hyper-classified since the only planet that currently has a Nowhere Agency is Earth. Though located in the Outer Rim, it has such primitive political and social structures that it remains unincorporated. Though an Outer Rim Ascendant operation has initiated a Contact Contingency in order to communicate with this organization.

- Additionally, The Ascendancy maintains watch over the planet and its more prominent organizations, up to and including the Nowhere Agency.

- Some known facts about the Nowhere Agency include:

- The Earth Nowhere Agency has several outposts scattered over the planet known as Nowhere Facilities in which they study and prepare for eventual First Contact. Though these outposts serve many purposes, in their Terminal Recovery Wings they care for Earthlings who have experienced extraterrestrial harm.

- Earth Nowhere Agents have rudimentary knowledge of extraterrestrial technology due to reverse engineering of at least one known crashed ship that was not an Act of Invasion, thereby not under the jurisdiction of The Ascendancy.

- Since it is so close to the NetNeg, it is suspected that there have been several encounters that are unofficial and/or have gone unregistered.

- Technology has been reverse engineered to give the Earth Nowhere Agency a technological advantage over other Earthbound organizations.

- It is unknown whether all of this technology originated in the UCA, NetNeg, or another unincorporated system. However, it is known that much of it came from an official UCA spacecraft that also provided Earthlings with rudimentary information about the UCA and its citizens.

- Though currently in rudimentary contact with the Outer Rim Ascendancy, there has been no official First Contact due to the planet's lack of evolutionary, social, and political achievements.

- The Earth Nowhere Agency's cooperative structure coincidentally emulates The Ascendancy's structure with different colored uniforms possessing different skills and duties (Black, White, Red, Gray, and Blue).

  - Black—soldiers/investigators

  - White—scientists

  - Gray—hyper-classified

  - Blue—laborers

  - Red—guards

For more information and for answers to specific questions, please see **Talmund's Legal Library Complete Entry: Nowhere Agency**.

Much like this file, accessing any files regarding the Nowhere Agency requires an unwritable, hyper-classified, secure clearance code. If you do not possess a clearance code, or if you obtained one through illegal means, Ascendant Officers will be on their way to your location before you finish reading this entry.

Chapter 11
Evidence

MARY SURVEYED THE CRATER in the massive empty lot where a meteorite supposedly had crashed. Her fists rested on her hips, her black suit fluttered in a spring breeze that was doing its best to blow away the fog and dust. From a distance, in the haze she looked like a dark, avenging angel with a halo of flames.

"No meteorite," she said, her nose wrinkling as the scent of rotten meat battled the scent of chlorine around her. "Stinks a little like lighter fluid, but I bet there is no dangerous radiation either. You know what that means."

"That is very interesting." Eugene looked down at the empty crater, one hand on his fedora, the other on his hip. Just like Mary, he stood out in this charred Nebraskan field. He took off his hat and ran a hand through his thick hair. "There should be something here though." He sniffed and pulled a small cube-like metallic device from his jacket. Clicking it to life with a button on its side, he pointed it toward the crater. Two small glowing orange arms flung from its base and the unit hummed to life. The green-hued screen on the device's trunk washed Ha's face in an eerie light that gave his fawn skin a sickly hue.

Mary thought it made him look like a zombie. "This is more than interesting," she insisted, looking away from him, hoping the sun would be high enough in the sky so that when she turned back, his skin would look normal again. She could not handle that sickly color. It reminded her of her family. It reminded her of their deaths.

"Yep. Very low radiation levels. And it really doesn't smell that bad." A hint of irritation fell from the edge of Eugene's voice. "After last night, if there had been a lot of radiation there would be lots of dead bodies."

Mary pointed upward. "That's always the way when something falls from the heavens."

"Hot with radiation?" Eugene laughed. It was an unenthusiastic sound. "Americans, always bringing religion into everything." He waved the device around as he circled the crater. "It's low everywhere," he said. "Nothing."

"Koreans, always bringing technology into everything." Mary offered her partner a sly smile and winked, hoping it would get him to smile back, to look up, to do anything that would make him look alive again. She looked away. Though she had seen more death than she cared to think about, this pseudo-death before her was the most unnerving of them all. Eugene was alive. Eugene was her partner.

"Just doing my job, ma'am," Eugene said, saluting her with weak, mocking sincerity.

"So, we have no meteorite but we have a crater that indicates there was a meteorite." Mary looked upwards. "What's that mean?"

"Whatever created this just got up and walked away?"

"It would seem so."

"And that's actually less interesting than the fact that there is little by way of lingering smell."

"Yep. Only the rocks smell, my man."

"We're going to need to double down on keeping this quiet."

"We're way beyond that."

"We need a smokescreen then. And we need it now. We might have to wipe the whole town."

"Still wouldn't be as bad as Florida," Mary offered.

Eugene put his hat back on, put away his first device and pulled out another. This one was smaller and more rectangular. With a flick of his wrist, he flipped it open to reveal a small touch pad and accompanying screen. "I'm calling Local now."

"You think he'll be okay with you using that thing out here in the public?"

"This is an emergency."

***

"Linc found his bike and paper bag in the street, Goddammit! What more evidence do you need?" Del hollered at the police chief. He was inches away, the smell of whiskey hot on his breath. The cracks in the middle-aged man's face were as large and deep as a man twice his age. But heavy drink and steel mill work could do that. So could losing a son in Vietnam, not to mention another right up the street from his home.

Ben sat at the Sims' dinner table in their cramped olive green kitchen and stared at Del with sympathetic hound dog eyes. "I'm sorry, Mr. Sims, but that isn't a lot to go on, we—"

"Isn't a lot to go on?" Del interrupted, the shock and anger mixing in his mind to force the words out like a lion's growl. "Maybe you could've gone on it yesterday, but you were too busy running your damn festival! That damn festival that . . . what was it even for?" Del turned away as a sob escaped his throat. He stared out the small window above the sink. A little rectangle, the thing reminded Ben of a mail slot.

What can you even see out of that thing except your neighbor's bathroom window? Ben ignored Del. It was the right idea.

He always took a beat when he could feel himself getting angry. This man didn't deserve Ben's anger. Ben deserved his though. He never should have kowtowed to the mayor. Charlie was right about him. He never should've agreed to put his whole crew on patrol at that ridiculous festival last night, that ridiculous festival that ended early thanks to that ridiculous meteorite.

He scanned the room quickly while Del fumed. There was a pan on the stove top, fried eggs that looked like they had been sitting there for twenty-four hours, stiff and crispy, their yellow going orange.

He sniffed. They smelled like they'd been sitting there for twenty-four hours too. Ben supposed he couldn't rightly blame the Sims for that. He cleared his throat and let his eyes fall to the refrigerator. It matched the color scheme of the kitchen, so it was terrible to look at. Ben could never understand what had happened in the 1970s to make everyone think olive and yam were *the* colors. They didn't even match the frightening tiles on the floor. Various shades of brown in shapes that made you think you were floating, that made you think none of this was real.

He wished he was in his own unassuming kitchen, with his own wife, his own children and grandchildren. His refrigerator at home looked a lot like this one, or at least it had when his kids had been young. There were bad drawings, report cards, mimeographed notes about school events, and Polaroid photos of happier times all stuck on with broken magnets that no one could bring themselves to get rid of. Ben wondered why happier times were always stuck to the fridge.

Del faced Ben once again, yanking him from his philosophical musings. His face was blotchy with drunken, red anger and his eyes looked as though they were about to pop out of his head.

"Well?" he asked pointedly.

"Now, Mr. Sims, I don't see how—"

"You don't see a whole lot, do you, Chief?" Del said. He slammed his fist on the cracked Formica table. The small cup of coffee by Ben's hand trembled and sent splashes of his heavily sugared drink onto his skin. He pulled away as slowly as he could manage and battled the burning.

"I am here now, Mr. Sims," he stood, "ready to speak with you, send out search teams, do everything that we can do. But you have to understand, with the meteorite last night, and now the feds have shown up, we have a lot on our plates at the moment."

"Have a lot on your plates at the moment, do you?" Del asked. Ben caught the way his fingers formed fists, two meaty hammers poking from the ends of his grimy flannel sleeves.

"The feds are here?" Jenny Sims asked, her voice as far away as the stars though she was only a few steps from the kitchen table.

She was sitting in the living room on their orange—*because of course,* Ben thought—and brown flower-patterned couch. Ben realized as he looked toward the woman that it was not so much a living room in the same way the kitchen was not so much a kitchen. There was just one large room in this part of the trailer. One side had vinyl, cabinets, a refrigerator, and a stove, and the other had carpet, a couch, and a television. He knew there were only two bedrooms and a bathroom down that skinny, shag carpeted hallway.

How do four people live here? he asked himself. *Three,* he corrected. *Two.* "Yes, ma'am," Ben said. "They were in touch last night shortly after the meteorite. They're here to investigate the scene"

"They're not here for Ricky. They're here because of the meteorite." Jenny stared out the large bay window on the end of the trailer. Her fingers fiddled with the dog tags hanging from her neck, the only part of their older son that had come back from Vietnam. Though her eyes seemed unfocused, her mind was quite the opposite. From where she sat in her pale pink nightgown and matching robe whose sleeves were stained with coffee, she had a solid view of the corner of Vineyard Lane and Iowa Drive.

Ben knew she kept hoping she'd see Ricky come riding through it, all bright eyed and happy, that stupid red Cornhuskers cap bouncing on his head. If she concentrated really hard, he thought she even saw it. Maybe she saw their older boy too, following Ricky and laughing at his antics. But he knew they always appeared more like an apparition in her imagination. No matter how bright they were, she could see right through them. He was gone even though he was there. It was as though she knew the truth even though she did not know. A sensible woman, Ben knew she was not one for flights of fancy.

"Maybe they can help with Ricky, ma'am," Ben said, relieved to be speaking to Jenny now instead of Del, who he was afraid he'd have to arrest before the morning was over. "A couple of agents are supposed to relieve my men this morning. If they're not there already, they will be soon." Ben was so tired. It had been after two in the morning when he finally made it home and he had been up since six.

"I'll go talk to them now." Del moved toward the front door which, Ben noted, was actually a side door that acted as the divider between the pseudo kitchen and living room. He hated having to be in a trailer, hated how it reminded him of the fact that there were those far less fortunate than him. When speaking with most of the people who lived in Oakview Lanes in their dirty little metal rectangular hovels, he mostly hated that he could not blame them for their situation.

A few slight changes to his life and he could have easily ended up here in this dead-end little village full of sadness and void of hope.

"Don't bother," Ben said using his best 'Chief Wilton' voice. "When they get here, I will speak to them before I send out official word that we're starting a new search party." He looked at the notes he had written down before, when Del had sounded reasonable if upset, not over the last few minutes when he had become a broken fire hydrant, spewing out anger like water. "We will start in Oakview Lanes, gathering people to comb through the area." He picked up the coffee and sipped. "My officers will see if anyone saw anything."

"Linc already did that. No one saw anything."

In his defense, Ben tried very hard not to roll his eyes, very hard. Though he did fail.

"You don't think Linc is as good as your Barney Fife twats?" Del asked. This time he crossed his arms before his chest, a strange prideful display.

Ben raised his hands, palms out, and took a step back. "I'm sorry, Mr. Sims, it's just that we need to be official."

"Fuck official," Del said. "I want my son. We already went through the field, the woods too. You and your boys need to be getting on down to the truck stop, talk to drifters, get in touch with the highway patrol or—"

"Drifters? Highway patrol?" Ben put his tan service cap back on over his slicked salt and pepper hair to try and hide his confusion. Though he was a solid foot taller than Del and a good fifteen years his senior, he felt defensive in Del's presence. There hadn't been an abduction around these parts for more than twenty years, and now in less than twenty-four hours there was not only a missing child but a meteorite that nearly killed one of the kid's neighbors. This was too much for an overfed, old police chief who only wanted to retire quietly.

"It could be anyone!"

"Look," Ben said, "I understand your frustration."

"You don't understand anything, Chief Wilton," Jenny said, her voice still distant, unbothered with emotion. "Your children are adults. They have families of their own. You have grandchildren."

Del moved across the room in two quick strides and placed one baseball mitt of a hand on Jenny's thin shoulder, squeezing slightly. The gesture made Ben want to cry.

Instead, he closed his eyes and rubbed his forehead. "We have the bike and the bag and headphones. We're dusting them for prints. We're combing the ground where it was found, we're releasing his name and appearance to the press, and we're starting a search party, an official search party." Returning the notebook to his front pocket, he frowned, getting to the hard part. "We're going to need to have you two come in at some point too."

"Get the fuck out of my house," Del said, his anger more subdued than it had been a moment ago, but somehow more terrifying. And to think, Ben was the one with the gun.

Ben stepped out, hoping his day couldn't get any worse but knowing full well that was exactly what was going to happen. His two officers, Banks and Shackelworth, were heading down the road toward him. That meant the feds were here.

He rubbed his eyes and wished he still smoked.

***

Eugene looked up from the rectangular device. "Local wants us to see what we can see here before we do anything rash like Croatoa the whole town."

"I heard him," Mary said. "I think they heard him up in Omaha."

"He's such an asshole."

"Should be simple enough, especially if this is nothing."

"A crater with no rock and little radiation tells us it's probably something big."

"I thought that would make you happy."

Eugene frowned and looked back and forth across the field. It was covered in footprints from who knew how many people running back and forth. There were also tire tracks from what he knew were emergency vehicles. What might have been the most intriguing sight however was the completely destroyed Jeep in the distance. He could barely make it out through the dust. "Shall we study the area now?"

"No time like the present."

"What do you want to do about the people who were here last night?" Mary asked.

"I guess that depends on what we've stumbled onto here," Eugene replied. "No. Never mind. One thing at a time."

Mary opened the suitcase and pulled two pairs of binoculars from it, handing one to Eugene.

The two set off in opposite directions. As they walked, their heads bent toward the earth, their binoculars scanned the rocky, upturned ground before them, sending data across the lenses and saving it on a mini-disc drive attached at their waists.

"I'm not seeing anything," Eugene said into a wrist communicator after a ten minute walk.

His voice came through tiny speakers on Mary's binoculars near her ears. "Yeah," she replied, clicking her matching comm. "It looks pretty standard. Maybe you were right. Maybe this is another wild goose chase. Maybe it was just a freak meteorite that just exploded upon impact or something like that. It is possible. Are there any strange rocks around?"

Eugene thought for a moment and studied the ground around him, adjusting the binoculars so that he could focus on the mineral content of the dirt there. "All I'm seeing is upturned earth and broken bits of fence." He looked to the tree line a few miles in the distance and squinted, adjusting his binoculars again. Two little boys were crawling through the spring overgrowth there. It looked as though they were in serious conversation.

"A couple of little kids are in the woods out there. Should I subdue them?"

Mary had to laugh. "And wipe them?"

"I mean . . ." Eugene shrugged, unsure.

"Are they approaching the impact site?"

"No. They're going the opposite direction."

"Let them be. Out here in the real world, kids entertain themselves by exploring woods and doing stupid shit. Or you could join them, it might be fun."

"Why did I sign on for this?" Eugene asked.

"Because you have a crush on me?" Mary suggested.

"Very funny," Eugene replied dryly. "Seriously, if something is out there, it could hurt those kids."

"I hate to say it," Mary said, her voice coming through with a static warble, "but we need to stay on mission. Stay focused on the site. Find the end of the blast zone, we'll make our lines and go from there. We're going to have to check out the woods eventually. I don't imagine a couple of little kids can cause much damage. And frankly, if something crashed out here, I find it hard to believe it would stumble into the woods. It's more likely that it headed for the houses where it could be helped."

"Famous last words," Eugene said.

"You find your side yet?"

"Yeah, I'm circling around. The blast zone isn't very big. You?"

"I can see it. Land is trashed but the zone is almost too small for the crater. Everything is pretty standard other than that. I'm going to drift over to where that Jeep is."

"I'll meet you there."

A few minutes later, both agents stared at the broken husk of Jack's Jeep.

"Wonder if he died."

"That man back at the trailer park didn't say anything about someone dying."

Eugene turned away from the ruined vehicle. "Let's look around."

They bent their heads to the ground once more, letting their binoculars do the work, zooming in on the dirt and scanning the area for anything out of the ordinary. There were less than normal levels of radiation for a meteorite impact, various footprints from the people who had been here the night before.

"This is going to be nothing, isn't it?" Mary asked. Her arms hung limply at her side. "At least it'll be easy. Local will probably be pissed about it, probably send us to the Arctic when we're done or worse, back to Florida. This is going to be just like—"

"I don't think so," Eugene interrupted. His words came out slowly, as though he wasn't sure of what he was saying.

Mary perked up and approached him. "What is it?"

"Look at this print." Eugene pointed to the ground.

Mary cocked her head to the side, looking down, her eyebrows raised behind the strapped on binoculars. "Now that is interesting, isn't it?" she said, squatting to stare at a long skinny footprint that appeared to have four long skinny toes, two in the front and two in the back.

"That's alien is what that is. I'd say Whitley."

Mary stood and clicked a few buttons on her watch. "Call Local again. Use the phone. We need to lock this down now."

"And to think, when they sent us out here, you said it was going to be pointless." Eugene laughed, eyes focused on the strange shape in the dirt.

"That was you," Mary said.

"Holy shit," Eugene said, more to himself than to his partner. "This is huge." But as he formulated plans for the next few steps, he heard a screaming the likes of which he'd never heard before, not even on one of his red assignments, and he looked over at the tree line.

The two little boys from earlier were running in their direction. Their faces were animated with terror and their words were a garbled mess of fear.

Eugene could make out one word through their cries:

"Ricky."

Chapter 12
The Body

AS TWELVE-YEAR-OLD Wyatt Kincaid walked along the bank of the Missouri River, unconcerned with what was taking place in the trailer park where he lived or the large field that rested between the trailer park and Oakview, he made a conscious effort to appear as though he was simply wandering. "Meandering" as his mama would have said. Behind him, at two years his junior, Sammy Nice did the same thing. Sometimes they'd stop for a moment and study the Missouri's swift current, throw a rock or two in its rushing waters, or their heads would jolt up at the sound of a bird cawing or a squirrel squeaking.

But there was a seriousness in the air between them that anyone within shouting distance could have felt. These boys were on a mission. Weaving in and out of the forest and onto the beach, they made their way to their destination as though trying to keep from being followed.

"We're going to be there soon," Wyatt whispered. His squeaking, prepubescent voice carried over the beach and lost itself in the nearby woods from which they had just emerged.

"Are you sure?" Sammy asked. "I don't want any space monsters to get us. My dad was telling me about this movie, *Alien*, and I didn't like it. I didn't like it at all." They weren't even supposed to be here. If his parents knew where Sammy was right now, they would have killed him before any alien could. Why had he followed Wyatt? Wyatt was always doing stupid things that got him into trouble. He did not want to get into trouble.

But space. Space. Sammy loved space. Even though he was terrified of aliens.

"*Alien* isn't real, dumb ass. Now, *Star Wars*, that's real."

"*Star Wars* is real?"

Wyatt nodded knowingly. He was ready to drop knowledge on this kid. "Kind of, Sammy," he said, his voice heavy with the condescension his age allowed him. "*Star Wars* isn't really real, but," he raised his hand, pointing his finger to the sky like a college professor about to reveal a hidden truth to a room full of freshmen, "it happened a long time ago in a galaxy far, far away, so it could be real."

Sammy let that idea wander around his head for a few seconds before he wrinkled his nose as though he smelled something disgusting. "You're kidding."

"Very good." Wyatt laughed.

"This is kind of dangerous though, yeah?"

"I don't know, Sammy." He let his head fall back and arms hang slack at his side. "Maybe?" Pursing his lips, he looked at Sammy. "You didn't have to come. It's not like I put a gun to your head or anything."

"What else was I going to do?" Sammy replied, feeling real anger for the first time that morning.

"I don't care what you do," Wyatt said, turning and huffing over the beach away from Sammy.

"Come on!" Sammy cried and ran to keep up.

"Look," Wyatt pointed to the east as he stopped. Their argument was forgotten. "Do you see that black line on the beach?"

"Way over there?" Sammy squinted, shading his eyes with an already dirt covered hand. Though the air was still hazy with dust, the sun was starting to shine now, chasing away the fog.

"Yeah, that's the property line between the field which is city property and some state property or something. I don't know. My dad said the city built the wall to mark the line before I was even born. He said it is there to make sure trailer park folk know where they can't go."

"Where can't they go?"

"Where we can't go."

"We?"

"Trailer park folk."

"We can't go in the field?"

"Yes."

"But we go there all the time. We were all there last night, looking for—" He let the word 'Ricky' fall away before it was spoken. A part of him didn't want to say the name. He wasn't sure why, but he thought that if he spoke the name then he could disappear too. And he did not want to disappear.

"Yeah," Wyatt said. "Grownups do weird stuff and make weird rules and then they break them."

"What does that mean?"

"It means even though this is all public land, that area is off limits."

"Why?"

Wyatt shrugged. "Because Oakview doesn't like trailer park folk on their land."

"But we play in the field all the time. No one cares."

"I'm not a grownup, man. I don't know why. All I know is that there are weird rules that grownups make."

Sammy nodded as if Wyatt had made the most profound statement ever made by a boy.

"Anyway, if there are space rocks, they'll be on the other side of that! It's where they crashed!"

"Why don't we just go through the field? I thought they crashed there. I don't understand why we had to go all the way around the park and come back this way. It's a lot of walking."

"Well, you know how we always play in the field and there are never cops there and it's basically the best?"

"Yeah."

"Well, there are cops there now, you idiot! Have been since last night. After they got the search party out of there, they blocked it off, said it was off limits."

"How do you know all this?"

"My dad."

"Wow."

"FBI is coming too. Don't want to mess with that."

"Like secret agents?"

"I don't know."

"Yeah, but—"

"Don't 'yeah but' me, Sammy. We're on a mission here."

"By God," Sammy said, awe wavering with fear in his voice. "A mission. Will they be . . . you know . . . dangerous?"

"Will what be dangerous?"

"The rocks. The space rocks. Maybe they'll be, like eggs and these, like octopus things will climb on our faces, and—"

"Shut up, Sammy," Wyatt said, pulling him from the brink of panic.

"Maybe that's what happened to Jack," Sammy said. Thanks to Wyatt, he had escaped panic's clutches, but fear was still very much on his tail.

"For Christ's sake." Wyatt threw up his arms. "Fine! Go home!"

Sammy thought about it, he really did. But ultimately to his ten-year-old mind, boredom was far more dangerous than danger, imagined or actual.

"No. I'm coming with you," he said.

Wyatt shrugged. "Those rocks were pretty dangerous to Jack though, weren't they?"

"My dad said this morning he's going to be fine. He said that Dr. Broyles was there as quick as spit and he saved him." Sammy was hoping that saying these words out loud would make them real.

"Did he say that? Then why are you scared of alien egg pods or octopuses or whatever?" Wyatt grinned.

"I don't know," Sammy replied through a sigh.

"Well, my dad said it'll be a miracle if Jack makes it to the end of the week. He was there last night too. He saw him. He said he ain't never seen so much blood and he's been an EMT for years. Your dad's a janitor. What's he know?"

Sammy whistled. "I hope your dad's wrong. I like Jack."

Wyatt nodded knowingly. "Me too. He takes off his leg and shows me sometimes."

"He was in the war."

"Yeah, so nothing can kill him, right?" He shrugged. "Except maybe a giant space rock with, like, an octopus that lays eggs in your face in it."

"So, they are dangerous?"

"Not now. There ain't no more falling. It can't be dangerous." He paused and looked Sammy up and down. He was pale and skinny and wore clothes about two sizes too big for him. A sudden pang of pity rushed through Wyatt. "Look," he said quietly, "there are no space monsters either, in case you're still worried about that." He tried to sound confident, but his words trembled, as though hanging on a branch, ready to fall.

"I'm more scared of—"

"Don't be such a baby, Sammy," Wyatt said and punched him in the shoulder. "Whoever got Ricky, got him when he was alone. You ain't alone. I'll protect you."

"Don't joke," Sammy said. "Don't talk about him. My mom said Ricky Sims ain't never coming back. I still don't know why we had to come all the way out here."

"I told you, if the meteorite fell in the field, Jack and May would be dead."

"I know, but—"

"And it couldn't have fallen in the woods, because it would've gotten someone in the search party and knocked down some trees."

"Sure, that makes sense, but still—"

"Still nothing," Wyatt said. "Follow me." All these questions had gotten him thinking about Ricky. He had never really liked him. Always showing off, Ricky was a try-hard. And he thought he was better than everyone in the park. He thought he was going to get out, going to be something, a big baseball star or some bullshit like that.

Ricky acted like he didn't know. But he had to know.

Once you were in, you never got out of Oakview Lanes, not alive anyway. It was like a prison you could leave sometimes. But you always had to come back. How long had Linc been at Oakview Lanes? Or some of those old couples? The Welkers? Wyatt didn't know but he thought he'd find out someday, when he was an old man. He just hoped he had a job that paid enough money to get him a nice trailer. Not one like the dead end lane trailers that opened up to the field. Please not one like that.

He walked on. Unlike Sammy, Wyatt would never leave his fears behind as childish.

Sammy stood still, his head moving from side to side. He studied the sandy beach and flowing river, longing for something—some animal or fish—to do something, anything to take Wyatt's attention away from his goal of space rocks. There was nothing though. Nothing that could end Wyatt's drive.

Some broken black branches clawed out of the sand. The river's current pulled all sound away, its cool, fishy scent at ease. Then there was the forest, a large dark maze even in the morning sun. It was full of beasts and wonder. Sammy gulped, knowing he had lied to Wyatt when he told him the woods were not scary. Even with the sun fully up now, the air was still dusty. It worked together to create a grim setting. How he had managed to walk through these woods to reach the beach without falling victim to some foul-smelling alien monster wielding a space laser was beyond Sammy. That idea sent a tremor through his body and he ran after Wyatt, fear unhidden as he screamed, "Wyatt, wait up!"

Somewhere in the woods, an animal chirped.

Sammy ran to catch up to his older, more sensible friend. As he moved, he kept his eyes firmly glued to what was behind him, certain that an animal or a monster or space monster was going to come crashing from the trees to eat them both. It was with a sudden jolt that he ran into Wyatt's stiff back and fell.

"Wyatt, what the hell?" he said, rubbing his backside as he stood.

Wyatt only pointed in front of him.

Sammy peeked over his shoulder at what had stopped his friend. Just on the other side of the wall they had been looking at a moment ago was the worst thing he had ever seen. The worst thing he would ever see. It was no space monster, no wild animal, no bloodthirsty thing.

It was the mangled and mutilated body of a little boy wearing a Snoopy watch.

It was Ricky.

* * *

A few minutes later, the boys, covered in scratches and grasping for breath, came pounding through the woods and running toward the first adult they saw, a man in black suit and matching hat, standing in the destroyed field.

***

DEAD BODY DISCOVERED ON MISSOURI RIVERBANK

The mangled child's body sat on the beach for approximately twelve hours.

By Charlie McKinstrey, staff writer

A morning jaunt through the woods led to a gruesome discovery for two young Oakview residents. Wyatt Kincaide (12) and Samuel Nice (10) had big plans for the day after the meteor shower. They were going to explore and find something 'alien.'

"We just wanted to see what was out there," Kincaide said.

Riding their bikes down Highway 275, the boys looped around Five Mile Field where it is purported a team of FBI agents are investigating the supposed meteorite. Once around the cordoned off field, the boys trekked down a trail most commonly used by forest animals and into a small patch of forest near the Missouri Riverbank.

"With all the dust in the air, it was scary," Nice said.

Traveling through the woods was not out of the ordinary for these two boys, both of whom had spent hours there during the summer months, so they knew their way.

"We went a little deeper into the woods than we normally do, but we wanted to find some space rocks, not this," Kincaide said through tears.

The small forest eventually gives way to a sandy beach where the boys marched toward a wall that predates the establishment of Oakview. University of Nebraska at Omaha Professor of History Eugenia Banks said that the wall must be the last remaining part of a Native American structure. Though she was unable to confirm it on such short notice.

The boys, however, believe the wall is there as a symbol for the people who live in Oakview Lanes. According to both Kincaide and Nice, it is there to tell them where they can and cannot go. This afternoon, both boys wish they would have heeded that wall.

Once they neared it, they discovered the mangled body of an as yet unidentified child. Chief Ben Wilton is working in conjunction with the FBI to identify the body and investigate the crime scene.

More news as it occurs.

Chapter 13
Separation Anxiety

AURORA ROLLED HER HEAD to one side and saw that she was lying on the floor in a blank metallic cell. She hoped it wasn't an Echo Chamber even as she knew it was. Resigned to her fate, she could feel the cold through the Correlative mask. Peel was weak. Their connection was still strong, despite the Bracing. Aurora knew this because not only could she feel the Correlative's weakness, but her pain as well. She had heard of Bracings causing a Severing. To be Severed from Peel . . . she didn't want to ponder what that would feel like. But how long would the Alliance let them maintain their connection? In her studies she had learned of Ascendants who had dared break the law.

Some were derelict, ignoring their duties, and using their connection to their Correlative as a way to get what they wanted. Others had stolen from the evidence halls, the temptation of otherworldly jewels being too great. Murder had been a problem as well. Sometimes it was fueled by a need for revenge for those who thought the Cosmic Tribunal's justice was feeble or worse: unjust—something Aurora could relate to. Like everyone else, sometimes when an Ascendant broke the law, it was fueled by desire and jealousy.

This wasn't that. It wasn't any of that. She knew that ultimately it was love that had caused her actions. She would have laughed if it did not hurt so much. The love she felt for Jon'Oh wasn't natural at all. Whitley, it was said, simply did not have that capacity. They loved their mothers and their sisters. They loved their homes, their pets. They loved. But they did not love the way she loved Jon'Oh, the way he had loved her. It simply was not what they did.

But that was specific to her people. In general, Ascendant Officers were not, nor had they ever been, immune to emotion. The cosmos as a whole misunderstood the fluidity of Whitley love. They had no opposite sex to bother with, no other gender at all. Yes, many Whitley were attracted to one another and together made homes and found a certain kind of love. But the attraction was never romantic. It was always about the easy joy of being with another Whitley, not this strange untenable thing she had made with Jon'Oh. She could remember, back in her podling days, the amazement she had felt when her older sisters had introduced her to romance reels from across the cosmos. They were so unreal as to be unfathomable. Ironically, she had loved them.

When Aurora had met Jon'Oh that strange, that unreal, that impossible love had stirred inside her. How had it happened? She couldn't be sure. She'd never be sure. But that unquantifiable feeling had been the realest thing in her life.

Now Jon'Oh was gone.

She was jailed.

Why didn't she get a happy ending like she had seen in all of those reels?

Did she deserve one?

She closed her eyes and cried. She cried for Jon'Oh, she cried for Peel, she cried for their failed plan, she cried for the woman on

Earth who held the spark of Essan DNA inside her, and she cried for herself, for her own foolishness, for her own guilt. Most of all though, as much as she wished the majority of her tears were for her dead lover or his doomed planet and people, or even the Earthling she had pulled into her machinations, they were for her Correlative. As punishment for what she had done, her connection to Peel would be Severed completely. She knew it. The one similarity between all of the Ascendant Officers convicted of a severe crime was Severing.

And what she had done, she knew, was severe.

Thoughts on Severing always led her to the tale of Ascendant Frid-Ron Neer. Some said it was just a fable, but others claimed that on Pelora there were ancient tomes about the Nietzschean Ascendant who had set himself up as a Dark God on an unnamed backward planet in the NetNeg. He had been so far removed from a place where other Ascendants actively patrolled that he had thought there was no way he'd be discovered. His plan had been elaborate and impressive, if doomed to fail.

After faking his death in a raid gone wrong, he ventured to the NetNeg planet he had first discovered on one of his mandatory scouting missions there. All officers had to do it once per Annam Standard Cycle, though it was always accomplished with a crew on a ship that kept them connected to the ExoNet, instead of alone with nothing but the vacuum of space and the Correlative to keep them company. Discovering the planet with other officers present was his first mistake.

Legend had it, Frid-Ron had been miserable in the Ascendancy and wanted out. Of course, this was always an option. Though appointed for life, if an Ascendant chose to leave, they could. It was a process but not an impossibility. But Frid-Ron found the Correlative connection to be too good to give up; instead, he planned and paced himself and eventually went AWOL and set up his kingdom. Of course he was found, of course he was arrested, and of course he was Severed. Severed from his Correlative and sentenced to live out his days on his primitive, warlike planet in the NetNeg, Frid-Ron was a cautionary figure from ages past. But was his story true? Did it really happen?

In one way or another, yes.

Was Aurora destined for Frid-Ron's fate, all because of her love for Jon'Oh?

No, she thought, it can't be that.

"You're in an Echo Chamber, Aurora," a voice broke through her thoughts. It came from the walls all around her.

"Wh-what?" she muttered.

"It's to keep you from thinking too freely while we transport you. It actively pulls the negative thoughts from your mind and force feeds them to you over and over in a negative loop. The mind finds the thoughts without any help though. It's actually quite fascinating, I believe the—"

"I know what an Echo Chamber is," Aurora interrupted and rolled over, knowing there was no escaping the voice. Prisoner transport trains that could withstand the rigor of HyperRift travel were all the same and the intercom system on every one was embedded in the fabric of the walls. There was no privacy. No secrecy. This voice could come from anywhere at any time. There was no use fighting it.

Peel? she thought, hoping her Correlative was strong enough to answer. *Are you sure you sensed a CorreAxe on Earth?*

There was a small vibration at the back of Aurora's head. It was frail and apologetic.

It's not your fault, Aurora thought, suppressing a sob for her closest friend.

The Correlative quivered around her. To be Braced was to come close to death for their kind. Those Ascendants who managed to learn the skill of Bracing called it an art. All others called it torture. Were there times when it was necessary to Brace a Correlative? Yes. On the rare occasion that an officer went rogue, there needed to be someone there who could stop them. Still, it was an ugly thing. Aurora had known that on an intellectual level before today. Now she knew it on a physical one, an emotional one, a personal one.

Peel did too.

And it was Aurora's fault.

She stood on wobbly legs. The Bracing had hurt her, but not nearly as bad as it had hurt Peel. The guilt was almost unbearable. She blamed herself the way Peel blamed herself. The only difference was, Aurora was right. This was her fault. All of it. She used Peel the same way she used that Earthling.

I'm going to get you out of this, she thought. *I'm going to save you, Peel.*

She reached out and touched the four walls. There was very little space in this metallic cage of a room. She looked up and down, the floor and ceiling matched the walls in its beige plainness. This Echo Chamber was efficient, small. Peel hung on Aurora loosely and was even dripping away in places. Aurora had to quickly step on the black puddles Peel left behind to reabsorb them.

But there were so many.

"Hello?" Aurora called. "I know you're there, Mia."

"Your interpreter still works. That's a good sign that the Bracing wasn't too bad," Mia's voice sounded from everywhere.

"How would you know? We speak the same language."

"Good point," Mia said.

"Mia?" Aurora said. "Can you localize your wavelength please? I know it's not procedure, but—"

"Flux thought it would be best if I was the one you woke up to," Mia said, her voice now coming only from a small section of the wall directly in front of Aurora.

"How could you do this?"

"It's my job, Aurora. I catch criminals. Of which, you are now one."

Mia's words were even but Aurora thought she could detect a subtle trembling beneath her sister's cadence. Was she angry? Sorry? Afraid? Sad? All of the above?

"Emotions getting the better of you, sister?" Aurora asked, a small part of her hoping to hear a sob.

"Not while I'm on duty."

"Wouldn't our podmother be proud," Aurora said, sneering. Peel dripped away from her face revealing a white chalk etching of anger and black almond shaped eyes of accusation.

"Aurora," her name blew out like a sigh from the wall, "what happened to you?"

"Love."

Mia mocked her with laughter. It was sudden and hurtful.

"What are you going to do to me?" Aurora asked. Her question was indignant with wounded pride and a hurt heart. She quickly wiped a tear from the corner of her eye and hoped her sister couldn't see it.

"You know the answer to that question, sister," Mia snapped back, her own indignation on display in her words.

"You have a Severing Chamber on this ship?"

"We're on the HyperRift Highway headed to Annam where you'll be jailed until your court date."

"You didn't answer my question."

"Do you know how Severing Chambers work?"

"I know enough."

"I don't think you do."

"What are you talking about?"

A sigh.

"Mia?"

"This is one of the latest model transports, Aur. You're in a Severing Chamber right now. An Echo Chamber and a Severing Chamber no longer have to be mutually exclusive. It won't be long now before you feel Separation Anxiety."

"What? No!" Aurora shouted, slamming her fists against the nearest wall. "Mia! You can't!" Black splotchy stains remained on the wall when she let her hands fall away.

"I'm sorry Aurora. We cannot bring you to Annam while you're still connected to your Correlative. You are a high criminal. You know the law."

As if on cue, the anxiety hit. But it was more than that. Anxiety, or fear of uncertainty, was like a pinprick when compared to what Aurora felt in that moment. Peel slipped away, her blackness slowly leaking from Aurora, from her soul. Peel tried to fight it. Tendrils and thin strings clung fruitlessly to her host. Aurora's pores felt as though they were being slowly pried open as Peel was pulled from her, struggling to hang on. That feeling of joined comfort that both had become accustomed to over the years grew weaker. The two-as-one sensation that had seemed foreign ages earlier when they had first Bonded was slipping away.

It was when Peel's inner connection to Aurora's mind snapped that the real pain hit. It was beyond physical, beyond emotional. It was deeper, primordial. Something that should have always been was suddenly no more. The end of a never-ending story. The alpha torn from the omega. It was as though a significant piece of Aurora's essence was popping from existence, leaving her naked in every way possible.

"You can't!" Aurora screamed through tears of rage and pain and sorrow, her fists pounding away on the rounded walls of her cell. She couldn't stop crying. "Mia, we're sisters! You can't." She slid down the wall, leaving black smears of Correlative in her wake, and fell into a dark puddle that was Peel, an inky blotch that she was only loosely connected to now. "Peel?" she whimpered. "Peel?"

The Correlative sent a weak spark for Aurora's brain but couldn't find it. Instead, her black skin slowly bubbled and deflated as though she was losing breath. She tried to reconnect with Aurora's physical form. Her tentacles climbed at Aurora's body, a child longing to reconnect, longing to join Aurora again. Failing. Dripping away, Peel used her last store of strength to pour one last message into Aurora.

The message was clear:

Et'a, Draconian.

Then nothing.

Their connection had been completely Severed. A mechanical whirring sounded from below and the floor shifted from solid to vented. Peel leaked through the slats. Aurora tried to reach her fingers through, hoping that she could pull her best friend, her partner, herself back up. She cried out. She reached. She pleaded.

Nothing.

No connection.

Peel was gone.

Aurora was alone.

Really and truly.

Alone.

"No," she whimpered, the word like a dead leaf falling from her lips. Staring through the slats at a vast tube where Peel lay motionless like nothing more than a puddle after one of Whit's night rains, Aurora was unable to cry, unable to scream. The emptiness was too large.

Two Red Stars guarded the tank, stoic and silent, while a third pressed a series of buttons at the tube's buzzing, whirring base. It hummed to life as the slats shut, hiding Peel from Aurora's view.

"Aurora?" Mia's voice sounded again. Regret settled below her podsister's name like Peel had settled in the tube below them. Also like Peel, it was a black mess of a thing, barely alive.

"What?" Aurora was beyond pain now. All that resonated in her mind was anger. "What do you want, *sister*?" The bile in her last word was as offensive as she meant it to be.

"Peel will be fine," Mia said. "She is being kept comfortably in a stasis tube. If you are found innocent, she will be returned to you promptly."

"If I'm found guilty?"

"You know what happens to her then, *sister*." Mia matched the bile on her last word.

"I hate you," Aurora said.

"You hate yourself," Mia replied.

Silence save for the sound of Aurora's heavy breathing. "Peel sensed a CorreAxe on Earth," she finally said. "Did you know about that?"

"What?"

Aurora heard surprise in her sister's voice. "You didn't."

"There is nothing on Earth, it's a backwards planet. We are watching Nowhere Agents—"

"Agents?" Now it was Aurora's turn to be surprised. "What are Nowhere Agents?"

The intercom hummed with the sound of Mia's sigh. "How much did you actually study Earth?"

"Enough," Aurora spat.

"Apparently not."

"What are you trying to do?"

"I'm trying to understand why you would claim a Draconian weapon is on Earth."

"Let me investigate."

Mia laughed. "You can't be trusted."

"When's my trial?" Aurora snapped.

"I don't know," Mia said. "But however long it is, I'll be there with you."

"What?"

"Flux's doing. I wanted to go back to the Outer Rim immediately."

"I don't need you there."

"I don't want to be there," Mia returned. "But unlike you, I take the oath seriously. I do my job." She clicked her tongue. "And now I have to contact Flux with this information."

"You're going to tell Flux about the CorreAxe?"

"If I send him on a wild goose chase, it's just one more thing we can report to the Cosmic Tribunal."

"Do what you have to do."

"My Correlative already has."

Aurora had no response to that. Instead, against her will, she whimpered, her fingers gently touching the floor, longing for her connection to Peel.

***

TALMUND'S SCIENTIFIC ADVANCEMENT INDEX BRIEF ENTRY: ECHO CHAMBER

- The Echo Chamber was created by Psyerrigen scientist Hel Lux Sofi (Sofi 2) as a negative weapon that forced Psyerrigen minds to fold in on themselves emotionally so that their defenses were down.

- Since Psyerrigen psychic powers are so strong, it took a tool with a vast array of electrical and conducive power to maintain the emotional stronghold.

- An unintentional side-effect of the Echo Chamber's use was that it forced its victims to think about their own regrets over and over again. While those who are incapacitated in an Echo Chamber are effectively disabled on a psychic level, their emotional well-being suffers as well since they are, seemingly stuck in a repeating ordeal of bad memories.

- Considered by many to be barbaric torture, several political committees and social organizations across the cosmos have unsuccessfully petitioned the Zenith as well as the Cosmic Tribunal to outlaw it entirely.

- Though rarely used in an official capacity, those Ascendant agents accused of crimes against the cosmos are still held in these for transport.

- Additionally, Echo Chamber technology can be combined with Severing Chamber technology in order to more swiftly separate an Ascendant Officer from their Correlative partner.

Status

- Official Creation Date: 1.25347.6AST

- Inventor: Hel Lux Sofi (Sofi2) 1.25300.6-1.25399.6AST

- Psygerrigen Accessibility Status: Uncommon/Official

- UCA Accessibility Status: Uncommon/Official

- UCA Patent Registration: 11111.27p-2.37762/Psyerrigen/

Top Factual Documentation

- Echo Chamber: The Inner Workings of a Mind Numbing Device

- Echo Chamber: Accidental Torture

- Echo Chamber: A Complete Record of The Echo Chamber's Legal Battles

- Echo Chamber: Wonder of Psyerrigen Science

- Echo Chamber: The Unauthorized Biography of Hel Lux Sofi (Sofi 2)

Top Opinions/Entertainment

- Echo Chamber: To Hell in an Echo Chamber

- Echo Chamber: Memories Like Needles in My Mind

- Echo Chamber: Echo Echo Echo Echo

- Echo Chamber: Tool of Oppression

- Echo Chamber: Why Isn't This Outlawed?

For more information and for answers to specific questions, please see **Talmund's Scientific Advancement Index Complete Entry: Echo Chamber**.

***

TALMUND'S SCIENTIFIC ADVANCEMENT INDEX BRIEF ENTRY: SEVERING CHAMBER

- The Severing Chamber was created by a classified Ascendant Tech (or Techs) at an unknown point early in the life of the Ascendancy to use as a technique for separating Ascendant Officers from their Correlative partners if their behavior necessitated such an action.

- Severing Chambers can have lasting negative side-effects on both the Correlative and the Ascendant lifeform being separated.

- There is no known record of a volunteer Severing causing any lasting negative side-effects.

- Severing Chambers work through an alteration of sound waves directly surrounding the Ascendant, causing the Correlative to experience deep confusion. This confusion weakens the connection between the Correlative and Ascendant. The chamber monitors this connection and when it is at the proper point (which is different for each Ascendant), it amplifies the sound wave alteration thereby tearing the Correlative from the Ascendant.

- Considered by many to be barbaric torture, several political committees and social organizations across the cosmos have unsuccessfully petitioned the Zenith as well as the Cosmic Tribunal to outlaw it entirely. Most notably, the Ascendant Officer Union (AOU) has proudly brought cases before the Zenith and Cosmic Tribunal at a semi-regular rate for centuries.

- Additionally, Severing Chamber technology can be combined with Echo Chamber technology in order to more swiftly separate an Ascendant Officer from their Correlative partner.

Status

- Official Creation Date: Hyper-Classified

- Inventor: Hyper-Classified

- UCA Accessibility Status: Hyper-Classified

- UCA Patent Registration: Hyper-Classified

Top Factual Documentation

- Severing Chamber: Unclassified 1022.22.12

- Severing Chamber: Accidental Torture 2

- Severing Chamber: A Complete Record of The Severing Chamber's Legal Battles

- Severing Chamber: The AOU's Stance

- Severing Chamber: A History

Top Opinions/Entertainment

- Severing Chamber: Two Halves

- Severing Chamber: The Pain is Real

- Severing Chamber: The Hypothetical Weapon of Mass Destruction: Echo/Severing Chamber

- Severing Chamber: Tool of Oppression 2

- Severing Chamber: Creation Myths: A Reel

For more information and for answers to specific questions, please see **Talmund's Scientific Advancement Index Complete Entry: Severing Chamber**.

***

TALMUND'S SCIENTIFIC ADVANCEMENT INDEX BRIEF ENTRY: REELS

- The term 'reel' is a universal and all-encompassing definition for any form of sensory entertainment found on the ExoNet.

- Though 'reel', in the literal sense, is an outdated and unused technological form of motion entertainment, the term has stuck and is used for everything from mind-directed enterros to eyeslice indicators UCA citizens can access over the ExoNet.

Status

- Official Creation Date: Multiple Dates (see individual reel types)

- Inventor: Multiple Dates (see individual reel types)

- UCA Accessibility Status: Common

- UCA Patent Registration: Public

Top Factual Documentation

- Reels: The History of Motion Entertainment

- Reels: Master Actors Through the Ages

- Reels: Master Directors Through the Ages

- Reels: Overcoming Cosmic Bias Through Entertainment

- Reels: We All Need Laughs and Frights: A Psychological Study of Award Winning Comedy & Horror Reels In Five Parts

Top Opinions/Entertainment

- Reels: Into the Unknown

- Reels: Lawrence & Agi: A Love Story

- Reels: Retrograde 2

- Reels: Shirk The Wanderer

- Reels: Giving Him Something He Can Feel: The Adventures of Sam Dingus Jones III

For more information and for answers to specific questions, please see **Talmund's Scientific Advancement Index Complete Entry: Reels** in which a complete list of the various types of reels can be found.

***

TALMUND'S BESTIARY BRIEF ENTRY: NIETZCHEAN

UCA Designation: ZraNietzchean-Prime

- A culture bearing, verbal communicating, land dwelling, bipedal evolutionary mammalian primaticus that presents itself as, overall, average in that class and order. They possess social and political structures based on an underlying religious belief that permeates the entire planet. Though it has been studied and discussed by anthropologists and social psychologists from all over the cosmos, there is no common agreement on its purported belief system, other than one of hopelessness. Or, as those Nietzchean who are ardent followers of their religion put it, 'meaning is a myth.' They reproduce through sexual contact and have a gestation period of approximately forty Annam Standard Weeks.

- Nietzcheans are distinguished by an invariably dark complexion, eyes, and facial hair (in the males) considered long and unruly.

- As they are the dominant species on Nietsch, they are classified by Talmund as homo nietzchean. Nietzchean are anatomically similar to others in the primaticus order in evolutionary traits. Like many in the primaticus order, Nietzcheans display an erectness of body carriage that frees their dual hands of five digits each (four fingers and one thumb per hand) for use as manipulative members.

Status

- Average Height: 1.70 meters

- Average Weight: 70 kilograms

- Average Lifespan: 500 Annam Standard Years

- Home Planet: Nietsch/Zra System/Inner Rim

- Planetary Status: Dominant Lifeform

- System Status: UCA Equality Inner Rim

- Cosmotic Status: UCA Member Inner Rim (Strong Standing)

Classification

- **RIM: Inner**

- **SYSTEM: Zra**

- **PLANET: Nietsch**

- **DOMAIN: Eukarya**

- **KINGDOM: Animalia**

- **PHYLUM: Chordata**

- **CLASS: Evolutionary Mammalian**

- **ORDER: Primaticus**

- **FAMILY: Hominidae**

- **TRIBE: Homini**

- **GENUS: Homo**

- **SPECIES: Nietzchean**

Factual Documentation

- Nietzchean: Hopeless Realism: A Rudimentary Understanding of Nietzchean Society

- Nietzchean: The Myth That Makes Man

- Nietzchean: Riding Solo: The Happy Nietzchean

- Nietzchean: Frid-Ron Neer: Cautionary Tale, Myth, or Man?

- Nietzchean: Frid-Ron Neer's NetNeg: A Collection of Historical Data Regarding Nietsch's Most Famous Non-Fictional Fictional Hero Villain

Top Opinions/Entertainment

- Nietzchean: Lost on Nietsch

- Nietzchean: Hope

- Nietzchean: Hope 2

- Nietzchean: No One Understands This Song

- Nietzchean: Reels and Reels and Reels

For more information and for answers to specific questions, please see **Talmund's Bestiary Primary Entry: Nietzchean**.

***

TALMUND'S SCIENTIFIC ADVANCEMENT INDEX BRIEF ENTRY: ANNAM STANDARD TIME

- Annam Standard Time (AST) is based on the amount of time it takes for the planet Annam to travel around its sun.

- Official inter-rim meetings, hearings, organizations, and events throughout the UCA are based on AST.

- AST was adopted throughout the UCA in order to maintain and sustain a more equitable traveling and interfacing schedule between planets and systems.

- There are three official zones considered AST: Inner, Outer, and Mid.

- These zones are oftentimes presented as AST.I, AST.O, and AST.M but the I, O, and M designations are not mandatory.

Status

- Official UCA Adoption Date: 2.44895.9AST

- Inventor: N/A

- UCA Accessibility Status: N/A

- UCA Patent Registration: N/A

Top Factual Documentation

- Annam Standard Time: A Cosmotic Explanation of the Zones

- Annam Standard Time: Communicating Across Zones

- Annam Standard Time: Dividing Hours

- Annam Standard Time: The Math of It All

- Annam Standard Time: Redefining Time

Top Opinions/Entertainment

- Annam Standard Time: Leave It Up To The Scientists

- Annam Standard Time: Open Up and Leave

- Annam Standard Time: Free Yourself of the Binds Of Time

- Annam Standard Time: Reactionary Redux

- Annam Standard Time: In the NetNeg There Is No Time

For more information and for answers to specific questions, please see **Talmund's Scientific Advancement Index Complete Entry: Annam Standard Time**.

Chapter 14
Interrogations

A DEAD BODY. ACTUALLY, no. Not just a dead body.

A mutilated child.

"This can't be happening," Eugene lamented.

"It can and it is," Mary replied. Her normally cheery disposition was hidden under the gray storm clouds of the discovery.

How she had managed to calm those boys was beyond Eugene's ability to understand. They had been in a worse state than his buddies had been when they came back from their first test flight of that experimental jet. All of them who weren't dead were currently under forced psychiatric care. (And would be for the rest of their miserable lives.) Those boys, with their pale faces, tears, and panic, had been miniature versions of the pilots, the ones he had once called friends. He wanted to ask Mary how she had done it, how she had managed to keep her cool and pull those boys back from the brink of madness. But he knew it didn't matter. Even if he did know how she did it, he would never be able to replicate it, not for his friends anyway. Thanks to that experimental jet they had all volunteered to fly, they were mad.

And he was a Nowhere Agent. He was a Nowhere Agent because he had no other options. On his flight, he had seen terrible things, unbelievable things, things that should have put him in psychiatric care or the graveyard with all of his friends. But Eugene had been able to defy logic and keep his grip on sanity. The scientists had warned them all that the mind-ship connection they had concocted built from reverse engineered alien hardware was dangerous. Like all birdmen throughout history, Eugene and his friends had laughed it off. Like all birdmen since the Wright Brothers, their arrogance had known no bounds. Seeing those boys cry about their dead friend had reminded Eugene that he hadn't been to visit his own friends in a long time. He suppressed the guilt he knew was creeping up to destroy him.

Mary had become a Nowhere Agent because she had seen a different sort of unbelievable thing. She had seen the thing that had killed her family. Where he had almost been broken, she had been hardened. It was that hardness, Eugene thought, that she had used to calm the boys, to get their story, and ultimately, to seek out the dead body. Strangely, it was that hardness that kept her cheery.

Yes, he had gone with her through the forest toward that little desecrated beach. But he hadn't wanted to. Had Mary? Maybe. Where the true depth of madness he had witnessed is what had driven him into the open arms of the Nowhere Agency, for Mary, it was the true depths of pain.

They were very different people.

Maybe that's why they made such good partners.

They sat in a portable office at a fiberglass table. It was really just a modified Airstream. For all of the technology the Nowhere Agency had at its disposal, it were still considerably lacking when compared to the rest of the universe, or cosmos, or whatever it was called by the lifeforms who existed on other planets. As if to compensate for their weakness and lack of technological advancement, everything here was blindingly white and sterile and was doing its best to give off a sense of power.

Eugene knew the truth about this flimsy trailer. It was less powerful and more like that house from Ray Bradbury's short story, "There Will Come Soft Rains." Maybe it would be the last thing standing if shit got ugly. But it would be alone and it would be sad.

At least it had been brought in within hours of Eugene's last phone call to Local. And Local had come with it so that he could do face-to-face with public officials. That, after all, was not Eugene's job.

Eugene thought that below the scientific sterility of this trailer he could detect a hint of new car smell. The state-of-the-art computer equipment lining the walls beeped and hummed with static heat as it did whatever the lab coats said it did. He looked out the small window like a porthole and watched as some blues erected cameras on poles all over the field. A number of others stood guard over the spot where Eugene had found the footprint. And while the trailer and the poles and the little, white, round huts popping up all over the field were indicators that things were not right here outside of Oakview, NE, Eugene knew it was the makeshift wall going up around the perimeter of the impact event that would piss most people off.

After all, one of their own had been murdered out here. Another was in the hospital. Were these events related? Eugene wasn't sure, but he wanted to find out.

"How are we going to make the people forget all of this?"

He stood up on knees that popped far too much for a man his age and peered more closely out the porthole window. The blues, so named because they were all clad in bright blue overalls, were divided into two groups. One group was strictly construction. They came in with a small army of nondescript blue trucks filled with equipment and began the work of throwing up the wall, placing cameras everywhere, and raising small, rounded work buildings for the white lab coats. The second group of blues walked the perimeter, keeping their weapons out in the open and ready to fire.

"Didn't you say Local already spoke with the governor and the actual FBI?" Mary asked.

"Yes," Eugene said, knowing how she'd respond. "And the mayor."

"Then we're fine."

"We're not making any friends with this." Eugene studied the cement barriers that made up the quickly growing wall and the stoic men and women in those unmarked blue overalls and dark sunglasses that guarded it.

"There is nothing else to do." Mary joined him at the window and followed his eyes across the blues to stop on the ones at the growing wall. There were several residents of Oakview Lanes standing opposite them with arms crossed and deep disgruntled looks etched across their hardened faces. "Jesus, it's like a photo from the 1930s," she said.

"A Goddamned dead kid," Eugene said. "Missing was bad enough. But this?" He whistled through his teeth. "I don't know about this."

"All we can do now is work fast, figure out this shit with the footprint, and get gone before the media gets any serious wind of it. Because no matter what we do, they will. This is too big, too much a conflagration of events. It can't stay hidden."

"Local said he'd run interference with the media if they get wind of this. That'll help," Eugene said.

"Well, he was too slow for that McKinstrey person," Mary said, pointing at the paper open on the table.

"Nothing important really there though." He frowned. "What do you think he'll want to do if things get too big?"

"I don't know. I hope he doesn't have anything too serious in mind. We don't need any more dead bodies. One is more than enough."

"This is crazy. And that means a lot coming from me."

Mary threw Eugene a pity laugh. "What a coincidence, huh?" she said.

"Is it?" Eugene sat down on the bench by the table and leaned back. It creaked its discomfort but he ignored it.

"You think some kind of space monster murdered that kid?" Mary sat across from him. "Everything we know about Whitleys says they're basically peaceful."

"We've only just pieced together information from files on that downed ship from 1947 though. We don't know what's going on now. Hell, we don't know if other organizations or governments know more than us. How many Russian assets do we even have? Chinese?"

"Not enough." Mary nodded.

Eugene rolled his eyes. "It just doesn't feel right, you know? It's too much. I can't believe it."

"I can't believe we don't have a contingency plan for an alien crash landing in a small Nebraska town the same night that a little boy is killed." Mary stifled a sardonic laugh. "Wait. Yes, I can."

"But that's just it. It's too weird, right?" Eugene leaned forward, resting his elbows on the table between them. "It's like things are being set up to explode." He locked eyes with his partner and tried to hold her in place with only willpower. He needed her to see what he was saying.

"I don't know." She looked away. "We have no records of anything off planet that would A) do this or B) be able to get here even if they could do that. I mean the planet is monitored."

"The Normans," Eugene said.

"What?"

"The couple that was in the field when whatever it was crash landed, we need to talk to them. If something from out there landed without a ship—and it looks like there was no ship—that can only mean an Ascendant. If an Ascendant came to Earth, it sure as shit wasn't sanctioned. We would have known about it."

"Would we?"

Eugene shrugged. "I hope so. I mean, that's our job, right? Mike would've at least."

Mary took a breath. "According to the police chief, the man, uh," she dug in her pocket for a notebook and when she found it, flipped it open to read, "Jack, is in the hospital fighting for his life right now."

"What did they say about the wife again?"

"The chief didn't know how she was but said she seemed okay last night. Didn't you take notes when we were talking with him after we found the boy?"

"I was watching that old man."

"Linc?"

"He doesn't trust us."

She nodded. "I know. He's the smartest person we've met in this damn town. Or it might just be the fact that we wear these G-Man suits."

Eugene nodded. "Well, maybe the Normans are smarter."

"Or maybe they had something to do with that murder."

"I can't believe Local let the townies take the body."

"There was no evidence of anything off-world murdering that kid. What else was he going to do? I mean, he went with them."

"Well," Eugene stood and pulled on his jacket, "I think I'm going to go speak with these Normans."

Mary pursed her lips. "I don't think that's a good idea."

Eugene's eyebrows raised of their own volition. "What?" There was a snap to his word that he knew sounded angry.

Mary stood and patted him on the shoulder. "Listen man, the husband is either being operated on or in an ICU right now and the wife isn't going to answer any questions coming from your grim mug."

"What is that supposed to—"

"I'll talk to her." She elbowed her way past him and reached for the door. "You hold down the fort and remember to get me a good room when this trailer is taken away and they give us our own little igloo set up." She paused, looking out the window again. "Though it's not going to take much to be better than that motel from last night."

"But, Jones, Mary, you can't go to a hospital, it's—"

"Don't." Her words were a sudden gust of winter wind.

"I'm sorry, Mary," he said. "I just don't think it would be a good idea for you to go to a hospital."

Mary looked out the window, forcing away memories of her last hospital stay, forcing away the sight of her husband's emaciated form rotting on a bed before her, her children, folding in on themselves as they spent their last living hours vomiting.

"I'll be fine," she lied.

The two stared at each other for a few moments. Through the walls they could hear the dulled sounds of speedy construction. Gruff blues shouted at each other to get things done and help out here or there. Hammers banged; saws buzzed. Inside, computers beeped. There was so much noise. None between them.

There was never any noise between them.

"All right," Eugene said finally. "Just take care of Betty. I'll make sure the blues get the parameters built and do my best to keep the people away. If there is collateral damage, Local will have to clean it up himself."

"Hoer Verde all over again," Jones said. "Or MV Joyita."

"Or worse."

"That's not our concern right now."

Eugene looked at his watch. "As soon as the white coats get here, I'll send a team out to the crater to do a deep dive."

"Good luck," Mary said and she left and shut the door behind her.

Eugene wondered if maybe it actually would've been better if this had ended up being nothing.

***

"You can't do this!" Linc shouted. He was inches away from the car, eyes bulging madly, as he leaned forward and pounded on the roof.

"I can and I will," Mary mumbled and turned on the car radio. "The Tide is High" blared from the speakers. It wasn't loud enough. She was driving past the perimeter into the trailer park and the first person standing at the gate was that old man, Linc.

He was attracting a crowd and his anger was spreading. Mary could see it in their faces. Some were a lot closer to full blown panic than Linc, while others hovered around a disgruntled confusion. She clicked a small round device attached to her ear and raised her wrist comm to her lips. "It's going to get worse before it gets better out here," she said.

"I can see it from here. The blues are getting antsy too."

"Don't let them kill anyone until you speak with Local."

"Don't worry. I'm not making that mistake again."

"We really need to stop thinking about Florida."

***

At the police station, Chief Wilton had no idea what was going on at Oakview Lanes. He was busy dealing with a contingent of reporters and the parents of the Sims boy. The feds had allowed him to send a coroner and one officer out there to study the mess and bring the body back, but beyond that his hands were tied.

"This is a federal matter now," that red-headed woman, Agent Jones, had said. But since that man that both agents referred to as Local had arrived with the body, and monitored everything that had happened to it, Ben had wondered if this was something more.

He had wanted to tell the agents, the man called Local, anyone who would listen, that he was happy it was a federal matter, that he didn't want anything to do with this murder investigation, this meteorite, all of this mess. They had official paperwork that he didn't even want to look at. They had a letter from the governor that he didn't care to read. He wanted to go back in time to the festival where he could eat corn dogs and drink beer to his heart's content.

When they had come in with their black suits, badges, and documentation, he had been relieved. Sure, he had made it appear as though he was angry about this, that this should be his case, that the boy was an Oakviewian and his responsibility. But the truth was, he didn't care. Or rather, he didn't want it. Because he did care. He felt terrible for the Sims. He just didn't want to deal with all this mess.

Local had disappeared, saying something about the mayor. The agents had stayed at the site. His officers were out of their element. And Charlie McKinstrey had already accosted him to write a damn news brief about that poor boy.

Meanwhile, all Ben had was the Sims boy's father in a holding cell. As sorry as he felt for the man, you couldn't start throwing punches at police officers because someone—not a police officer—killed your son, even if there was a reporter egging it on. You especially couldn't do it in a crowded police station with a government agent standing right there.

He tapped his pen on the blank piece of paper before him. "This can't be happening," he said. His head hurt. His stomach gurgled. Was he hungry? Had he eaten this morning?

A knock sounded on his door, weak, unsure.

He rubbed his temples.

The knock sounded again, a little more insistent this time.

"What now?" he asked himself.

The knocking became a pounding followed by the grating of his executive secretary's voice. "Chief!" The sound resided somewhere between an annoying small child's screech and the scratching rasp of a sixty-year-old morbidly obese, chain-smoking man's cough.

"What?" he called, hopefully his tone let her in on the fact that she was the last person he wanted to hear at that moment.

She opened the door and entered uninvited, bringing with her the tragic noises from the station. "That Sims man is mad," she said. "He won't stop screaming about murder." A stark woman, all bones and anger, and glasses that made her eyes seem two sizes too big, Dora Langstrom was all business all the time.

"Well, Dora, his son was murdered."

"I know. I read about it in the special edition," she said, raising her fingers to mock air quotes. "So were mine, sir," she grumbled her derision, unable and unwilling to go one conversation without mentioning her two dead sons, taken from her by what she liked to call Johnson's Biggest Mistake. "No special report about them from Charlie."

"I'm sorry," Ben said, giving her exactly what he knew she wanted and not explaining that Charlie McKinstrey couldn't have been more than twelve at the time of her boys' deaths. "Is that all you needed to tell me?"

"No." She removed the glasses and let them dangle from a chain around her neck. Her blue eyes, now human sized, peered at him.

This was more of Dora's show. In times like these he wondered why he employed her. Then he remembered his files and how perfectly organized they were. He remembered his phone calls and how he only received the ones he absolutely needed to receive. And he remembered the way she ignored his growing belly and his doctor's orders to stop eating so many sweets. When he did this, he wondered why he hadn't married her instead of his wife.

"What else?"

"Sims' wife is still waiting to be questioned and there are more than a few reporters wanting statements. At least McKinstrey is gone. Oh," she raised a finger and flipped through a notebook in her hand, "Linc from Oakview Lanes has called about a hundred times about those feds at the trailer park."

"Did you tell that guy, Local, about it?"

"Before he left, yes. But he didn't seem to care. Said he needed to talk to . . ." she tapped her chin with the end of her pen as she thought, "Oh yes!" she brightened up in mock excitement, "'more important people' were his words."

Ben stood, feeling sure his belly would pop the buttons on his shirt before much longer. "Okay. I'll talk to Jenny first. Keep holding off the vultures."

***

"I know this may seem a little strange, ma'am," Mary said, standing across from May Norman in a hallway outside of Jack's recovery room at Draco General Hospital. "But my people need to work fast if we are to maintain the integrity of the impact crater and surrounding area."

"Isn't Ricky's body being discovered in the area going to make it impossible to 'maintain the integrity of the impact crater and surrounding area'?" The mockery was as sharp as the stone that must have sliced through Mary's face when the meteorite hit.

"You've heard about that?"

"It's a small town, Agent Jones. And even though I'm preoccupied, I read the newspaper. I've also already spoken to a reporter."

Mary stumbled for a response. The electric lights buzzed above them and cast the women in a ghostly blue. The white walls and matching tiles reflected the color in all directions, making the hall seem an endless azure hell. Mary felt woozy but hid it, placing one hand on the cold brick wall to hold herself steady.

She cleared her throat.

"All the more reason to answer my questions swiftly. I know it's somewhat strange, but—"

"It's actually very strange," May said. Her voice was a confident whip. It was impressive on such a young woman.

"Ah," Mary said. She was not used to being treated this way by people outside of the organization. They were usually frightened of the way she stood, her black suit, and her eyes that were trained to never look away. But being in a hospital again after so long had her off her game. "I assure you, Mrs. Norman, I am an agent in a particular branch of the FBI and we—"

"You keep saying that. But you won't tell me which one. All I'm getting from you is G-Man vibes. Is this the 1950s? Are you going to arrest me for being a Communist?"

Mary pulled her badge from her jacket's inner pocket once again and held it out to May. It was gold and there was a triangle with an open eye etched into its center. Below the triangle was the Latin word nusquam.

"This is real, ma'am," she said. "I assure you."

"It doesn't look like any FBI badge I've ever seen."

"Have you seen a lot, ma'am?"

May breathed deeply and rubbed her temples with one hand. "And you want to know what my husband and I saw last night?"

"Yes, ma'am. We want to know more about the rock that fell to Earth. We want to know if it will have any lasting effects on the area, on you . . . on your husband. There may also be tests involved."

"Why would there be tests?" May asked, turning her head to look out the window down the hall. The sky was so peaceful, so calm, so unlike it had been the night before. The dirt that the alien's crash landing had thrown into the sky caused a slight hint of brown to mask the blue, giving it a thicker, slower feel, as though outside the world was steeped in the slight sepia tones of a more innocent time.

Mary squinted at May, sensing that for a moment anyway, May's defiance had been replaced with something else. Fear? "Did you . . . did you see anything strange last night, Mrs. Norman?" she asked, her voice rising a few octaves as the words fell. "It could pertain to the murder if not the meteorite. They could be related."

"I told you a reporter has already been here this morning. Didn't I? And I've talked to Chief Wilton's men. You could talk to any of them about all of this."

"Yes ma'am." Mary nodded. "But I'd rather talk to you. Reporters can be . . . difficult for someone in my line of work. And the police here—"

"Can they?" May interrupted. "Can't imagine why reporters would be difficult for a jackbooted good soldier like you to work with."

"I don't mean to disparage the fourth estate, it's just that some things need to be kept quiet and reporters don't tend to like that."

"Well, I'm pretty sure you won't get along with the one I spoke with then." May looked into Jack's room.

Mary thought it was strange how similar this round little window was to the one in the trailer she had just come from. "That's not very reassuring, ma'am," she said.

"I can't deal with this right now." May paused and her jaw tightened. "My husband is in that room battling for his life." She jerked her head back so that her eyes met Mary's fiercely. All the aggression had returned, and now it was stronger than before.

Mary would not back down. She nodded slowly. "I'm sorry ma'am. I was under the impression that he was out of the woods."

"Does he look out of the woods to you?" May said. The question was a simple thing, as if asked over coffee, but the anger that hovered below it was still strong.

Mary wasn't sure why there was so much anger in this small, prim woman. She knew a thing or two about racism and had initially chalked May Norman's behavior up to her defensiveness against that. After all, she knew she would not have wanted to be a Black woman married to a white man living in a trailer park in this little town. She could practically smell the 1960s era hate emanating from the streets. But there was something more to it. Anger, she knew well, was a secondary emotion. It was like worry and sadness's asshole little brother. This anger seemed a little too fresh to have stemmed from something she knew May had dealt with most of her life.

Racism was like that.

Earthlings really did have a long way to go.

Mary looked through the window at May's one-legged husband attached to several medical machines that to her experienced eyes seemed primitive. They had so much more at their bases. They were sleeker and more refined and, she knew, better at saving people than the monstrosities hooked up to Jack Norman.

She couldn't help but think of her husband and children once more, dying, each one alone, from the radiation of a downed space probe from places unknown. She felt the hard fabric of the Hazmat suit she was forced to wear when she saw them, smelling, even through the layers of protection, their deaths. Her eyes fell to the breathing tube sticking out of Jack Norman's mouth, taped to his lips. His hands covered in thick bandages, scratches criss-crossed over all of his visible skin.

Mary's husband had looked much the same when he died. And he had the support of the agency's advanced medical equipment.

No, she silently told herself. She had no time for empathy or sympathy. She had no time for sorrow. She had no time for a trip down memory lane.

"I'm sorry, ma'am—"

May looked away. "I don't want to talk about this. We don't even know if my husband is going to live."

Mary nodded. "I apologize. He's alone in there? No doctors or nurses?"

"Are you implying something, Agent Jones?"

"Only that in my experience, patients who are still in the woods need around the clock care."

"They'll be back momentarily." Her words were ice and fire.

"I see."

"And I am about to go in and be with him, so, if you'll excuse me." She looked up and down the hall, her neck craning as though she was trying to see around the corners at either end. "A nurse will be in soon too. Talk to her if you'd like. Everyone has something to say about the meteorite or my husband . . . or Ricky."

"Yes," Mary said, her eyes scanning the sterile hall. "This is such a large hospital for such a small area."

"It's been crowded in the past."

"I'm sure."

A moment of silence passed between the women as they stood, one with her arms crossed before her chest and the other with her hands on her hips.

"Have you lost loved ones?" May finally asked.

Mary found her eyes drawn to that same window that May had been looking out of moments earlier. The never ending hazy light out there was a direct contrast to the harsh bright one in here. The constant buzzing and smell of antiseptic made Mary want to head straight for that window and jump through it, away from this woman, away from this hospital, away from this life. If she could, she would have flown up through that cloudy blue away from this bright blue and never stop until she was far from it all. Isn't that why she had agreed to join the Nowhere Agency in the first place?

To just get away.

"Everyone has," she finally said.

May reached out a hand and squeezed Mary's arm. All defiance gone once more, all anger. "Look," May said, "I don't know what happened last night. I can barely hear right now. I'm still a little woozy from the painkillers they used on me to fix my face. I'm sorry I can't be of more help."

"Thank you, ma'am," Mary said and nodded. "I do hope your husband is okay. We will be in touch." She took May's hand and shook it. "When you're feeling up to it, I'd like to talk more."

May nodded and offered a half-hearted thanks.

"Just a couple more things, then I'm on my way," Mary said. "What was that reporter's name again, the one you said spoke with you earlier?"

"Charlie McKinstrey," May said.

"Thank you." She pulled a notebook from her jacket pocket and jotted the name down. "And your face, what happened to it exactly?" she asked, pointing at the line of small bandages running up and down her cheek.

She felt it and looked away. "Something hit me when the meteorite landed."

"No stitches though. Must not have been too bad."

"Must not have been."

Frowning, Mary nodded once more and turned away. "Thank you, Mrs. Norman," she said while she headed down the aisle toward the window.

The thought of crashing out that window shot through Mary's mind again and she shuddered, hearing the glass shatter in her mind. As she tossed the fantasy away and turned from the window, a rotund doctor with a bald head and an unlit cigar sticking out of his mouth bumped into her.

"Sorry ma'am," he said, hardly noticing her as he made his way down the hall toward Jack Norman's room.

***

"How are you feeling, Mrs. Sims?" Ben said as he sat down across from her in one of the two dingy brown interrogation rooms. There was an orange line painted in the middle of the wall opposite him that he'd always wondered about. Why was it here? What was the point? It had been here when he had been hired more years ago than he liked to remember and he thought it would be here until the station crumbled into the ground. Like so much he had seen today, it was hideous.

Jenny Sims did not seem to notice the orange line. She did not seem to notice Ben. Instead, she looked beyond him with big dark eyes that knew a pain he would never understand. The purple rings holding those eyes up and her thin, tight lips made her look as though she had aged ten years in three hours. His eyes couldn't help but find the woman's hands. They seemed brittle for a middle-aged woman, a little too hard, as they ran over her older son Ronny's dog tags.

He cleared his throat and looked away. Never had he felt so awkward in an interrogation room.

"I'm going to ask you a few questions," he said, after the silence of her gaze became too much. Knuckles on the mirror behind him, he tapped. "Before we start, though, a couple things. First, we're being monitored. But you've seen *ChiPS*, so you knew that." He smirked awkwardly at himself and his weak attempt at humor. "And second, I don't think you or your husband had anything to do with your son's abduction and murder. These questions are just to suss out any possibilities, anything you might have missed or we might have missed."

Still no response from Jenny. In fact, she barely moved, except for her fingers that couldn't stop rubbing those dog tags gently.

He noticed that she was wearing a flannel that was far too large for her and far too warm for this cramped little room. Like most heating and cooling systems in the Midwest, the one at the police station could never figure out how to behave in the early spring.

"You can take off your flannel, if you'd like, ma'am. I'm hot in here and I don't have a coat," he said. He was accustomed to being gruff whenever he sat in this room, accustomed to a perp across the table who had been caught shoplifting or spray painting, or even slinging pot. An awkward half-laugh tumbled from his lips.

"I'm fine," Jenny said, her voice someplace far away, so much so, Ben was surprised he could hear it.

"Okay then, these questions are going to be similar to the ones I asked at your trailer, but now that we know more and—"

"You've separated me from my husband," she finished his sentence.

"Um, yes, we do like to question you alone. And since he was," he paused, fidgeting, a student who hadn't done his homework. "Um . . . so upset, we thought it best to separate you."

"This is how it's done."

"We do question couples separately. How did you—"

"My father was murdered."

"Lord, I'm sorry, ma'am, I have people working on this case who should've told me that. I had no idea."

"It's all right. It was a long time ago, but I know the drill. We all do out there I think." She offered a vague motion in the direction of Oakview Lanes.

"Yes, well," Ben huffed, unsure if he should be defensive or apologetic. "Let's just get on with it, shall we?"

Again, no response. Just those eyes, those deep, dark eyes that mourned and mourned and mourned, and Ben knew they always would. He had seen eyes like that on his secretary enough to wonder if they would rub off on him and one day he'd look in the mirror and see nothing but loss.

A kid, he thought before beginning the basic interrogation. "Where were you the morning Ricky disappeared? What were you doing?

How about the night before?" They went on and on and Jenny answered his questions willingly, truthfully, and sadly.

When he was done, he stood and offered his hand. "Thank you for your time," he said. "I'm going to speak with your husband now, if he's calmed down. I am sorry for your loss."

Jenny did not take his hand. She only sat.

He left the room and two officers, Banks and Shackelworth, were waiting.

"That went well," Banks said, one of his young ones.

Banks, Ben thought, *a naive boy.*

"About as good as could be expected," Shackelworth offered.

Ben nodded. "How's the dad?"

"Calm."

"I'll talk to him then. Where are we with the body?"

"It's still here if that's what you're asking," Banks said.

"That guy, Local, left though."

"I know. He said there wasn't much on the body he needed."

"The coroner agrees. He's looking at it right now. He doesn't think he's going to find anything evidence wise though. It's a fucking mess."

"I know," Ben said. "I know."

Chapter 15
Inside Oakview Courier

CHARLIE LOOKED UP FROM her typewriter at the sound of the main door slamming. Frustration crawled its way across her pale round face as she watched the publisher storm in.

Shit, she thought, the color rising in her cheeks.

Barry Breathwite was rotund and red and appeared to have been sealed into his brown polyester suit like a Wimmer's hot dog burned into an overcooked bun. His bald head, poking out of his mustard yellow collar like a pig in a blanket, gleamed with sweat.

"Open some windows!" he shouted, waving a handful of newspapers around.

A reporter across the room jumped from his own typewriter like a jackrabbit and hopped to do Breathwite's bidding.

Charlie rolled her eyes.

"Mr. Breathwite," Ernest Clement said, opening his office door and spreading his arms in greeting. He showed his white teeth in an all-encompassing smile. The EiC was ten years Breathwite's junior and technically his employee but somehow managed to ingratiate himself like a peer to the larger, far more powerful man. Ernest was thin and had that early gray that made him look far more respectable than he actually was. Charlie always thought of him as a scoundrel with a good heart. He was kind of like Han Solo to her. And if he was Han, then she was Luke, not Leia (much to her mother's chagrin).

Breathwite huffed. "Ernest," he said, "we need to talk."

"Come right in," Ernest said, standing aside and motioning for Breathwite to lead the way into his office. As he pulled the door shut behind him, Ernest, in his unbuttoned flannel and loose blue jeans, was a visual contrast to Breathwite. He seemed calm, cool, collected. He offered a sly wink to Charlie that told her not to worry, everything would be okay, he could play Breathwite like a fiddle.

Charlie allowed herself a moment of ease as she looked over her latest story, staring back, unfinished on the white paper before her. It dangled from the typewriter's carriage like a child's tongue sticking out to mock her. A breeze from the windows Breathwite demanded be opened made the paper flutter. Now it was laughing at her. Now it was spitting a raspberry.

Of course it was.

The article was a puff piece on the meteor festival last night. Ernest had let her have the article about that poor murdered boy. Now she had to pay for it by writing up another mindless commentary on a mindless affair spearheaded by a mindless mayor. She supposed it was a small price to pay for being the only reporter who had been able to speak with the police chief about that Sims kid, for being the only reporter who had even approached May Norman.

Sure, Ernest was probably right. It was probably in bad taste for her to approach May when her husband was fighting for his life. But there was a connection there. Charlie knew it. She could smell it.

The boy's body was found not far from where the Norman couple had been when the meteorite hit last night. The body was near the woods where everyone from Oakview Lanes had been looking for the boy. After Charlie had talked to May at the hospital, she could tell she had been hiding something. Her gut told her so and she had learned a long time ago to listen to her gut. Sure, some of her colleagues laughed at her, told her she acted like a reporter from the movies, and proceeded to mock everything she wrote. But lately she'd been published far more than any of them.

And she could smell this story dammit. In fact, she could smell something bigger. Not the story but the *truth*. She had sensed a lie hidden below everything May Norman had said. She had been holding something back and the stench of that repression had seeped through every short, angry word she had said. And now that there was a rumor that feds were at the trailer park cordoning everything off, Charlie knew, *she absolutely knew* there was something more. All of it was connected. It had to be. She had followed her gut to talk to that Norman woman earlier that morning and she knew that if she could keep following her gut, a truth would pan out, probably the biggest one of her career . . . so far.

But Charlie was stuck behind her typewriter trying to figure out a way to throw quotes about pie eating contests into this asinine story about a festival that no one even cared about anymore thanks to everything that had happened over the last sixteen hours or so.

"What the fuck?" she whispered.

"What the fuck, what?" Jock Hensfold asked. He was a fellow reporter. As old as time but socially and politically stuck somewhere in the 1930s, Jock had never been Charlie's favorite colleague . . . or person. Naturally, he followed his question with, "Women shouldn't talk like that."

"Mind your business, Jock," Charlie spat, trying hard to listen to the conversation going on in Ernest's office.

From behind the office door, she could hear Breathwite's muffled voice. It grumbled and growled like a volcano ready to explode. It huffed and puffed like a dragon ready to light her on fire. Ernest was managing to keep him calm. No windows shook, no door handles rattled, but the underlying anger was enough to unnerve Charlie. She had thought this was coming for a while. The man had never liked that Ernest had hired a woman and she knew he had eyes everywhere. Someone probably told him that they had seen her harassing May Norman at Draco. And with all of last night's excitement, she assumed Breathwite would be coming in here to stop whatever she had planned.

She stood and crossed her arms. She couldn't be here anymore. She couldn't be surrounded by all of this brown and gray, all of these file cabinets and desks, all of the bubbles in the water cooler, and all of the stale cigarette smoke climbing up from Jock's ashtray.

"I'm going to get coffee. Anyone want something?" she asked the four other reporters in the room. All men, two older than Breathwite, and two younger than her, shook their heads in unison. It unnerved her. She mocked them with her own head shake and headed out as Ernest's door jangled open on unsteady joints.

"McKinstrey?" Ernest's voice sounded behind her.

Shit, she thought again as she turned to face him. "Yes?" she asked, using the best sing-song voice she could muster.

Ernest raised both his eyebrows. "Huh-uh," he said, indulgent if somewhat suspicious. "Mr. Breathwite and I need a word with you."

"I was about to get some coffee. How about first I run and get the both of you something too?"

"Isn't that supposed to be your job, anyway?" Jock said, laughing behind his liver-spotted hand as he lit up a cigarette.

Sudden anger surged through Charlie's frame. "Listen here, you old—"

"Charlie, now . . . please." Ernest's tone brokered no argument. He shot a quick and angry glare at Jock. "Mind your manners, Jock, especially around your betters," he said before allowing Charlie into his office and letting the door fall shut of its own accord. He paused after it clicked closed and opened it again, sticking his head out to yell, "And put that damn thing out!" to Jock.

Charlie laughed under her breath.

"I swear to God, Barry, it's like wrangling kittens sometimes," Ernest said through a sigh.

"You know what your problem is, Ern?" Breathwite said, leaning forward in the protesting chair. He rested one elbow on the desk in front of him and looked over Ernest and Charlie both.

Charlie could tell that the man had clearly cooled down some, but the way he leaned forward, almost like a predatory snake about to strike, despite his size and girth, unnerved her. She imagined an anaconda or, strangely enough, an evil Santa Claus, one who didn't bring presents. He brought pain . . . and enjoyed doing it. Barry Breathwite was Krampus without the horns and fur. She pictured him shaving it all off every morning and had to suppress a laugh.

"What's 'my problem' Barry?" Ernest asked, walking around his messy desk and leaning back in his own chair, his arms falling behind his head where he clasped his fingers and waited, a serene smile on his lips.

Breathwite turned to keep his eyes on Ernest.

Charlie was unsure how Ernest could act so nonchalant around Breathwite. The man signed his paycheck, ran the paper, and was generally known as the Southeastern Nebraska King of Journalism, which meant something, as it included the heavy hitters from Omaha and Lincoln as well as all the small towns like Oakview.

Breathwite was also terrible. A greasy guy in a sham of a marriage whose children had hightailed it away from Oakview as soon as they were old enough to leave, Barry Breathwite was not only powerful but angry. He was not the kind of man Charlie would speak to this way. She felt she could just as easily end up at the bottom of the Missouri River as fired if she pissed him off.

"Your problem is you're too nice." There was that growl behind Breathwite's words again, as though there was an animal inside him glaring at the bars of his cage, calculating, waiting for the perfect moment to pounce and shatter his prison.

"That's not what the politicians I report on say." Ernest laughed.

"Oh, oh, oh," Breathwite mocked, "I didn't mean you were too nice to your subjects." He turned his chair once more and the squeaking was like a screaming siren of pain in the small office. "I meant you're too nice to your reporters." He pointed one of his thick fingers at Charlie. "Too nice to you, in particular."

"Nice segue, Barry," Ernest said, leaning forward and resting his arms on a pile of newspaper on his desk.

Breathwite stood. His eyes slid over Charlie who had never felt so naked in her life. The sensible, blue cotton tea-length skirt and matching jacket that made up her suit wasn't enough to protect her from his gaze.

"It's sad," Breathwite said, "to see a . . . thick, four-eyed girl like you acting the way you do. You should really be out there thinking about getting a man, don't you think? I bet you could spit out a fine mess of babies with those hips."

At the mention of her glasses, Charlie instinctively reached for them and moved them up her nose. She tried to suppress the red glow to her cheeks when Breathwite mentioned her hips. She tried to dry the urgent angry tears sprouting in her eyes. She tried to calm her shaking fists.

She failed.

"Mr. Breathwite," she said slowly through gritted teeth. "I'm going to need you to explain what you mean."

"Well, I worry with your reporting, and your appearance, you're just turning yourself into an old maid no man wants to get near. I mean, do you want to be the next Betty Friedan?"

"Jesus Christ, Barry," Ernest spat his name like a wad of phlegm, "It's 1981. That's enough. If I knew this is how you were going to treat my reporter, I wouldn't have brought her in here."

Charlie tried to speak but found her voice pulled away in an undercurrent of anger. All she really wanted to do was hit. She felt her fingernails digging into her palms and hated the fact that she had painted them pink this morning, made them look pretty and shiny. In that moment she not only hated everything Breathwite would have considered feminine, but all men everywhere.

Breathwite, seemingly shocked, offered a sidelong look at his EiC. "You wouldn't have?" he asked, honest confusion in his voice. "You know how our relationship works, correct? I'm the publisher, which means I'm your boss, you do what I say, you—"

"Tell her what you told me and then you can be on your way unless we have more business."

Charlie had never seen Ernest like this. He was an easy-going, laid back Chief. Sure, he had a dedication to the truth that was genuinely inspiring when in the field, and Charlie had seen him land more than his fair share of one-two verbal punches to a corrupt politician, but this was different. This immediate anger spoke to a hurt she felt he understood. How could that be? She suddenly wanted to know Ernest better than she did.

"You're right. She's a lost cause anyway." Breathwite pulled the stack of papers from below Ernest's elbows.

"Barry."

Breathwite held the papers up so that they were inches from Charlie's face. "Do you see these headlines?" he asked, shaking them.

Charlie took them and flipped through. On every issue she saw one of her stories. She looked from Ernest to Breathwite. "My articles," she said, a pit opening in her stomach and pulling in all of her anger so it could be replaced with alarm.

"Yes," Breathwite said, triumphant. "These are your articles." He crossed his arms.

"What about the articles?" Ernest asked, pressing quietly, simply, like a teacher would a student with some dark secret he knew they wanted to share but were afraid to.

"They're getting people to talk about our paper more than they have for a long time, since the television news reporting started growing like a damnable weed in the garden."

Charlie, confused, looked to Ernest for help. He smiled and nodded. "Ask whatever questions you have, Charlie."

Charlie took a moment. Breathwite leered. Ernest stood once again, crossing his arms before his chest.

"What," she began tentatively, "what are people saying?"

"That was my first question," Ernest said, nodding.

Breathwite grumbled something under his breath that neither Charlie nor Ernest could hear.

"What's that Barry?" Ernest asked.

"Most of them are saying it's good reporting. They're interested. You have people reading. You may even be up for an award or two at the end of the year."

"And is that what you came here to tell my reporter?"

Breathwite side-eyed Ernest with evil intent, never turning his face from Charlie. "I came to tell her that when word gets out Charlie McKinstrey is a Goddamn woman there will be fallout."

"What?" the shock hit Charlie like a bullet. No one, not even those old school assholes Jock or Huey, ever spoke to her this way. "What did you say?" The tears from earlier had burned away with the heat of her anger.

Breathwite stepped back raising his hands. "Now, now, now, Charlie, you know I didn't mean—"

"Barry," Ernest interrupted, "if I may." He reached out both of his arms as if to separate the two as though they were children about to throw fists in a schoolyard. To be fair, at that moment, Charlie really wanted to throw fists. Ernest's head swung from one to the other.

"Fine," Breathwite said, disgruntled.

"Okay," Ernest rubbed a hand over his slightly receding hairline. "Charlie, Barry thinks you're a great reporter but is concerned about what will happen when people start to realize you're a woman covering all of this serious news—"

"I'm literally in the middle of writing a stupid puff piece on that fair or whatever it was last night right now!" Charlie shouted. A bird roosting just outside an open window called out in disgust and flew away. A breeze gusted through the window and brought with it dust and the fishy smell of the Missouri River. "This is the kind of thing women report on, this is—

"I know, I know, and I thank you for it. You write about more than just hard-hitting news and we," he looked at Breathwite, "both of us, appreciate it." He rubbed his hands together before interlocking his fingers as though about to pray. "Now, as I said, Barry is concerned. He came in today to make sure you weren't going to continue to report on what happened to that kid."

"And?" Charlie spat the word.

"And he said, 'no,' you little—"

"Barry!"

Breathwite huffed and pulled a handkerchief from his jacket. He dabbed his forehead and neck. "Why is it so fucking hot in here?"

"A storm is coming, by my guess," Ernest said.

"Fucking springtime in Nebraska," Breathwite growled.

"Anyway," Ernest continued, "we discussed it and though Barry is worried, we feel it would be best if you keep doing what you are doing, keep writing the articles you're writing, the puff pieces as well as the more hard-hitting stuff. After all, it'll just be more news when people start to realize a dainty little girl is writing about murders and the like." A note of sarcasm fell musically from his mouth.

Charlie was confused. She thought for sure Ernest had lost this battle. This newspaper had been part of Breathwite's enterprise for longer than she had been alive. She wanted to nod and leave before anything else could be said. But the reporter—the loud, obnoxious creature living in her gut that always wanted answers—refused to budge. She hung her head, succumbing to that creature's voice, that voice that screamed, that yelled, that shouted, "Why?"

She stood straight, eyes as fierce as she could make them, and looked at Ernest, trying hard to show her frustration at her EiC. "Then why am I here?"

Ernest shrugged. "I said I'd offer Barry the opportunity to convince you to stop reporting on the more serious matters you've covered.

Except for last night, there hadn't been anything too heinous to report on for awhile and—"

"What?"

He shrugged again. "It was the least I could do. This is his newspaper after all." He smiled, this time hiding his teeth, as though somewhat ashamed. "Barry here," he reached across his desk and placed one hand on the large man's shoulder, "screwed the pooch right out of the gate."

Breathwite knocked Ernest's hand from his shoulder and grunted, "Mixed metaphor."

Ernest directed his attention to Charlie. "You can go. I know you were about to step out to get some coffee. Will you bring me back one?"

She nodded, stammering, suddenly so confused by the situation that she had lost herself. "Yes, yes . . . of course. Black, right?"

"And hot please."

Breathwite huffed his indignation and stomped out of Ernest's office without another word. He charged through the newsroom as the other reporters looked on, some following their publisher's movements and others staring, mouths agape at Ernest and Charlie.

"What just happened?" Charlie asked.

"Hold on," Ernest said and stepped forward, leaning on his open door. "Don't you boys have a newspaper to write?" he shouted before slamming the door.

He faced Charlie, arms crossed, a knowing grin on his lips. "Barry, am I right?"

"How are you able to . . . control him like that?"

"I know his secrets, Charlie, and let me tell you, they are good."

"You want to share?" she asked.

"No," Ernest said. "But when I die, I'll make sure my will says to give you my journals." He winked. "Now go get that coffee please." He walked around his desk and sat back down, putting on his round wire frame glasses so he could read whatever rough copy sat before him. "Also, I know you went and talked with that Norman woman at the hospital this morning while these other idiots were at the cop shop harassing our poor police chief. Keep shit like that up for long and you'll have my job one day. Do you want my job?"

"Um, thank you but no," Charlie said but didn't know for sure. Maybe she did want Ernest's job one day.

"You're welcome," Ernest replied without looking up, "and by the way, stop writing that stupid meteor festival story. I'm giving it to Jock. You have bigger fish to fry, don't you?"

"Yes sir, yes sir," she said as she backed out of Ernest's office.

"You're probably going to want to go back to the hospital and talk to May Norman again, yeah?"

"I think so," Charlie said. "She was hiding something earlier. If her husband is doing better, she might be more open."

"I'm sure there are people at the trailer park who'd love to talk to you, too." Ernest nodded. "Don't forget my coffee before you do anything else though." He slid the wire frames up his nose.

Charlie left the office quietly. Her fellow reporters threw questions like baseballs at her but she refused to answer, mostly because she knew most of them knew what had transpired in there because the walls were paper thin and she wasn't going to give them the satisfaction of hearing her talk about the way Breathwite made her feel. This was a win and she was going to savor it while she figured out what to do next for this story.

***

METEOR FESTIVAL BRINGS LARGE CROWD

Willa Cather Park sees more guests than ever before.

By Charlie McKinstrey & Jock Hensfold, staff writers

IT HAD been called a fair, a festival, and a celebration, and Mayor Greyson Rose's day-long affair was one for the record books. With more than 10,000 visitors from all over the area and as far away as Rome and Tokyo, the Meteor Fair proved to be a success.

"We knew if we invited the public to a big party to see the meteors that we would get lots of attention, but we had no idea it would be this big," Mayor Rose said.

The crowds began gathering at the gates of Willa Cather Park early in the morning and the influx of curious visitors did not abate for hours. When, finally, it appeared that the police were going to have to start turning people away, an emergency road closure was set up that opened up more room for visitors. Tony Nguyen, from Tokyo, was excited to be here for this.

"It's just something you never expect to see in your life," Nguyen said.

Another visitor from afar, Leo Vecchio, of Rome, agreed.

"I'd have come anywhere to see this light show," Vecchio said.

Though Oakview's visitors seemed to enjoy themselves, there was at least one Oakview resident who was overworked during the festivities.

"No, I did not want to close streets and set up barricades, but with the number of people coming in from out of town, there was really no other option," Police Chief Ben Wilton said.

With some of Oakview's main thoroughfares closed, several businesses joined the fair as semi-official vendors.

"We normally keep our patio furniture in storage until well into June, you know, because this is Nebraska and our weather can be unpredictable. But with so many excited people here, it felt like the right thing to do," Janice Kalanowski, owner of Deliteful Deli, said.

Despite Kalinowski's misgivings about Nebraska weather, on the day of the fair, there were few clouds in the bright blue sky. This, naturally, kept people at the park until nightfall when the meteors could really be seen. When the bands began to play and the sky lit up with fiery wonders, there was little left for all of the gathered amateur astronomers other than to enjoy the sights and sounds.

"All in all, it was a massive success and we hope to use that success to help build future projects and bring Oakview into the 80s with a bang," Mayor Rose said.

Chapter 16
Croatoa

"YOU TWO HAVE REALLY screwed the pooch on this one, haven't you?" Local asked. He liked to yell at them in this small trailer with the white coat typing away madly at a keyboard behind him. He wanted an audience. And even though he knew the mousy little man staring at the computer and tapping its little keys was doing his best to make it look like he was not paying attention, he was taking in every Goddamned word.

Good. This meant it would get out that Local Mike Martinez wasn't one to be fucked with.

A small man in a suit that matched Mary and Eugene's but was somehow trimmer and more sophisticated, Local Mike Martinez commanded the North America region for the Nowhere Agency and was one degree away from official First Contact. When the time came, if the location was right, he was the point. Every time there was an incident here, he secretly prayed that it would be the real, official thing, that he would be the one seen on the news, read about in the papers, and listened to on the radio.

He would make history.

He was too important to be here dealing with these two morons and their idiocy. Mary Jones and Eugene Ha had been screw-ups since day one, and Mike was wondering how many chances they would get, how many times he would have to suffer their incompetence, before his bosses just let him Croatoa them. Any more chances, any more screw-ups, would be too many because here he was, again, less than twenty-four hours after an incident, coming in to clean up what Tweedledee and Tweedledum couldn't seem to fix.

"Don't see how this is our fault, Mike," Eugene said, openly trifling.

He was the one that really bothered Mike. He couldn't believe they had ever been partners. Along with his repetitive failures came a repetitive arrogance that he hadn't earned. The only reason he was even part of this organization was because he somehow had survived something that had killed or driven insane every other pilot who had manned an experimental jet. In other words, dumb luck had gotten him here, a stupid trick of genetics.

And the piece of shit couldn't even fly these days.

"You don't?" Mike said. He hoped Eugene could feel the fire behind his dark eyes because he sure as hell could. "Let me lay it out for you then, Agent Ha." He cleared his throat as he tapped on the binder resting on the table between them. "First, you were in a car accident on your way to the scene. How does that even happen in a car like that?" He pointed out the window to where the Cadillac sat, its fresh dent gleaming in the afternoon sun. "How did a pilot do that?"

"Deer. It's in our report," Eugene said through gritted teeth. "And you know as well as I that I haven't been a pilot for a long time."

Mike smirked. "Oh, but there is more!" he shouted, shaking the trailer. The white coat almost fell out of his chair.

Mike shot him a quick, sharp glance.

"Sorry," he mumbled under his breath as he reached for buttons on a control panel and made himself look busy typing away on the keyboard again. Green words filled out the black screen in front of him and danced on his glasses.

Exasperated, Mike faced Eugene. "You interacted with local residents without wiping their memories, you stumbled onto an unrelated murder, and you were unable to stop an army of idiots from traipsing through the crash site. It's a miracle you even found that print!"

"What can I say?" Eugene said, a grin crossing his face that would have pissed off his own grandmother. "We're miracle workers I guess."

Mike turned from him to Mary who had been standing quietly by the door. While she may have been as big a screw up as Eugene, she was at least humble and easy on the eyes. And what had brought her to the Nowhere Agency wasn't dumb luck like in Eugene's case. It was willfulness and strength. In the face of tragedy, Mary Jones had shown her true colors. Sometimes Mike wished he would have partnered her up with literally anybody else. But that wasn't the way it worked in the Nowhere Agency. Opposites were joined together until they made it to the top and they were happily, thankfully, put on solo duty, or, like him, made Local.

"Have you had any luck with anything?" Mike asked.

"Some," Mary said. "I'm sure the woman who was in this field when the meteorite hit knows something she's not telling anyone. I think she may have interacted with the Whitley. There is a cut on her face that she claims happened when the meteorite hit but it's far too healed, unless whoever helped her has access to better medicine than anyone on Earth."

"Maybe our dear leader can make her talk where you've failed," Eugene said. He looked down at Mike and sniffed, pursing his lips as if studying a scientific specimen. "You think you can?"

One of Mike's thin black eyebrows climbed into the vast barren field of his forehead.

"Watch your tone, Agent Ha."

"Sorry, sir." Eugene said, his tone indicating that not only was he not sorry, not at all, but that he had no intention of watching it either.

"You have more to say?"

Eugene's hands were clasped before him. "We've been here for less than twenty-four hours and in that time, we've discovered a murder, a Whitley footprint, and a crater with no meteorite. This is unprecedented and if you blame us for the way we are reacting to an unprecedented situation, maybe you should have come here yourself when the white coats first noticed there was going to be a meteor shower."

Mike's lip twitched. "That's not my job." He pointed a thin finger into Eugene's chest. "And even if it were, I would not have begun my investigation by getting into a car crash!"

"You're here now though, aren't you?" Eugene replied, looking down at the shorter man. "Can you figure this shit out?"

Undaunted, Mike let his hand fall to his side where he balled it into a fist. He stared hard right back at Eugene. They were two bulls in a China shop about to destroy everything. "You should know better than to talk to me like that, Agent Ha. With one word I can send you back where you came from."

"No one can send me back to where I came from, Mike," Eugene said. "You know that."

"Oh, your little nightmare world? The one from the flight that grounded you, that place?" Mike replied. His questions were soaked with intentional smarm. "I'm so sick of you bringing that up. How long until you get over it, man? How long?"

"You don't know anything!" Eugene exploded, pointing a finger at Mike's chest.

Mike batted the finger away. "I know a lot, Eugene, and if you want to continue down this path, keep talking. Let's see where it ends."

After a trembling pause followed by a gust of wind that rattled the trailer, Eugene spun away from their game of chicken. He took two large steps to the other side of the cramped trailer and violently shoved a curtain aside to look out a larger window upon the field. It was now populated with small white domes and several blue overall clad agents. Many sported automatic weapons. All sported angry grimaces. Eugene motioned toward them.

"There is more going on here than we know," he said, his voice even now. "And instead of coming here to help us with this, you come here with accusations about how we aren't doing our job." He crossed his arms before his chest and looked hard at Mike. "Now, I don't know what's going on with you, with your bosses, but there is no reason for you to be blaming us for all of this. It is not our fault."

"For once."

Eugene clenched his teeth. "I swear to God, if you bring up Florida again—"

"Are you about to threaten me, Agent?"

"Does it sound like a threat?"

"Gentlemen, gentlemen," Mary said, stepping between the two of them, "can we all just calm down?" She placed one hand on Eugene's chest but kept the other one a few inches from Mike. "Tensions are high. If a Whitley came here without a ship, we all know what that means."

"Obviously, it's a rogue Ascendant. And we're sure there is no evidence of a ship? A meteor shower would be the perfect cover." Mike cleared his throat, trying to find his professional voice once more.

"None," Mary said.

"The white coats haven't officially confirmed the print yet, correct?"

"No, but it is all but confirmed. A few more samples of the surrounding earth will tell us if there is any residue from a Correlative and we're sure that there will be."

Mike closed his eyes and clasped his hands together before his face.

"Also, like I said, May Norman knows more than she's saying," Mary said.

"What do you think she knows?" Mike asked, looking at her from behind his clasped hands.

"Honestly, all I know for certain is that she's hiding something."

"Something significant to us or the murder?"

"Jesus, Local." Eugene said. "It could be both."

"Tone, Ha," Mike replied. "The murder is terrible, but until you give me reason to believe otherwise, professionally, it is not our concern. We need to get someone in here whose job it is to deal with terrestrial murders and the like but we can't do that until we figure out what we're dealing with."

"Do we really want more people here?" Eugene asked. The edge that had been tearing through his words was somewhat softened. "More cops and Fed suits are only going to make more people suspicious. At this rate we're going to have to Croatoa 500 radius miles."

"Maybe if you would have arrived last night when everything was happening instead of spending a comfortable night in a motel, we wouldn't be at this point," Mike said. He frowned as if to simultaneously drive home the point and indicate that he could already smell Eugene's bullshit.

"You weren't here!" Eugene shouted. "There was nothing we could've done anyway! It was a madhouse! There were people running all over the place after the meteorite hit. So many of them were in the woods looking for the kid, that by the time we would have arrived, we would have had to Croatoa them to begin with. Then what would we know?"

"We would know that you two knew how to do your jobs."

"How could any of this be our fault when we weren't even here yet? Christ, Local, we were in a car accident!"

"Look," Mike said, closing his eyes and resting his nose on his clasped hands for a moment before looking back up at Eugene, "I don't care what happened to you two, right now we need—"

"Right now, we need to get to the bottom of this," Mary interrupted, her voice acting once more as a barrier between the two men. "And stop bickering like a couple of children." She focused on Mike. "Do you think you should contact your superiors?"

Mike laughed weakly. "I have to go through the other Locals before I can even think about making that happen. And we cannot contact them with questions, only discoveries and information."

"Well, we have none of that officially yet. But if you give us white coats a little more time, we will know," the white coat put in. He had swiveled in his chair so that he faced the group. His pinched face wore worry like makeup, but he seemed confident as he nodded at the three of them before returning his attention to the screens.

"Then what should we do in the meantime?" Mike asked.

"Isn't that what you're here to tell us, boss?"

Mike leaned heavily on the table in the middle of the trailer and looked from agent to agent to the white coat sitting at a humming computer monitor. "I'm here because we all know that a footprint with no evidence of a ship means chances are high a rogue Ascendant visited us."

"How do we know for sure they're rogue?"

"As far as we know, they're the only ones who can travel through space without a ship. And we would have been informed of a visit. It also wouldn't have happened here of all places. It would have been official."

"Is there any way the Ascendant could be official though? Could this just mean that the Alliance thinks we might be ready to join them?" Mary asked.

Eugene's laughter was sardonic and angry. "We're so far from ready, Jones."

"So what?"

"I don't know," Mike said. "I'm honestly unsure what to do from here." He motioned for them to sit at the table.

"Step one is to confirm beyond a shadow of a doubt that what we found is a Whitley print from someone wearing a Correlative. Once we are certain of that, I'll put the wheels in motion."

"We'll know soon," the white coat said without turning his eyes from the computer monitor.

"If it's not, we can pack up and get out of here," Mike said.

"What about the murder?" Mary said.

"What about it?"

"We have to help find out who killed this boy," Eugene said.

"That's not our jurisdiction."

"What if it is?"

"What do you propose?" Mike said.

"I should go talk to this May Norman woman again," Mary said. "This time I'll bring Eugene and we'll get far more serious if we have to. Maybe even bring her in."

Mike nodded.

"There's more."

"What?" The word was frozen with frustration.

"She's already spoken to a reporter."

"Jesus," Mike said. "What else could go wrong?"

"I have the reporter's name. She's just from some paper here in Oakview. We'll talk to her too."

Mike rubbed his forehead where he felt the dull beginnings of a migraine. "Fine," he said. "I'll stay here and monitor the white coats and the blues, help keep the perimeter safe. I may have to speak with the mayor again." He wiped his hands together as though he was cold. "Once everything is confirmed, I'll make contact if I have to."

"Then what?"

"Then they will deal with any extraterrestrial element here, if there is one, we wipe the town . . . or . . ." He trailed off and let his head hang weakly from his shoulders.

"Or something worse."

"Croatoa."

***

TALMUND'S LEGAL LIBRARY—ABOVE HYPER-CLASSIFIED—BRIEF ENTRY: CROATOA (EARTH)

- Croatoa is the name the Earth Nowhere Agency has given to the act of completely eradicating a group of people from not only their planet, but from their history as well.

• This is a brutal act that has only been recorded as happening on Earth twenty times, though it is suspected to have happened far more.

• The coordinated effort that the Nowhere Agency must put into a complete Croatoa is impressive if sadistic.

• As Earth evolves as a society and develops speedier forms of communication, the act of Croatoa will become less and less manageable.

• The word developed from a legend about a missing on planet colony.

For more information and for answers to specific questions, please see **Talmund's Legal Library Complete Entry: Nowhere Agency.** Much like this file, accessing any files regarding the Nowhere Agency requires an unwritten, secure, above hyper-classified, clearance code. If you do not possess a clearance code, or if you obtained one through illegal means, Ascendant Officers will be on their way to your location before you finish reading this entry.

Chapter 17
A Regular Superman

JACK AWOKE IN A hospital bed, his mind a jumbled mix of dreams and memories. Eyes wide with shock, he took in his surroundings like a good soldier. They made no sense. Shaking his head and rubbing his eyes with the palms of his hands, he thought he heard gunfire somewhere in the distance. He felt a sting on his arm and slapped at it. He felt another on his ear and slapped at that. His fingers tingled with little fibrous bites.

Mosquitoes? he thought. "No." He steadied himself. "Vietnam is over," he said. "The jungle is over." Another breath. "All will be well . . . all will be well . . . all will be . . ." He let his eyes fall past an empty chair with a sweater hanging on it to the window on his right as he lost track of his words.

Late afternoon Nebraska sun shone through, drowning him in a light that did nothing to help his addled mind, ease his throbbing headache, or dull the slight ringing in his ears. If he listened carefully, he could hear wind howling out there. It was like the call of a fast-approaching beast. There had been beasts in Vietnam. He had been one of them.

"Where am I?" his broken throat choked out. A small victorious voice cried somewhere in the depths of his brain, proclaiming that they were definitely not in a Vietcong prison.

But could he believe it?

"May?" he added, thinking that saying her name out loud might make her real, like some kind of magical chant. "Medic?" he called after that. Though his voice was small, it echoed in the empty room. "Is there a medic?"

He sat up and kicked off scratchy yellow blankets—not an easy task given his weak and wobbly leg—and let his foot fall to the cold blue tiles. As he tried to move, he felt a sharp pulling on his wrist and noticed the IV bandaged there, as well as several more bandages around his hands. He hissed at the sight as a memory of hitting hard metal slammed into his thoughts. At his intake, a keen pulling yanked at his gut.

"What did I do?" he asked.

The room, with all of its modern comforts, air conditioning, and medical equipment, had no answer. Its silent sterility offered no help. It felt too organized, too real.

"This must be a dream," he whispered. He cleared his throat and readied himself to yell again, knowing full well it was going to feel like razors in his throat but maybe it would wake him up. "Medic!" His voice cracked through the dull ringing in his ears. His throat pleaded for moisture.

He yanked a breathing tube from his nose but dropped it immediately and hissed as his hands throbbed with a stabbing, pulling pain. Again, his stomach felt as though it was being torn apart. Burning in the back of his throat ignited a series of coughs he couldn't control. The pain doubled and tripled like Hydra's heads as he wrestled with it.

The coughing finally subsided, leaving his body wet with the sweat of pain. He looked around the room searching for his prosthetic leg until he lost his balance and fell back. All he saw now was the ceiling.

It was a speckled thing, some sort of generic hanging tile that looked as though it had a maze carved into it. Wandering through that maze of off-white confusion he realized this was not the first time he had been lost in an inescapable hell.

The Vietnamese jungle was a maze more powerful than he could comprehend. Even being there wasn't enough to truly understand its power. It was bigger than mankind's ability to understand. The tiles above him morphed into leaves as big as cars. The heat wrapped around him. An insect buzzed in his ear. He was lost in the jungle again. He found his heart hitting at his chest as though it wanted out. He found his idea of reality falling away as more sweat beaded a headband across his forehead. He struggled to sit up, managing only to do it after he pushed down the pain he felt everywhere.

It was this pain that brought him back to reality. Blinking upwards at the ceiling tiles, something akin to relief washed over him.

Out of breath and shaking as his neck muscles strained, he managed to scan the room for his prosthetic again. It wasn't there.

There wasn't even a wheelchair.

Taking a few calming breaths, he told himself once more that he was not in Vietnam. He was not in a makeshift military hospital. He was in Oakview. He had to find May. He gulped. The last conversation they had flew up from his memories like a bullet ripping through his brain.

"Shit," he said. "Shit," he said again. He looked around the room for a cane, a walker, anything that could help him get moving.

Nothing.

I guess I'm hopping out of here, he thought. *Or crawling.*

Finally noticing that his hands were covered in bandages, he ripped heart monitors from his chest and let them fall to the floor like discarded trash. The machines around his bed shouted angry high-pitched screams as he grappled with the IV.

He was a bitter mess of frustration as a young nurse's face appeared in the small round window on the door. Her curious eyes went wide as the door flung open with an urgency that sent Jack falling backward once more.

"Mr. Norman! You have to lie down! You've been seriously injured!" she shouted, worry alive in her words. She ran to him, placed a hand on his shoulder and another on his arm, gently trying to move him to his pillow.

"No!" He jerked free. "Where's my wife?"

The nurse fell back and looked around the room. Jack followed her eyes to the empty chair in front of the window. A crumpled newspaper he hadn't noticed before rested on the seat. Jack struggled to focus on the headline and felt himself jump at its words: "METEORITE IMPACT EVENT SHOCKS SCIENTISTS."

"I—I don't know," the nurse said. "She was here and—"

"Jack!" Again, the door opened. This time May stood at the threshold, her eyes and face shining with a radiance that melted Jack.

"May," he said, tears welling as he approached her. "Thank God."

She reached him and they embraced warily. His bandages, sore sides and belly, and the bloody holes in his hand where an IV had been attached made Jack a delicate specimen at best.

"I'm here," she said. "I'm here, Jack. You're awake. All will be well." Her tears dampened his shoulder as they embraced.

"What happened to your face?" he asked, studying the dull scar running down her cheek into her lip.

She reached for his hand but stopped short of touching the bandages there. Instead, she placed gentle fingers on his wrist and turned to the nurse with apologetic eyes. "We need some privacy. Please."

"As you say, ma'am." The nurse left as quickly as she had arrived. "I'll be back in a few minutes to get Mr. Norman all hooked back up again."

"Thank you," May said, then turned her attention back to her husband. "Let's get you situated, shall we?" She helped Jack slide up so that his head once more found the pillow.

After Jack was comfortably beneath his blankets again, May sat and smoothed her skirt before she took a drink of coffee. "Would you like a sip?" she offered.

"I don't think I can hold it," Jack said, raising his bandaged hands before him.

"Let me help." May sat up and gently tipped the cup to Jack's lips.

Though it was a small amount, the coffee felt good easing its way through him. He savored its taste. "How long have I been out?" he asked after May had pulled the cup away and sat it down.

"Since the meteorite hit," May said. "On and off . . . mostly off. That's roughly," she looked at the watch on her wrist, "eighteen hours."

He nodded. "Where's my leg?"

"I don't know. I'm sorry." Even those words sounded like summertime honey. When she spoke with that subtle concern for his well-being that so few people possessed, Jack fell in love again. He was always falling in love with her again. In that moment, he always wanted to be.

"How?" There was more confusion in his tone than anything else.

"We couldn't find it at the . . . crash site."

"What happened exactly?"

"We have a lot to talk about Jack. Do you remember anything?" she asked.

"It's cloudy," he replied.

"You remember the meteorite?"

He nodded. "I remember—" He reached one bandaged hand up, falling short of touching her cheek. "What happened to your face?" he said, his voice soft and shaking.

"It's minor. A rock or something cut me. Nothing to worry about." She kissed him gently. "The baby is fine."

"Thank God," was all he could say.

"Yes," May said. "All will be well."

"May," Jack began, pulling away, "I'm so sorry about . . . about everything."

"Oh Jackie, don't be," she said. "None of this was your fault."

"We shouldn't have been out there. If I," he gulped, "if I would've just admitted I was useless in the search after dark—"

"No," she said. "It was smart. There needed to be someone in the field in case Ricky came back."

"Still," he said sheepishly, "I feel terrible."

May smiled and wrapped one hand around the back of his neck so that she could pull him closer. Her lips inches from his, she opened her mouth to whisper. Before she could say more, Dr. Broyles banged the door open and swooped in like a giant bird of prey, chewing on an unlit cigar and looking pleased with himself.

May sat up in her chair, back straight, and eyes suddenly hard where they had been soft. They were aimed directly at Dr. Broyles. Jack moved his head to the side and was about to whisper if everything was okay, when May turned away.

"Mr. Jackson Norman!" Dr. Broyles shouted, raising his hands like a revival preacher on the last night's final altar call. "You are a sight for sore eyes! Look at you!" His boisterous voice outweighed his massive frame.

The doctor's grin stretched across his face like a demented clown's. Jack, gaping, wondered if he was even human. But before he had time to really chew on that thought the way he felt it deserved to be chewed on, Dr. Broyles continued:

"You are a Goddamn miracle, a superman even!"

Jack eyed the big man weakly. "Thanks," he said. "But I feel like shit."

"You look like it too!" Dr. Broyles laughed as he pulled up a chair and made himself comfortable at Jack's bedside across from May. "At least you got some privacy here, am I right?" He looked around the room and puffed up his chest pridefully, stretching the medical jacket. "State of the art." He patted Jack's leg. "It's a good place to die, but an even better place to recover."

Jack nodded.

"Jesus Jack, I'm sorry. I forgot about your dad," Dr. Broyles said, deflating some. "He died in this hospital, didn't he? Oh God, I'm sorry." He looked away and seemed authentic in his apology. "I forgot, and only a few years after your mama's heart attack and your tour in Vietnam. I'm sorry, son. I'll be damned, you've had a rough go of it."

"It's okay," Jack said, weakness wrapping him like a blanket. "My pa isn't the only one who has died in this hospital. We've all lost people."

Dr. Broyles squeezed Jack's shoulder and eyed him. Though Jack thought the doctor was trying to show concern, he could have sworn he saw a look of expectancy masked by his rough, sympathetic face. It was as though he was nervous but for what, Jack had no idea.

"Did you need something, Dr. Broyles?" May asked, looking up once again. There was a coldness to her Jack could not miss. "We were in the middle of something."

"Not going to attack me again, are you?" Dr. Broyles laughed, happily leaving the moribund topic behind.

"What?" Jack asked.

"Well," Dr. Broyles continued to laugh through his words, "Mrs. Norman here got a little excited when I came upon you in the field last night."

"Got excited?"

"She bum rushed me away from you."

Jack faced May. "What?"

"I was scared." May's cheeks flushed. "It was all so scary." Her voice was meek like Jack had never heard.

"Hmph," Dr. Broyles exhaled. "You didn't seem scared."

"May, what's going on? Are you—"

"I'm just embarrassed," she interrupted, running a nervous hand through her hair. "Can I speak with my husband alone?" she pleaded with Dr. Broyles.

"Oh yes, I'll give you your privacy in a moment," Dr. Broyles said. "The nurse told me our patient here was awake and I wanted to check on him before anyone else did. She's coming back in a minute to get his IV situated and get the monitors back on him." He looked across the bed at May and leaned in, whispering, "Also wanted to see how you were doing, Mama."

"We're fine, thank you," she said. "We're all fine." She felt her belly and was comforted by the life there. "And no one else is here."

"Not yet," Dr. Broyles said.

"What are you two talking about?" Jack asked. Weak with frustration, he looked from one to the other quickly. His head felt light and cloudy.

Dr. Broyles exchanged a quick glance with May.

"I'll explain everything soon," May said.

"So," Dr. Broyles turned his attention back to Jack, "you're still alive. You have to tell me, son. How'd you do it? I mean, when I saw you last night . . ." He laughed. "Lordy, I thought for sure you'd be dead before we made it to town. Truth be told, you shouldn't have been alive when we got there. I don't think I'll ever figure it."

Jack shrugged. "I don't think I will either."

"Well, thank the good lord for Jeep, am I right?"

"Jeep?" Jack asked.

"Your Jeep flipped over and you were stuck under it," May said, sipping her coffee.

Jack almost laughed. "I didn't do anything but get myself buried."

"Yes. And you tried pounding your way through the floor. That's how we found you. We could hear your fists hitting the thing. By God, you're an honest to God superman," Dr. Broyles added.

"Right." Jack raised up his bandaged hands as if to show Dr. Broyles how wrong he was. "You said that, but . . ."

"I know, I know." Dr. Broyles' eyes went wide and wet. "But I thought for sure that meteor had gotten you, boy." His eyes made Jack feel exposed. "You're made of strong stock."

"Yes, he is," May said. "And so am I and," she quieted, "so is our baby."

Dr. Broyles pulled a handkerchief from his jacket pocket to dab his forehead. "Look, Mrs. Norman—May—I am sorry about all of the adoption stuff from yesterday, but I firmly believe—"

"Let's not bring that up now," Jack demanded, a sudden temper firing inside him. He tried to sit up straighter but Dr. Broyles held him down with one of his monstrous hands.

"Jack, stay down. Jesus, man, there were pieces of your Jeep stuck in your abdomen. Stop moving."

"What?"

"Don't believe me? Lift up your gown and have a gander at the scars. I sewed you up myself."

"But you're not—you don't do that . . ." Jack's hands dug under his blanket and went to the hem of his gown. He pulled it up so he could see his stomach clearly. A monster's twisted mouth tied shut with black wire stared back at him. "Christ on a cornstalk," he whispered.

"Well, I assisted. I was one of the firsts with any medical knowledge on the scene out there so I did some minor field dressing. And when we got you to Draco, I couldn't let Dr. Henry work on you alone," Dr. Broyles said quietly. "I know I'm just an OB/GYN, but still, this is my hospital and you're my patient. Well, your wife is. That's worth something."

Jack stared at the remnants of the gash, about ten inches long, running around his stomach, inches below his belly button, surrounded by several smaller stitched-up wounds. "How did this happen?" he asked.

"As near as we can tell, a piece of your Jeep went flying and found a temporary home in your belly and knocked you over before the rest of the damn thing landed over top of you. Frankly, that thing saved your life."

"You said you were one of the first on scene?" Jack asked.

Dr. Broyles shrugged. "I happened to be out on my porch enjoying the light show and when I saw the explosion I came running. There were several people from the search party for the Sims boy who beat me there, but I managed to beat the EMTs."

"The explosion was so loud." Jack looked at the hazy blue sky out the window before he continued. "Did anyone die?"

Dr. Broyles shrugged. "A few cows, some varmints. A fair amount of that field is gone. Yours was the worst injury from the meteorite though."

"Wow," Jack said, unable to find any other words.

"Wow indeed," Dr. Broyles said, puffing up like an agitated walrus for a moment before appearing to think better of it. "Well," he picked up Jack's hand and looked at the small wound where the IV had been. "This isn't too bad and I should get going anyway. I'm sure Dr. Henry will want to come take a look at you. The nurse should be here soon to fix that IV you pulled out and take care of all of," he waved a finger at Jack's chest where small, round red marks told him where the monitors had been attached, "that." He laughed heartily. "And anyway, it looks like your May wants some alone time." He gave her a half-hearted smile that she returned in kind.

"Have they found Ricky yet?" Jack asked.

Dr. Broyles trundled through the room and out the swishing door as though he hadn't heard Jack.

Jack faced his wife. "Ricky?"

May looked away. "They found his body."

"His body?" he echoed.

May nodded.

"How are Jenny and Del?"

"Not good."

"They catch who did it?"

"Not yet." She returned her eyes to Jack.

"Has Broyles bothered you about adoption at all?"

"He's actually apologized more times than I can count."

"I still don't trust him," Jack said. "I'm glad we're both okay at least." He fell back onto his pillow.

"Well, I don't know if I'd exactly call you okay, Jack."

"I survived, right?"

"You did."

"But there is more?"

She nodded. "Let's wait until you're off the painkillers."

"I don't want—"

The nurse poked her head in the room before Jack could finish. Jack and May both eyed her with a mix of suspicion and anger. "That woman from earlier today is here to see you again," the nurse stuttered, "she looks serious. And there is a man with her this time. I don't like the look of him at all. Should I send them away?"

"Dear God."

"May, what's going on?" Jack said.

"I'll be back, honey." She stood. "I'll explain everything as soon as I can." She left the room and followed the nurse down the hall.

****

METEORITE IMPACT EVENT SHOCKS SCIENTISTS

Northern Ignotus not what astronomers expected.

By Ernest Clement, Editor-in-Chief

ACCORDING TO DR. THADEUS BIRCH of the University of Nebraska at Lincoln's astronomy department, the meteor shower known to astronomers as the Northern Ignotus was supposed to be little more than a fun light show akin to Independence Day displays.

"Think of The Fourth of July," Birch said. "The meteors are coming so close to the planet that they will light up the sky like fireworks."

But things changed. In a twist of events that no scientist "Oakview Courier" was able to contact saw coming, a meteor became a meteorite. In Five Mile Field, an impact event occurred. Though there is no explanation about how this happened or what it means on a cosmic scale (if anything), Birch is concerned.

"We are not experts on anything when it comes to space," Birch said. "However, we know that we do not know enough. Events like this only serve to prove it. My concern is that even with all of our studying, all of our observing, and all of our supposed expertise, we did not see this coming. What else could we not see?"

According to Police Chief Ben Wilton, the meteorite is nothing for Oakview citizens to be concerned about, at least in the immediate future.

"There was no evidence of anything toxic landing, so everyone can just calm down about it," Wilton said.

However, as was reported earlier, the impact event did directly affect at least two Oakview citizens: Jackson and May Norman. The Normans, who happened to be close to the location of the meteorite's landing, survived. May walked away with only a few bumps and bruises, but Jackson is currently in intensive care at Draco General.

More news as it develops.

Chapter 18
Without Peel

AURORA COULDN'T SHAKE THE sick feeling creeping through her body like an army of insects. They weren't hurting her, there was no biting, no pinching. It was just an unwelcome presence, an invasive crawling, another creature sharing her body, her thoughts.

The irony was not lost on her as she sat, naked, alone—really and truly alone—for the first time since she had Bonded with Peel and begun the second half of her training to become an Ascendant. Now, though Peel was gone, all she felt was that there was something else there with her, something *wrong*. Longing for Peel to wrap her up and protect her from such things, she stifled a cry. She had been waiting for the ship to land for some time. The jolt when they had left the HyperRift Highway wouldn't have bothered her had she been coated in her Correlative's symbiotic embrace. But without Peel, the jolt and following drag as the ship bounced into standard space was an almost unbearable strain on her body. They hadn't even allowed her a space suit to protect her from this because Ascendant ships were never built with consideration for those called "naked" amongst the ranks. If you didn't have a Correlative or were at least somehow encased in a stasis pod, you were just going to be miserable on one of their ships. There was nothing for it.

Though Aurora was miserable and in pain, she held back her tears. She would not give her sister or any of the Red Stars manning this thing the pleasure of seeing her cry.

On Annam she would be tried before the Cosmic Tribunal. The Zenith, including Ascendant Pinnacle Oz would probably be present for her hearing. High Prosecutor Fluctioner would prosecute and they would demand to punish her to the fullest extent of the law. There would be a great audience. When was the last time an Ascendant had committed a crime such as this? Had an Ascendant ever committed a crime such as this? Aurora wasn't sure she'd be able to hold her tears back when she stood before the Cosmic Tribunal because the more she thought about it, the more she thought she did deserve to be punished.

Lost in thoughts of the impending trial and of her own guilt, she didn't feel the wall she leaned on hum to life. Peel would've felt it and warned her. But Peel was gone so when the wall melted away, Aurora fell to the floor with all the grace of a newborn podling.

She looked up into her sister's Correlative covered eyes. They were white and unfeeling where they would've been black and reflective had she deigned to show her face. Those eyes were like two bright voids. This is what Aurora herself looked like when she wore her Correlative. Looking at this reflection of sorts without Peel gave her pause. Before she could speak, Mia's Correlative melted from her face. Aurora turned away from her sister's naked black eyes and sneered.

"What's going on?" Forcing the words out was a chore. She had forgotten what speaking without a Correlative there to help was like. Everything was just a little too difficult. It was far from impossible, but Peel had always sensed what she was thinking and given her body a little extra nudge to ensure her thoughts morphed quickly to fine words and swift actions. Without Peel, everything was a chore. Living was a struggle.

Mia threw heavy coverall prison blues at Aurora. "These are your size. I'm not having my sister be seen naked in public for the first time since she was caught."

Aurora put the coveralls on. "What about the Draconian on Earth? Did you look into that?"

"Give me your hands."

Aurora reached out and Mia placed electro-fiber cuffs on her wrists. "Your ankles now," she said and, bending down while Aurora gingerly kicked out her feet, Mia clasped another set of cuffs around her ankles. "Are you ready?"

"No."

"Too bad," Mia said, tugging her by the wrists and spinning her around so that she could shove her in the back. Aurora shuffled along, her ankles and wrists cuffed so tightly that movement was a trial in and of itself. The heavy fabric of the prison blues and the cold buttons resting against her skin only forced a perpetual reminder that she was without Peel.

Without Peel, she felt as though nothing worked right, not her, not those around her, and definitely not the cosmos. Sounds and scents were off. It was as though she knew there was something there but it was all just out of reach of her understanding, something she had known before but felt she'd never quite grasp again. Everything looked dull. Everything felt dull. The ship should have been communicating with Peel who should have been communicating with the ExoNet and Aurora herself so that she knew what was going to happen before it did, so she knew every twist and turn before she met them. She knew everything . . . or as much as she possibly could. Now, naked, she was disconnected.

Pulled along like a mewling child, Aurora stumbled. "Where are you taking me?" she asked as she struggled. Somewhere between sluggish and spastic, she felt like a baby.

"Comm bay, Aur. You're going to tell Captain Flux about this crazy CorreAxe theory yourself," Mia huffed. "I want no part of it."

"But you're letting me tell him?" Aurora felt the smile in her words. In all that had gone wrong, perhaps one thing was right.

Mia spun to face her sister. Her almond eyes were slits on her smooth, gray face. "Don't think this means I have any desire to understand what you've done." As she spoke, her own Correlative climbed back up her neck toward her face, tendrils and tentacles longing to wrap her in its embrace. "I'm simply allowing you to share your story with my captain so I don't have to." She turned away. "Now come along."

Aurora followed her sister up a ramp into a room with a single, large screen on one wall and a handful of smaller ones lining the others. Commboards attached to each screen made several connections possible. A series of stark, dim hololights lit a walkway through the screens. Mia marched through the walkway passed blinking azure keyboard hovers and buzzing signals and placed her hand to the right of the largest screen.

"Ascendant 6161938.M, Outer Rim Officer Mia Nova, requests Sol Galaxy Captain Flux," she said.

A moment later the large screen came to life and a larger Flux looked out of it at them. As a Tholin, he was already an imposing figure, but on this screen, he seemed almost godlike. His Correlative fell from his face and his protuberant, tubular eyes blinked. Their rectangular pupils that stretched around their curved endings were as black as deep space and when he blinked, his cloud-like skin rushed to dampen the constantly moving things. His face, craggy in spots where his bones protruded through the gloom of his skin, made Aurora think of the Stone Beaches on Whit. The way fog formed above the water and the jagged boulders protruding through it like blades through skin had always both frightened and enticed her.

"Present," he said. His voice sounded like rushing rapids in a deep cave without the Correlative over his mouth to modulate it. Teeth like stalagmites and stalactites gleamed with moist residue from his vaporous skin and though Aurora wanted to look away, she couldn't.

"Captain Flux?" she said dumbly.

His Correlative morphed so that it looked like clothes, a strange hat, a button up white shirt with a black vest hanging open over top of it, and a pair of blue pants. On his hip were two belts, one holding up the pants and the other keeping what looked like a pair of pistols within his reach. Behind him, Aurora noticed a series of paintings of what might have been Essans or Earthlings riding four-legged animals with magnificent manes and flowing tails.

Horses, she thought. *They're called horses.* The landscape on the paintings could have been pulled from the desert planet Dryke. But it was neither Dryke, nor Essa. It was Earth.

"Drink it in, Vega," he said, grinning.

"I told you, Captain Flux is a student of Earth."

"This is . . . Earthling attire?" Aurora asked.

Flux shrugged. "An approximation. My Correlative is still learning how to make these things. It's having trouble with the hat." He leaned back in a wooden chair and placed his feet on a desk before him. They were clad in the strangest boots Aurora had ever seen. The spurs jingled. "What do you need?"

"Um . . ." Aurora began but couldn't find the words.

"I wanted to let you know we made it to Annam and Aurora has a big claim for you."

"Is that right?" Flux said, uninterested.

"My Correlative sensed a CorreAxe on Earth," Aurora said quickly.

Flux's tubal eyes widened and crawled forward, blinking. "Is that so? Doesn't seem likely on Earth."

"What do you know about Earth?" Aurora asked.

"A sight bit more than you, it seems," Flux said. "How much research did you do anyway?"

"Why do you want to know how much research we did?"

"You don't get to ask questions, Aurora," Mia said.

"Let her be, Nova. This is fine. I know a lot about Earth, Vega. I've watched it for years. You might say I'm a rarity out here. I'm fond of it."

"Have you ever seen a CorreAxe? Has your Correlative ever felt one?"

Flux laughed.

Mia joined him but where his laughter was loud, hers was soft.

"We aren't allowed planet-side unless it's an emergency, girl. You know that. It's one of the laws you broke. It's not part of the UCA yet."

"Just in the running."

"The very early running," Flux said.

"Very early," Mia emphasized.

"So nothing?"

"No, but you know not just any Correlative can sense a CorreAxe. They have to be related somehow."

"The closer the relation, the stronger the sensation," Aurora repeated an old mantra she had been taught during her studies.

"Indeed," Flux said. He looked to Mia. "We've wasted enough time, correct? There's this Earth reel called *Magnum P.I.* that I've grown fond of and it's about to start."

"Wasted enough time?" Aurora asked.

"We needed you preoccupied while we removed your Correlative, Aurora," Mia said. She placed her hand on the device next to the screen. "Thank you, Captain," she said and the image of Flux blinked away.

"Wait. Is he even taking this seriously?" Aurora said. "Is he?" she demanded.

"I don't know," Mia said. "I just knew it was a way to keep you busy while we removed your Correlative. If you were near it when we had to remove it, we thought it might seek you out. So, we tucked you away in the comm room. Worked like a charm." She wiped her hands as though removing crumbs.

"Peel, her name is Peel," Aurora said.

"Come with me," Mia replied, leaving the room.

Annam.

There was always a slight static in the atmosphere that made Aurora somewhat uneasy. When Peel was with her, that uneasiness was nothing. Peel regulated her physically so that she could survive in any atmosphere without fear but it was those little adjustments that had always meant a lot. When it was a little too cold or a little too hot, or the planet's atmosphere wasn't exactly what was needed for a Whitley's physiology, Peel found the proper mixture of elements in the environment and made sure Aurora received them. Physical comfort was easy when you were bonded with a Correlative.

But Annam was a sight to behold, even without Correlative aid. With its massive structures, some of which sprawled over entire continents, formed of compressed light and particulate sound, functioning in perfect harmony with the forests and wildlife of the planet, there was a mysterious magic to it. It should not have been possible to mix such ordered science and technology with such unordered natural madness. But here it was, light and sound molded around and apart from the forests, mountains, and plains of Annam. Somehow, despite the separation, they weaved together, one great beautiful multi-colored glowing quilt of existence.

The capital planet and oldest member of the United Cosmic Alliance tucked comfortably at the center of the Inner Rim near a bright, life-giving star, Annam was considered by some to be the closest thing to paradise one could find in the known cosmos. Even its massive prison structures, one of which Aurora found herself approaching, was magnificent. The building was a dark place. Its compressed light was hardened and darkened to indicate to anyone who could see it from a distance that this was not a place they wanted to approach. Likewise, the particulate sound that made up its inner bones and jutted out in strategic locations to help keep the walls of negative light standing, moaned with a deep sadness that didn't necessarily hurt the ears, but stung slightly, a constant reminder that this was not a good place. More than that though, it was a dangerous place. Had Aurora been escorted off the ship anywhere else, there would have been crowds to gape at her. There would have been ExoNet cams hovering at a respectful distance, focusing on her, force feeding any information they could garner out to the people of all the rims. Somewhere nearby, Aurora knew, there would have been producers editing the footage into various montages, some making her look like a villain, others like a victim. It all depended on where the footage would be shown and who was producing it. In a system as vast as the UCA everyone was someone's hero and someone else's villain. There really was no truth.

No one would come here though. Not even producers. No one came to the Black Boxes of Annam unless they had to.

The Red Star Ascendant who stood guard over this gargantuan prison building had specially trained Correlatives to help them keep their sanity in the face of all of this twisted dark light and dull concussive sound. The guards on either side of Aurora were clearly paired with such Correlatives.

Her sister was not though.

"You should go back to the ship," Aurora whispered to Mia.

"Find out more about the Draconians and the CorreAxe."

"I can handle a Black Box for a while, sister. Don't worry about me. Worry about yourself."

"Mia, you know these places are dangerous. I'm a lost cause. Just get out of here."

"I will not."

"You must. If not to save yourself, then to find out what exactly Peel felt on Earth. If there's a Draconian presence—"

"Stop," one of the guards demanded in a horrible approximation of the Whitley language.

"Where are you taking me?" Aurora asked, knowing full well that even if they were to answer, she wouldn't be able to understand either of them when they spoke in more than single word commandments. Without Peel, she understood little. And these guards had no intention of using their own Correlatives to modulate their speech and communication to make it easier for her to understand. That wasn't their job. Unlike their white, blue, and gray counterparts, the Red Stars were not ambassadors.

"They're not going to talk to you. Or did you forget that part of your training as well?" Mia asked.

"I didn't forget anything."

"Even if they did speak, you wouldn't understand them unless you spoke Annalang fluently. That's what they are, that's what most Red

Stars are. Or did you forget it was your Correlative that helped you communicate?"

"Why are you staying?" Aurora snapped. "You hate me. Just go!"

One of the guards tapped Aurora on the shoulder, warning her to stay calm.

"I don't hate you, Aurora." Mia looked away from her sister, back at the ship. "My commanding officer assigned me to stay with you until your court date. He wants the Zenith to see that it was Outer Rim Ascendants that brought you in," she said. "He would do it himself but he has a galaxy to captain."

"He sends you on his little errand to make himself look good?"

"I am an officer in the Ascendancy and I do my job."

Aurora rolled her eyes. "You do your job?" she asked. "How? By ignoring my tip?"

The guard at Aurora's other side tapped her shoulder with a little more force.

"You get one more warning before one of them gets violent. Do you remember that from your lessons?"

Aurora cursed her sister and the guards under her breath. She knew they understood her. They all had their own Correlatives. They had to be able to understand all languages, to always be prepared, to always know what was going on. As a prisoner, Aurora did not have the luxury of knowledge and communication. As a prisoner Aurora did not have the luxury of freedom. Anger welled up inside her and she clenched her jaw, fighting the desire to take a swing at one of the guards. She knew she'd be stopped mid-swing anyway, but the idea that she could try was appealing. Her teeth scraped together and her fingers dug into her palms.

Without Peel, she was powerless.

The guard to her left made a strange grunting sound from behind its own Correlative mask. The red star on its chest caged in a sea of black spoke of its own rage. This was a career guard. There would be no sympathy from him. Aurora looked to her left. The other Red Star was the same. There would be no peace here, not that she expected it anyway.

The air stunk of mold and stone. It shouldn't have, not here, not on Annam. But the compressed light and particulate sound of this Black Box was doing its job already.

It was driving her crazy.

***

TALMUND'S PLANETARY LIBRARY BRIEF ENTRY: ANNAM

UCA Designation: AnnAnnam-Incorporated

- Annam is the third planet from the star Ann and one of eighteen astronomical objects in Ann's system known to harbor and support life. Fifty percent of Annam's surface is land consisting of continents and islands. The remaining 50% of the planet is water. It is situated at the center of the Inner Rim and is the capital planet of the UCA where The Cosmic Tribunal holds court and where the Zenith regularly convenes to discuss inter-rim matters and law.

- The dominant species on Annam evolved and disappeared

eons ago and is said to have "achieved higher purpose." The theories of what this means are countless and range from an evolution to higher spiritual form of existence to a breakthrough in HyperRift research that allowed them to find a new home in an entirely different cosmos. None have been scientifically confirmed but several are the basis for the dominant religious beliefs in the Inner and Mid Rims. In their absence, several lifeforms have taken up residence on Annam, making it the only known planet in the cosmos inhabited entirely by immigrants, save one: The Cosmic Tribunal who is just as much a part of the planet as it is a part of the citizens of the UCA.

- Being the capital planet of the UCA, it holds all primary governmental buildings including those responsible for infrastructure, interplanetary dispute, ExoNet observation and maintenance, etc. It is also the physical home of Talmund's Library, Ascendancy Central, inter-rim prisons (Black Boxes), and many others.

Status

- Planetary Status: Incorporated

- System Status: UCA Inner Rim

- Cosmotic Status: UCA Member Inner Rim Prime Standing

Top Factual Documentation

- Annam: The Origins of the UCA

- Annam: Theoretics in Theology

- Annam: Birthplace of the UCA

- Annam: Government Operations Handbook

- Annam: Black Box Journals Vol. #1

Top Opinions/Entertainment

- Annam: We Are All Annalang

- Annam: Jungle Quest With Queen Marie Drone

- Annam: Heaven in Hell

- Annam: Flight of the First Annalang

- Annam: Immigrant Song

For more information and for answers to specific questions, please see **Talmund's Planetary Library Primary Entry: AnnAnnam-Incorporated** and **Talmund's Library of Cosmotic Legends Primary Entry: Annalang**.

***

TALMUND'S BESTIARY BRIEF ENTRY: ANNALANG

USA Designation: AnnAnnalang-Immigrant

- A culture bearing mixed species that has various classifications. Annalang are all lifeforms who have given up citizenship in their home systems and/or planets to live on Annam. They may also petition for dual citizenship on Annam as well as their home system and/or planet. The language spoken on Annam is called Annalang. This is also the designation for those who live there. The language is a hybrid mix of verbal and physical communication styles. Difficult to learn for most lifeforms, it is a mandatory requirement for all seeking citizenship on Annam. This is a way to ensure that only the most intelligent lifeforms from all systems can maintain permanent residence on Annam.

- There is no single description for the Annalang save that they are considered some of the wisest and most intelligent lifeforms in the cosmos.

Status

- Average Height: Cannot be calculated due to the diverse nature of Annalangs.

- Average Weight: Cannot be calculated due to the diverse nature of Annalangs.

- Average Lifespan: Cannot be calculated due to the diverse

nature of Annalangs.

- Home Planet: Annam/Ann System/Inner Rim

- Planetary Status: Dominant Lifeform

- System Status: UCA Equality Inner Rim

- Cosmotic Status: UCA Member Inner Rim (Strong Standing)

CLASSIFICATION

- None

Factual Documentation

- Annalang: Learn the Language

- Annalang: A Complete History of the Language

- Annalang: Father Grippus Magnum, the Creator of Annalang

- Annalang: One World for All

- Annalang: A Living Document for a Living World

Top Opinions/Entertainment

- Annalang: Elitism

- Annalang: The Center of the System or the System of the Center?

- Annalang: A Proud People, A Proud Home

- Annalang: An Award

- Annalang: Slangish Slugs Wrecked

For more information and for answers to specific questions, please see **Talmund's Bestiary Primary Entry: Annalang**.

***

TALMUND'S SCIENTIFIC ADVANCEMENT INDEX BRIEF ENTRY: COMMBOARDS

- Though there have been several inventions that minimize size and maximize communicative ability and physical space of ExoNet connections since the invention of Sam-I GreenBlox's commboard in 2.18294.9AST, since it is essentially the home of the ExoNet, it is still the primary tool most lifeforms use to access the ExoNet and communicate across galaxies.

- GreenBlox created the first commboards using technology derived from his own metallic and transformable flesh.

- Greenblox's home planet of Nortrebyc is the location of

all primary manufacturers of commboards throughout all three rims. Though there are other brands manufactured in many galaxies. These other brands are never quite as strong or efficient as Nortrebyc originals.

- The Nortrebyc technology is a highly guarded secret with layers of patent protection which serves to keep the gap between True Greenblox and imitators.

- The commboards work in an almost rudimentary manner, forming a net of digital information that surrounds the galaxy.

- Greenblox himself once explained it as a grid or net that holds all of the information in the cosmos.

- When traveling on the HyperRift Highway only Greenblox commboards are effective for reaching the ExoNet and communicating.

Status

- Official Creation Date: 2.18294.9AST

- Inventor: Sam-I GreenBlox 2.18180.9-2.18332AST

- Cromlonican Accessibility Status: Common

- UCA Accessibility Status: Common

- UCA Patent Registration: 13579.86n-4.28/Nortrebycian/

Top Factual Documentation

- Commboards: Greenblox's Gift

- Commboards: Integral Design Mechanisms Book 1

- Commboards: Integral Design mechanisms Book 2

- Commboards: Transforming the Cosmos

- Commboards: Operators Guide (updated)

Top Opinions/Entertainment

- Commboards: Out With The Old And In With The New

- Commboards: Reeling and Dealing

- Commboards: On A Ship, Click-Clack

- Commboards: Recordings From the Edge

- Commboards: Four Journals

For more information and for answers to specific questions, please see **Talmund's Scientific Advancement Index Complete Entry: Commboards.**

***

TALMUND'S SCIENTIFIC ADVANCEMENT INDEX BRIEF ENTRY: HOLOLIGHTS

- An invention of a team of engineers from the Mid Rim who create under the White Lotus banner, hololights are self-sufficient, nearly immortal, near-living creations that have in no uncertain terms made space travel that much easier.

- Hololights are powered by an immortal engine that senses activity and can activate, deactivate, dim, and brighten as needed.

- White Lotus never patented the inner workings of hololights so, as long as a lifeform can get access to the midiparticles that sustain their immortal engines as well as the directions for hololight construction found on the ExoNet they can create their own.

- As midiparticles are difficult to come by in both the Inner and Outer Rims, there are often Mid Rim visitors mining for midiparticles on various systems there.

Status

- Official Creation Date: 2.37843.1AST

- Inventor: White Lotus (organization) 2.11111.1-current AST

- Cromlonican Accessibility Status: Common

- UCA Accessibility Status: Common

- UCA Patent Registration: None

Top Factual Documentation

- Hololights: Where To Find midiparticles

- Hololights: Midiparticle Hunting Parties Resources and Materials

- Hololights: Midiparticles Explained

- Hololights: You Can Make Your Own Immortal Engine!

- Hololights: Seeing Through The Stars

Top Opinions/Entertainment

- Hololights: Blinding Lights

- Hololights: What If They Lived?

- Hololights: Horror Ball

- Hololights: A Trick Of The Light

- Hololights: The Ballad Of The White Lotus

For more information and for answers to specific questions, please see **Talmund's Scientific Advancement Index Complete Entry: Hololights**.

***

TALMUND'S SCIENTIFIC ADVANCEMENT INDEX BRIEF ENTRY: KEYBOARD HOVERS

- Keyboard Hovers are the most efficient way for all lifeforms to access the ExoNet through commboards. Made from molded light particulate grown primarily on Annam but known to originate on as many as 27,000,000 other planets throughout all three rims, keyboard hovers are moldable and elastic.

- Once connected to the ExoNet through an inter-rim access device they can be programmed to understand and communicate through all known languages.

- Created on Annam during the First Great Immigration as a way to aid the various disparate lifeforms in communication, they became essential to ExoNet.

- Cromqulan Zeep of Moro 5 Velco in the Inner Rim first perfected keyboard hovers, but since his creation it has evolved with society. Several inventors, mechanics, and engineers across the cosmos have added their intelligence to perfecting these communication tools.

- It is considered an honor amongst those in the field of communicative hardware to work on the original key to cosmotic communication and though it is a patented and guarded invention, it is also a highly honored and respected one that many travel through the rims to simply watch being made.

Status

- Official Creation Date: 1.12311.1AST

- Inventor: Cromqulan Zeep 1.11111.1-1.12455AST

- Cromlonican Accessibility Status: Common

- UCA Accessibility Status: Common

- UCA Patent Registration: 11111.11.a-1.11/Annalang/

Top Factual Documentation

- Keyboard Hovers: A Complete Guide

- Keyboard Hovers: Simple/Complex

- Keyboard Hovers: Communication is Key

- Keyboard Hovers: Willing Connection Through Science

- Keyboard Hovers: Migrants Maintain

Top Opinions/Entertainment

- Keyboard Hovers: Tools

- Keyboard Hovers: Whispering Tears

- Keyboard Hovers: Linked In

- Keyboard Hovers: Galaxy Quest 5

- Keyboard Hovers: Unknown Territory

For more information and for answers to specific questions, please see **Talmund's Scientific Advancement Index Complete Entry: Keyboard Hovers**.

***

TALMUND'S PLANETARY LIBRARY BRIEF ENTRY: DRYKE

UCA Designation: MasDryke-Incorporated

- Dryke is the second planet from the star Mas and one of sixteen astronomical objects in Mas's system known to harbor and support sentient life. Ninety percent of Dryke's surface is land consisting of one large desert. Ten percent of Dryke's surface is water. It is situated on the edge of the Inner Rim and, along with the other fifteen life supporting planets in the Mas System, is often considered the last outpost of civilization before one of the dead zones that separates each rim. The dominant species lives on land and cannot consume water so they freely offer it to travelers. Their single world government is based on a series of monetary and geographical exchanges that have left the planet one of the richest in the known cosmos. There has only been one Drykan Ascendant in recorded history. Theories abound as to why, but it is most commonly assumed that Drykan life is so tranquil that few harbor any desire to venture through the cosmos.

Status

- Planetary Status: Incorporated

- System Status: UCA Inner Rim

- Cosmotic Status: UCA Member Inner Rim Prime Standing

Top Factual Documentation

- Dryke: The Desert Jewel

- Dryke: Traders of Peace

- Dryke: Drykan Society

- Dryke: Ascendant Sirius Rise-Dryke: The Autobiography

Top Opinions/Entertainment

- Dryke: Desert Adventure

- Dryke: Desert Adventure 2

- Dryke: Psalm of the Sand

- Dryke: Hydro-cutioner

- Dryke: Outpost One

For more information and for answers to specific questions, please see **Talmund's Planetary Library Primary Entry: MasDryke-Incorporated** and **Talmund's Bestiary Primary Entry: Drykans**.

***

TALMUND'S SCIENTIFIC ADVANCEMENT INDEX BRIEF ENTRY: BLACK BOX

- The discovery/creation (debated) of the Black Boxes of Annam is said to have happened early in the growth of the United Cosmic Alliance. Though the science behind how they work is just as debated as the date of their discovery and/or creation, they are highly studied by the brightest engineering and scientific minds in the cosmos.

- Black Boxes are sedentary stone formations considered absolute black in much the same way Correlatives are. There are no other known similarities between the two.

- These sedentary stone formations are highly malleable and can be formed into buildings with rooms, halls, doorways, etc. with little effort. They are also sturdy. Never has a Black Box been known to crumble or break in any way.

- Black Boxes emit a strange audio frequency that no lifeform is able to hear. This frequency does injure unprotected minds though to the point that prolonged exposure can cause madness. Only one known lifeform is able to withstand the frequency Black Boxes emit: Correlatives, and of those, only Correlatives who grow the Red Star of the Ascendant Guard are able to withstand it for long periods of time.

- Black Boxes are used as holding cells for inter-rim criminals awaiting trial in front of the Zenith and/or The Cosmic Tribunal.

Status

- Official Creation Date: Classified

- Inventor: Classified

- Annalang Accessibility Status: Limited

- UCA Accessibility Status: Limited

- UCA Patent Registration: Classified

Top Factual Documentation

- Black Box: Knowledge is Power Vol #16: Black Boxes of Annam

- Black Box: Corruption Inside the Black Box of Verendi: An Expose

- Black Box: Making Art in Prison

- Black Box: I Tiptoed Toward Madness: My Time in The Black Box

- Black Box: Special Report: Is It Time To Move Away From Black Boxes?

Top Opinions/Entertainment

- Black Box: Escape From Verendi

- Black Box: Escape From Verendi 2: Return To Verendi

- Black Box: Trial Trail: An Ascendant Vollum Case

- Black Box: Sing Me A Song Of Sadness

- Black Box: Going Dark

For more information and for answers to specific questions, please see **Talmund's Scientific Advancement Index Complete Entry: Black Box**.

Chapter 19
The Truth

"YOU HAVE TO UNDERSTAND, Mrs. Norman, we're not here to hurt you," Mary said. She leaned away from May, rested her right ankle on her left knee. She was calm, cool, collected, a powerful statue of a woman in a black suit. She was doing everything to exude importance, but also kindness and understanding. In many ways, May thought of Mary as a high school dean. She was just doing her job.

That fiery red hair though? It made May think of the devil.

They sat across from one another at a dewy green Formica table in the hospital cafeteria. Quiet chatter and subtle muzak did its best to mask the tension from any onlookers. Its best was not good enough. The women radiated tension. Both of them. Hospital employees from custodians to surgeons were used to tension. The walls were built of the stuff. It was the plaster that held the bricks in place. The tension a man felt as his wife gave birth. The tension adult children felt as their elderly parents clung to life. The tension of the cancer patient as he battled his fate. The tension of the victim of a drunk driver, who screamed that she couldn't feel her legs. The tension of the drunk driver, who stumbled into the emergency room with nothing more than a small cut. The hospital and its denizens knew about that, knew about all of that. To some degree they fed on it. Tension was their lifeblood.

But the tension between Mary and May was something more. It was like the tension of two warring armies as they came upon each other across a vast field of tall grass. Everyone wondered who would be the first to actually start the war but everyone knew that when it was over that field of green would be a sea of red. Beyond that?

The tiles on the floor and on the wall, blue, beige, and unremarkable, seemed intent on leaning toward them to listen to what they said, to be there to record this meeting of two mighty forces.

"Is that why your man back there keeps pacing and touching the gun he clearly has holstered at his side?" May asked, eyeing the other agent, who stood behind Mary with his hands on his hips. The black suits they wore were ridiculous and reminded May of something out of one of those noir films her mama used to love. But the man's fedora was too much. May could tell that he thought it made him seem as important as the red-headed agent. But it didn't work. It almost made him look like a cartoon.

His lip twitched as he stared back at May. But May didn't notice. Instead, she studied his eyes. They were hard and dark, like two frozen puddles on his face. What would happen, May wondered, if she broke through that thin layer of ice?

"Your attitude isn't helping, ma'am," he said.

"Who are you again?" May asked, pounding on the icy layer above his dark eyes. She would be defiant until the end.

"My name is Agent Eugene Ha."

"Uh-huh," May said and took a sip of her hospital coffee, sniffing it to cover the stench of hospital food invading her nostrils. At least the coffee smelled good. Its taste may have left something to be desired but Jack had liked it so she sipped it and was reminded of him, of his strength. "And you two are here to ask me more questions about last night, correct?"

"We've already gone over this, ma'am. My partner," Eugene motioned toward Mary, "thought you may have more information that you . . . forgot. We'd like to do something of a swap with you."

"I've already told you everything I know."

"Have you?" Mary asked, cocking her head to the side. The inflection in her voice told May that the question was innocent enough. She was only curious if maybe May had missed something this morning. They were two friends talking over a cup of coffee. This was nothing serious. This was nothing to be worried about. But the way Mary's green eyes focused, unblinking, told May that this was a lie.

"What is it you think I know?"

***

Eugene studied the cafeteria. It was relatively empty this late in the afternoon. A couple of doctors at a corner table discussing some surgery or procedure probably. A handful of cafeteria workers milling about here and there. A middle-aged couple sat by a window quietly eating what passed for food here. He wondered specifically what was going through their minds, what sort of pain had brought them here to pretend things were normal. If it hadn't been for the muzak floating over everything, he may have been able to lose himself wondering about that couple. It would have taken him back to the last time he had visited his old friends in the Terminal Wing of the Nowhere Agency's unnamed hospital. He would have remembered a conversation with Billy Yi and he would've cried because Billy would have had no idea what he was talking about. Thanks to interminable speeds, Billy's mind was gone.

But that muzak, a twisted version of some terrible old Bee Gees song if he wasn't mistaken, kept pulling him out of his memories. And he was thankful for it.

He kind of wanted to just pull his gun out, point it at May Norman, and force her to talk. Kindness, it seemed, was getting them nowhere fast.

"We don't have time to play games," he said. He sat down between the two women and smacked his hand on the table.

Every other person in the cafeteria paused, forks full of salad hanging before their mouths or straws full of Coke dangling near their lips as they turned to face the two black suited agents and the young woman sitting with them. The imitation Bee Gees played on and eventually that was enough to get the doctors, nurses, patients, and hourly wage earners to go back to their respective business.

Eugene took no notice and instead leaned in closer to May, trying to use his proximity where his voice had failed, trying to scare her. "We know you saw something otherworldly," he hissed, "and we need to know exactly what it was."

May did not betray her fear but sat composed. "Like I already told your partner," she said, pulling a napkin to her lips and dabbing the coffee away. "I didn't see anything. Why are you so worried about a meteorite anyway? Shouldn't you be looking into that dead boy? Isn't that the sort of thing that the FBI does?" She cleared her throat. "He is my friend's son."

"Was," Eugene said. "He was your friend's son."

May let a grim smile form on her lips and focused all her attention on Eugene. "Just because he is dead does not mean that he is no longer her son. His name is Ricky Sims and you would do well to put your sophisticated government agency to work in finding out who killed him instead of harassing a pregnant woman whose husband almost died last night." Curling her lip, she turned to Mary. "And your attempt to frighten me is failing, Agent Jones. I've seen enough in my short time on Earth that a red-headed white girl and her tall Korean boy toy can do little to shake me." She paused pointedly and swung her head from one agent to the other and back again. "Even if you're both packing."

"Mrs. Norman," Mary said through a sigh, "we know you're lying and we will pull the truth out of you if we have to." She ran her hands over her face. "We do not want to do anything . . . untoward . . . but we will. This could be a matter of international security."

"International security?" May asked, her cool veneer melting a bit. "What do you mean?"

"What did you see?" Eugene asked. The demand in his tone was enough to bring May's cool back with a vengeance.

"Nothing," she said. The word was a blade.

"Mrs. Norman, May," Mary said, "I need you to understand that we do not want to hurt you—"

"But we will. We will hurt you, your husband, and any other loved ones you might have."

"Is this some kind of Cold War, nuclear nonsense? Or do you think I'm a Communist, Mr. Hoover?" May asked sarcastically. Though she laughed through her words, she felt fear tremble below them.

"Interesting conversation," a sweet-sounding voice announced itself from behind the agents, "to have with an American citizen."

They turned as one to see a short woman with intelligent blue eyes and a grin reaching from one crabapple cheek to the other. She wore a *Star Wars* t-shirt, jean jacket, and matching blue jeans and looked innocent enough but she didn't sound that way.

"May I join you?" she asked, pulling out a tape recorder. "My name is Charlie McKinstrey and I'm a reporter."

"Fuck," Eugene said. He looked at Mary. "Croatoa?" he asked.

"Slow down, cowboy," Mary said. "We need to take them in, though."

"Croatoa?" May asked but before she could finish the question, she felt the barrel of a gun dig into her side.

"You're both coming with us," Mary said, pressing a similar barrel into Charlie's side. "You're going to be quiet or we will kill you and everyone else in this cafeteria. After we do this, we will wipe the memory of everyone here from the world."

"Then I will walk upstairs to your husband's room and kill him," Eugene added.

Charlie gulped, her bravado lost somewhere on the tip of the gun.

"Where are you taking us?" May asked.

***

"What happened to your car?" Charlie asked as Eugene shoved her past the dented front fender.

"Never mind," he said and opened the back door. The wind had grown more severe as the day stretched toward evening. It blew the door open so severely that Eugene lost his grip. "Get in." With one hand holding his hat on his head, he shoved Charlie in. Opposite her, Mary did the same thing to May.

When they were in the car, May noticed that the outside world was closed off. No sounds or smells came through. Even the wind, which was blowing so hard that she knew nothing short of a severe thunderstorm was headed their way, couldn't be heard. May could hardly even tell they were moving. There was a beeping sound and the windows, which were tinted on the outside, tinted on the inside too. Her world had become the backseat of a dented black Cadillac and the only other person in it she thought she could trust was a reporter she didn't think she particularly liked.

"This sucks," Charlie said under her breath.

"What an astute observation," Eugene said, turning to face them.

"Why did you tint the windows?" Mary asked. "They know where we're taking them."

Eugene shrugged. "Force of habit."

"We know where you're taking us?"

"The field, obviously," Mary said. She started the car and sped out of the parking lot. "And you seemed so smart earlier."

May looked over at the reporter who had been bothering her earlier that day. She was fidgeting, her eyes darting back and forth, her hands needling the hem of her jacket.

"You okay?" she asked.

"Not really," Charlie said.

May took her hand. In a way this Charlie person had come to her rescue—or at least had tried—and that was worth something. Linc liked her, she knew, from an earlier story she had written, but still, she had her suspicions. And she had pissed May off earlier that day with all of her invasive questions. Here and now though, she was all May had.

"It's okay," she whispered. "We'll get out of here."

Mary looked in the rearview mirror. "You two trying to come up with some sort of escape plan, Mrs. Norman?" she asked.

May gulped.

Charlie spat out a rapid-fire response bereft of thought and brought up by fear. "If you think I haven't been in tighter spots than this, you're—"

Eugene rested his gun on the back of his seat and pointed it at Charlie. "Shut up, McKinstrey," he said. "Jones was talking with Mrs. Norman."

May frowned and looked away.

"You brought this on yourself by being quiet," Mary said, keeping her eyes on the road. "All you had to do was talk to us then this whole mess would have been over for you."

"But you decided whatever information is in your head is more valuable than your life, I guess," Eugene added.

"And this poor intrepid reporter's life here," Mary added.

"You're going to kill us?" May asked.

"We don't want to kill you," Mary said. "We're taking you to our boss and he'll decide what we're going to do with you."

"This is . . . this is a crime, what you're doing, it's a crime," Charlie said "You, you sound like gangsters."

Do we though?" Mary asked. "Or maybe we have a few more powers than the people you're used to reporting on, Charlotte Macy McKinstrey."

"How do you know my middle name?" Charlie asked.

"I do my homework on anyone I think I might have to speak with," Mary said. "You're actually a great journalist. It's unfortunate that you're stuck in this Podunk little town in the middle of nowhere." She felt pity for Charlie. "Maybe we could change that."

"I don't know anything."

"But we could always use someone who knows how to get to the bottom of a story."

"Obviously," Charlie said. "You two idiots can't seem to do it without resorting to threats and violence."

"Hey, we haven't been violent!" Eugene blinked.

"Yet," Mary added, winking at Charlie in the rearview mirror. "We're almost there." She leaned forward and pressed a few buttons on the dashboard. "Look Mrs. Norman, we're at Oakview Lanes."

Another beep and her window cleared so May could see the trailer park, her home. She hadn't seen it since this morning when she had run home to pick up some new clothes. She had wanted to see Jenny but she had been gone. Police had been everywhere. Those gruff people in blue coveralls were marching through the field. Nothing had seemed right. Now, things were even worse. There were several people at the laundromat milling around as though confused. A few police officers here and there seemed to be directing groups one way or another. And though she couldn't hear it, she could see the way the wind was shaking the trees and trailers alike. She wondered why there were so many people about when they should have been somewhere hiding from the incoming storm.

"What are they doing?" May asked.

"The same thing most people do, standing around being confused," Eugene said. "We've cordoned off the field and the forest all the way to the river. A bunch of them led by that old man—"

"Linc, his name is Linc," May said.

"Yeah, Linc. Now there is a character. Anyway, Linc wants to go back out to comb through the woods looking for clues and he's pissed that we won't let him, as if the local cops would," Eugene said. "Anyway, a bunch of your trailer park folks are just kind of wondering what to do. Frankly, I think they wish your husband was here. As best as I can tell he's something of a leader to them."

May nodded. "He is. What about Jenny and Del?"

"The couple whose kid was killed? Haven't been out of their trailer since the cops brought them back from the station earlier."

"How do you know all this?"

"We've been monitoring this place all damn day. It's amazing what you can learn by just looking and listening, isn't that right, McKinstrey?" Eugene said, his gun still pointed at her.

Charlie did not respond.

A few minutes later the car was driving through a temporary wall on the border of the trailer park and the field, being flagged in by two men in blue coveralls with automatic weapons hanging from their shoulders. A few minutes after that, the agents were getting out of the car. But before they did so, Eugene pressed a button on the edge of the dashboard and a clear barrier rose between the front and backseats.

"Impenetrable," Eugene said, tapping it with his knuckles, "as is everything else. Don't get any ideas." He opened his door, climbed out, and stuck his head back in. "We'll be back. Seriously, don't bother trying to get out. It isn't going to happen."

Charlie and May were alone.

"Why did you come back?" May asked.

"I thought you were hiding something so I went back to the hospital to talk to you some more." She shrugged. "When I went up to your husband's room, a nurse told me you were in the cafeteria with those two suits."

"I am hiding something," she said. "There is more. A lot more."

"These black suits know it too, don't they?" Charlie asked.

May nodded. "They know I'm holding something back."

"Well," Charlie said, smiling, "I wouldn't worry too much. Neither of them have the cojones to back up what they're saying."

"What?"

"They're full of shit. All this badassery we're seeing, it's crap."

"How do you know that?"

"The same way I knew you were lying this morning."

"I wasn't lying."

"Withholding the truth?" Charlie rolled her eyes. "Is that better?"

"Either way, we need to get out of here. I'm sure there is someone here who will back up all that talk."

"Probably," Charlie said. She looked out the window and saw a few blue coverall clad men walking up and down in what she knew were premade lines. These men were soldiers through and through and the black suits were spies or feds or some weird mix of the two and the ones in white coats that ran from one strange, rounded building to the next were obviously scientists. "It'll be another black suit who gives the order anyway. It might be one of the blue guys who pulls the trigger." She turned back to May. "What are you hiding?"

May looked away. "I was visited," she said. Her eyes fell to the floor.

"Visited? By who?"

"I . . ." A pause. Another sigh. "An alien."

Charlie laughed. "Okay,"

"I have proof." May said.

"What? Where?"

"Do you think all of this is happening because of a normal meteorite and a little kid getting killed?"

"Can you show me?"

"If we can get out of here."

Charlie studied their surroundings. "This place is locked down. But it's getting dark and there is definitely a storm coming though so maybe . . . it's possible."

"There has to be something we can do."

"Make a run for it when they open the doors. They don't want to kill us."

"Don't they?"

"Well, they don't want to kill you."

"How do you propose we get away?"

"I don't know." Charlie grunted. "Do you have any weapons?"

"I don't even have my purse."

"This is ridiculous."

"Well, you don't even have a purse, so—"

The door swung open and Mary looked down upon the women, an angry red god. "I need you two to get out and follow me."

"Why?"

"Where are you taking us?"

Mary said nothing but stared down at the women.

"Fine." Charlie climbed out, pulling May along with her. "But we're not going anywhere until you tell us what is going on."

"Right," Mary said and pulled a small metallic device from her jacket pocket. It looked suspiciously like a small cattle prod. Just the sight of it sent shivers down May's spine.

"What is that?" she asked.

"It's not what you think it is," Mary said. "But it will make you do whatever I say."

"I don't know—"

Mary aimed the device at Charlie and clicked a small button at its base. There was no blast or bullet, no electrical charge. Charlie simply stopped talking. Within seconds she grabbed her throat and her face started turning blue.

"I've sucked all of the oxygen from the air directly surrounding you, Ms. McKinstrey. Do you want to do as I say now?" She clicked the button again as Charlie fell to her knees.

"Do," she coughed, "do as you say."

May helped her to her feet and the two of them went with Mary.

After an uneventful walk through the field littered with small white domes, they were led to what appeared to be the most official one. A bit larger and somewhat more ornate than the others, it was surrounded by a series of guards all clad in the blue coveralls.

"Is this a cult?" May mumbled to herself.

Mary laughed. "Only if the highest form of government this planet has can be considered a cult."

"Historically, this could be—" Charlie began but was cut short by a sharp look from Mary.

They entered the building and saw Eugene standing next to a shorter man with a trim goatee and a matching black suit. Eugene grimaced and the shorter man smiled, motioning for the pot of coffee resting on the table between them.

"Ladies," he said, "please take a seat, have a drink."

Another prod from Mary and both women were seated.

"First let me apologize for my agents' behavior. You may call me Local." He reached out a hand but neither woman took it. "Very well," he said, "we started out on a bad foot. Let me explain everything."

"Everything?" Charlie was skeptical.

Mike nodded. "Everything. Why don't I start with First Contact?"

"First Contact?" May asked.

"It's unofficial since nothing came of it really, but," Mike leaned toward the women, "it happened in July 1947."

"Roswell," Charlie said.

Mike nodded. "A delegation of lifeforms from the capital planet of the UCA crashed on Earth. They were headed to the Saturnian moon Tho, what we call Titan."

"You can't be serious."

"Look around you Mrs. Norman, I'm all too serious."

"What does the UCA call Saturn then?"

"What?"

"You're making up names for moons that already have names, why not planets? Seems to be a small hole in your plot." She crossed her arms. "Or a large one."

Mike looked from Eugene to Mary.

"This is what we've been dealing with," Eugene said.

"Then I know why you brought them in," Mike said. "Let me tell you this story, ladies, and then you can ask questions."

"Go ahead," Charlie said. The feeling of her lungs being sucked of oxygen made her weak but she stared at Mike as though unafraid.

"Thank you," Mike said, leaning back. "Our organization saved as many as we could, but so much of the ship had fallen apart upon entry into our atmosphere that it was very difficult." He cleared his throat as though remembering the horror of it all, but there was no way he could have been there, he looked hardly over forty. He would've been a little boy in 1947.

"And what, the aliens still live here?"

"Oh no," Mike laughed. The girl was foolish. He was wise. "There was a rescue mission sent out relatively quickly. They made contact with us after that and saw that our American government had done its best to take care of the people aboard their ship and the next thing we knew, we were placed on probationary status to join the UCA."

"What?"

"Probationary status can last hundreds of years and right now that status is a closely guarded secret. To actually be admitted many things have to happen, one world government, an end to in-fighting amongst leaders, that sort of thing."

"We're a far fucking cry from that."

"Yes, Ms. McKinstrey," Mike said, his voice going down an octave and his eyes somehow growing darker, "which is why what happened last night is very disturbing, Mrs. Norman."

"I don't know what you're—"

"Stop with the games, Mrs. Norman, we saw the footprint. We know there was a Whitley here and we know it was an Ascendant."

"I don't understand."

"What did the Ascendant say to you?"

"You don't know what you're—"

"Mrs. Norman," Mike said slowly, "stop lying." He turned away as though it was difficult to look at her. "The Ascendant who met with you is working outside of their jurisdiction and may have committed crime atop crime on a cosmic level. We need the information in your head and we can get it forcibly or you can cooperate."

"Forcibly?"

"How is your husband, Mrs. Norman?"

"What is that supposed to mean?" Charlie asked as May groped for a response.

"It means that this lifeform that *you* interacted with," he pointed at May, "could have dire plans for the entire planet and it is our job to make sure those plans do not come to fruition. We will use any means necessary to get to the bottom of this," Mike said. His tone was soft but his words were hard. "So, I ask one more time Mrs. Norman, what happened last night?"

"I—I—"

"We already listened in on your conversation in the car," Eugene said. "Please just tell us the truth."

May looked from Charlie to Mike to the other two agents. "Fine," she said. "I'll talk," and she began her story.

Chapter 20
The Return

THE LONELY ONE SAT on the sandy bank of the Missouri River some miles from Oakview. His feet, crossed before him, rested in the water's cool current. He leaned back and opened his ears. The river whispered words no one could understand, not even him. For the stagnants, these words were ancient. For him, they were merely old. Nevertheless, they were soothing, familiar. So much here was soothing and familiar. So much on this planet was soothing and familiar. Even the storm that he felt was coming, soothed him. It was going to be terrible. With any luck, maybe there'd even be a tornado to destroy that trailer park.

This little green and blue marble on the edge of the Outer Rim was such a nice place. Yes, the stagnants were doing their best to destroy it, much like the fools on Essa. But they had not yet accomplished it. He wondered for a moment what had become of Essa. Had the people there ever seen the error of their ways? Had they finally come back around to the knowledge that they had forgotten, that their planet was not a tool but a living thing? That they were not its possessors but its caretakers? They had masked scientific advancement as order, but Draconians knew real order, true order. And they had brought it to the UCA.

Only to be denied thanks to the machinations of a wild planet of women.

Growling at that memory, The Lonely One prayed there was still hope for Essa. If for no other reason than one day the Draconian Reign would rise again and begin anew. And Essa, he knew, was a wonderful little jewel, much like Earth, only better. It was a wonderful little jewel begging for order, begging to be ruled by his people.

By him.

He grunted. Sometimes it could be difficult living out here, cut off from the rest of society on a planet full of stagnants. He had been on Earth for so long, living through so many of the all too short ages of man, it was easy to get complacent. And he had been, there was no denying that. Killing stagnants, deceiving stagnants, and generally being a terrifying thorn in their collective side had kept his attention for he didn't know how many Earth years. Long life had proven to be a blessing on this world ruled by short lived stagnants. He had been able to experiment as well, playing with their DNA, manipulating their genes here and there. There was a part of him that thought the stagnant could make good fodder, slaves to feed the Draconian Reign.

But now things had to change. His fun and games had to come to an end. His time spent dipping his claws into the Earthling ooze was over. There would be no more experiments with their DNA. There would be no more wanton murders. There would be no more mad manipulations. He would have no more entertainment or education here.

He needed to make contact with his brethren.

Not only had he witnessed a Whitley Ascendant interacting with an Earthling, but last night he had almost been hit by what he knew had to be a human operative for a contact team. Then at the hospital earlier today he had bumped into a Nowhere Agent. He had suspected an agency had been set up here years earlier, but thought he had years before he had to worry about actual contact, what the UCA had dubbed "Official First Contact," an erroneous term he knew only meant contact the Zenith approved. The Zenith. Now there was a joke. He chuckled but the thread of laughter frayed. He had no time for it.

This situation however was no joke.

As best as he could tell, there were two possibilities at play. One was that there were rogue officers in the Ascendancy working with Earthlings for one reason or another. The other was that Earth was actually in the beginning stages of admittance into the UCA. Or maybe it was a combination of both? Either way, he knew what he must do. He must call his fellow Draconian believers here to Earth. When he called, they would come. Had it been anything other than a Whitley he would have let it go and burrowed deep into the Earth to sleep as he had when he had first arrived on this beautiful planet with its people of mud.

Or perhaps he would have simply escaped to a different planet. He had been on Earth for a long, long time after all. He could have taken his CorreAxe and slunk off to the NetNeg and found another planet and its people to quietly study and harass for ages.

But a Whitley had landed on Earth alone, a Whitley had interacted with an Earthling. This meant something. It had been a long time since he had read the Prophecies of A'Kai, but he remembered from his childhood in the class caves. And he knew his Draconian brethren in the Reign would remember as well. They would know that this was a signal from a higher power, not from him alone, but from the Great Scale as well. The ending of the First Draconian Reign had begun with an ill-thought-out invasion of Whitley and now, the

Second Draconian Reign would begin thanks to the foolish actions of a Whitley. An Earthling stagnant would call this poetry.

So would his brethren who had read the Prophecies of A'Kai, his brethren of the Reign. The Lonely One knew he could get them to come here and help him find that Whitley and once again, the Draconian Reign would rise as A'Kai predicted. It was only natural that this whole thing would begin with him, The Lonely One, a Draconian who never faltered in his beliefs, who never succumbed to fear, who never bowed down to the cosmic criminals who ran the UCA.

First, he needed to get the ax though.

Then he needed to get May Norman.

Then he would know the truth about what had happened during the meteor shower.

When he did, CorreAxe in hand, he would share it.

And he knew his brethren would come. They'd see the ax, they'd hear his story, and they'd agree. Last he had heard there were only twelve left and eight of them were in the UCA's possession, locked away someplace secret, someplace safe. The fact that he still had one made him worthy to follow. He had witnessed a Whitley Ascendant on Earth. That fact made his message urgent.

He would retrieve the ax.

He would capture May.

He would safeguard his labs.

He would contact his fellow Draconians.

That was the rub though, wasn't it? When he made contact, his signal would be heard. You could not send a signal like he'd need to send without being noticed by every Ascendant Tech in the rim. He'd need that ax when the UCA sent Ascendants for him. It was the only weapon in his arsenal that could slice through living Correlatives.

After he called them, his brethren would arrive quickly, but since they had to take back roads from the HyperRift Highway, he doubted they would arrive before an Ascendant force. And when they did arrive, they would not be the formidable army they had once been. How many Ascendants would he have to kill before the rest of the Reign joined him and war was officially declared once more? How many inexperienced Draconian hatchlings would fall at the hands of Ascendant stormtroopers? It didn't matter. The fact that an Ascendant was here mingling with Earthlings meant he had few options. Truth be told, he was ready. Exile had been an experience he was glad to have lived, but the time had come for a change.

He knew it.

The signs were clear.

The Lonely One wanted to shout into the night, the terrible conflagration of events played on his nerves. He was not scared; he was energized in a way he hadn't been since the Draconian Reign had marched across the cosmos and nearly controlled the entirety of the UCA with its unquestionable order.

He released the breath and let himself morph fully into his Draconian form, something he hadn't done in such a public place for a long, long time. He hadn't dared since he had nearly been caught so many years earlier. Once mankind had left their gods behind for the dual seduction of technology and science, it hadn't been safe to show his true form. His green and brown, thick scaly skin, mud and moss intermingling like lovers on his hide, his gangling arms and his digitigrades legs, ending in sharp talons, made him a monster in stagnant eyes. The way his tongue slithered over his army of pointed teeth and his diamond-shaped pupils moved seemingly of their own volition, made him a beast from their darkest nightmares. Even the way he smelled when he was in his true form—hyper rich and slightly sour—caused a fear in the stagnants that would have been offensive if it wasn't so amusing.

It mattered not. Soon the ax would return to him if its connection held true, which it would. He was its ruler and it was his subject. There was no fighting that.

The ax was near and it would feel his anger. It would know it needed to return.

He fell back into the sand, spreading his arms wide and feeling the sharp grains press into his scales. He licked his waxen lips and wiped his tongue over the pointed teeth he hid so often. There was a chill in the air and though he shivered, he welcomed it. If he was colder, he'd be calmer. He needed that to focus.

"Come to me," he whispered softly. His voice was a subtle hiss, a warning. There was no shame in his tone, no fear that he was being heard. The ax was everything to the Draconian people. It wasn't just a powerful nearly sentient undead weapon, it was a symbol, a symbol of all they had lost and all they would one day gain if they were only patient.

"Patience," he said, as though channeling the ax itself.

He knew it would join him. He could feel it. He closed his eyes and let that feeling climb through him, tingling everywhere. He had only ever gotten rid of it twice before and each time when he needed to retrieve it had been like this. When the calm had come over him, the blade had manifested.

Tonight there was something of a struggle, though. The Lonely One didn't know if it was because of the river's powerful current or his own internal turmoil and anxiety over what he knew was going to occur. He looked at his watch. Still four hours before sunrise, and he thought he could lie here until then if he had to. But what would he say to the people combing the river for that boy's body if they saw him?

They didn't know he was The Lonely One after all. Even if he morphed back into his less offensive stagnant form, the form he wore in his daily life, seeing a respectable doctor, the most respectable doctor in the area in fact, naked, lounging on the beach with an ax mysteriously at his side, might cause suspicion. No matter. He'd probably be able to explain it away. After all, these stagnants were fools, all of them.

"When did life get so hard?" he asked the heavens.

They did not answer.

Instead, an ax handle bumped against his foot. He shot up and thrust his hands into the water. A moment later he pulled out the CorreAxe and felt relief mixed with anxiety. It was a good feeling. It reminded him that everything was going to change soon—and for the better.

"They'll come," he said to the ax. "When I show you to them, they will obey me. They'll come quick."

A strange sensation washed over him as he stood. He was calm but he was also elated. It had been a little more than twenty-four hours since the meteorite. The stagnants had discovered something out there in that field and had made it nearly impossible to approach the area. He knew it had to have been a footprint or some other sign that a Whitley had made contact. But that was little information. May Norman had more and he would get it from her before anyone else. He ran one finger over the edge of the ax blade.

He hissed, "May Norman," into the night like a song. His scales, viridescent and patchy with brindle stains and hanging moss, glowed as he slowly shifted back into his stagnant form. His hide was nearly impenetrable by stagnant means, but now he felt it crumble into his body so that the weak skin of a flabby stagnant could grow. He felt his tail, a huge swinging thing that slunk on the ground as he stood, shrink into his back, melting away like a diseased appendage. His eyes, dark slits that saw everything, reformed to those of a stagnant. Hair popped from newly developed pores and sprung to ragged, sweaty life. The final part of his body to change itself back into the stagnant form was his mouth. As it happened, he let his tongue glide over every tooth while their sharp points dulled to flat molars and weaker incisors.

"May Norman," he said again, "I'll start with you and your planet." When he turned from the slow rumble of the Missouri River, he once more was a man, he once more was a stagnant, or at least he once more looked like one. But below the visage pumped the heart of a Draconian bent on bringing his once mighty empire back to life. "Now, where did I place my clothes?"

He spat on the beach and headed for the trees as in the distance he noticed the first fork of lightning strike. A moment later, he heard the thunder.

***

TALMUND'S HISTORICAL DOCUMENT LIBRARY BRIEF ENTRY: THE PROPHECIES OF A'KAI

- A'Kai is a mythological-religious figure in Draconian culture who is said to have written prophecies predicting the Draconian Reign's march across the cosmos.

- Often referred to as the Great Scale.

- His prophet, Great Reign Lord and Past and Future Emperor Ch'oke D'Amon Karak was the primary voice behind the first Draconian Reign.

- In the prophecies, through his prophet, A'Kai predicted that the Draconian Reign would one day rule the entire cosmos with order. In the book, it is said that Ch'oke D'Amon Karak will return time and again until the prophecies are all achieved. Once they are, A'Kai will take his seat on the Cosmos Throne.

- There are only two known print copies of The Prophecies of A'Kai in existence, both of which are held by Talmund's Library. Though it is rumored that other copies exist and are being held by various members of the Draconian Diaspora as historical documents.

- With proper documentation and approval, digital copies can be obtained on a temporary basis through the Talmund Library Secure ExoNet Hub.

- The Prophecies of A'Kai contain some of the only semi-publicly accessible information on Draconians.

Top Factual Documentation

- The Prophecies of A'Kai: An Exploration and Understanding

- The Prophecies of A'Kai: A History

- The Prophecies of A'Kai: Later Introduction to Draconian Beliefs

- The Prophecies of A'Kai: Structural Representation in Current Societies

- The Prophecies of A'Kai: The Bad and the... Good?

Top Opinions/Entertainment

- The Prophecies of A'Kai: Monster Mash

- The Prophecies of A'Kai: A Comical Rendering

- The Prophecies of A'Kai: Mock the Madness Tour

- The Prophecies of A'Kai: Why "Alone Together" Makes No Sense

- The Prophecies of A'Kai: Hibernation: The Secret to Longevity

For more information and for answers to specific questions, please see **Talmund's Historical Document Library Complete Entry: The Prophecies of A'Kai**.

Chapter 21
Legal Matters

A GREAT CRYSTALLINE GATE that Aurora knew was far stronger than it looked opened before them. The Red Stars shoved her through. As she stumbled forward, her bare feet scraping on the gravelly ground, she heard one of the guards grumble derisively and was reminded, once again, how powerless she was without Peel. A short journey down a solitary path in the middle of a barren garden and they were at the main entrance.

"Rules," growled one guard in another terrible parody of Whitley.

"You know you can speak clearly in my language if you'd like to. Your Correlative—"

A backhand to Aurora's face shut her up. She nearly fell, knowing the guard had held back. If he hadn't, she'd have been dead.

Behind them, Mia gasped.

"Rules," the guard said again. "Three." He lifted the three fingered hand he had slapped her with. "One." One finger went down. "Do as guards say, always. Two." A second finger fell. "Keep your time tight. Three." A third finger went down to form a fist. "Speak only when asked questions." He raised the fist to her face. "Understand?"

Aurora nodded.

"Speak your answer," he growled. "It must be spoken." He pointed above them to the hovering black cameras that swept through the air like birds. "We are all watched and heard here."

"Yes," Aurora said.

"Good." He opened the fist and pressed it against the wall. The wall absorbed his hand, made clicking, licking sounds, and released his hand. The door before them struggled open on ripping, elastic cords to a long, claustrophobic hall. "We go through here. We cross the process room. Waiting. Then down holding cell hall to free room where you meet your legal advisor."

Aurora wanted to reach out to the walls, break through them with Peel's Correlative strength, and free the prisoners trapped in this monstrosity of a building. If they were anything like her, didn't they deserve their freedom? Didn't she?

Did she?

The people in here were alone and scared in their cells but they were regularly released into common areas away from this Black Box, where at least they were allowed interaction with other living things and some respite from the madness inducing building. This was only temporary torture until their trials and convictions. In a way, Aurora was happy for them, even as she was jealous and sad. Some of them would be convicted and sent to the mines. Based on what she knew, that wasn't a terrible life. And though she had joked with Peel about it and DC had even suggested it, that would not be her fate. There was a SoloPen waiting for her somewhere in the vast nothingness of the cosmos. She knew what her future held, what she didn't know was whether or not she deserved this punishment.

All she had wanted to do was help her lover's people. All she had wanted to do was give them another chance at life. She could concede that things did not go as planned. She could concede that she wished she would have had more time with the Earthling, with more Earthlings, to properly educate them. But here she was on Annam preparing for what she knew would be a terrible sentence and no one seemed to be concerned with Earth, about the Draconian with a CorreAxe she knew had to be there.

She had to accomplish the impossible. She had to escape. She had to get back to Earth. She had to make right what she had made wrong.

The processing room at the end of the hall was manned with a handful of other Red Star guards, each with a specific duty. One scanned her, inside and out; another took her finger prints; another bathed her in a cleansing gel that not only purified her skin but her clothes as well. There was a blood, flesh, and body fluid test to check for illicit substances and undetected illnesses. There was a physical test in an encasement field to determine her strength and fitness level so that she would be placed in a cell that, for her, would be impenetrable. Finally, she was given an intelligence and emotional stamina test that determined how long she could stay imprisoned in a Black Box before she'd lose her mind. The results of this test had no bearing on the SoloPens—that was a different kind of torture. Being imprisoned in one of those caused a different kind of madness—a madness she knew couldn't be reversed. After you had been in a SoloPen for long enough, nothing mattered anymore except the SoloPen.

She gulped, remembering her brief stay in one when she had been training.

As the process went on and Aurora became more certain that it would never end, she could not free her mind from the possibility that there was a Draconian present on Earth and close to where she had met the Earthling. Had she put that Earthling in more danger? Had she inadvertently caused harm where she only wanted to help? Every time she attempted to speak with Mia, who watched stoically, seemingly detached from the proceedings, she was met with a severe warning from whatever guard was administering whatever test at that particular processing point. Forever became a solid stone wall whose shadow Aurora walked in as she was shuffled from one station to another in a room that never ended.

Until finally, blessedly, it did, and the guards who had escorted her there, moved her down another hall that seemed elastic and eternally black.

"Where are you taking me?" she asked.

One of the guards smacked the back of her head. Aurora thought she heard Mia, still following behind them, suck in her breath, but couldn't be sure. The Black Box was already affecting her senses. How long before it would take her mind? They couldn't allow that though. She had to be able to stand trial. If she was mad, she couldn't. They'd let her sit in her own misery up to her breaking point, then pull back. It was masterful. It was genius. It was torture.

The guards led her around a bend and she noticed an open door at the end of the hall where she could make out the vague image of a Vastaloose sitting at a table in a miraculously lighter room. He was studying a blue hued screen projected from the table. Aurora could remember some information about the Vastaloose from Peel. They were a small but firm people. Made of joints that twisted, turned, and bent in all directions, whenever they did move, the clicking and clacking of their many interconnected and multiple jointed bones sounded like gnashing teeth—of which they also had several. With shell-like chromotaphoric skin that absorbed color and molted away every few years, and eight beady eyes embedded in varying spots encircling the top of their skull in a different pattern on each, the Vastaloose were universally known for their cunning. The cosmos was filled with empires put in place by the shrewd mind of one Vastaloose or another. There was more about the Vastaloose people, their home planet of Vastaloo, their mating rituals, the history of their society, their wars, their religion, their family structures, but Aurora no longer had unrestricted access to Talmund's Library since she was without Peel. All that she had were memories of information dumps.

As they grew nearer to this Vastaloose, Aurora didn't think he fit the stereotype. All of his six arms were up, his clawed hands clenched before him as though he was in a state of panic. The suit he wore in various shades of brown was a weak imitation of traditional professional Vastaloose attire. Where Vastaloosians prided themselves on their sleek and well-kept clothing, this one's was a loose, frumpy semblance of respectability with dark stains on the multiple scarves, cuffs, and collars. And the colors clashed with his skin, which seemed to be absorbing the essence of the dark gray walls around them. Apparently, an uncontrollable side-effect of the chromatophores to Annam's sound and light environment. Though he had those strange eight eyes circling his head like a crown, their blackness didn't seem shrewd, but lost.

He pointed one hand in their direction, snapping his claws as they approached. The floating screen disappeared in a blink.

"Hello," he said in broken Whitley, standing in a whirl of beige, brown, and stained white scarves and walking around the table to greet Aurora.

She was certain he was going to trip on one of the longer scarves, but his rawboned legs somehow made the delicate dance through the waving fabric to her. He reached out one knotted and clawed hand in greeting, a hand Aurora was unable to take.

"I am your . . . uh . . . Tribunal Appointed Counsel, J4rr0ck'L334v3r." He smiled. It was meant to be a friendly, inviting expression, but it revealed an enormous mouth of layered, sharp, broken teeth below a small fleshy hump of a nose.

Aurora shuddered.

One of the guards grunted and pushed her forward.

The Vastaloose caught her with all six of his hands and huffed his powerless indignation at the guard.

The guard simply turned away and mumbled something else Aurora couldn't understand.

"I know how . . . er . . . much time we have . . . uh . . . guard," the Vastaloose replied with an indignant rage that surprised Aurora. "Don't forget to turn off the cameras!" he added sharply as the guards trundled away. He cursed in Vastaloosian under his breath. No matter what language, Aurora knew a curse when she heard it. This quick streak of hot anger seemed out of place with all of her initial notions of this creature. She examined him for a moment, trying to figure out which was the real personality and which was the show.

Mia, however, stood motionless at the threshold and cleared her throat, snapping Aurora out of her rumination.

"Can I . . . er . . . can I help you, Officer?" J4rr0ck'L334v3r asked.

"I will be waiting with the guards," Mia said to Aurora before turning away.

"Your very . . . er . . . uh . . . own Gray Star, and another Whitley . . . er . . . by the looks of her," J4rr0ck'L334v3r said to Aurora. "You are important." He pressed one of his hands into the wall. Like when the guards had opened the door outside, the wall absorbed it. After a quick buzzing and what felt like an atmospheric scan hummed over them, the door slid shut. Pressure melted away from the room and the dull sensation that there was something else there, something digging at Aurora's mind, faded.

"She's my sister. Her Galaxy Captain wants the Zenith to know who captured me," Aurora replied. "She's going to be my shadow for a while."

J4rr0ck'L334v3r nodded. "Come, sit," he said. "We have much to . . . ah . . . er . . . discuss." He helped Aurora into a seat at the small table where the screen had been hovering. "I'm sorry for my . . . er . . . accent. I do not speak Whitley . . . often."

"How's Peel, J4rr0ck'L334v3r?" Aurora asked, sitting hard as the Vastaloose walked around the room, eying the cameras in every corner before he joined her.

"Please call me . . . er . . . 0ck," he said, all eight of his eyes revolving around his crown-like skull to study the tiny black cameras. When the small blinking red lights on each one clicked off, 0ck's shoulders fell slightly and Aurora picked up on a clear ease in his tension.

"I asked a question, 0ck."

0ck pressed buttons on a light energy keyboard that hovered above the table between them. The blue screen he had been staring at earlier appeared above it. A file folder shone bright white against the electric blue. 0ck touched it with one of his claws and it flew open, revealing several more holographic folders. Aurora squinted, reading her name again, her sister's name, Jon'Oh's name, and even Peel's all written in the standard tongue of Annam, of the cosmos. There was another subset of folders piled one on top of the other with locations: Whit, Essa, Earth, Draco, and more she could not see.

0ck clicked Peel's folder.

A video of a dark room fanned out from the folder and floated above them. Aurora and 0ck's eyes followed it as it slipped to the wall to their right and embedded itself there. 0ck reached up and hit the PLAY button hovering in the middle of the screen. The video grew brighter but that only truly revealed how dark it was in that room. There were humming red lights sprinkled throughout the walls, ceiling, and floor in an audio station pattern designed specifically to hold a Correlative in place. It was not necessarily a guaranteed preventative measure, but when holding a Correlative, the Ascendancy always erred on the side of caution, adding as many restraints as possible, no matter their efficacy. At the center of this dark room stood a large clear tube. Connected to the ceiling and floor through a series of smaller, humming multi-colored tubes that shot various audio fluids into and out of the larger tube, this thing was a Correlative's worst nightmare.

"No!" Aurora shouted. "They have her in a Sound Cell?" She leapt from her seat, anger coursing through her. "No! No! She'll die!"

0ck, raised four of his hands. "Your Correlative is not going to . . . er . . . die, ma'am," he said. "The audial . . . liquid . . . is . . . uh . . . just enough to keep it . . . er . . . uh . . . docile. It's in something of a . . . er . . . stasis . . . holding . . . uh . . . ah . . . awaiting your trial. I inspected it before your arrival . . . er . . . myself. The settings . . . are . . . uh . . . programmed to hold only. It is in no . . . er . . . pain.

"She," Aurora corrected sternly.

0ck nodded. "Very well. She is going to be a . . . ah . . . prosecution witness at your . . . er . . . trial. Once your trial is complete, the Tribunal will decide . . . er . . . what's to be done . . . what's to be done . . . er . . . with her."

Aurora breathed a sigh of relief. "Thank the Podmother."

"Indeed," 0ck said. "Shall we . . . ah . . . get down to business now? I have only had . . . um . . . your information for a short . . . er . . . short time and I need . . . er . . . I need you to fill me in . . . um . . . on some . . . things."

Aurora returned to her seat. "Do you know how long I've been in transit?"

"By standard passing . . . only a few hours. You were . . . er . . . on the HyperRift Highway for an even shorter period of time. The . . . the . . . whole highway was . . . er . . . uh . . . shut down for you," 0ck said. "You're . . . er . . . something of a . . . ah . . . celebrity. Anti-celebrity? Famous? Infamous?" He pressed buttons on the table once more so that folders appeared and disappeared as he moved. "They have moved your trial through to the front of the cue. But the Gray Star ship . . . er . . . uh . . . had a long cue of its own to . . . to wait in before we could get you . . . er . . . planet-side."

"Why?"

He shrugged. "Annam is always busy, but it became especially so . . . er . . . when . . . word got . . . out that you . . . er . . . uh . . . that an Ascendant . . . was caught after committing . . . er . . . some sort of crime. The public . . . um . . . isn't quite sure. You've . . . er . . . um . . . or your crimes rather . . . many of them . . . uh . . . have been classified for now. In any case, many . . . uh . . . gamblers lost money. Others . . . others won." He playfully pointed at her. "You were supposed to last longer . . . on the run. And then there are the . . . uh . . . curious who've come . . . who've come for the trial itself. After Essa fell, it didn't take long . . . for word to get out . . . er . . . on the ExoNet that an Ascendant was involved in . . . um . . . some underhanded dealings—"

"'Underhanded dealings'?" Aurora asked.

0ck blinked, four of his eyes looking directly at Aurora. "You did break that law, Aurora. Though . . . er . . . I offer no . . . um . . . judgment."

"That's not—"

"It is a fact. There is . . . um . . . irrefutable . . . evidence. I am not here to . . . exonerate you. I am here to . . . I am here to help prove . . . it was . . . uh . . . ah . . . necessary, that inter-rim laws should be changed . . . that you were legally wrong but . . . er . . . morally right."

"What?"

"I . . . er . . . sought out your case when . . . when news first . . . um . . . er . . . hit the legal channels, so to speak."

"What?"

"No one . . . er . . . no one wanted it."

"Aren't you public defenders assigned cases through the Ascendancy? Isn't there a special class just for Ascendant?"

"There is, yes . . . but . . . several . . . uh . . . of my . . . er . . . colleagues turned down the case because of . . . well," he fumbled with the scarves tied around his arms, "they do not . . . uh . . . want to be associated with what you did."

"I thought you were here to defend me."

"Well," Ock said, flitting his claws in the air as though this was obvious, "that . . . er . . . uh . . . goes without saying. It's my . . . job."

"I see." Aurora's thin lips curled as she tried to figure Ock out. "Why?"

"Though my colleagues are . . . weak, there are . . . er . . . many . . . uh . . . citizens who agree with me." He tapped the table. "There is a large contingent of citizenry who believe the Conservation City practice is outdated and that the UCA should take a hand in . . . er . . . um . . . helping all citizens, even . . . uh . . . those whose planetary rulers are . . . circumspect or . . . or worse. Because . . . uh . . . it is traditionally . . . er . . . not the people who make the poor choices . . . er . . . um . . . but the rulers." He cleared his throat. "Does that . . . make sense?"

She nodded. "Stop punishing the people for the actions of their leaders."

"Something . . . like that, yes." He returned the nod. "So you can imagine the interest from lifeforms with those beliefs . . . when bits and . . . er . . . pieces of your story . . . dribbled onto the ExoNet alongside . . . um . . . images of Essa's destruction."

"There are images of it?"

"Vids from the Ascendancy Techs who monitored the whole . . . the whole thing." He paused and swiped away the screen between them. "Would you . . . would you like to see one?"

Aurora frowned, twitched against her will, and leaned away from Ock so that her back almost hurt as it pressed against the cold, hard seat. The dull, daily physical pain of living without a Correlative was almost too much for her and she hunched forward and away from the backrest, placing her elbows on the table.

"I do," she said, though beneath her prison blues, her body twitched. Cold sweat. Muscles ached. Her clear set of eyelids fluttered uncontrollably.

Maybe she didn't.

Ock's several arms moved too fast for her to object. Within seconds he had pulled up a vid from his Essa folder and hit the hovering PLAY button at the screen's center. Essa stood out in a sea of black space. It looked so much like Earth, or, more accurately, like a mud covered and rotted version of it. It was like a broken and burnt cookie, what should have been beautiful was instead a symbol of excess.

"If you look closely here," Ock tapped the wavering screen and it ballooned up, zooming in on a dark line firing away from the planet, "you will . . . uh . . . see a black streak shooting from planet-side toward space. That's . . . that's you." He leaned away and the screen fell back to its original size. "Your Correlative is so . . . um . . . dark that it wouldn't have been noticed had the . . . er . . . techs not been looking for it."

She laughed sarcastically.

Ock cleared his throat. "Anyway," he said, "you'll see the spark of the HyperRift Window opening . . . er . . . here," he pointed again and Aurora caught the brief, small explosion of white blink in and out. "Opening a HyperRift Window . . . ah . . . so close to a planet's atmosphere is a . . . er . . . uh . . . dangerous business," he observed.

"I know," Aurora said, slowly bobbing her head as her eyes grew dry watching the wreck of Essa dangle in space like a broken toy. "We planned it just right so that it would work."

"Here it . . . er . . . comes," 0ck whispered, some reverence in his stuttering voice. He pressed a few buttons on the base of the screen. "I'm going to . . . er . . . speed it up. Actual destruction took upwards of fifteen standard hours."

Aurora nodded, not really hearing him. Before her, Essa's brown and black splotches grew lighter. The red clouds like blood swirling through the atmosphere took on a violent nervousness, splitting and colliding as below them, great glowing orange fissures appeared on a surface that seemed to be melting at the edges. The crust took on an almost blinding whiteness as water from clouds, lakes, and oceans alike split and fell upward through the vaporizing atmosphere into space. It wasn't long before chunks of broken earth, hundreds of kilometers wide, were shoved from the planet's mantle. It was like there was some kind of terrible, angry fire giant beneath the surface, shoving piles of fetid mud into space. It was an egg hatching and the thing that came from it was an explosive beast.

The gargantuan heaps of rock and mud careened this way and that through space as the ocherous cracks opened up into hungry maws eating anything that didn't fall away. The monster was rising. It was conceived in the mad minds of selfish Essans, a monster that would not exist if it weren't for the rulers who had lived on the planet, who had ignored the man she loved.

Aurora imagined she heard Jon'Oh cry out. She felt his pain. She shuddered and reached one hand out to the screen. "Oh, Jon'Oh," she said softly.

"Yes, well," 0ck said, clicking the screen off, "that's . . . er . . . about that. The rest is . . . er . . . uh . . . mostly repetitive . . . until . . ." He cleared his throat, "until the planet is totally gone. And trust me . . . er . . . uh . . . you do not want to see the aftermath."

Wiping the tears from her eyes, Aurora thanked 0ck.

"My pleasure," he said. "Now, if you don't mind . . . let's er . . . get down to business." He clawed a few of his collars and scarves and pulled on them to illustrate his seriousness. "I've spent much time reading up on you, contacting your co-workers, family . . . er . . . etc."

"You're different," Aurora observed, sniffling.

"What?" His forward-facing eyes jumped from the hovering folders between them and landed upon Aurora.

"When those guards were escorting me down here, I saw you and you looked . . . panicked. Unsure. Weak."

"It is . . . er . . . nice to see your . . . uh . . . powers of observation are still intact Ms. Vega, despite the loss of your . . . Correlative."

"Right," she said. "You don't get the Correlative until you prove your own skills."

"Apologies," he said. "Whenever I come to a prison . . . er . . . I convey an image of . . . weakness and ingratiate myself to the . . . to the guards. I am the Beta to their self-perceived . . . er . . . Alpha."

"Mine didn't seem to like you."

"I don't need them to . . . uh . . . like me per se," he said. "It helps but it doesn't matter, not really. I need them to . . . er . . . underestimate me."

"Why?"

"You know . . . er . . . uh . . . you know you're no longer an Ascendant, correct, Ms. Vega?" He smiled at her, joking, but once more his attempt at kindness failed thanks to his several jagged teeth.

Aurora leaned back, never so consciously aware that Peel was no longer part of her.

"I'm sorry," 0ck replied, hard lips falling down around his teeth. "Our mouths can be . . . er . . . off-putting. It's these . . . uh . . . teeth. They grow in, fall out, grow back in. Such is the life of a . . . a . . . Vastaloose. My great uncle collected his. He was . . . er . . . uh . . . strange."

"I'm sorry too," Aurora said, ignoring 0ck's last statement, "about all the questions I mean. Old habits."

"It's quite alright." He waved her apology away with half of his arms, the clicking of his joints was strong in the small room. "To answer your last question . . . er . . . though, if the guards think I am weak, then they let their own . . . um . . . guards . . . uh . . . so to speak . . . down and I am able to . . . learn." He pulled the lapels on his baggy jacket, pride puffing up his ticking chest. "For example, because . . . er . . . uh . . . the guards thought I was weak and incompetent, I learned where they were . . . ah . . . keeping your Correlative and was . . . able to speak with it—her—er . . . uh . . . before I was scheduled to."

"Is that legal?"

"Strictly speaking . . . er . . . it's more appropriate to say it is not illegal."

Aurora smiled despite herself. "I think I like you, 0ck."

0ck fumbled with the screen before him for a moment and a series of reports appeared between them. "This is . . . this is . . . well . . . a highly unusual case, Ms. Vega," he said, eyes scanning the words so quickly Aurora couldn't keep up. "You have been accused of crimes against the Alliance and there is, like I said . . . er . . . irrefutable evidence as such."

"On to business then."

0ck leaned back. "I admire you, in a way."

"Admire me?"

"You have . . . uh . . . convictions. Your record . . . shows that." He clicked a few buttons and an image of all of Aurora's citations and awards appeared before them. "You were a great Ascendant."

"If I'm so great, why am I here?"

"Because," Ock smiled, revealing those broken sharp teeth once more, broken sharp teeth that so much resembled those of your average Draconian that Aurora had to wonder if this was some trick, "you . . . er . . . also love."

"Don't say it like it's a great thing. Love has gotten me here, imprisoned, alone for the first time since I can remember. Peel is alone, probably terrified, probably going to be retired. Love is a cruel joke played on all of us by an evil god."

"And yet you thank your Great Podmother quite a bit," Ock observed.

"It's a figure of speech. If you've studied up on me then you know I'm not the religious type."

"But you are the loving type."

"What do you mean?"

"Peel, that is . . . er . . . interesting to me. You named your Correlative."

She nodded. "I couldn't refer to her as 'Correlative' whenever we spoke."

"And you gendered her as well. Fascinating. That's . . . er . . . hardly noted in any of the records about you."

"Guess the record keepers didn't deem it relevant."

"Record keepers," he pushed a few more buttons, "are not infallible."

"Don't I know it."

"Aurora," he said, leaning forward so that his face hovered through the glowing screen between them. It dissipated in a splash of blue sparkles. "I have scoured the ExoNet . . . uh . . . researching you and Dr. Jon'Oh Lox, all of Essa. The . . . er . . . Tribunal has given me permission to take my time so I can . . . er . . . do this right."

"You actually think I have a chance of being freed?"

"As your crimes were . . . uh . . . mostly non-violent and your and Dr. Lox's machinations achieved . . . er . . . uh . . . nothing of any significance, and there is a great . . . outpouring of . . . er . . . support for your actions, I believe I can convince the Tribunal to let you off easy and use your . . . actions . . . to help bring about real change in the cosmos. But I need some . . . er . . . information from you."

"I don't care what they do to me," she replied. "I want Peel to be safe. I want Earth to be safe. That's all."

"The arresting officer told me you'd say something like that."

"You've spoken with Captain Flux?"

"I have. And I intend to . . . er . . . speak with everyone I can . . . can . . . about this case before and during the trial. But before I do . . . I need to hear the story from . . . er . . . uh . . . you."

"Are you trying to be funny?"

"No." He cleared his throat. "Aurora, I am here to hear your side of the story. The ExoNet is already filled with . . . um . . . so many versions of your story from . . . er . . . uh . . . those masquerading as journalists and those . . . ah . . . uh . . . more legitimate. But . . . I want to know your story from you. Anyone telling the story out there in the . . . er . . . vastness of the cosmos doesn't actually . . . uh . . . know it. Much is being kept from the masses. You . . . er . . . you . . . need to tell me everything."

"Everything?"

He nodded. "Please, start by explaining . . . by explaining . . . er . . . why you did . . . uh . . . what you did. And understand that I have . . . I have been trained as a Truthteller."

"You'll know if I'm lying?"

He nodded. "Detection is the most ancient . . . er . . . and most difficult art of my people. Few master . . . uh . . . it."

"Can you tell me something first?"

"Maybe."

"How did the Ascendancy know?"

"Your lover, Jon'Oh Lox, had a technoid called DC. DC's virtual membranes were attached to the ExoNet. Though Lox had a blocking mechanism installed in it, which would have worked, the very . . . er . . . act of adding one set off alarm bells within the . . . uh . . . Ascendancy. Technoids have no . . . nature . . . natural . . . blocking mechanisms like Correlatives, so adding one that was even stronger . . . er . . . than anything a Correlative could naturally create was . . . er—

"How we were caught," Aurora finished for him.

"It was . . . er . . . a minor oversight." He cleared his throat. "You avoided adding a . . . uh . . . an additional block on your . . . ah . . . Correlative, which was smart . . . since . . . since they are . . . er . . . so heavily monitored by the Ascendancy. I'm sure . . . er . . . given some time Dr. Lox . . . uh . . . would have devised some . . . some sort of lock that would have gone unnoticed . . . but," Ock said, "normally the block would never be observed closely, a normal byproduct or evolution of physico-mechanical life within the ExoNet. The science is still . . . er . . . uh . . . um . . . unsure, unclear, about much of that. But when you told your captain you . . . er . . . were taking time off . . . around the same time . . . er . . . uh . . . Essa was schedule to . . . when it was about to fall, his gears—"

"Tram, that bastard robot, son of—"

"He was simply doing his job, something you would have done in any other . . . er . . . circumstance. With all of your recent . . . er . . . activity involving Essa, you were suspect."

"And so was Jon'Oh." She crossed her arms over her chest.

He nodded. "I have answered your question," he said, "please . . . uh . . . please tell me your story."

She closed her eyes and leaned back, letting her head fall behind her so that she could see the ceiling. "I loved Jon'Oh," she began.

***

TALMUND'S BESTIARY BRIEF ENTRY: VASTALOOSE

USA Designation: Nav Vastaloosian-Prime

- A culture bearing, verbal communicating, land dwelling, quadrupedal evolutionary arthropoda insectahumanoid that presents itself as, overall, average in that class and order.

- Vastaloose are distinguished by an innate ability to know when someone is speaking the truth. Though Vastaloose naturally possess this ability to varying degrees, there are those among them who perfect what they consider, culturally, an artform. These Vastaloose are honored with the title of Truthteller. In all of recorded history, no officially ordained Truthteller has been fooled. Physically, it is theorized that their ability to detect lies so well stems from their multiple eyes (that each serve their own distinct purposes) as well as the small, stiff sensory hairs all over their body.

- Their reproduction rights are private and kept secure. However, it is rumored that they reproduce through an egg infestation ceremony in which their most highly regarded females release their eggs only to be fought over by all males in the vicinity. Evolutionarily, this fighting is said to have transformed from actual physical altercations to games of cunning.

- As they are the dominant species on Vastaloo, they are classified by Talmund as vespula vastaloosian. Vastaloose are anatomically similar to others in the hymenoptera order in evolutionary traits though they lack the ability to fly. Like many in the hymenoptera order, Vastaloose possess a thorax with several appendages (different numbers depending on what part of Vastaloo they originate) with hypermobility allowing them to display an erectness of body carriage or multipedal body carriage depending on the level of freedom their hands need for movement. Their arms and legs are indistinguishable and each possess two fingers and one thumb per hand that can act as manipulative members or pincers.

Status

- Average Height: 1.5 meters

- Average Weight: 50 kilograms

- Average Lifespan: 100 Annam Standard Years

- Home Planet: Vastaloo/Nav System/Inner Rim

- Planetary Status: Dominant Lifeform

- System Status: UCA Equality Inner Rim

- Cosmotic Status: UCA Member Outer Rim (Official Standing)

Classification

- **RIM**: Inner

- **SYSTEM**: Nav

- **PLANET**: Vastaloo

- **DOMAIN**:Eukarya

- **KINGDOM**: Animalia

- **PHYLUM**: Anthropoda

- **CLASS**: Insectahumanoid

- **ORDER**: Hymenoptera

- **FAMILY**: Formicavespidea

- **TRIBE**: Apocrita

- **GENUS: Vespula**

- **SPECIES: Vastaloosian**

Top Factual Documentation

- Vastaloose: A Complete History of a People

- Vastaloose: Truthteller: The Journey

- Vastaloose: Accomplished Vastaloose Throughout the Cosmos

- Vastaloose: A Society of Honesty

- Vastaloose: Shrewd Commanders of Truth

Top Opinions/Entertainment

- Vastaloose: Saviors or Villains?

- Vastaloose: The True Draconian?

- Vastaloose: Truth and Lies Throughout the Cosmos

- Vastaloose: Truthteller or Truth Manipulator?

- Vastaloose: Judgment

For more information and for answers to specific questions, please see **Talmund's Bestiary Primary Entry: Vastaloose.**

***

TALMUND'S SCIENTIFIC ADVANCEMENT INDEX BRIEF ENTRY: SOUND CELL

- Developed in 1.45682.1AST by Annalang Doctor Gerald0 Lan1x, the Sound Cell today is only used by Ascendant Officers.

- The only lifeform-created machine that can successfully contain a Correlative, the Sound Cell is a prison that emits audio frequencies that do not weaken a Correlative, but keep it in a weakened and docile state after a Severing.

- Sound Cells are used during rare situations in which Correlatives have to be Severed from their Ascendant partners and contained for transfer to Pelora or holding while they wait to take the witness stand during a trial.

- While scientists and other Correlative experts consider Sound Cells to be safe and comfortable kennel-like temporary homes for the Correlatives, some consider them tantamount to torture.

Status

- Official Creation Date: 1.45682.1AST

- Inventor: Doctor   Gerald0-Lan1x (1.45601.1-1.45726.1AST)

- Annalang Accessibility Status: Limited

- UCA Accessibility Status: Limited

- UCA Patent Registration: 26438.11.a-1.27/Annalang/

Top Factual Documentation

- Sound Cell: The Science of The Cage

- Sound Cell: A Complete Biography of Doctor Gerald0 Lan1x

- Sound Cell: Living In A Dream

- Sound Cell: Correlative: One Year Later

- Sound Cell: Audio Computations on Sound Cell Science

Top Opinions/Entertainment

- Sound Cell: I'm Living In A Box

- Sound Cell: Retreating

- Sound Cell: Escape From The Ascendancy

- Sound Cell: Audio Nightmares

- Sound Cell: Audio Nightmares 2

For more information and for answers to specific questions, please see **Talmund's Scientific Advancement Index Complete Entry: Sound Cell**.

***

TALMUND'S SCIENTIFIC ADVANCEMENT INDEX BRIEF ENTRY: CONSERVATION CITY

- The Conservation Cities of Monmoth (Annam) are, for all intents and purposes, prisons. Developed when the United Cosmic Alliance was expanding to include two rims (currently there are three), the science behind how they are created is above hyper-classified.

- Developed in 2.13459.9AST by Annalang Ascendant Tech Dramman Ro Koi No, the Conservation City process (conserving or diminishing), is the non-reversible shrinking of an entire city and all of its citizens on a doomed planet. Once conserved, those who dwell in the city are unable to leave and/or communicate with the outside world beyond the most rudimentary visual messages, though they can be closely observed and monitored.

- This process only takes place if a planet, through no outside influence, is on the verge of destruction. Conserving is voluntary for all lifeforms on the planet, save select cosmotic prisoners from the planet. When the threshold number is reached (different for each lifeform), the conserving begins. Once fully Conserved, the cities are moved to the city of Monmoth on Annam where they are studied by teams of scientists in many practices from geology to behavior, until every citizen encased therein dies, what the UCA officially refers to as a Peaceful End.

- Conserving is done because the UCA decided millennia ago that lifeforms from a planet that are so destructive that they manage to destroy their home planet, have no place in cosmotic society. Additionally, they are studied to help prevent more lifeforms from falling victim to themselves.

- There is much debate over the efficacy and humanity of conserving, with cases demanding a complete abolishment of the practice being brought before The Cosmic Tribunal regularly.

Status

- Official Creation Date: 2.13459.9AST

- Inventor: Ascendant Tech Dramman Ro Koi No (2.13359.9-2.13659.9AST)

- Annalang Accessibility Status: Limited

- UCA Accessibility Status: Limited

- UCA Patent Registration: 46698.12.a-1.39/Annalang/

Top Factual Documentation

- Conservation City: The Complete Study of Ro'Chall of Nargo-1

- Conservation City: Conserving the Cancer

- Conservation City: The Case of Jerik Null vs. The UCA

- Conservation City: An ExoNet Tour of the Conservation Cities of Monmoth

- Conservation City: Implementation And Effects of Conserving

Top Opinions/Entertainment

- Conservation City: Escape From Monmoth (series)

- Conservation City: Ghosts in Monmoth

- Conservation City: I Was Conserved!

- Conservation City: Conserve Me Up And Take Me Home

- Conservation City: Growth

For more information and for answers to specific questions, please see **Talmund's Scientific Advancement Index Complete Entry: Conservation City.**

Chapter 22
Aurora's Story

"I DIDN'T THINK I could love the way I loved him. The way I love him."

"And that's . . . that's because of Essan . . . er . . . or Whitley physiology?"

"No," Aurora said coldly. "We love on Whit. We share our lives. We share our bodies. It's different though. Outsiders don't understand."

"I am sorry . . . er . . . uh . . . I meant no disrespect."

Aurora crossed her arms before her chest, slumping back in her seat. "It's nothing," she said. "Most lifeforms don't understand us."

"I am . . . er . . . trying."

She offered 0ck the smallest smile she could manage—it was all she felt he deserved. "What I mean to say is that I never loved like that. I never wanted a relationship, physically, emotionally . . . I never wanted any of it with anyone, Whitley or otherwise. That's more common on Whitley than on other planets."

"Then Jon'Oh appeared in your life?"

She nodded, a wistful remembrance passing over her face. "Then Jon'Oh." She was silent as she lost herself in the memory of him.

"By all records, he was a fine Essan."

"When I first visited Essa because of his distress call, I should've arrested him on the spot." Aurora laughed, her recollection of his bearded face bringing joy even in this place, even in this prison.

"Why?" Ock asked.

"His distress call was bogus."

"Bogus?"

"It was a violation. He claimed to have seen a Slag War Cruiser Sanction VIII within the Essan system. He sent video evidence."

"All faked?"

She nodded. "All faked. Quality deep, but fake. There was no inter-rim reason necessitating Ascendancy presence beyond the officers already assigned to the sector. Their rounds would have had them on Essa eventually."

"But their rounds would only allow them to do mandatory checks for inter-rim issues . . . er . . . correct?" Ock asked.

"Yes, and honestly, that area of the Inner Rim was quiet, is quiet. Had been for some time." Echoes of her burgeoning relationship with Jon'Oh pulled her lips into a smile. "Ascendants who petitioned to patrol that sector called it early retirement."

"Not a lot of . . . er . . . inter-rim law breaking going on in Essan . . . um . . . territory," Ock said.

"Right," she agreed. "When I received the signal with the video evidence, I had to check it out because I was closest even though it wasn't technically my sector at the moment."

"And you found he . . . broke the . . . er . . . law."

"I did." She raised her pointer finger and leaned toward Ock. "But he only broke the law because he was afraid. Afraid for his people. His planet. Himself." She picked two of Ock's eyes and locked onto them with her own. "I understand fear."

"Yes, your planet was where the Draconian Reign finally ended . . . at the cost of many Whitley lives." He paused. "No . . . that's not right. It didn't . . . er . . . uh . . . end there."

"We like to say that the end began there," Aurora said.

"Indeed." 0ck nodded. His neck clicked and clacked with the shifting of his skin plates and articulated bones.

"They killed so many of us, so many of my ancestors." Aurora fell into a past she had learned of again and again, a time of slaughter, a time of misery, and finally, a time of rebirth.

"And this informed your feelings for Jon'Oh?" 0ck asked. His voice was like a clock ticking out of beat and yanked her from her memory of memories.

"This informs my feelings for everything, 0ck. It informs every Whitley's feelings for everything." She was almost shocked that 0ck had to ask this. Then again, she supposed, his people had never survived something so heinous.

"Yes. Yes." He typed up notes with fast moving fingers. "Continue please."

"We fought when he told me the real reason for the distress call."

"Which was?"

"He wanted the UCA to do something about Essa's . . . problems."

"Fighting?" Two more hands joined the ones typing. "Please continue."

"I threatened to haul him in, throw him in a SoloPen, not that his crime would have been punished with something so severe. He didn't know that though." Her lips slid into a frown. "He said, 'Good! Take me to Annam! I want to plead my case to the Cosmic Tribunal itself!' or something like that, something foolish and bold." She laughed.

"Are you describing your lover as foolish and bold?" 0ck asked.

"My lover?" Aurora smiled once again, but it was clouded with mourning. "He was my lover, wasn't he?"

Ock shrugged. "It . . . er . . . seems that way."

Aurora rubbed tears from her cheeks. "I told him that wasn't how it worked and laughed. He threw a holomodel of Essa in the air between us and sped it through to its destruction. It looked an awful lot like what we just saw."

"His simulation was . . . ah . . . accurate?"

"'Billions of Essans will die!' he said. He was so angry, so scared. He was crying unabashedly. He didn't care. And," a lump caught in her throat, "and I felt sorry for him."

"You pitied him?"

"It was more than that though. I felt empathy. I knew what it was like to see your planet suffer. I was born into a world that was all but dead because of what the Draconians had done. I lived in it, I helped rebuild it."

"But the Draconian Reign happened long before you were born. How much was left to rebuild?"

"Whit is a mature planet. We can't measure her growth in any way that any of us would understand."

"Every planet is a god."

Aurora's eyes rolled against her will. "Well, that's one way to put it."

"The way Whitleys would put it."

"The way religious Whitleys would put it."

Ock's fingers danced across the keyboard. "But Whit's issues were due to nothing the Whitley people did. Your people, along with a long line of lifeforms on other planets, were attacked by the Draconian Reign. The Essans alone were strictly at fault for Essa's problems, no one else."

"Are you my lawyer or . . . ?"

"I'm simply . . . er . . . trying to think like the . . . uh . . . prosecutors. They will . . . er . . . bring up the actual laws."

"I don't know what happened," Aurora said, exasperated. "Something was triggered inside me, I guess. Was it love?"

"I hear it's a many splendored thing."

"What did you say?" Aurora asked. The words sparked a loose memory somewhere in her mind. She had heard that phrase before recently. But where? From whom?

"Never mind." 0ck waved away Aurora's concern. "Continue your story."

Aurora blinked and pursed her thin lips before continuing, "Jon'Oh convinced me to return legally, and I did, again and again and again." She sat up straight now, the telling of her story somehow re-energizing her. "Our relationship was clumsy at first, silly even. We both went out of our way to meet each other. He'd send messages over the ExoNet, asking simple legal questions, playing dumb. I'd come calling when I could.

"My sister warned me not to get too attached. All the science said that Essa was as good as dead and since it was, like you said, only through the fault of the planet's inhabitants and not through any illegal invasion or some accidental infection through an Alliance connection, they were on their own."

"You know the laws well."

Aurora's hands fell to her lap and she let her eyes land on them. She studied the way they made sad, smooth little fists and thought of the hours she had spent holding Jon'Oh's hands, feeling their strange warmth, his five digits that fit so perfectly intertwined with her four.

"Anyway, we grew closer. We petitioned. When I was off-duty I was there. When he could leave Essa, I took him to Whit and even Annam a few times. We fell in love and I swore I'd help him." The tears came like a torrent now. "I still remember our first kiss." Head up, she looked at Ock. "Kissing, the way lifeforms like Essans do it, like Whits do," she sniffled, "it's so strange when you think about it."

"We don't . . . er . . . uh . . . express our emotions that way on Vastaloose," Ock said awkwardly.

"You should," she said dreamily, studying Ock's strange, hardly existent lips.

"Yes, well—"

"Anyway," Aurora continued, as if waking from a dream, "our petitions grew more heated. We gathered some compatriots, none of which had the stomach to do what we ultimately did."

"And what . . . what became of . . . er . . . them?"

"Are you asking me if we murdered our friends?"

"I'm simply searching for the . . . facts," he said. "Again . . . er . . . uh . . . the prosecutors will ask. If you could give me names . . . that would help."

She nodded. "We didn't kill anyone. Everyone left our group of their own accord. They claimed that they would keep our secret and we had no reason to doubt them."

"Are you certain they kept it?"

"I'm not certain of anything," she said.

"Did you ever suspect, er . . . uh . . . any of them?"

"I suspect everyone . . . now."

Ock typed something down quickly. "Why not just leave Essa?" he asked. "Several did. They're in their Conservation City right here on Annam, in Monmoth."

"Leave Essa to die in a zoo? How many Essans took the Alliance up on that offer, really?" she asked, disgust dripped from her words. "How many people from other planets ever do?"

0ck flipped through a holographic folder that appeared in the air above them when he flicked his clicking wrist. "Um, it looks like . . . yes . . . a few hundred thousand are in the sanctuary, 3,000 or so of which were . . . er . . . inter-rim prisoners beforehand and still . . . er . . . uh . . . um . . . are. I don't have the numbers for the other . . . um . . . cities in Monmoth at my claw tips, but I can get them if you'd like. It'll only take a moment."

"It doesn't matter. They're all prisoners. Past the extinction threshold." A quick, angry laugh slipped from her lips. "Sanctuary? How many conservation cities have ever grown beyond the confines of their bottle or bell jar or tube or whatever you want to call it?"

"None." 0ck said. "That's not . . . uh . . . that's not what they're for. The prediction is that . . . within . . . uh . . . ten generations, the Essans, like those lifeforms who went to Monmoth before, will be no more."

"And there is no reversing the conservation process. They'll die in their tiny cage," she said.

"The Tribunal prefers to call it a . . . uh . . . er . . . a Peaceful End."

Aurora rolled her eyes. "And why are they forced in these cages?"

0ck's jaw tick-tocked like a dying clock on its several hinges. "Legally, they're not allowed to mingle with those from . . . er . . . other systems or planets even."

"Because?"

"No one is forced. Er . . . save a handful of . . . er . . . uh . . . prisoners. You know this."

"Accept life in the bell, under the UCA's watchful eye or die when your planet does." Aurora sneered. "The Tribunal does not want their destructive behavior to spread. Studied? Sure. Spread? Absolutely not."

"The option to run is always available," 0ck said.

"The NetNeg?" Aurora blinked. "The Ascendancy would find us. They always find the runners. Always. Then The Tribunal would find us guilty of . . . so many crimes."

"We are the Tribunal, Ms. Vega. All . . . uh . . . of us . . . me, you . . . even everyone in Monmoth has a link to the Tribunal."

"That's what they say," Aurora said and leaned back again, looking away from 0ck. "But I don't know if I believe it."

"Your revolutionary group . . . floundered?"

"It couldn't flounder. It never even swam." She crossed her arms on the table and let her chin rest on them. "The Tribunal, the Alliance, the Ascendancy, no one would help, no one would listen. Our ideas were 'crazy,' they said. We were talking about breaking ancient laws that had been held up as sacred for eons. We couldn't do it. It was over."

"Jon'Oh's plan then?"

She nodded. "It was perfect."

"Except for DC."

"If that were the only thing." She rolled her head back and forth across her arms. "How did we miss that?"

0ck shrugged. "Hubris? Ignorance? A godlike hand in your machinations?" Who can . . . er . . . say? But . . . er . . ." he trailed off, his wide mouth opening and closing as if having trouble thinking.

"Yes?"

"You said 'if that were the only thing' a moment ago. What did you mean?"

She leaned back. Her head felt light. She squinted suspiciously at 0ck. "Isn't the Black Box not supposed to affect me in this room?"

0ck nodded. "It isn't affecting you, Aurora. Your Separation Anxiety is high right now and you traveled on a HyperRift Highway without your Correlative for the first time in . . ." he stretched out the last word as he brought up some of his own notes in the hovering blue-hued screen between them, "seventeen standard years."

"Has it been that long?"

"That's what the . . . er . . . records say."

"What did you ask?"

"What else besides the techs discovering DC's connection to the ExoNet were you talking about?"

"I don't understand the science of it, but Jon'Oh found Earth, a planet on the edge of the Outer Rim, not part of the Alliance, so far behind in its development that it wouldn't be for lifetimes of its people. It was populated with so many creatures that seemed to have counterparts on Essa. Jon'Oh created the Helix Needles, we determined that a meteor shower would hide my jump there right before Essa fell—"

"Interesting coincidence."

"A godlike hand in our machinations."

"Indeed. Go on."

"Anyway, like I said, we did it. We determined that Essan DNA was compatible with Earthling DNA, perfected the Helix Needles, and I went."

"And over a few generations, Earthlings . . . er . . . of all stripes would become Essans."

"Yes!" she almost shouted. "Only I was supposed to be there to teach them about the Alliance, about what had happened, about everything. I was supposed to bring them up, so that—"

"When the Alliance came calling, they were ready, willing, and . . . uh . . . able to join."

She nodded. "It would've been harmless."

"And, according to my records," he said, flipping through another holographic folder, "they would have become an . . . um . . . improved species because of the way the Essan DNA would react to Earth's sun."

"Yes. Something different, something . . ."

"Yes?"

"Something wrong."

"Why do you . . . er . . . say . . . uh . . . wrong?"

"I'm beginning to think the whole plan was selfish."

"How so?"

"It doesn't matter. I failed. The Helix Needles were destroyed. I was caught. And when I did make it to Earth, Peel sensed a CorreAxe. We left in a panic and ran into the Gray Stars. And here I am."

"Yes, yes, I was informed of that. The CorreAxe is your other problem?" He tapped on the keyboard. "Anything else?"

"The Gray Stars said that Earth is being monitored. They made it sound like there was a Contact Contingency in place. We didn't know that."

0ck nodded. When his head tipped up and down it looked as though he was trying to eat something off the tabletop. "Yes, I was informed of this today as well. You know . . . as . . . er . . . an Ascendant how these . . . er . . . things are. They're very . . . very secret, hyper-classified. Only a handful even know about things like this when they're in the . . . er . . . early stages."

"Still," she said, a pleading tinge in her words, "we should have discovered it. We looked so closely at Earth."

"Do not fault yourself too . . . er . . . uh . . . much . . . Aurora," 0ck said, reaching across the table so that his arm sent one of the screens evaporating into millions of tiny blue dots that slipped back into the tabletop. He patted her on the shoulder.

Ock's hard, cold claws on her shoulder did little to alleviate any of Aurora's self-loathing. Still, she felt herself smile.

"You were two lifeforms devising a plan to outwit an inter-rim police force, a government that spans galaxies and millennia, and a Tribunal that is connected to your very brain."

"The connection is only one way."

"Yes, but still . . . I'm feeling a bit overwhelmed with all of the . . . er . . . information . . . uh . . . I've received in just a short amount of time."

"What are you getting at?"

"This is your story, all of it?" Ock asked, shrewdly. "Remember, I'll know a lie."

There was a pause. Aurora folded her arms around her chest. "All of it that I care to share."

Ock nodded. "I'm afraid . . . er . . . that won't do."

"Why? How?"

Ock clicked all of the folders away and leaned across the table toward Aurora. "The Contact Contingent is made up of Earthlings from various parts of the planet who are referred to as Nowhere Agents because while . . . er . . . uh . . . technically they are citizens of every country on the planet, they are also . . . also citizens of none of them as they are now technically . . . citizens . . . er . . . of the UCA. Probationary, but still."

"What are you getting—"

He held up two hands to stop her. "Primitive planets tend to have several governments, several rulers, even several languages. They divide themselves in . . . um . . . tribal ways. It's all very . . . er . . . uh . . . barbaric."

"I know. We knew. We thought that I could hide there in the chaos and help pull the people away from it." She rubbed her head. "How do you know this?"

"Well, you . . . er . . . know . . . I am . . . er . . . uh . . . good at my job," he said.

Aurora laughed sardonically. "Do you know when they were planning on actually making official contact?"

Ock shrugged. "I have only read references to an upcoming predicted technological boom on Earth that could possibly initiate things. It's highly classified . . . er . . . I only received access to it when I . . . uh . . . took this case. But, as best as I can tell, the years for official contact to happen . . . are . . . er . . . uh . . . countless."

"Sometime within the next six to ten generations?"

"You remember some of the lessons from your . . . er . . . Alliance Building 101 classes," Ock chuckled. "But with this planet . . . er . . . probably a little longer. It's people are . . . something . . . something else."

"But if Earth is being observed, if there is a Contact Contingent, then that means—"

"That means if you did have contact . . . um . . . I need to know before the Alliance does because that could contaminate the planet and . . . er . . . change their plans. Connected to Essa . . . er . . . uh . . . like that, it could—"

"Podmother, they could—"

"Destroy Earth too, if it is determined to be contaminated with your . . . presence . . . er, so to speak," Ock finished for her. He leaned in closer. "And legally they wouldn't need to provide a conservation alternative since Earth isn't . . . er . . . an Alliance planet. But," he sat back again, "such knowledge could also . . . sway people about things . . . er . . . things like Conservation Cities and . . . uh . . . the like. I need to know everything, Aurora. I also need you to . . . uh . . . understand that I am on your side. No matter . . . er . . . what . . . I do not want this to happen."

"Why?"

"I am Truthteller. We believe . . . er . . . all life is . . . sacred. Why do you think I am a public defender?"

"Fine," she said, then let silence hover between them like one of 0ck's folders of information. "I made it to Earth and met an Earthling."

"And?" 0ck asked, pressing.

"I used a Helix Needle."

"On what? Who?"

"A pregnant Earthling female . . . the homo sapien."

"The dominant species?"

"I believe so, yes."

"Others?"

"They were destroyed."

"You're lying."

She grunted. "One more survived."

"Where is it?"

"With the Earthling."

"What you're telling me, Ms. Vega—Aurora—is that there is an Earthling carrying a fetus with . . . er . . . Essan DNA in its blood right now. This same Earthling also possesses a second . . . ah . . . Helix Needle?"

She nodded, sheepish.

He gulped, his mouth gone dry. "Er . . . if this pregnancy . . . is . . . er . . . viable it could . . . uh . . . change everything."

"I know. It could paint a target on Earth."

All six of 0ck's hands came together and he began clicking his talons. "I have been working under the assumption that you . . . er . . . failed. All of us have."

"What are you saying?"

"A failure on your part could . . . uh . . . bring an awareness to the . . . um . . . cosmos about the unjust laws. But if you . . . er . . . uh . . . succeeded in creating a new . . . er . . . uh lifeform . . . and you did not do so neglectfully . . . perhaps . . . perhaps we can . . . we can . . . er . . . put a stop to this whole mess." He thought for a few moments before suddenly snapping his head toward Aurora. "I need to find that Earthling," 0ck said. "Do you know . . . uh . . . er . . . where you landed?"

"I don't—"

"Never mind," he said and clicked on the table between them. A new folder appeared. "I'll find it. I need . . . er . . . uh . . . to contact the Gray Stars. I need—."

"I don't—"

"It doesn't matter," he said sharply. "If this Earthling births a perfectly healthy baby, then your plan was a success and it could help change, well, everything."

"You're not making any sense. You just said that it could mean the UCA will destroy Earth."

"Precisely. I have to find this lifeform before the Ascendancy does."

"Why?"

"She could be the perfect witness. She could—" he stopped, eyes going round with realization. "How did you . . . uh . . . administer the needle?" he said suddenly.

"I don't know, I talked to her and explained she was saving the world—"

"Did you force it upon her?" he asked. "Was there a fight?"

"There was no fight. I even helped her with an injury."

"And this was not an Act of Invasion?"

"I—no!" Aurora shouted. "I wanted to help. I wanted to stay, to explain, to make sure she knew what she was getting into."

"But you were rushed because you were caught?" he asked.

"Yes, that's right, that and Peel felt the CorreAxe—"

"Good, good. I must be going. This is all coming into place. We'll be in touch!" he stood and headed for the door.

"What about me?" Aurora asked.

"You're going to have to stay in your . . . er . . . cell. I will be back as soon as I can."

"What?"

"You can't be removed, Ms. Vega. But . . . er . . . if I can do this . . . uh . . . it could change the cosmos," Ock said. He grabbed her hand and squeezed it gently with two of his. He offered a half smile, doing his best to keep his sharp teeth hidden. "I am sincere," he added. "You will . . . er . . . see me again."

He left the room and a moment later her two guards stomped back in and forced Aurora down the long hall to another door that led through another hall and into a massive room filled with cells. They directed her to her own. After shoving her in and slamming the black bars closed, they said something unintelligible in an approximation of her language and stomped away.

As Aurora sat down on the edge of a rock-hard bed, she couldn't help but wonder what had just happened.

***

TALMUND'S SCIENTIFIC ADVANCEMENT INDEX BRIEF ENTRY: SLAG WAR CRUISER SANCTION VIII

- Slag Cruiser series spaceships were originally created by Chirrupian Healy Gray as a way of traversing the stars prior to the discovery of the HyperRift Highway. Outfitted with the latest technological advances in weaponry and space travel, for millennia, the Slag Cruiser series was the standard choice for traveling across the cosmos.

- With HyperRift travel the standard since its discovery, the Slag Cruiser took on a new role, one of war. Ascendancy manned ships can be nearly anywhere in the cosmos in a matter of seconds to aid a planet, system, or galaxy that is being unjustly attacked or invaded by another.

- Still maintaining the latest weaponry and space travel equipment, Slag (now) War Cruisers are the go-to ship when The Ascendancy has to convert from police force to military force.

- The latest version, Sanction VIII, can hold upwards of 50,000 officers of Annalang Standard physicality, has HyperRift capabilities, and is outfitted with standard weaponry that can be molded for the ship's intended purposes.

Status

- Official Creation Date: 1.87492.7AST

- Inventor: Healy Gray (1.87345.7-1.87555.7AST)

- Chirrupian Accessibility Status: Limited

- UCA Accessibility Status: Limited

- UCA Patent Registration: 19372.13.c-8.54/Chirrupian/

Top Factual Documentation

- Slag War Cruiser Sanction VIII: Latest Specs

- Slag War Cruiser Sanction VIII: A Complete Tour

- Slag War Cruiser Sanction VIII: Caption L30 Nox's Guide Volume #1

- Slag War Cruiser Sanction VIII: A History

- Slag War Cruiser Sanction VIII: Floating Ghost: The Husk of Mary

Top Opinions/Entertainment

- Slag War Cruiser Sanction VIII: Mazerunner

- Slag War Cruiser Sanction VIII: Space Ghost

- Slag War Cruiser Sanction VIII: Deep

- Slag War Cruiser Sanction VIII: Nearly Able

- Slag War Cruiser Sanction VIII: The Ghosts of Mary

For more information and for answers to specific questions, please see **Talmund's Scientific Advancement Index Complete Entry: Slag War Cruiser Sanction VIII**.

Chapter 23
House Call

THE NIGHT WAS LONG, dark, and quiet. After everything that had happened a mere twenty-four hours earlier, The Lonely One could hardly blame the stagnants for their fear. Of course they were keeping themselves secreted away in their homes. A boy had been murdered. What they thought was a meteorite had crashed into the earth, nearly killing a man.

They didn't know that it was actually an alien whose intent was . . . What was her intent? No matter. If the stagnants had known it was an alien, how would their fear be playing out? Would they be running through the streets in a panic induced frenzy like they had in the 1930s when that madman had broadcast that infantile story? Or what was it that had happened on the West Coast a few years later? The Battle of Los Angeles. These stagnants and their various hysterias were so amusing. Today if the threat of aliens loomed as large as it had then, would they, out of fear, violently attack all who were different? Or would they continue cowering in their homes under the fragile mask of safety the way they were doing now? Would they pretend that buildings of wood and mortar could withstand the powers of alien civilizations millions of years older than their own? How could they?

He wrapped his hands around the CorreAxe, feeling its lifeless but emotive response to his strength. "You are mine," he hissed, "and we have much work to do."

Even the Correlatives that Ascendant wore could be destroyed by these monstrosities formed from the cosmically burned and hardened corpses of their deceased ancestors. He would easily scare May with this. He would easily kill her husband. Then he would take her and keep her alive until she answered all of his questions. Then he would contact his brethren and they would begin the reign anew. Maybe he could even keep May alive until she birthed her baby. He could take it, raise it as his own, teaching it Draconian Order so that when the Second Reign flew forth from the burnt-out husk of Earth's stagnant society, they could place an Earthling regent on this planet.

His regent.

This was a new beginning, something he had been dreaming of since he had first gone into hiding. First, they would take Earth, then they would move their way through the rims. The Great Draconian Diaspora would end and all those who had bowed to the whims of the UCA would fall. His people who never lost their way would finally claim their place, finally rid the cosmos of any and all who would oppose them, finally create an ordered, brilliant Draconian cosmos.

He was almost gleeful when he walked to his car near the beach and put on his clothes. Listening to the river's night songs as he thought about his plans for the future had put him in a mood the likes of which only killing had ever done. It was a strange release, a powerful glow that both emanated from him as it fell into him. This, then, he knew, was joy. He hopped in his car, as gleeful as a hatchling and turned on the radio, giggling as Juice Newton's "Angel of the Morning" sounded out of the speakers. If there was one thing the stagnants were truly skilled at, it was music. He thought for a moment he would miss it as his head bobbed back and forth.

"Perfect timing," he cackled, unable to get enough. Smacking his hands against the steering wheel in a euphoric display, he drove toward the trailer park.

Soon, he'd have that woman in his grasp. He would learn all he needed to know. He would contact his brethren.

They would come.

***

The trailer park was a gloomy place as night fell. Normally, The Lonely One imagined, it was louder. He grimaced wondering what this place was like every other night. Normally, drunken parents probably wailed at one another while children cried. He was certain there should have been some inebriated laughter accompanying the sounds of sloppy sexual encounters. But there was nothing like that.

Fear had pocketed them all quietly in their homes where he imagined they huddled together waiting for a killing blow. These stagnants really were the perfect victims. But there was something else creeping through his thoughts as he pulled up to the small white aluminum trailer, criss-crossed with fading painted on brown bars in some mockery of decor. A gurgling sensation in his belly was causing what the stagnants referred to as heartburn. Was he nervous? The Lonely One did not get nervous. Draconians did not get nervous when they were facing an enemy they knew they could easily destroy. He grabbed the CorreAxe from the backseat. He stepped out of the car and let the growing breeze wash over him.

The air was cool.

The quiet was enchanting.

He looked around. Light spat from open windows in a few trailers illuminated the pathetic yards of patchy brown grass around them. Some of the light posts offered weak glowing cones of supposed safety up and down the street. They were shining, mocking bright buttons here only to remind these people of all they did not have. Most of the light posts offered no such thing though for they were shattered. They were dead guardians unaware that their time had passed. Pairs of dirty shoes dangled from wires that made tracks in the sky. They flopped in the increasing wind as though holding on for dear life. The Lonely One closed his eyes and forced a small change in his ears to make them stronger, those of a Draconian instead of a stagnant, at least on the inside. He heard people milling about their homes. He heard short conversations, voices quivering with fear. He focused on the Norman trailer. Someone moved about in the darkness there. He leaned in closer. It was definitely not the petite May Norman. It was a man . . . a man with two legs. Not that he thought Jack Norman would have been released from the hospital at this point.

Still, this was a curious turn.

Walking to the front door, he told himself to stay calm. Even if it was a Nowhere Agent, he had a CorreAxe in his hand and could make short work of them. He could defeat any of them and whatever pathetic weapons they might have. He knew that if the UCA had begun interaction with them they'd have a little more power than your average Earthling. But not much. That was against the law. He almost laughed as he thought of breaking the law.

He knocked, certain that everything would be fine, that everything old was new again, that everything would be as he had known it one day would be.

"Who's there?" came a voice that did not belong to either Norman. It sounded soft, hazy, sloppy, drunk.

The Lonely One opened the door. "Hello," he said, using his silkiest voice.

"Dr. Broyles?" Del Sims said from the kitchen. "What are you doing here?

"Hello Mr. Sims," Dr. Broyles said. "I could ask you the same thing, couldn't I?" He entered and clicked the light switch next to the door. Light illuminated a comfortably messy kitchen and living room combo. There was a hand quilted Afghan of many colors spread across a patched couch, a television with broken antenna, and a coffee table sprinkled with books, magazines, and empty glasses. Dr. Broyles sniffed, noticing a hint of cinnamon.

"That's the scented candles. May loves them," Del said, noticing the way Dr. Broyles' nose twitched as if irritated.

"How quaint," Dr. Broyles said. And it was. Though small, it felt homey. It felt loved. Dr. Broyles' upper lip twitched in disgust.

"I'm just getting something to drink. We ran out," Del said with only a hint of shame in his voice. "I know where they keep the booze."

"And you need it," Dr. Broyles said, crossing the room toward him. He grinned, knowingly, like he was in on a fun secret with Del. His chin fell to his chest and hid the grin. "I am sorry for your loss, Mr. Sims."

"Thank you," Del said, leaning his back on the counter and struggling to open a bottle of vodka he had just removed from a high shelf above the humming green refrigerator. "Call me Del." With a final, triumphant tug, Del managed to yank off the vodka lid. He dropped it. It clattered to the floor.

Dr. Broyles looked up again. This time his smile seemed a little wider than it should have been, like the doctor was a little less or a little more than human. Not quite right. Then again, it could have been the booze making Del see the world differently. He'd been drunk now for at least eighteen hours he reckoned. Maybe longer.

"What time is it?" Del asked.

Dr. Broyles did not reply. He stepped closer.

Del heard a small voice hollering out from below the bottles that had helped him through the day. It was squeaky and weak. It was scared. It wanted him to run.

"Dr. Broyles." Del, trying his best to drink himself blind, took a wobbly step toward the round, wooden kitchen table where a paper bag rested next to a pair of white coffee cups, one with the word HIS emblazoned on it, and the other with the word HERS. "Can I help you?" He sat down and took a swig of the vodka. Drips dribbled down his chin. He rubbed his eyes with one hand and held the vodka bottle tightly with the other, placing it precariously on his thigh. "Is everything alright, Doctor?"

Dr. Broyles lifted the CorreAxe. "Maybe," he said. "Where are the Normans and why are you here?"

"Is that an ax?" Del asked. He opened his eyes wide, using the hand holding the bottle of vodka to point. Laughing slowly, he belched. "Listen, I know you're their doctor, man, but this is cool. We're friends. There's no reason for," he hiccuped, "axes." More laughter.

"It is," Dr. Broyles said. He was going to kill Del anyway. He didn't have to keep any secrets. "It's made of the strongest material in the cosmos."

"Cool," Del said. "Why do you have it?"

"I use it to kill people."

Del laughed. "Right. You're a baby doctor."

Dr. Broyles laughed. "Where is your son, Del?"

Del frowned. "My son is dead, both of them," he said. "Everyone knows that." His head hung like a broken branch from his neck and bobbed there as he hiccuped and cried.

Dr. Broyles sat down in the chair across from him. "Do you understand what I am saying, Del?"

"Look," Del said, leaning away, the drink holding off an army of realization like a well-built wall. "If you're joking that you killed my boy with that ax, I don't think I can handle that kind of thing right now. Why would you even joke about that?" A squeaking whine raced through his voice. He took another drink and turned away from the doctor. "They really do keep a nice place."

Dr. Broyles ran a thick finger delicately down the side of his ax. "Do I look like I'm joking, Del?" he said.

"You really did it?" Del blinked. The words that came out of his mouth weren't his own. They were the slurred and heavy words of a stranger analyzing the situation and failing to process what he was hearing. "But . . . what? That doesn't—"

"Oh Del, I really do wish you were sober."

Sobriety stood against the booze and took a swing. "Why?" Del gently placed one hand on the bag on the table. He hoped there was something in it that could save him because he knew at that moment that he needed to be saved.

Dr. Broyles raised an eyebrow. "Do you know what, Del?" he asked. Somehow, his voice seemed slithery.

"Dr. Broyles, I—"

Dr. Broyles let the ax fall on the table between them. It seemed to vibrate with life.

"I'm not answering any of your questions." Dr. Broyles swung again and cut a chunk off the table. "But you're going to answer mine."

Del flailed in drunken shock as he fell from his chair. He managed to grab the bag but opened it to see nothing more than a small silver box and a delicate little pouch. He threw it at the doctor who easily sidestepped it.

Dr. Broyles stood over him, hands wrapped firmly around the ax's hilt as his skin changed. A cracking and stretching noise filled the room. Del felt the booze demand to come back up and out his throat as an otherworldly stench permeated the small trailer. In the doctor's mouth teeth multiplied, grew, and sharpened, stretching his jaw in a grotesque mockery of a human smile as they forced themselves from his lips and cheeks with wet, sloppy thuds.

"Jesus," Del muttered, looking up at something that was no longer a large human doctor, but a green and brown scaled lizard with yellow eyes of malice. Del thought, *Dinosaur?* drunkenly as ripped clothes fell off of the doctor. An image of Bill Bixby morphing into Lou Ferrigno danced through Del's thoughts. "More like the Abomination," he slurred.

"Tell me the truth now, Del," the thing that was no longer Dr. Broyles replied. "Where is May?"

No words came from Del's mouth, only fear made sound.

***

"I can't believe she left two Goddamned pieces of intergalactic hardware in a Goddamned paper bag on her Goddamned kitchen table!" Eugene banged on the steering wheel as his foot fell like a stone on the gas pedal.

"You heard her talk. She wasn't even sure it had actually happened; she doesn't understand," Mary said. She was holding onto the dashboard as the car veered through the cordoned off area of the field toward the makeshift gate. "Shit." Her eyes went wide. "They haven't opened the gate!"

Eugene hit the brakes and rolled down the window, screaming at the blues stationed there. Less than a minute later, their Cadillac was screaming through the trailer park toward May and Jack Norman's home.

Emerging from behind a trailer and following significantly behind the Cadillac, was a golf cart holding an elderly man and his large red-headed assistant.

The Cadillac screeched to a halt in front of the Norman trailer and the agents sprung out with their guns pulled. Jenny Sims opened her trailer door and watched while they crept up on her neighbor's home.

"What's going on?" she asked in her wispy, faraway voice.

"Back in your home!" Mary shouted.

"Del is in there," Jenny replied, raising a finger to point at the Norman trailer where Mary and Eugene were headed. There was no urgency in her words. It was simply a statement of fact forcing itself out from behind the terrible knowledge on repeat in her mind, that her son had been murdered.

"Ma'am, return to your—"

Del's ear-piercing screams cut off Eugene.

He reached the door first and flung it open to a Draconian holding a CorreAxe above his head, ready to drop it on a terrified Del Sims.

Eugene fired every bullet in his clip.

The Draconian fell.

"Holy shit. Is that a . . . a CorreAxe?" Mary said, standing behind Eugene and looking over his shoulder at The Lonely One's fallen body.

"I didn't think they were real." She holstered her gun and followed Eugene inside.

"Del Sims?" Eugene asked.

"Over here," Del's weak, warbly voice sounded from under a pile of rubble in the kitchen.

Eugene ran over to help dig out the drunken, frightened man as Mary eyed the Draconian and spoke into her wrist comm. "Local, you're never going to believe what we have here."

"What now?" Mike's tone was one of defeat. "You know I'm trying to make contact now. I do not need anything else."

"You're going to need this," Mary said and lifted her wrist so that she could point the comm at the Draconian's bleeding body, the ax just out of reach of his fingertips. She clicked a button on the device's side and took a photo.

A moment later, Mike gasped in her ear. "What did you use to shoot it?" he asked.

"Standard issue."

"Get out of there!" he screamed. "You know you need heavy artillery to kill one of those things!"

"I didn't exactly have time to get the suitcase!"

"It's not dead! Get out of there!"

"This is not your concern, Agent," the Draconian said softly from the floor. "There is nothing you Nowhere Agents can do about it."

"It might not kill it, but it'll hurt." Mary fired one shot at the Draconian's face. "Ha! We need to go!"

Eugene lifted Del to his feet while crouching at the sound of the gunshot. "What the hell?"

The Draconian climbed up and peered down at Eugene and Del. He reached for the CorreAxe fallen at his side. "I need May Norman," he said, his voice sounding like lizards skittering over pebbles.

"I don't think so," Eugene said.

The Draconian swung the ax so quickly that the air whistled until it stopped abruptly in a wet gurgle of slippery flesh. Del fell back, blood spurting from his mouth. "Wha-what?" he said through the escaping ichor.

"Del?" Jenny asked quietly from the doorway.

"Shit," Eugene said.

"Ha! Eugene! Come on!" Mary shouted.

Eugene dropped his gun and stared at Del as blood gushed from a hole in his chest.

The Draconian faced Mary. "Where is May Norman?" he asked.

Mary shot again.

The Draconian swung again. Mary fell back against Jenny and both women tumbled out the door into Linc.

"What is going on over here?" Linc demanded.

Behind him, Bucky keened, pointing at the Draconian standing in the doorway.

"My husband," Jenny muttered.

"Up! Up! Up!" Mary screamed, pulling the woman to her feet.

"You can't—"

"Linc, run!" Mary shouted, shoving the older man away. "Run!"

The Draconian smashed his way out of the door and took a deep breath, his stomach pulling in so that for a moment he looked like nothing but skin and bones. When he released the breath, a high, multi-pitched roaring rose from his throat as a massive leathery collar unfurled from the layers of hard green skin on his neck. He reached out, placed one giant claw on the handlebar of a nearby motorcycle, and flung it. The motorcycle tore through the trailer park, smashing into poles and slamming holes through trailers before it exploded against a large tree. Satisfied, The Lonely One grabbed the awning, and flipped, landing on the roof. Mary fired at the monster in vain as it leaped from one trailer to another, scurrying into the blackness of the night and swinging his ax at anything he felt needed to fall.

"What in the name of all things good and holy was that?" Linc screamed, spittle flying from his mouth in Mary's general direction.

Mary lifted her gun toward him. "I'm honestly not sure how many bullets I just fired, Linc, but I'm willing to bet I have at least one more."

Linc stepped back, holding his hands up while placing himself between Mary and Bucky. "Now, hold on, I—"

"Get in the car or get shot, Linc. You decide." The direction was fierce and her eyes told no lies.

"I'll get in the car," Linc said. "Come on Bucky," he added, grabbing the crying young man by the arm.

"I don't want to go with them!" he screamed. "I want to go home."

"Now, come on Bucky," Linc said, leaning in and reaching one arm around the bigger boy's shoulders. "I'll keep you safe, just come with me."

Mary holstered her gun. "I'm sorry. I'll keep you safe too, Bucky." She turned to look back through the trailer's doorway. She saw Eugene digging through the rubble, saw Del Sims' dead body sprawled out next to him. There was blood, so much blood. She faced Bucky and Linc again. "I really am sorry," she repeated herself. "We just need everyone to come with us."

"My husband?" Jenny asked.

Eugene came through the door, a bloody paper bag in his hands.

"Oh," Jenny said. There was a sadness in the way that single word fell from her. It was a sadness muted by exhaustion, humbled by shock.

"Please come with us," Mary said. She placed one hand on her back to escort her toward the car.

"We'll get blues out here right away to clean the scene," Eugene said to Mary as he walked down the trailer's front steps toward her. "Everything was in a paper bag just like she said."

"Well, that's one win, I guess," Mary replied, helping Jenny into the car. "One of us needs to get on the trail of that Draconian."

"We have no idea where he's going, Jones. We need to get this," he lifted the bloody bag, "to Local now."

"It was Dr. Broyles," Jenny said. "That monster was Dr. Broyles. I saw him walk into May's house after Del went in. It has to be him."

"What? Who?"

"Dr. Broyles, he opened the hospital in town. He's the richest man in these parts," Linc added helpfully.

"He's a large man?" Mary asked, remembering the doctor she had bumped into at the hospital the day before, seeing his name embroidered on the white coat he wore.

"Yes," Jenny said. "Very large."

"I know where he lives," offered Linc.

"In that case, take me there," Mary said.

"Local won't like this," Eugene said, raising an eyebrow at his partner.

"Local doesn't like anything ever, does he?" she asked.

"Suppose not." Eugene's half-cocked grin told Mary that he approved.

"Let's stop yammering and go!" Linc exclaimed.

"No! Wait! I want to go with you!" Bucky pleaded, grabbing onto the much older man. His large hands encircled Linc's forearm. He squeezed.

Linc winced but allowed it.

"I know this is difficult to process," Mary said, her words as subdued as she could make them, her voice the one she used to use with her own children when they were hurt, before they had died and this life with the Nowhere Agency had changed her. "It's going to be very dangerous where we're going. If you go with Agent Ha, he will take you somewhere safe."

Bucky leaned in closer to Linc, trying to bury his head in the much smaller man's shoulder. "But, Linc, I—"

"Now listen here, boy!" Linc shouted, wrenching his arm away. "We don't need you getting in the way when we chase that thing!"

"I just—"

"Bucky, I will tell your mama you've been uncooperative and then she won't take you to the comic book store!"

"But, but . . ." Bucky trailed off, fear of the Draconian battling with fear of his mother's wrath.

"Look," Linc said, growing softer, "I need you to stay with Mrs. Sims, okay? She's had a bad day. And it looks like it's going to storm." He waved his hands at the darkening clouds. "It's in the wind, can you feel it? It's bad."

Bucky nodded.

"Mrs. Sims needs someone to take care of her. Can you do that for me?"

Bucky sniffled. "Will you be okay?"

"I don't know, Buck, I don't know."

Bucky nodded through whimpers. "Fine," he finally said.

"Glad that little drama is over," Eugene grumbled. "Everyone in the car with me unless you're going with her."

Jenny and Bucky joined Eugene as he sat in the front seat and started the car. "Stay in touch," he said. "I'll get out there as fast as I can."

Mary nodded. "Open the trunk. I'm going to need the suitcase."

Eugene pressed a button on the dash. "Done," he said as the trunk flung open. Mary walked around and reached in. She pulled out a sleek black suitcase.

Eugene sped away and Mary looked from the disappearing taillights to Linc. "What will we take?" she asked.

Linc grinned and pointed at his golf cart while around them people emerged from their trailers, groggy and afraid but still possessed of that single trait Earthlings could not seem to shake: curiosity.

Chapter 24
Contact

THE LONELY ONE RACED down the roadside. Earlier, the cool early spring air had been pleasant on his scales. Now it made him quiver. To his right, trees swayed in the growing breeze, scraping their violent music to the beating of his pulse. Thunder bellowed in the clouds and lightning vomited forth from the sky. The darkness, normally his friend, seemed alight with danger. But he was swift as any bird, powerful as any bull. All pretense dropped, he could release his full, unadulterated strength on any and all attackers. His daily life as a stagnant was over. Since the Nowhere Agency knew he was here, there was no need to be conservative. He looked toward those ominous trees, studying their black outlines for anything, anyone else he could kill. That drunk, pathetic man had not been enough.

Nothing.

It was just his nerves. Still, he had to be quick. They would be after him. Contact needed to be made. And it needed to be made now. And his brethren needed to come fast.

Headlights appeared around a nearby bend, sending the shadows of the trees across the highway over The Lonely One. He ignored the car. He ignored the shadows. His secret was out. It did not matter who saw him. It did not matter what lurked in the shadows. It did not matter what nightmares he'd cause, what investigations would ensue. It did not matter who was after him. These stagnants were not going to rule this planet for much longer anyway.

The car grew closer. He kept running but looked back, curious. The car's headlight beams reflected off of his serpentine eyes. He blinked but he would not be stopped. Not now. The car came to a screeching halt. The Lonely One smiled. The car was red. His favorite color. Four doors. Full. He heard people, a child crying. No. Two children.

They sounded delicious.

The car went into reverse. The wide-eyed middle-aged woman at the wheel panicked. The Lonely One heard her screaming for the children to stay calm. The boy next to her in the passenger seat peed himself. The urine smelled strong with fear. The child in the backseat mumbled something about wanting his mother.

Enough, The Lonely One thought.

He roared and rose up on hind legs, stretching his body out as long as it would go. His tail rested on the asphalt to help him balance. His head swung from side to side as he sniffed the air. His tongue danced across his razor-like teeth.

"You." He pointed one clawed finger at the woman behind the wheel.

The woman whined like a trapped animal, angry and afraid, unwilling to resign itself to the fact that it was going to die. The Lonely One let loose another roar. This one was like a nightmare come to life. He hadn't made a sound like that since sometime in the 1700s.

New Jersey, was it?

No matter.

He roared.

He howled.

He broke the night.

The first drop of rain fell.

An oncoming semi rounded the same bend behind the reversing car. It honked to compete with The Lonely One's roar. But it was too late.

When the vehicles collided, the explosion of metal and flame was immediate. It lit up the night much like the meteor shower had. Bright orange and dancing yellows flew from a billowing black cloud that mingled between the semi's front bumper and the car's rear.

The Lonely One had always loved the smell of gasoline.

"Burn," he whispered. "Burn."

The glow was enticing to a creature such as The Lonely One, a monster from space that liked to see the worlds he conquered flip over on themselves, become parodies of what they once were, a creature who knew the only true way to conquer was first to destroy. The only sure way to bring order was to first bring chaos.

For a moment, he thought about darting over to the destruction like a hero, rescuing the victims, and taking them to safety just so he could see the looks in their stagnant eyes when he went in for the kill. He thought better of it and continued, giving the burning wreckage as wide a berth as he could. He was, after all, in a hurry.

He had to make contact. Now.

***

"Everything has been verified," Mike said to a hulking monstrosity clad all in black. Bulbous white eyes sprung from its hump-like head and his mammoth fingers on his mammoth fists on his mammoth arms tapped incessantly on a table made of stone. It was like a whale with arms and legs, a whale with arms and legs that was made of clouds. It was unnerving to see. "One of your Ascendant Officers gave an Earthling what we think may be an Essan DieCyclo and a Helix Needle. My agents are on route to retrieve them now."

"Send me all the information you have." The words rolled from the Tholin's tongue like rocks down a muddy hill. "Your agents won't be enough."

"Why won't my agents be enough, sir?" Mike asked, almost defensively.

"We have reason to believe there are more troubling circumstances on your little planet."

"We have a lasgun," Mike said, hating that he sounded like Mary.

"Good for you," the Tholin replied, an indulgent smile hiding in the dark water below the surface of his words. "You are aware of the fact that I am Ascendant Galaxy Captain Flux, correct?"

Mike nodded.

"Then I'll assume you are aware of the fact that I know what I am talking about."

Mike grimaced as he pressed a few buttons on a keyboard jutting from the wall. "Done." He spun away from the screen and eyed the one on the opposite side of the dome. Erratic static fluctuated over the black and white image of May Norman and Charlie McKinstrey as they sat in a holding cell a few domes away. They were in deep discussion but it didn't matter. Mike would be wiping the reporter's mind soon. He didn't even want to think about what was going to happen to the other woman. He'd pass her off to someone with a little less power than him, force them to deal with it. He might even actually have to Croatoa all of these people, this whole town. Maybe the entire area. That was never good. He needed to bring that up with Flux.

"Received," came the rocky voice.

Mike faced Captain Flux again and felt his undeniable smallness in the galaxy, the universe. "Everything in order then?" he asked.

Flux nodded. Or at least Mike thought he nodded. It was difficult to tell with a Tholin. "This is highly disturbing information, Local Michael Martinez."

"Please, uh, sir, just call me Local."

Flux nodded again or at least his head moved in a mockery of a nod.

"I'm going to need an audience with this human woman." He scanned a translucent screen floating near his eyes. "May Amen Norman is her name?"

"That's correct, sir."

"Thank you very much. I'll be sending a team to pick her up soon. The UCA may want to speak to her in a more official capacity."

Mike nodded and a heavy silence fell between the two of them. Flux appeared to hover between wanting to say something else and wanting to get off the line and forget this conversation ever happened. It was strange, the way he could read Flux's emotions even though he was masked. The Correlatives, based on what little he knew about them, were fascinating creatures.

Flux reached off screen to a button Mike couldn't see. But he knew what it would do. It would end the call. He couldn't have that.

"Okay, then—"

"Sir," Mike interrupted, his voice shaking. "There is more."

"Yes?"

"Your Ascendant used a Helix Needle on May Norman."

"Well, that," Flux said through a sigh, "is something."

"That's not all." Mike's words hung heavy with apprehension.

Flux's eyes squinted and inched toward the screen like two overstuffed snakes. "And what else might there be, Local?" he asked.

"There is a Draconian present on Earth as well."

"A Draconian? From the Diaspora?" Shock laced his words. He looked away and brought a hand to what would have been a chin on a human.

For a moment, Mike was struck at how, of the few aliens he'd met, they all seemed to have the same mannerisms as Earthlings. For some reason to him that only served to illustrate the smallness of his kind. "The Diaspora, sir?" he asked. "I don't understand."

"She was speaking the truth then?" Flux said to himself.

"We don't know anything about the Draconian other than he was at the woman's house when he was found. Two of my agents fought him and he escaped. But one is trailing him now."

"Well let's hope they're successful in subduing him." Under his Correlative mask, Flux frowned. "Your agent has the lasgun?"

"Yes, sir."

"Good. In the meantime, I have work to do. I think I'll be leading a team directly to Earth soon. If there really is a Draconian, I am going to need to be there."

"He has a CorreAxe sir."

"That tracks with everything Ascendant Vega told us. Be careful." He clicked a button off screen and his image vanished.

Mike chuckled sadly to himself. "I need a drink," he said to the empty room.

***

Before Captain Flux could call Nash and the others to follow him to Earth and retrieve this Earthling woman, another call came through, this one not from the private line to Earth only possessed by a handful of agents, but through his common ExoNet connection that his Correlative upheld.

"Who could this be?" he grumbled as he clicked on his holoscreen to see the defense lawyer J4rr0ck'L334v3r beamed there. Flux's frown, which was hidden by his Correlative, grew until it wasn't hidden very well at all. "Well, if it isn't my favorite public defender," he said through a sigh. "What can I do for you?"

The tone of his voice told 0ck that Flux did not want to do anything for him. His tone, in fact, told 0ck that the Ascendant was busy, busier, he imagined, than Flux had ever been. It was, after all, pretty quiet out there on the edge of the Outer Rim.

"It is less what you can do for me and more what I can do for you, Captain Flux." 0ck said, smiling wide, knowing full well it would not turn a Tholin into a mewling mess. Tholin could not be scared by something as minor as a mouth full of jagged teeth.

"Don't talk in Vastaloosian riddles. Explain."

"Your rogue Ascendant is my client."

"I am well aware of that," Flux said. "I have a lot on my plate right now, 0ck. Whatever you need, make it quick."

"Aurora Vega used a Helix Needle on an Earthling."

"I just received a report from Earth giving me details that line up perfectly with that. She also reported that there was a Draconian with a CorreAxe present. That's just been confirmed. This is something I must take care of. I am in a hurry. What do you want?"

"I need access to the Earthling," 0ck replied. "I can make it worth your while."

"How so? And don't make this worth my while, make this quick," Flux huffed, standing. "If there is a Draconian with a CorreAxe on Earth, I do not believe he is on vacation."

"Can you make sure I get to speak with this Earthling?"

"What is your game, 0ck? Spit it out now. Or I'm severing the connection. I have work to do. And I'm certain you do too."

0ck clasped his claws together before his face. He cleared his throat. "I have always believed that certain laws are . . . barbaric."

"I know your standing on Conservation Cities, 0ck. Get. To. It."

"What do you think is going to happen to Aurora?"

Flux gritted his teeth. "Obviously, the Tribunal will judge her guilty." He put his tongue between his teeth and hissed. "She'll get a reduced sentence because of her record. Maybe they'll even put her in the Conservation City with the surviving Essans."

"That doesn't seem reduced. That seems downright harsh for the person responsible for creating a new and better cosmos."

"The Earthling?"

"Yes. She could be the key to changing outdated laws. Aurora Vega could be a hero, not a villain."

Flux rolled his eyes. "That's not up to me, counselor. And, since I am an officer of the law, frankly I think this line of discussion is inappropriate." He paused. "How do you even know if I have connections on Earth?"

"Don't play coy with me, Flux. The Tribunal itself gave me access to classified information when I took this case. I know." 0ck let his eyes swivel over his head and spread his arms wide. The clicking reminded Flux of the rock-hop game he played as a child. "It is my job to know everything. I know all about your fascination with that planet. I know all about that planet."

"Top secret, my ass," Flux grumbled.

"I merely want this Earthling Aurora injected with the Helix Needle to be a witness."

"That is also not up to me. But the law says that since she isn't a citizen of—"

"She has interacted with an Ascendant—a Whitley Ascendant no less—and, seemingly, a fugitive member of the Draconian Reign. Furthermore, she may be carrying DNA that could change not only her world but the entire cosmos."

"You're not suggesting that this Earthling—who is not a UCA citizen—be brought before the Tribunal?"

"Stop with your indignation, Flux. There is no law against it." He placed his clawed fingertips together and leaned back, relaxed. "In fact, now that I've contacted you and told you all of this, now that you have corroborated this information, there might be a law against the Ascendancy keeping her from the trial. I could contact High Prosecutor Fluctioner and hear his thoughts before you make any decisions if you'd like."

Flux nodded, irritation glowing from his eyes. "You are quite the legal scholar, Ock.

***

The Lonely One knew the crash would bring the police and any other stagnant that wanted to see the grotesquery of charred bodies. As the sirens blared in the distance, he was already home, slinking up the front steps of his modest farmhouse, dragging his ax along the ground just to hear the sound it made as it sliced through everything. It was a slick noise, and constant. It jingled through the air like music with each raindrop that hit it. The storm was coming.

A Nowhere Agent would be here soon, he knew, so he had to be quick. He couldn't take the time to enjoy the ax's musicality. He took the stairs three at a time and ran down the hall like a giddy child to reach the attic. He pulled open the hatch and scrambled up the ladder to his lair within a lair. The walls were coated in a mixture of sand and mud with black and brown sticks woven throughout, making it seem less like an attic and more like a hut. It dripped with a mucilaginous ooze that would have been a mess if it wasn't for the system regulator that manipulated all of the natural developments in this attic to The Lonely One's will. With it running, the slime dripped in time and landed on the floor, gathering into a small globulous bump that slid to an elaborate stone basin across the room. With ancient runes carved around its rim, this basin served one purpose and one purpose only.

The Lonely One approached it.

The floor, covered in smooth, damp stones, creaked as he stepped over it. He smelled the moist, wetness of home. It was an approximation of Draco, made up of bits and pieces of his long destroyed home world he had managed to save before his people were purged and exiled. The system regulator, a small, tubal, mechanical device wedged into the slime covered wall sent robotic arms throughout the room. Its silver bends and twists found a humming base on the stone floor. It kept the moisture where it was supposed to be and spared the rest of his house from its growth. It was ordered. It was how all things should be.

The Lonely One approached the stone basin. He set his CorreAxe in it and pulled a stone mask of a giant Draconian skull from the slime on the wall. It oozed out, the slime almost fighting The Lonely One to retain its possession. But The Lonely One was stronger. He controlled the slime. He controlled the room. One day soon, he would control this world and the worlds beyond.

He raised the mask to his eyes and studied the painted visage of Great Reign Lord and Future Emperor Ch'oke D'Amon Karak. He held this thing with reverence, a small part of him fearing he'd drop it.

Cradling it in one arm, he pressed a small, nearly imperceptible button on its forehead then raised it toward the CorreAxe. Its eyes glowed red and scanned it.

"I have a CorreAxe," The Lonely One said through a cool whisper. "You must listen. It is urgent." He turned the mask so that it faced him and spoke his demand that all his brethren who still held true come to Earth, that this planet would be the new birthplace of the Draconian Reign. The time was now.

He imagined the accolades he'd receive when they all came. He imagined historians writing of this moment and placing the records in Talmund's Library. He imagined his name finally, after what felt like lifetimes piled upon lifetimes, being known.

He ended his speech with one decisive sentence: "You need to come now."

From below, his front door crashed open.

Chapter 25
Fires

"DR. BROYLES!" MARY SHOUTED from the front door, "I know you're here! You left a pretty clear fucking trail." She entered and held the angular black lasgun before her. With one hand, she clicked a small button on the side of the binoculars she wore. "If you don't come out, I can just find you!" She scanned every opening the way she had been trained. The goggle-like binoculars converted the world into clear, solid lines that stood out before a stark background allowing her to see literally everything within her line of sight. The first time she had used these reverse engineered monstrosities she had almost passed out from the sheer clarity invading her eyes. But now she was old hat.

"Come on, Broyles. In case you haven't figured it out yet, I'm not a typical Earthling." She looked around, knowing that Draconians tended to do most of their working underground and most of their living above. Flipping another switch on the binoculars, she stared at the floor. The wood faded away revealing a nondescript basement with an open chest resting in its center. She blinked and clicked that button again.

This time, the cement faded away revealing a bunker of sorts. In that bunker she saw a mad scientist's lab of grotesqueries. Walls were lined with human and animal body parts of all ages. Tubes, bubbling and filled with pustular gore, hummed an eerie warmth.

Tables of aligned shining medical instruments waiting to be used for this monster's studies stood over thirsty drains. The dust free environment of cleanliness that mocked the terror of this thing's experiments was almost overpowering. She almost wanted it to be dirty, at least if it was dirty, she could take Broyles for a madman. But this chamber of secrets was clean, so clean it was clear he knew what he was doing, it was clear he had plans.

"Dear God," Mary breathed, reminded of the hospital where her family died, remembering what she had been told, why she had agreed to join the Nowhere Agency. Vomit slid up her throat and she forced it back down. "Broyles!" she screamed, turning away from the horror chamber.

Dr. Broyles had to smile at the stagnant's arrogance. "How did you get around the car accident?" he asked from the top of the stairs where he emerged from the shadows, as confident as she was arrogant. Clad in a loose-fitting Styx t-shirt, blue jeans, and a smile, he winked at her. A cigar poked out of his lips almost jauntily. He was playful. In one hand, he held the CorreAxe. He rested it on his shoulder, doing his best to emanate the aura of an unconcerned rock & roll woodsman.

"Let's just say my driver knows what he's doing," Mary replied. Lasgun pointed at him, she removed the goggles.

"Ah," Dr. Broyles said, pointing his cigar at the gun in Mary's hand, "I see you've given up on the peashooter. Graduated to something with a little more kick."

"Yes. I have a weapon that can kill you now," Mary said. "And I'm a crack shot. So you can come willingly or I can take the shot, Broyles."

With eyes like slits, Dr. Broyles studied the weapon in Mary's hand. He had seen them before, years ago. An army of Ascendant had rained down upon Draco, CorreBlades and CorreBeams sprouting from some hands and lasguns silently firing from others. They were terrible things of condensed power. Their heavy metallic hides held a centralized concussive gamma force that could indeed kill him. It was curious that an Earthling had one, even a Nowhere Agent.

"How did you find yourself in possession of such a weapon?" Dr. Broyles asked, hiding any tension in his voice with a stretch of his vocal cords.

"None of your business." The lasgun felt heavy. Mary's fingers were wet with sweat. She had never been so close to an alien entity before. For much of her career with the Nowhere Agency there had been a small voice whispering in the back of her mind, telling her this was all bullshit. With every mission she had completed or every incident she had studied, that voice had grown more and more confident, no matter what her superiors had said. She had known of the most famous one, Roswell, before joining the Nowhere Agency, and even though that was where the alien tech in her hand supposedly came from, she still suspected that the whole incident could have been a weather balloon malfunction. The weapon could just have been advanced tech. Then there had been the Tehran incident, which was surely propaganda, despite what the Local from that part of the world claimed. Even that nonsense in Rendlesham could have been faked for one reason or another. The strange space radiation poisoning that had killed her entire family—her entire town—could even have been a governmental mistake.

She had never minded the perceived lie. The Nowhere Agency paid the bills and kept her busy, kept her mind off the life she had once had. Plus, it had introduced her to Eugene who she thought might have been the first real friend she had since her husband died.

Then Florida had happened. Deep down, despite the fact that nothing significant had panned out from it, Mary knew that something otherworldly had taken place there. For the first time, she had felt it. Eugene had told her about that feeling several times before, but she had laughed him away. She had been a happy cynic until then. Now, with all of the madness they had run into in Oakview, she knew her days of cynicism were completely over. Even if they weren't, even if there was a small chance that the cynic shrinking in her gut like a piece of half-digested potato was strong enough to swim to freedom, Dr. Ignatius Broyles cut the lifesaving rope of hope in all things mundane.

"You're not going to tell me?" His tongue, suddenly inhuman in length, slid from his mouth. Its pointed, unnatural tip slithered up his cheek and licked the sweat from across his brow before slinking back into its cave.

Mary pulled a small lever on the barrel of the lasgun and it buzzed to life, a hazy hue of wavering green light glowing from its tip and fading the further away it floated.

"I'm not," she said.

"I bumped into you at the hospital, didn't I?"

"You did," Mary said, offering no emotion.

He sniffed the air. "You smell nice." He spat out his cigar. It landed on the carpeted stairway and smoldered there. His grin grew wider. His lips pointed like knives on each end carved their way up his cheeks. Slicing, slicing, slicing.

"You're not fast, stagnant, not like me," he said and morphed so quickly that Mary's eyes had trouble keeping up. For a moment her brain, still hypnotized by the strange slow way his lips were cutting into his face, refused to believe what it had seen. It was impossible. Even to a Nowhere Agent, this was difficult to process. Where seconds ago a man had stood with a disgustingly inhuman smile stretched across the very human skin of his face, now was a giant lizard-like humanoid, made of green and brown nightmares. Its pink tongue whipped out from beneath row upon row of incisors.

Mary fired a bolt of green condensed gamma energy.

She missed The Lonely One but blew a hole the size of a man through the side of his house.

"This little dance could be fun," The Lonely One hissed while broken beams and shattered plaster fell to the floor around them with a loud clatter. "But I have miles to go before I sleep." He scrambled down the stairs, white dust following him, and past the smoldering cigar. With one switch of his tail, he slammed into Mary's side and raced past her before she could pull the trigger a second time. He took a swing with the CorreAxe. Mary dodged it. She fell to the floor and spun to fire once more. The gamma ray flew over The Lonely One's head to silently dissipate in the night sky.

When The Lonely One made it outside his front door, he saw Linc digging through a toolbox strapped to the end of his golf cart. He charged him.

"What the fu—"

Before he could finish, The Lonely One reached out and wrapped his claws around the golf cart's front bumper. With an eerie ease, he wrenched it from the ground and flung it into his house. Linc fell from it as its contents showered down upon him.

Mary leapt away from the front door as the golf cart crashed through the wall. More debris rained down. There were torn photos, she noticed, that she thought must have been the images that came with the frames. There were electrical wires wrenched free from the walls. Shattered pipes dripped what she hoped was water splattering on her back. She forced herself up, her legs having trouble cooperating.

"Oh no," she whispered, watching The Lonely One approach Linc.

Crawling on all fours, Linc rifled through the tools that had spilled from the back end of the golf cart when The Lonely One had thrown it. He came upon a small gas can as the monster approached. Linc dug a lighter from his pocket and climbed to his feet, gas can in one hand, lighter in the other.

The Lonely One stood before him, a hulking green and brown lizard with evil eyes that Linc could tell guarded real thoughts, a man's thoughts, not an animal's. "I am going to kill you now, stagnant," The Lonely One growled.

Linc looked over the beast's shoulder as he unscrewed the gas can's cap. That black clad, red headed woman stood on a destroyed front porch. She held that strange little gun in one hand and a dazed, sad expression on her face. Her suit no longer looked imposing.

The Lonely One huffed while he wrapped one claw around Linc's torso. "I am an eternal nightmare to your kind," he said.

"And I'm a fucking alarm clock," Linc replied, then he lit his lighter and dropped it down the open gas can.

A wave of flames sprung forth. The explosion knocked them both off their feet, Linc in a heap of burning flesh, and The Lonely One in a screaming mass of scorched scales and fire.

Mary pulled the trigger once more. The Lonely One dodged the blast but fell against the car in his driveway—his car. Thinking he should morph and dive in, he almost didn't notice Linc. Screaming an inarticulate cry of rage, the old man had somehow managed to stand and charge The Lonely One.

Mary fired again. This time, the beam nicked The Lonely One's shoulder as he tried to spin away from Linc and failed.

Screaming, burning, The Lonely One bounded toward Mary as he shrugged Linc off. Mary tumbled out of the way. The Lonely One's flailing hands were unable to find purchase on Mary and he fell headlong into the hole in his house.

Mary turned and fired again, but the fire The Lonely One had brought with him, burned everything it touched. The house filled with flames and smoke faster than Mary could pull the trigger. Growing black smoke forced her away. Squinting her eyes as the flames crackled and cried before her, she almost didn't hear Linc moan behind her.

She backed away from the burning house toward Linc's moans and watched as The Lonely One emerged from a second story window to leap into the sky, morphing into a burning bird that reminded her of the Phoenix as it flew toward Oakview.

"Agent, come here," Linc asked. His words were wobbly, as though they weren't quite sure how to make it from his lips.

Mary looked from the burning house to the dying man. She hesitated, knowing that every second not going after The Lonely One, probably meant a new stack of bodies.

Her eyes went from the flames to the sky where The Lonely One had disappeared. The clouds were dark now. Thunder cracked; the dark clouds exploded. The real storm had arrived. Shaking her head, she finally decided to approach Linc.

"Linc," she said as she knelt beside him.

"Did I . . . did I help?" Linc asked. "I just . . . I just want to keep the park safe."

Mary glanced up and back at Linc. "You sure did, Linc," she said. "You helped."

With a smile, the old man closed his eyes and was gone.

***

"He escaped," Mary said into her wrist comm. "And killed Linc."

"Who?"

"The civilian who was with me."

"Of course he did," Mike said. "Where is he going now?"

"Toward Oakview. But he is injured."

"How badly?"

"I hit his shoulder and Linc . . . Linc set him on fire . . . or blew him up or something."

"Impressive," Mike said.

"Maybe he's headed to the hospital," Eugene added. "It's his."

"May Norman's husband is still there."

"Could be his target now."

"Do you know what he was doing at his house?" Mike asked.

"No idea."

"Did you investigate?"

"He burned it down. He also caused a car accident up the road." Mary looked in the distance where she could see the lights of emergency vehicles spreading across the highway to surround a raging fire. In the rushing rain it reminded her of a painting. "It's chaos out here. There's this fire," she motioned toward the house burning behind her though no one was there to see it, "and there's the fire on the road. The rain is doing its best to put it out, but . . . I don't think it's going to work."

"Not to mention what happened at the Normans' trailer. Panic in the streets now and all that," Eugene added. "I mean, people saw the Draconian and felt him jump on their trailers. The trailer park is a mess."

"Lord. We have no solid idea what he's doing, where he's going? Anything?" Mike asked.

Mary could hear the defeat in Mike's voice and while she was not fond of the anger, she often heard in it, this felt worse. "I'll check the hospital," she said.

"I'll meet you there," Eugene called.

"No. Ha will wait until The Ascendancy arrives. He'll lead them to the hospital. Do not engage without backup again. What you already did was foolish enough."

"I'm sorry sir, Ascendants are coming?"

"Yes. They have experience with Draconians. Even with the lasgun, you cannot handle this alone. You have to wait."

"I just—"

"Stop talking, Agent Jones. Make your way to the hospital and wait for Ha and the Ascendancy. Again, even with the lasgun, you cannot take a Draconian alone. You've proven that tonight. Do you understand me?"

"Yes sir," she said. Would she obey? She was not sure of that.

Frustrated, she opened the door to The Lonely One's car and sat in the driver's seat. Reaching over the sunshade, she found the keys.

"Just like in the movies," she whispered as she started the car. She pulled to the end of the lane as the smoke billowed out of the open windows and large maw of a hole in the house behind her.

***

Jack had waited long enough. His wife had disappeared and he knew what had happened last time someone in this damn town had disappeared . . . yesterday. He hit the nurse call button repeatedly. His bandaged hands pressed through the pain.

"Mr. Norman," an older, demanding nurse entered his recovery room, "you have to stop this." Her gray hair looked like a dirty crown around her head and she held herself like someone used to being obeyed. With her rigid back and black, hard eyes, she reminded Jack of his old drill sergeant, Ross. The way she spoke, like each word was a whip crack of an order, reminded Jack of Ross too.

But Ross was long dead, and Jack had always wanted to yell at that man.

"I need to get up and find my damn wife!" Though it made him lightheaded, though it made his throat feel like someone was sharpening a knife against it, though it made his heart beat much faster than he knew it should have been beating, he gave as good as he received.

"I already told you," the nurse said, approaching his bed while she brought her stethoscope to her ears, "we've searched the hospital up and down. She's not here. Did you call home?" Her lips pursed together, creating a thin dark line across her face.

"I already told you," he repeated, mocking the woman with her own words, "the line is dead."

"Very funny, Mr. Norman," she said. "I know people like you can be . . . excitable, but—"

"What do you mean, 'people like me'?" Jack asked.

The nurse released an exasperated sigh. Her shoulders climbed up and fell down like a cartoon character's shrug. She cocked her head to the side and smiled meekly. "You know, she said, "soldiers."

"You think this is because I was in Vietnam?"

Her eyes found purchase on one wall, then another, and finally the storm outside the window. "I don't know, sir," she said, some of the angry energy fading. "After that and then almost dying, you might not be in the right state of mind."

"I'm not sure you are in the right state of mind," Jack said quietly, suddenly too shocked to be angry.

"We're doing all we can," she said.

"Did you call the police?"

She groaned. "Why would we call the police, Mr. Norman?"

"Because," Jack began through gritted teeth, his anger manifesting far quicker than he was comfortable with, "my wife is missing."

"Your wife is hardly missing, Mr. Norman," she leaned in and fluffed his pillow, "though your heart rate is somewhat elevated. You need to relax." She stepped back and reached for the television remote. "Why don't you watch TV for a bit? I think *The Facts of Life* is on."

"I don't want to watch TV." Jack's jaw clenched. His words fought their way out like escaping prisoners. "I want to find my wife."

"Let me see what I can do." The nurse spun on her heels to walk out of the room.

Jack screamed unintelligibly and grabbed the closest thing he could find to throw at her. It was a half empty Styrofoam coffee cup. It splattered against the wall, leaving a dark splotch like the one on Jack's life. He squinted and thought it looked like an outline of Vietnam.

***

Though his shoulder throbbed where the Nowhere Agent's lasgun had skimmed him, and the rest of his body ached with burns, The Lonely One easily reached his hospital, the one he had aptly named after himself, or a version of himself from centuries earlier. These Earthlings and their short, short lives had been a real blessing to him.

And though he was happy to have reached the hospital, he had never doubted he would. He was, after all, far better than any stagnant sent to subdue him, even a stagnant with a weapon designed to kill his kind.

Smiling to himself, he morphed into the form of Dr. Ignatius Broyles. His clothes were tattered and burned and were falling off of his stagnant form so there was no way he was going to get into Draco without causing a fuss. He couldn't have that, after all, he was there to retrieve May Norman, then he'd go into hiding until his brethren arrived.

Crouching behind a series of bushes near the main parking lot, he watched as a night janitor pulled into the parking lot in a rusty blue El Camino. What was the scruffy old man's name again? Sigmund? Sam? Samson?

"Bah," he said to noone. That wizened stagnant's name did not matter. As he parked his jalopy, The Lonely One made his move. It was almost too easy.

The kill was quick. Unfortunately, it was also relatively painless to the man who was far younger than he appeared. Gently, The Lonely One pulled off his clothes and shoved the body into the passenger seat where he covered him in an old blanket that had been in the car's bed. He studied the overalls he was sliding into. The man's last name, "Nice," was emblazoned above a chest pocket.

"Of course." The Lonely One had to laugh. "How appropriate."

Entering disguised as the night janitor, The Lonely One raised no eyebrows, not that he thought he would. Even with his injuries, it was an easy thing to make himself look like the custodian. Stagnants were simple to emulate. Their basic biological structure was not one of advanced evolution, but simple. In that way, they were almost beautiful. With a flick of the wrist, he could morph from one to another. It was the same for most creatures on this backwoods little planet.

Making his way through the halls toward his own office wasn't difficult. Stagnants, he knew, gave little consideration for their servant class. He wasn't even noticed as he approached the heavy wooden door with a golden plaque etched with his false name screwed into it. No one paid any mind as he clicked it open and entered. Once the door fell shut behind him, he changed back into the familiar form of Dr. Broyles and opened his private closet for a set of clothes that made him look respectable. It was all too easy. He wondered how much time he had before he was publicly accused of murder, before he became a pariah here in Oakview. As he looked around this office where he had spent hours and hours pretending, hours and hours in what he called his daily life, he morphed back into the janitor. Dr. Broyles' clothes hung baggily on his thin frame. He ran an affectionate finger over the official looking degrees hung on the walls, all of the books, all of the superiority.

He had loved it.

But it was over.

He clapped once as if applauding his own success at the end of a show. He was a master actor and this had been a master performance. A strange, bittersweet feeling of regret formed in the coldest corner of his mind. He had not accomplished much here in the middle of nowhere save a few messy murders. What more could have been done had he not wasted so much time pretending to care? With a mind heavy from wondering about the what ifs, he left the room, never to return. He didn't have time for that nonsense anyway.

Jack Norman's room was not that far away.

***

Mary smacked the steering wheel in frustration. The wreck The Lonely One had caused had brought the authorities. Police, firefighters, and EMTs were scattered over the road. The noise of the dying flames, falling rain, crashing thunder, and shouts of firefighters, were of little interest to her. To be brutally honest, she wasn't even that concerned about the two dead bodies, she could clearly see in the fire. Charred husks of humans whose stories were over could not help her now.

Even the third person, a small boy, clearly still alive because the EMTs buzzed around him like bees, was not her concern. Everyone here, dead or alive, was either part of the mess, or cleaning it up. She needed to get around it. And Dr. Broyles' ostentatious automobile could not do that.

Sighing, she pulled over and opened the car door. Even though the firefighters had been hard at work, and the rain was pouring, the heat in the air was overpowering. She wondered what that semi had been shipping for only a moment. It did not matter. She had to get these guys out of the way.

"Hey!" she screamed, stepping out of the car, and digging in her tattered jacket pocket for her badge. "Hey!"

A handful of firefighters and police officers turned to face her. Collectively, they all seemed to be asking, "What?" in the rudest way possible.

She did not have time for this so she put on her scared girl face and stashed her badge.

"There's a house fire a few miles back!" she cried, even forcing a few tears to help. "I saw it! It was terrifying!" Her eyes were wide with fear. Her hands trembled. *I'm just a damsel in distress,* she thought, laughing to herself.

One of the firefighters, a large man covered in soot and red faced from the heat, ran over to her. "What are you saying, ma'am?"

"There's a fire!" she screamed now, her voice cracked with false fear. "It's a house. Someone might be in it." It didn't matter that they would find Linc's body when they arrived and have a laundry list of questions for her. She had to find that Draconian.

"Where?"

"Back a few miles! I think a doctor lives there!"

"What?"

"It's Broyles' place!" Another firefighter ran to them. "We just got the call! We have to go!"

"Thank you, ma'am," the first firefighter said as the bunch headed toward one of two firetrucks blocking the road with its ambulance and police car pals. A quick discussion took place and someone shouted a few orders to a handful of other firefighters who jumped to attention. They ran toward one truck and piled on. The firetruck's sirens roared to life and the giant thing sped toward the growing flames of Dr. Broyles' house in the distance.

Mary studied the empty space in the road where the firetruck had been parked and realized she could now fit Dr. Broyles' car through the mess.

"Are you alright, ma'am?" a police officer with too much belly and not enough hair asked before she could jump in the car and speed away. He approached her with his hands out, as though he wanted to wrap her in a fatherly hug.

Mary smiled weakly and looked away. "It was just so scary," she said. "And I need to get going. Is there any way I can get around this?"

"Uh," the police officer said, and took off his hat to wipe his brow. "I don't know if that—"

"Agent Jones," Chief Ben Wilton called, approaching her from the shoulder. "Did I hear right? Dr. Broyles' house is on fire?" he asked. He was not offering comfort or help. This was an interrogation.

Mary could hear it in his tone even through the rain. *Game recognizes game,* she thought. She had to change tactics. She nodded quickly, straightened up, and became the consummate professional. "Yes sir, and I am in a hurry, so—"

"Where are you going? Back to the trailer park? I've gotten some calls of a disturbance; some strange things were seen around the Norman place. I don't have enough officers to head out there just yet, but I intend—"

"I'm sure we have people on it."

"I hope so, Agent. Are your people prepared for this storm? We might get a tornado before the night is over."

Mary looked past the chief. "Can I go, please?"

"How did you know about Broyles' house?" Ben asked.

"I drove by it."

"Uh-huh," he said. "Where are you off to now?"

"Chief, I don't think—"

Ben gave the officer a quick scathing glare to stop him.

"Back to base."

"What?" Ben snapped.

"I'm going back to base."

"Indeed." He didn't move.

"Can I go?" she asked.

"I don't know if that would be such a good idea," Ben said. He looked from side to side. "I'm not sure I can trust you." He pointed at the car. "Pretty sure this is Dr. Broyles' car."

Mary blinked and offered a forced smile. "I'm not sure I can trust you, Ben."

"Can you tell me what's really going on in my town?" he asked. His hand, Mary noticed, was hovering over the butt of the gun at his waist. Next to him, the chubby officer was taking hesitant steps back, his eyes darting from the chief to Mary. Were one of these men really The Lonely One? Mary had witnessed him change, after all. He could be anyone.

"I can't tell you anything," she said. "It's all classified."

"Well, you know what isn't classified?"

"No sir."

"The names of the people who died in this car wreck."

"That seems—"

"Danielle and Wyatt Kincaid!" Ben yelled. He was taller than Mary and as he yelled, he seemed to grow taller still. Spittle flew from his mouth as he added, pointing a hard finger at the boy surrounded by EMTs, "And that one is Sammy Nice!"

She looked from the smoldering vehicles to the boy on a gurney, wordless.

"Goddammit, they discovered the Sims boy!" Ben's eyes bulged from their sockets, forced out by his anger.

"I'm sorry, Chief," Mary said, trying hard to keep calm. "What about the truck driver?"

"I do not know who the goddamned truck driver is, but we'll probably have to identify his body through dental records!"

"Are you really supposed to be sharing this information?"

"Can you share anything with me?"

"Anything I know about any of this is classified."

"Uh-huh," Ben said, running his tongue over his teeth. "Classified it is." He sniffed and looked down at her. "Is this madness going to continue?"

"Unless my agency and I can do something to stop it, yes."

"And I have to let you leave in order for that to happen?"

"I'm afraid so, Chief."

His fingers twitched above his pistol. "I don't think that will work for me."

Mary rubbed her temples with one hand before taking a step back. "Don't make me do this, Chief Wilton."

"Do what, missy?" he asked. His hand was now firmly on the butt of his pistol.

She looked down at the gravel they were both standing on and slowly reached for Ben's shoulders. He jerked slightly, his gun shaking. She caught his eyes with hers. "Ben," she said softly, "I need to go."

Ben hesitated. He ran his tongue over his upper lip. Rain fell. Finally, he lowered his weapon and let his head hang.

For a moment, Mary knew that the two of them could have been mistaken for sad lovers, coming together once again at the sight of a shared tragedy. That image ended when she kneed him, as hard as she could, in the groin.

He fell with a hollow gasp that impressed her. She thought for sure he was going to squeal like a little girl. Before he could get his senses about him, before he could even look up from the gravel where he rocked back and forth, she was in Dr. Broyles' car and burning down the highway toward Oakview.

***

"Hello, Jackson," Dr. Broyles said as he opened the door, morphing from the janitor to the doctor. His voice was slippery. He walked into the room on light feet. "I hear you've been having a rough day."

"Dr. Broyles!" Jack yelled, seeing the familiar face of a man he did not like was somehow better than seeing the faces of all of the unhelpful nurses he had been dealing with. "Thank God, someone here who can help me!"

"Help you?"

"Get me out of here! I need a leg! Even a peg and a cane would do! You've got to be able to get me one, right?" he asked, exasperated. "These nurses have been no help!"

"Calm down, Jackson," Dr. Broyles said, pulling a stethoscope out of his coat pocket. "I'm only here to check on you."

"I don't need to be checked on, dammit, I need my wife!"

"Where is your wife?"

"I don't know!"

"Calm down, Jackson, calm down," Dr. Broyles said as he approached. "Let me just give you a quick check and you can tell me all about it."

"My wife left to speak with someone about the meteorite and she never returned. She's not answering the phone at home and no one, none of the nurses or doctors, no one, can tell me what is going on," Jack raced through an explanation.

"Well, unfortunately, I can't either," Dr. Broyles said, inching closer, eyes fluttering from human to Draconian.

"What are you—"

Dr. Broyles wrapped a hand around Jack's neck. "Quiet," he said. "Your pain will be over soon."

Jack struggled to free himself from Dr. Broyles' grip. But the more he did, the tighter the man's fingers squeezed. They also grew heavier, colder. Harder.

"What—what—"

"Don't talk," Dr. Broyles hissed into Jack's ear. "Your war is over, Jackson. Mine has just begun." He squeezed a little tighter and Jack fell asleep, the image of a lizard burned into his eyes.

***

"He must be here," Mary said into her wrist comm. "Are the Ascendant there yet?" She looked at the castle-like structure from the front seat of Dr. Broyles' car and grimaced at how ordinary it seemed.

"No," Mike's voice came through like a whip. "Just monitor."

A fist knocked on the passenger side window of the car. She looked to see Chief Ben Wilton's grimace. "This isn't your base, Agent Jones, is it?"

***

Dr. Broyles pushed a wheelchair down the hall. Jack Norman sat passed out in it, covered in a blanket and lost in a nightmare world full of gunfire and giant lizards. Broyles smiled at nurses and waved at his fellow doctors.

"This is fun," he whispered into Jack's ear as they reached an elevator. "I'm going to kill so many of these people someday. In the meantime, we have to—" He stopped, looking out the window. "Wait," he said. "What's that?" He studied the sky. The storm was in full swing now. Lightning flashed; thunder called out. And the rain, the rain fell and fell and fell. But Dr. Broyles could focus through all of it with his Draconian eyes. He squinted at the dark clouds and saw it.

"The Ascendancy," he said, watching quick black streaks dissipate in the sky. No one else would have noticed in this storm. They were cloaking. But his Draconian eyes could not be fooled. The Lonely One looked at Jack whose head rolled from one side to the other. "And they told me I put too many windows in this building. Can you believe that?" He laughed. "Well, it looks like my plan is changing . . . again."

The elevator opened and he pushed Jack inside. Then he pushed the button for the basement. A moment later Dr. Broyles rolled Jack into the damp coolness of the underground. The morgue was there, all the dead bodies. The boy he had killed last night, what felt like a lifetime ago. He looked at the watch on his wrist and wondered if the other bodies would make it here: Del Sims, whoever was in that car and truck.

"Hey," Jack's weak voice sounded from the wheelchair. "What is happening?" he said, half-awake.

Dr. Broyles smiled. "Go back to sleep, Jack."

"What?" Jack asked, his head heavy on his neck.

Dr. Broyles wheeled Jack toward a cement wall and pushed him off to the side as he morphed once more into his true form. He placed his Draconian hand on the wall and it melted away; behind it was a large, Ovoid Bomb. It hummed with imprisoned might and offered subtle yellow light from small circular holes sprinkled over its surface.

***

"Chief Wilton, I'm sure you understand that I cannot share everything I do with you."

"Actually," he said, getting out of the rain and into the passenger seat next to her, "I don't rightly understand that at all." He pointed his gun at her. "Now what is going on, ma'am? And why the hell did you think you needed to knee me in the nuts?"

"You know I can't tell you that."

"Well, I guess if you're going to stay silent, I'm going to just sit here with you and wait."

"I don't think that's such a good idea, Chief, I don't—"

A sudden rumbling interrupted her. It wasn't thunder.

"What's that?" Ben said.

"Shit." Mary's eyes went wide. "A bomb," she said. "Get down."

A moment later the hospital exploded in a sea of flames.

***

TALMUND'S SCIENTIFIC ADVANCEMENT INDEX BRIEF ENTRY: OVOID BOMB

- Ovoid Bombs function at semi-sentient levels and can hibernate for an undetermined amount of time until triggered by their creator(s). Invented in 1.65432.9 by Androgonion Dr. Belladora Carol, Ovoid Bombs were outlawed in 1.99999.8AST.

- Androgonion physiology is resistant to fire at temperatures as high as 3000°C, so the Ovoid Bomb was created as a way to protect themselves from invaders.

- Ovoid Bombs work as extensions of their creators and can be made to flame on for limited amounts of time in limited areas or they can be set free to multiply and produce at will.

- The recipe and instructions for Ovoid Bomb creation is hyper-classified and is currently only used for scientific purposes.

Status

- Official Creation Date: 1.65432.9AST

- Inventor: Dr. Belladora Carol (1.65390.9-1.65466.9AST)

- Androgonion Accessibility Status: Illegal

- UCA Accessibility Status: Illegal

- UCA Patent Registration: 25341.9.a-6.43/Androgonion/

Top Factual Documentation

- Ovoid Bomb: Fire Baby (documentary)

- Ovoid Bomb: Lost in The Tombs of Androg

- Ovoid Bomb: Living Fire Exhibit

- Ovoid Bomb: A Complete Record of the

Androgonion/Ramulok War

* Ovoid Bomb: The Final Bomb

Top Opinions/Entertainment

* •Ovoid Bomb: Fire Baby (song)

* •Ovoid Bomb: To Battle a Sleeping Flame

* •Ovoid Bomb: Level Up IV

* •Ovoid Bomb: Defeating the Ovoids

* •Ovoid Bomb: Sentient Salute

For more information and for answers to specific questions, please see **Talmund's Scientific Advancement Index Complete Entry: Ovoid Bomb**.

Chapter 26
The Ascendancy

"HUH, THAT'S SOMETHING," BEN said, looking at the great ball of fire where Draco General Hospital used to be. "Something indeed." A blast of heat rolled their way, turning the downpour into steam as it approached. The car rumbled with its power. Ben squinted at the flames and saw that they were behaving strangely. It was as if they were glued to the burning building. When they grew strong enough to catch a nearby structure on fire, they died down or danced back to their source. Maybe it was more like the flames were attached to the burning building by elastic strings that would only allow them to move so far from their source. Ben shrugged. All he knew for certain was that this was bizarre. "I'd call this in if I thought anyone could do anything about it."

"Wow," Mary said softly, rubbing her eyes as though what she saw was a mirage.

"That is definitely something you do not see every day." Ben faced Mary. "Do you know what the hell that is?"

"Not exactly," Mary said. "But it is alien."

"Well shit," Ben said.

"Chief," Mary opened her door, "we need to get out of here now."

"Uh-huh," Ben said, opening his door as well, "you might have to, but I have to stay. I have to deal with these sorts of things. You know, car wrecks, dead bodies, exploding fucking hospitals." He cleared his throat. "Things of Earth."

"Right."

The flames, though self-contained, were violent with heat and were serious enough to be attracting a crowd even in a storm like this one. Though the town had all but shut itself down in the wake of Ricky Sims' murder, an exploding hospital could pull out even the most frightened.

"People are starting to gather 'round," Ben said, his eyes scanning the growing numbers. There were murmurs of subdued shock sounding here and there. A few whimpers. He noticed a woman on her knees crying softly to herself. "Some of them had family in that building. Some of my officers had family in that building."

"Chief, I," Mary struggled with her words, "I think this is . . . this is going to get bigger than—"

"We don't have but two firetrucks in this town, Agent Jones," Ben interrupted. "Fuck it." He strode across the parking lot to his own police cruiser and reached in for the radio. "We have a little problem at the hospital," he said into it.

"It exploded," came a garbled voice from the other end. "We saw it from here."

"Dora, why are you at the radio?"

"No one else is here, Chief."

Ben wiped his brow. "And the firetrucks are outside of town dealing with a car accident and the good Dr. Broyles' house." He leaned against his car and felt sweat trickle down his back and sides. Or maybe it was the rain. He wiped his forehead and pulled his hat down closer to his eyes.

"I'll see if I can't rustle up some volunteers and get at least one truck called in from Ames," Dora said.

"You do that." He threw the radio back in the car and eyed Mary from across the parking lot with a fury that rivaled the flames. His, of course, wasn't contained to its source. "You need to tell me what's going on, Jones. Everything," he yelled.

"I'm afraid she does not, Officer," a voice sounded behind them.

Ben turned to see Galaxy Captain Flux flanked by four of his Ascendant Officers hovering in the sky. The chief's mouth hung open in a limp display of shock.

"You, however, need to move aside because we have reason to believe there is a wanted inter-rim war criminal in that burning structure."

Ben's hat flew from his head as a massive gust of heat bloomed forth from the burning building. It landed at Captain Flux's feet just as Flux himself touched down softly. Even Mary, who had seen images of these aliens and knew much about them, found herself dumbstruck in their presence. There were clearly two Tholin, Flux was one of them. They were accompanied by a third one who looked humanoid, but with six arms, a long head, and what appeared to be his own watery bubble. It must have been a Lubbol. Still another gave the impression of a great black horse with four strangely jointed arms protruding from an oddly stretched torso. This one was a Craddackian. At first glance, it was clearly a centaur with a few extra appendages. But for the very horse-like head and extra arms, it would have been one. The last one could have been a human woman with a violent pink mohawk balanced like a blade atop her head. Mary knew a Psyerrigen when she saw one. They all were clad in dark black suits with a gray star on their chests and a gray belt at their waists.

Mary gulped. "What do you need from me, sir?" she asked, staring up at the Tholin whose eyes seemed to be looping around his head to take in all of its surroundings.

"I need you to stand still," he said as one eye flitted to the woman with the mohawk. "Neo, you know what to do."

The one with the pink mohawk stepped forward and reached out a hand toward Mary's forehead. The agent flinched but stood still while the blackness slithered up the woman's arm and away from her hand so that her bare blue skin could touch Mary's. The moment her finger met Mary's forehead a glaring light flashed across her vision.

She wavered but stayed on her feet.

"Impressive," Neo said. "Most at least fall after a psionic touch. These Earthlings are made of stern stuff." She turned from Mary and touched Flux's head.

"Some of them, yes," Flux said as he closed his eyes. "Quite the story," he added while Neo walked around and touched all of the Ascendants on their heads.

"If this Nowhere Agent is correct, the Draconian is in that building."

"That hospital," Ben said, shuddering away his shock, "is full of people! They are burning to death!" he yelled. "We need to do something!"

"There are no people alive in that building anymore, sir," the horse-like being said. "No." He tilted his head toward the fire. "There are two. My Correlative believes one is the Draconian and the other is an Earthling. But the Earthling is not doing well."

"What?"

"The Draconian clearly set a semi-sentient Ovoid Bomb. They are localized and immediate. Terrible weapons, outlawed by the Tribunal many standard years ago," the one in the bubble said. "The Draconian must have a Prime Shield to protect it from the intense heat."

"Good thing we have Correlatives," Flux said. "Follow me." He headed toward the burning building and his Ascendants followed.

***

As the Ascendants disappeared into the flames, Eugene pulled up in his dented Cadillac. He had to drive slowly as the gathering crowd was making the parking lot a minefield of moving bodies, but he managed to maneuver through to where Mary stood next to Ben. He stepped out of the car to see Mary crouch before Ben who crumbled to his knees.

"This isn't happening," Ben kept saying over and over.

"He saw the Ascendant?" Eugene asked.

"I thought you were going to bring them out."

"The mohawk touched my head and pulled out the location. Then they left. They hardly paid Mike any attention. They were far more concerned about that woman, May Norman. Their leader left two to guard her."

Ben snapped his head up at her name. "Her husband was in the hospital."

"I don't think he died in the fire, Chief," Eugene said. "But if those Ascendants can't find him, I'm pretty sure he will die soon . . . and it will be ugly." He turned from them and studied the crowd, the sky. "We should probably disperse these people," he said.

"Yeah, yeah," Ben said, and stood on wobbly legs but kept his head between his knees. "People," he said, far too softly, "we need to get someplace safe. This storm is going to be bad."

Above them, raindrops were turning into small pebbles of hail.

***

Flux ordered his Ascendant to split up. The fire was not nearly hot enough to break through their Correlatives but the smoke did make it difficult to see and if the Draconian really did have a CorreAxe—and Flux had no reason to believe he didn't—they were in dangerous territory. Fire had always unnerved him. Those who inhabited the moon of Tho were not accustomed to it, not the way it was on Earth anyway. The way it seemed to cry and snap like an angry bird was troubling. It wasn't alive but it somehow was.

"Pure oxygen," he scoffed.

He didn't like the idea of splitting up. He'd been observing Earth long enough to know that here, particularly, it was a bad idea. That is, if rudimentary reels had any basis in truth.

But they had to find the Draconian before he could do any more damage. It already seemed like they were going to have to Croatoa this whole town, maybe even the surrounding area. Thankfully they had no ExoNet system to deliver news immediately across the planet. Here, information moved relatively slowly. With any luck they could wrap this up cleanly and put a pretty bow on it for the Tribunal and Zenith.

Flux announced that he would take the lowest level, looking for a way to get below ground, as that would have been the most likely place for the Ovoid Bomb to have been stored. A cool, damp place where it wouldn't have been able to grow very large. He made his way through the mess of burning walls, flinging molten rebar and brick out of his way as the flames tried in vain to break through his Correlative. Finally reaching an elevator, or what was once an elevator and now nothing more than a smoke-filled shaft, he paused.

"Can everyone hear me?" he asked.

"Yes sir," Nash said.

"Loud and clear," Neo's deep voice sounded in his mind.

"Aye," Nelumbaum Black called out through his rubbery neigh. Flux normally gave the Craddackian a hard time for the verbal ticks that found their way into the mental voice connecting them all through their Correlatives. But not today.

"Coldbloom?" Flux asked. "Daw?" The urgency in his thoughts could not be hidden.

"Here, Captain. I'm here. I'm battling the burning structure at the moment."

"Aren't we all?" Flux said, ripping the blackened elevator doors from the wall and leaping down the shaft. "I'm heading to the basement. If you can't find anything, follow me down."

When he landed in the basement, he took in the ruination with a mix of awe and fear. The Ovoid Bomb had definitely been down here. He could tell by the blast marks on what remained of the walls. The way they climbed with clear purpose showed evidence of semi-sentient flames. All Flux had to do was follow the evidence and he knew he'd find the source, and chances were, the Draconian who operated it as well. His eyes danced through the smoke, searching. Squinting, he tried to dissect the hazy environment.

"You're hiding," he growled into the fire. "I know you Draconians are particularly well versed at that."

Something clattered.

"Come out, come out, wherever you are," Flux said playfully.

Something large was knocked over. It crashed, blasting a mix of dust and flames toward Flux.

"A Tholin," came a slithering, wet voice, dulled behind the safety of a Prime Shield.

"A Draconian," Flux said as The Lonely One appeared a few feet behind the wave of soot and fire, clouds of smoke parting like an entourage for their leader.

"Hello Lonely One," Flux said. Silently, he contacted his Ascendant. "I could smell you even through the smoke."

"I'm impressed you can tell me apart from my brethren," The Lonely One said.

"Don't be. There isn't an Ascendant in the cosmos unaware of your particular appearance."

"You mean there isn't a Correlative."

"I know what I mean."

"And I know you're bringing your troops," The Lonely One said. "This isn't, as the Earthlings say, my first rodeo."

"I hereby arrest you for high crimes against the United Cosmic Alliance. You may speak your dissent but you may not refuse to comply with your arrest."

The Lonely One laughed and took a step to the side to reveal Jack passed out in his wheelchair. "What about this one?"

"What about that one?" Flux asked. "He's an Earthling. He is outside my jurisdiction."

"Is he?" The Lonely One asked. "Then you won't care if I do this?" He took one razor sharp claw and slid it across Jack's face. A red trail tore through his skin.

Jack screamed himself awake, eyes wide in panic.

"What are you doing?" Flux asked, an almost exhausted disinterest in his voice. "Stalling?"

"Why would I be stalling, so your Ascendants can show up?"

"We're already here," Nash said from behind The Lonely One. "Nice ax. Where did you get it?"

The Lonely One grinned. "I've had it a long, long time," he said.

"Shall we dance?"

"Try not to hurt the Earthling," Flux said.

The attack launched. The Lonely One's CorreAxe slid like water from a sheath on his back. He swung it as though it was an outgrowth of his arm. The Ascendants attacked as one, each moving with keen strength and fierce determination. But they were not used to fighting a being with a weapon so dangerous to them. Even their Correlatives feared the blade in his hand so their movements were a bit slower, a bit more repressed. For the Ascendants, fear of the CorreAxe was the ultimate equalizer.

All the while, The Lonely One laughed.

***

"What the hell is going on?"

Ernest Clement had seen a lot in his forty years. He had witnessed firsthand the naive and willfully ignorant 1950s that had given birth to the drug-addled and hopelessly optimistic 1960s, and finally he had come into his own in the hedonistic and overindulgent 1970s. After having covered multiple assassinations and attempts, the moon landing, and that farce that was Watergate, he did not think anything could surprise him. Even seeing that down-home peanut farmer or that dufus who used to act with monkeys become presidents hadn't been shocks after Nixon . . . or Ford for that matter.

As he pulled up to the burning hospital, whose flames seemed to be folding in on themselves while several spectators surrounded it, almost too shocked to be scared, Ernest realized he could still be blindsided. He really wished he had some cocaine right now too.

No.

He needed some downers after this, something to mellow him out. For a second he wished he was back in that Indian opium den he had visited a few years earlier and he had been beautifully and gratefully high.

"What the hell is going on?" he repeated himself, pulling into the large parking lot milling with people. He parked and jumped out, moving as close to the fire as he could until he came upon the chief of police standing hunched over, a red-headed woman in a black suit patting his back, and a tall, skinny Asian man (also in a black suit—but with a matching fedora) pacing in the rain. His eyes met the Asian man's.

"What's going on?" he asked.

"Move along," the Asian man said.

"I asked a question," Ernest said as he approached and looked from person to person. He had been in the game long enough to know how to hide his anxiety from someone that was clearly a government official. "What the hell is going on here?"

"I wish I knew, son," Ben said. "I wish I knew." He never looked up from the concrete. He laughed a little weak thing. "Remember when all we had to deal with were drunks when the Huskers lost?"

"What is wrong with him?" Ernest asked.

"The things he's seen, buddy, they're too much," the Asian man said.

"I don't understand what that means," Ernest replied. "Why the hell isn't there a firetruck here?"

People gathered closer as Ernest's voice rose over the blowing wind and falling rain.

"Yeah, Chief!" someone in the crowd shouted. "What's going on?"

Ben stood up straight. He was pale-faced and clearly shaken. "There are no firetrucks yet," he said through a sigh. "They're dealing with two other fires out on the highway and over to Dr. Broyles' home."

"Why are there so many fires?" another person called out from the growing crowd.

"Shouldn't somebody be doing something?" came another voice.

"Everyone calm down," Ben said, raising his arms as though he could silence them with a wave of his hands. He was doing everything in his power to prevent himself from puking. "I've got dispatch looking for firetrucks from outside of Oakview. We'll get somebody here soon! In the meantime, you should all leave. This storm is getting nasty!" Though Ben was trying his mightiest to give off the posture and power of a police chief, he was unable to pull it off.

Sure, the man was a bit soft around the middle and his thin gray hair gave little impression of manliness. But Ernest knew there had always been something about him that had commanded respect; he had interviewed him enough times to know that. Whatever it was, it was gone. And Ernest wanted to know what had taken it.

"This fire isn't . . . normal," Ernest said.

Others agreed.

"Nothing is normal here anymore," the Asian man said.

"And who are you?" Ernest took one step toward him.

"My name is Eugene Ha," he said, pulling a badge out of his jacket pocket and flicking it out at Ernest so quickly it looked like a golden blur. "I'm with the FBI."

"I suppose with the black suit, I should've known," Ernest said. His shrewd eyes noticed the bulge where Eugene kept his gun holstered below his jacket.

"If you don't have any business here, I'm going to have to ask you to leave."

"I'm here looking for my best reporter. Last I heard, she was headed here." Ernest pointed one thumb at the burning mess. "If she was in that hospital when it went up in flames, I will find out who is responsible and I will use everything in my power to bring that man to justice."

"How do you know it's a man?" Mary asked, smirking.

"It's always a man, isn't it?" Ernest looked around as if suddenly realizing something. "Where are all of the police?"

"Occupied I guess," Eugene shrugged. "Didn't you hear the chief?"

"Occupied?"

"Alien invasions will do that to emergency services." Mary shrugged.

"Alien invasion?" Ernest sounded insulted. "What kind of hayseed reporter do you take me for?"

"I honestly thought we'd have more to do when this all went down," Eugene said, wistful.

"You're not making any sense," Ernest said.

"I kind of did too," Mary said.

"What—"

"Stop, Clement. They're telling the truth," Ben said. He approached the agitated crowd.

"What?"

"I'm going to move this crowd away. I think things are going to get uglier before they get better."

"Should we head into that burning building to help?" one more bystander asked. Behind him, a group of townsfolk were ready.

"No survivors anyway," Mary said. "Not with something like that."

"Two," Ben put in.

Mary laughed. "The Draconian and his hostage."

"Dear God."

"Still better than Florida."

"What the hell happened in Florida?" Ernest asked as he stared at the flames. Somewhere in the distance, sirens sounded. But these were different than police or firetruck wails. This was the early warning system. Ernest didn't have time to ask the obvious question ("What's a Draconian?"). Instead, he simply said, "Tornado siren."

The agents turned from him, both staring at the fire as if trying to find some life in it. The chief rounded on the citizens.

"Alright now, everyone move along," Ben called out, keeping the sound of his voice somewhere between authoritarian and pleading, or at least trying to. But it was the pleading sound that ultimately won. "You all know what that sound means!"

"What the hell is going on?" Ernest asked no one. Everyone.

"Just get out of here, Clement," Ben said. His words didn't sound like an order though. No. They were more like half-hearted suggestions from a little boy who just learned Santa Claus was a lie. Behind him, above him, around him, the tornado sirens blared.

"Well shit," Ernest said softly. He looked from one of those black suited G-Men to the other and knew he wasn't going to get any information from them. He decided to get back into his car to drive the few miles to Barry's house. If anyone could get to the bottom of this madness, it was his publisher. He only hoped he'd beat the tornado.

***

"Why did you do this?" Nash asked as he jabbed at the Prime Shield with a CorreBlade nearly as large as The Lonely One.

"Honestly?" The Lonely One asked. "I had other plans!" He laughed at his own mistake. "Then I sensed your arrival and thought I could blow this place up and nab your attention before I fled!"

"Your glee makes no sense," Neo said, swooping down to aid Nash.

"Nothing makes sense to small minds like yours," The Lonely One growled from behind the relative safety of his Prime Shield.

"This thing won't last forever!" Nash bellowed, smashing it with the dull end of his CorreBlade so that a few small cracks danced through the shield's humming static.

"This could go on forever, Captain Flux," Neo said through their Correlative link, "despite what Nash says." She sliced a small hole into the Prime Shield with her CorreBlade and was about to reach in and start prying it open when The Lonely One's CorreAxe flew in her direction. She flipped out of the way and as the ax fell near her, the hole resealed. The Lonely One's tail, as if it had a mind of its own, flung out at the same moment to trip Nash. Meanwhile, The Lonely One's free hand slashed at Dawlish.

"He's too highly trained. And since he has that CorreAxe, we don't have the proper weaponry to take him down without hurting the Earthling," Neo said within the confines of their shared Correlative connection.

"I know how Correlatives work!" The Lonely One shouted. "What are you saying, Ascendant? Speak freely!"

Flux grumbled. "Fall back everyone," he said.

The Ascendants complied.

"What do you want?" Flux asked, staring hard at The Lonely One.

"Free passage."

"Free passage to where?"

"To wherever they're keeping this man's mate. I really, really want to know what is going on with her." He laughed. "I suspect I know, but I'd like to make sure."

"We're not taking you to her."

"Why not? She's just an Earthling. Outside your jurisdiction, right?"

Flux growled and took two heavy steps forward. He hardened his feet into the cement ground and expanded. "Everyone out," he shouted.

"Flux, I know what you're thinking!" Dawlish said. "It's too dangerous."

"Is it?" Flux asked.

"You can't—

"I took an oath."

"If you stretch to full size in here, your Correlative won't be able to maintain the cover! The fire!" Dawlish screamed so that all could hear.

"I took an oath!" Flux shouted. He hunched over The Lonely One and his shoulders hit the ceiling, flames dancing around them all. "Now get out!" He spun on his Ascendants. "All of you!"

"Captain—"

"Nelumbaum, do as I say!"

"Aye, Captain," the Ascendant said.

He looked to Neo. "You're in charge now, Neo," he said, nodding.

Neo lifted her head to eye Flux. "Are you sure?"

"Do I look sure?" Flux asked through gritted teeth as his body bulged and the Correlative stretched around him. It snapped in places and its black skin flapped in the flames, mindlessly reaching out to encase a partner it no longer could.

Neo nodded. "Everyone out!"

The Ascendants flew away, leaving Flux alone with The Lonely One and Jack, once more passed out in a wheelchair.

The Lonely One, for the first time since the battle began, seemed worried. "What are you doing?" he asked meekly.

"I'm going to smash you and be done with it," Flux said. "What's one more dead Draconian hate monger?"

"No!" The Lonely One snapped. His teeth bulged and he charged forward, seeing that Flux's wispy, cloud-like skin was no longer protected by the Correlative. But it was too late.

Flux's Correlative could not maintain its coverage. His Tholin body, stretched to its full capacity, was simply too large. Even Correlatives had their limit. Though it held on as long as it could, eventually, its thin layer of protective skin stretched to the breaking point, leaving Flux entirely open to the elements. His Correlative struggled to cover its partner, but the fire burned through Flux's skin to dig at his bones.

Screaming in a garbled language of molten stone and steam, Flux managed to drop one huge hand on The Lonely One. Though The Lonely One swung the CorreAxe one last time, it did not help. The cracking of bones and rending of flesh sounded under Flux's fist as The Lonely One's tail twitched and his blood oozed from beneath Flux's quickly hardening and burnt skin.

Flux coughed, breathing in the strange and irritating atmosphere. His eyes swung limply around the burning room to rest upon his Correlative. It looked like a puddle trying to climb a wall as it approached Flux.

"No," Flux said. "Save the Earthling," Fire forced a cave in around them. "It is our job."

***

Jack woke up feeling energized. His head swiveled from side to side as his eyes took in a sea of flames. He blinked. A voice—but not a voice—sounded somewhere deep in the recesses of his brain telling him that he had to get up and leave. He argued that he couldn't stand, that he didn't have a leg. The voice told him it did not matter. A leg would be provided. But it was less a voice and more a sensation that felt as though it grew from both outside and inside himself. Grunting, he struggled against it. His hands gripped the wheelchair's arms. His teeth gnashed.

Be calm, the voice that wasn't a voice said. *I am friend. Flux loves Earthlings. I love Earthlings.*

"Friend?" Jack said.

A pleasant warmth ran from the base of Jack's skull through his spinal column and spread out to his appendages.

"What . . . what are you?"

Friend, the thought that wasn't a thought, the voice that wasn't a voice, came again. And this time Jack felt its fear. He felt its simple intelligence that was somehow both vast and shallow. Above it all though, Jack felt its honesty. This voice that wasn't a voice was a pure thing. It was almost godlike.

So he let it take over.

Jack stood. He blinked, unsure why the smoke wasn't burning his eyes. Unsure how he could breathe in all this smoke. Unsure how he could stand. He spun around and wavered as he saw what looked like a globulous monstrosity soaking a series of dark bones as flames ate at it.

What is that? he thought. What is going on? Where am I?

A feeling—no—knowledge—that his questions would be answered in due time washed over him and he closed his eyes.

A black rope flew from Jack's hand and latched onto a strange ax, pulling it toward him.

A moment later, CorreAxe in hand, Jack, now covered in the dark black skin of a Correlative, blasted through the flames and to safety.

***

TALMUND'S BESTIARY BRIEF ENTRY: LUBBOL

UCA Designation: NalLubbolian-Prime

- The Lubbol is a culture bearing, verbal communicating, land dwelling, bipedal evolutionary mammalian primaticus that presents itself as, overall, average in that class and order, save for its six arms which they use to climb through the massive trees on their forest planet of Lubb. They possess social and political structures based on a benevolent dictatorship of hereditary hierarchy in which the ruling class appoints various family members to various governing positions. They reproduce through sexual contact and tend to mate together for life.

- Though they are known for their six arms, it is their elongated heads that house their double brains that truly makes them stand out amongst their mammalian primaticus brethren.

- Each brain only controls three arms and the controlling mechanisms therein are different from Lubbol to Lubbol.

- Hailing from the Mid Rim planet of Lubb, Lubbol also possess a subtle elasticity of physical and chemical structure that allows them to maneuver through tight spaces and easily survive in some of the harshest environments.

- As they are the dominant species on Lubb, they are classified by Talmund as homo lubbolian. Lubbol are anatomically similar to others in the primaticus order in evolutionary traits. Like many in the primaticus order, Lubbol display an erectness of body carriage that frees their six hands of five digits each (four fingers and one thumb per hand) for use as manipulative members.

- The Lubbol are also known for their ability to create 'liquid armor' out of the moisture in the air. While this armor is not very effective in combat with multiple lifeforms beyond thier home planet, it is an instinctual reaction to danger.

Status

- Average Height: 1.70 meters

- Average Weight: 100 kilograms

- Average Lifespan: 200 Annam Standard Years

- Home Planet: Lubb/Nal System/Mid Rim

- Planetary Status: Dominant Lifeform

- System Status: UCA Equality Inner Rim

- Cosmotic Status: UCA Member Inner Rim (Strong Standing)

Classification

- **RIM:Mid**

- **SYSTEM: Nal**

- **PLANET: Lubb**

- **DOMAIN: Eukarya**

- **KINGDOM: Animalia**

- **PHYLUM: Vertebrata**

- **CLASS: Evolutionary Mammalian**

- **ORDER: Primaticus-Sexlaticus**

- **FAMILY: Hominidae**

- **TRIBE: Homini**

- **GENUS: Homo**

- **SPECIES: Lubbolian**

Factual Documentation

- Lubbol: Fruits from the Wee Tree: The Complete History of Lubb

- Lubbol: Mid Rim Paradise

- Lubbol: An Introspective Dive into My Two Brains

- Lubbol: The Trees of My Grandmother

- Lubbol: The Trees of My Mother

Top Opinions/Entertainment

- Lubbol: Sunrise on Lubb

- Lubbol: Snub Lubb

- Lubbol: Keeping Up with The L'Oreals

- Lubbol: Lubbin And Clubbin And Dubbin

- Lubbol: Surface

For more information and for answers to specific questions, please see **Talmund's Bestiary Primary Entry: Lubbol**.

***

TALMUND'S BESTIARY BRIEF ENTRY: CRADDACKIAN

UCA Designation: LanCraddackian-Prime

- The Craddackian is a culture bearing, verbal communicating, land dwelling, quadrupedal evolutionary mammalian primatico-perissodactyla that presents itself as, overall, average in that class and order. Its elongated torso and arms evolved as a way to help them contend with their primary predators, the flying Sheermoffs of Craddack. They possess social and political structures based on tribal needs and desires and though they have a one world government that sees to planetary needs, their tribes are vast and spread over a planet that is 50% water and 50% land. They reproduce through sexual contact and tend to mate together for life.

- The Craddackian were longtime foes of the Lubbol for millennia until both planets were admitted into the UCA and hostilities were officially ended (2.11111.1ACU).

- The Craddack's true enemy is the Sheermoff. These flying lizard-like creatures are not the dominant lifeform on Craddack but during their mating season, they do essentially shut the entire planet down for six Annam Standard weeks in which the Craddackians move underground and cease all activities both planet-side and inter-rimally.

- This practice is primarily a survival mechanism that their ancestors discovered but has grown to be an important religious and social activity for many Craddackians. Called the Great Under, this time period is set aside as a kind of rebirthing period for the Craddackians.

- As they are the dominant species on Craddack, they are classified by Talmund as homo craddackian (though some scientists have petitioned The Cosmic Tribunal to change their classification to subdominant). Craddackians are anatomically similar to others in the primatico-perissodactyla order in evolutionary traits. Like many in the primatico-perissodactyla order, Craddackians display an erectness of body carriage that frees their two hands of five digits each (four fingers and one thumb per hand) for use as manipulative members while their four feet of three toes each are designed for speed

Status

- Average Height: 2 meters

- Average Weight: 500 kilograms

- Average Lifespan: 100 Annam Standard Years

- Home Planet: Craddack/Lan System/Mid Rim

- Planetary Status: Dominant Lifeform

- System Status: UCA Equality Inner Rim

- Cosmotic Status: UCA Member Inner Rim (Strong Standing)

Classification

- **RIM: Mid**

- **SYSTEM: Lan**

- **PLANET: Craddack**

- **DOMAIN: Eukarya**

- **KINGDOM: Animalia**

- **PHYLUM: Vertebrata**

- **CLASS: Evolutionary Mammalian**

- **ORDER: Primatico-Perissodactyla**

- **FAMILY: Homoequidae**

- **TRIBE: Homini**

- **GENUS: Homo**

- **SPECIES: Craddackian**

Factual Documentation

- Craddackian: From Craddack to Lubb: A Journey

- Craddackian: Sheermoffs: A Study

- Craddackian: Tribes of Craddack

- Craddackian: Prairie Myths

- Craddackian: Calls of the Craddack: An Understanding of Culture

Top Opinions/Entertainment

- Craddackian: Lost On The Prairie

- Craddackian: Lord Youngun's Paste

- Craddackian: Ride the Sheermoff

- Craddackian: Unleash the Beast

- Craddackian: Welbo's Story

For more information and for answers to specific questions, please see **Talmund's Bestiary Primary Entry: Craddackian.**

***

TALMUND'S BESTIARY BRIEF ENTRY: PSYERRIGEN

UCA Designation: YonPsyerrigenian-Prime

- The Psyerrigen is a culture bearing, verbal communicating, land dwelling, bipedal evolutionary mammalian primaticus that presents itself as, overall, average in that class and order, save for its extreme telepathic and telekinetic abilities and blue skin (which is an evolutionary reaction to their sun's unique rays). They possess no overt social or political structures since knowledge of what one Psyerrigen truly feels is but a thought away. Though this makes it difficult for visitors, the Psyerrigen have found a way. Their loosely structured society can be said to be based on everyone depending on everyone else to make sure they all do what is right according to Psyerrigen culture.

* Though their culture is not rigid, it is also not anarchical. With small family units, usually made up of one parent and one child, they tend to keep their distances from one another except during their three annual holidays of celebration and apology.

* Though the Psyerrigen can telepathically connect to one another with little to no effort, around the cosmos their abilities differ on different lifeforms. For instance, they cannot break through the natural psychic defenses of an average adult Vastaloose.

* As they are the dominant species on Psyerr, they are classified by Talmund as homo psyerrigen. Psyerrigen are anatomically similar to others in the primaticus order in evolutionary traits. Like many in the primaticus order, Psyerrigen display an erectness of body carriage that frees their two hands of five digits each (four fingers and one thumb per hand) for use as manipulative members).

Status

- Average Height: 1.70 meters

- Average Weight: 70 kilograms

- Average Lifespan: 80 Annam Standard Years

- Home Planet: Psyerr/Yon System/Inner Rim

- Planetary Status: Dominant Lifeform

- System Status: UCA Equality Inner Rim

- Cosmotic Status: UCA Member Inner Rim (Strong Standing)

Classification

- **RIM: Inner**

- **SYSTEM: Yon**

- **PLANET: Psyerr**

- **DOMAIN: Eukarya**

- **KINGDOM: Animalia**

- **PHYLUM: Vertebrata**

- **CLASS: Evolutionary Mammalian**

- **ORDER: Primaticus**

- **FAMILY: Hominidae**

- **TRIBE: Homini-Psy**

- **GENUS: Homo**

- **SPECIES: Psyerrigen**

Factual Documentation

- Psyerrigen: A Scientific Study Vols. 1-4

- Psyerrigen: One Standard Year on Psyerr

- Psyerrigen: A Test of Telekinesis and Telepathy

- Psyerrigen: Ratio Effect on Psyerr

- Psyerrigen: Running With The Psyerrigen

Top Opinions/Entertainment

- Psyerrigen: Mind Numb

- Psyerigen: Home For The Holidays

- Psyerigen: Greetings

- Psyerigen: Formats and Funnels

- Psyerigen: Request Line

For more information and for answers to specific questions, please see **Talmund's Bestiary Primary Entry: Psyerrigen**.

***

TALMUND'S SCIENTIFIC ADVANCEMENT INDEX: PRIME SHIELD

- The Prime Shield, invented in 2.96732.1AST by Essan Dor'On Lox, is an effective offensive weapon that can temporarily withstand even Correlative attacks.

- Made up of condensed and semi-gelatinous energy suctioned from the nearest electromagnetic field, Prime Shields are used in everything from emergency situations to natural disasters to war.

- Though the shields themselves have limited lifespans that can and eventually will fail if bombarded with enough attacks, the sheer strength that they possess, even if it is temporary, is enough that The Ascendancy keeps a supply of them on every ship and transports them to planets in need on a regular basis.

Status

- Official Creation Date: 2.96732.1AST

- Inventor: Dor'On Lox (2.9667.1-2.96774.1AST)

- Essan Accessibility Status: Common

- UCA Accessibility Status: Common

- UCA Patent Registration: 16348.65e-1.465/Essan/

Top Factual Documentation

- Prime Shield: A Display of Power

- Prime Shield: Offensive Weaponry at Work

- Prime Shield: The Great Breaking of Borak 5

- Prime Shield: Cosmetic Record Book Vol. 34567

- Prime Shield: Weapons of War Special Edition: Prime Shield

Top Opinions/Entertainment

- •Prime Shield: When the Shield Fell (A Fictional Account of The Great Breaking of Borak 5)

- •Prime Shield: Level Up: Prime Shield

- •Prime Shield: Eternal Glow

- •Prime Shield: Leave it

- •Prime Shield: Alone Inside A Prime

For more information and for answers to specific questions, please see **Talmund's Scientific Advancement Index Complete Entry: Prime Shield**.

Chapter 27
Reunited

"WHAT . . . WHAT IS GOING on?" Jack spun and landed on the far end of the parking lot, facing the burning hospital. He stumbled as the Ascendants surrounded him. Paying no notice to them, he watched as the fire folded in on itself and took the hospital with it. Or was the crumbling hospital pulling the flames downward? As Jack looked up, he couldn't tell.

He turned toward the Ascendants and took an unsteady step toward them as the last of the fire dissipated.

"The Ovoid Bomb is dead," an Ascendant said.

"Bomb?" The CorreAxe in Jack's hand vibrated.

"You're wearing Captain Flux's Correlative," the largest Ascendant said. "Who are you?"

"I'm Jack Norman. You're Ascendant Nash from the moon Tho," Jack replied, receiving a quick imprint from the ExoNet the Correlative was sending to his brain.

Nash nodded. "How did you get it?" There was an anger below his words, an anger that the Correlative hugging Jack's body did not like. It rippled over him and sent one shocking word plowing through Jack's mind: *Defend.*

"I don't . . . I don't," Jack foundered as the Correlative sent an explanation into his brain far faster than he could handle. "Wait," he said, leaning on a car. "Flux told this . . ." he held his free hand before his face and watched as strands of the black, tar-like substance covering his body grew from his fingers and climbed upward. They wavered there for a moment, almost like they were dancing, almost like they were playful. "This is a . . . Correlative?" The thing that felt like a second skin slid from his face so that he could see all present with his own eyes. He blinked. "Captain Flux told it to save me then he . . . then he," he made a motion with his free hand as though it was a hammer, "he smashed that lizard thing that was Dr. Broyles." He looked around the group. "What is going on?"

"That's what I'd like to know," Ben said, holding his gun out and pointing it at the Ascendants. It shook. He shook. As far as he was concerned, the whole world shook.

"You are an Earthling peace officer, correct?" the Ascendant with the pink mohawk said.

"I am," Ben said through a shaking voice only matched by his shaking hand, his shaking body.

"We are peace officers of the cosmos," she said softly. "My name is Neo. These are my associates," she motioned to the others, "Ascendants Nash, Daw, and—"

"We don't have time for this," Jack interrupted. He reached up and pressed his forehead. "The Correlative is giving me Flux's thoughts." He stumbled back.

"This is highly unorthodox," Dawlish said.

"We . . . ah . . . we need to get May to . . . some place called Annam. Flux wanted it."

"Why?"

"And you. We need to take you to Annam as well." Dawlish said. "To be drafted into the Ascendancy on the battlefield, my Correlative says the last time that happened was during the Draconian Reign." He stared at Jack in awed reverence.

"How do you know about what Flux wanted?" asked Nash.

"The Correlative must have imparted Flux's knowledge onto the Earthling. It's protocol in times of battle when a Correlative has made a battlefield decision to draft someone into the Ascendancy," Nelumbaum said.

"I want this thing off of me." Jack leaned against a car, breathing heavily and pulling at the Correlative hugging his skin. "My soldier days are over."

"Everyone stop!" Ben shouted. "There is too much going on tonight for me to just let you all leave like this!" He waved his gun at the group, whipping left and right. Around them, the crowd of gawkers gasped. Though several people had scattered when the tornado sirens sounded, there were still too many present. "There is a tornado on the way! We all need to find safety!"

Ascendant Neo grimaced. "I am sorry for this," she said and with a movement that was almost too swift to see, she flung a Correlative tendril at the gun, grabbing it and yanking it from Ben's hand. She studied it for a moment. "You are so far from joining the UCA, the fact that we had to come here will be an outrage on Annam." She crunched the gun in her hand and let the pieces fall to the ground. Pressing a hand to the side of her head, she added, "I believe other protective forces are on the way. We will be leaving you here. But know that we will return," she said. "We'll have to."

"You're coming with us," Nash added, grabbing Jack by the arm.

"No!" Jack shouted and yanked his arm free. "Last I checked this was a free country."

"Earthling, you do not have a choice," Dawlish said. "You have been drafted."

"I won't—"

A clanging noise sounded in Jack's ears. He fell to his knees and grabbed his head. The Ascendants around him heard it as well, but instead of falling, they all looked to the skies.

"The klaxon," Neo said.

"What is going on?" Ben asked.

"Allow me," Neo said. Her Correlative rippled over her head and the klaxon that sounded within their Correlatives was released into the air and tore through the tornado sirens. It pulsed out over everyone there. Ben joined Jack. The small crowd of people who were still staring in awe at the Ascendant, fell back as if hit by a mighty wave. All of them grabbed their ears, screaming.

"What does it mean?" Jack shouted.

"You'll know in a moment," Dawlish said.

"I don't understand—"

A bright blue beam fired down from the sky and hovered before them. Inside the beam stood what looked to Jack like a squid covered in the same black suit that he wore. It nodded at the Ascendants. "I know this is highly unorthodox, considering Earth's status," he began, though he wasn't speaking, so much as sending visual representations of his words into their minds, "but the techs have discovered a powerful Draconian signal requesting immediate aid. It was sent from Earth near these coordinates. I originally beamed there but it appears the structure the signal originated from has been burned down." He looked beyond the Ascendants to the Earthlings.

"Was there a response, Slum?" Nash asked. His words quivered behind the mask.

"Aye," Slum answered. "We intercepted it but could not decipher the code. We have officers taking it to the diaspora now. They will know the code. But it does not matter because we will not be able to get to them and back here in time. The Reign is gathering its forces. It is coming here."

"Dear lord," Jack said. He looked around at the aliens who he could tell were afraid.

"The klaxon has been sent to your Correlatives and into official buildings throughout the Cosmos. This planet is going to be invaded and it is going to be invaded soon. We need to protect it."

"Where is May?" Jack asked.

***

"How long has it been?" Charlie asked when Mike entered the strange bubble house where she'd been imprisoned with May, Jenny, and Bucky. The door whizzed shut behind him with a finality Charlie did not like. "And what the hell was that ringing a minute ago?"

Mike eyes fell to the floor as Charlie strode toward him. "You're not—"

"I'm not scared of you or your black suit!" Charlie said firmly, hands on her hips.

Behind her, sitting on a white bench, with one arm wrapped around Jenny, May protested, "Charlie, I don't think—"

Mike rolled his shoulders back. "No," he said, looking Charlie in the eyes, "she's right to be angry." He pointed at Bucky who sat on the floor in front of Jenny. His eyes were red rimmed and bulging. He was sniffling and one of his hands rested on one of his broad shoulders. One of Jenny's hands rested on it, her fingers interlaced with his. "But the boy might have the better idea."

"What's that supposed to mean?" Charlie spat. Her naturally rosy cheeks were burning red with anger. "I'm not going to suffer another man's shit today!"

"He's scared," May said. "Bucky's scared. That's what he means."

"Are you threatening us now?" Charlie asked. She hadn't felt this kind of anger even earlier when she'd had to face her asshole publisher. "You are violating our rights! You can't do this! You can't—"

"It wasn't a threat!" Mike shouted. He turned away from her. "We should all be afraid," he added softly. He faced Charlie once more and raised two hands as if in surrender. "What you're about to see will be shocking," he said as behind him, the door opened.

Jack was first to enter. He limped in quickly as the Correlative drained away from his face. "May?" he said, looking at his wife.

"Jack!" she leapt from her seat and embraced him hard.

He pitched backward, still figuring out how to use his Correlative leg, but he held his ground against her warm body. "All will be well," he whispered in her ear.

"Jack, I can't believe it! How is this possible? How are you walking?" She reached up and ran a hand over a slight pinkish scar on his cheek. "What happened here?"

He touched her hand. "Just wanted to match you, I guess."

She breathed a short quiet laugh and smiled at him. For a moment they were alone, they had no real worries, and everything was as it should be. "Seriously," she whispered, breaking that imaginary world into a million little pieces, "what is going on?"

Jack thought about it, his eyes finding the ceiling for a second before returning to his wife's face. "It's a long story, baby, a long story, but this thing that I'm wearing, it's making me better somehow."

May's arms fell to her side and she backed away. One hand covered her mouth that hung open in a shocked 'O.' "Oh my God, you look like—"

"Someone else you've met?" Neo asked, entering behind Jack.

May peeked over Jack's shoulder, noticing all of the Ascendants following Neo in. "There are more of you?"

"So many, Ms. Norman, so many," Mike said. "Now this has been lovely, but we're in a hurry."

"Why?" May asked. She looked from Jack to Mike to all of the Ascendants gathering in the building where she had been held prisoner for hours.

Jack reached for his wife's hand. As if knowing she did not want to feel it again, the Correlative slipped away from Jack's fingers so that the couple could touch skin to skin. Still, May's eyes grew wide with fear as she watched it climb up Jack's arm.

"How did this happen?" She reached for Jack but stopped short of touching him.

Jack tried to answer but could not find the words.

"It's a long story," Dawlish said.

May looked over her husband's broad shoulder to the strange Ascendants. "I don't understand."

"Seems to be an Earthling trait," Nash said. He was partly amused and partly agitated by these Earthlings and was having trouble articulating these contradictory emotions.

Jack took a deep breath. "Apparently there's an invasion coming and we have to get out of here, and—"

"How do you know that?" Charlie asked.

Bucky cried softly and Jenny tried to comfort him.

"Dear Lord," May said. "Does this all have to do what happened to me?"

"What happened to you?" Jack asked.

Neo ran a hand over her pink mohawk and released an exasperated sigh. "I understand everyone's confusion here but please, we need to hurry. There is a force of powerful invaders heading this way and we must be ready for them. Not to mention this tornado you all are speaking about."

"Tornado?"

"You can't hear the sirens in here," Mike said.

"I need answers before I do anything," Charlie said sternly.

"A journalist," Neo said. "I smell it all over you."

"If you want a fight, Pinky, I can do that, I will—"

"You will do nothing," Neo said without a hint of challenge in her voice.

"Don't try to intimidate me." Charlie shoved past Mike and Jack to point a finger in the Ascendant's face. "Now tell us what the hell is going on."

"They're saying that we're all in danger!" Jack said, pulling away from May to reach for Charlie. "Something bad is happening."

"You're dressed like them," Charlie returned. "Why should I believe you?"

"Please stop this," Mike said but the wind was out of his sails.

"We can't! We have to—"

"Stop it! All of you!" Jenny shouted from the bench. The hand resting on Bucky's trembled. She stood. Bucky whimpered and made sure he kept hold of her hand. "I have no idea what's going on, but this poor boy here," she squeezed Bucky's hand, "is confused and frightened and cannot take much more of this! Both of my sons and my husband are dead. I cannot take much more of this!"

Silence followed this like night after day. And like night, it stretched out before them as all present stared, shock and shame mingling in their expressions.

"She's right. We need to get moving," Neo finally said as she faced Charlie. "I will give you all of the answers you seek, journalist," she said. "But I will do so as we move. Is that acceptable?"

Charlie nodded, her arms crossed before her chest.

Neo faced Mike. "Give us the DieCyclo and the Helix Needle. We need to get those off world before the invasion begins. If a Draconian gets hold of either of those devices, I'd hate to imagine what they could do with them."

"I thought you'd never ask," Mike said. "Follow me, everyone."

The group followed Mike across the quickly dismantling base through the storm to another building guarded by a group of blues. Charlie kept pace with Neo but found she had no idea what to ask her.

Once they arrived where Mike had directed, he retrieved the DieCyclo and the Helix Needle from a *Spider-Man and His Amazing Friends* tin lock box and handed them to Neo. When he placed them in Neo's hand, the Ascendant thanked him.

"Interesting container," she added.

Mike shrugged. "We found it in the trailer park."

"Indeed." She turned toward Nash. "You know what to do," she said.

"Yes," Nash said. "But I'm not happy about it."

"I didn't expect you to be," Neo said.

Nash grumbled a Tholin curse as he took the Helix Needle and DieCyclo from Neo's hand. He placed them in a pouch on his belt.

"Now it is time to go," Neo said and turned toward May. "You, more than anyone, need to leave this planet before the Draconians arrive."

"Why? What is going on?"

"If they arrive and they know that you interacted with a Whitley and they have even the remotest idea of what she did to you . . ." Neo's words fell away like leaves. "It would be better if I simply show you," she said, "show all of you, looking at the group of Earthlings and Ascendants before her. Her Correlative fell from her face and the blue skinned woman with large pink eyes offered only an earnestness that the Earthlings could not deny. "Please," she said, "hold hands."

As they did as she asked, Neo's Correlative slid from her hand so that she could touch May, skin to skin.

A shock of information swam through them all and within seconds, Charlie was retching, Bucky was crying even louder, and Jenny had fallen to her knees. May only took a wobbly step back.

"Oh my God," she said.

"There is no God," Mike said.

"Take her Nash," Neo said. "Take all of them. The Draconians will be here soon."

Before Jack could stop them, before he could say goodbye, Nash nodded and shot strands of his Correlative from his fingers which wrapped tightly around May, Charlie, Jenny, and Bucky. Screams and cries of fear following him, he charged from the building and fired into the sky.

"Don't worry," Neo said, as if picking up on Jack's shock. "He will only hold them like this for a few thousand feet, then they will be on our ship."

Chapter 28
The Draconian Reign Over Oakview, NE

"WHERE DID HE TAKE my wife?" Jack demanded.Without any prompting, his Correlative grew around his face and the tips of his fingers morphed into sharp points.

Neo raised a hand to stop him. "Jack Norman," she said, "you have been drafted into the Ascendancy. If you take up arms against me, your commanding officer, you will be in violation of several inter-rim laws."

"I don't care about inter-rim laws," Jack yelled. Around him, the Correlative trembled with empathetic rage.

"Neo is your commanding officer, Earthling," Dawlish said softly. "You are an Ascendant. It would not be wise to do what you are thinking of doing."

"I am not a soldier!"

"I'm afraid you are, Jack Norman," Neo said. "And so much more now."

"I can't—"

"All this is great, but can someone please tell me what the plan is?" Mike shouted. "You didn't share any of that shit when we did that mind-link thing, did you? Or did I just miss it?" He was on the verge of hyperventilating and he knew it. Trying to suppress it, he took deep breaths.

Neo stepped up to Mike. "You are the leader of the Nowhere Agency in this sector, correct?" she asked.

Mike nodded. "C-Call me Local."

"Local," Neo said. "You now know everything I know about this situation. I have already done mind-links more times this evening than I normally do in a standard month." She placed her hands on his face and pulled him gently toward her. "I cannot do another. You will take the information I have given you and make yourself useful. Do I make myself clear?"

Mike fell away and blinked. "Where are my agents?" he asked.

"They stayed in the town where, I presume, they can be useful when the Draconians attack."

"Things are about to get very ugly here on Earth," Nelumbaum said.

"How can we protect Earth from a Draconian army?" Mike asked.

"Your agency should correspond with the correct Earth authorities to let them know that their airspace is about to get crowded."

"They'll want to drop bombs," Mike said. "Shoot missiles."

"Do not let them," Dawlish said.

"The Ascendancy will be here. Members of all four factions are arriving. The sky will be rife with us. If missiles fired indiscriminately injure Ascendant officers, it will be bad for Earth."

"Is that a threat?" Mike asked. But there was no bravado in the question, no courage.

"No, Local," Neo said. "It is no threat. I only mean that if missiles are fired that can injure Ascendant officers, your planet will be in dire straits."

"What? How?"

"Fewer Ascendants here means less protection."

"The people are going to go crazy with this," Mike said. "We were supposed to do this whole thing slowly. There was supposed to be a process."

"Things change, Earthling," Nelumbaum said. "But there is much cover here due to the storm. A clever organization such as yours should be able to find a way to make this work."

The three Ascendants, along with the newest drafted officer, Jack Norman, heard a voice coming through their Correlative connection and looked to the sky.

"The first wave is here," Neo said. "Get as many Earthlings underground as you can," Neo said. She looked at Jack. "Are you with us, Jack Norman?"

"I fought in a war once," he said quietly. "I told myself I'd never do it again." He took a deep breath. "It left . . . it left scars."

Neo's Correlative fell from her face and her large pink eyes latched onto Jack's. He could feel their power even through the protective shield of his own Correlative. "I know what you have gone through. I know you do not want this. I know you do not deserve this," she said. "The last war you fought in was an unjust mistake that stole your leg and bits of your sanity."

"How do you—"

She raised a finger and the Correlative fell from it. Her blue skin seemed to be glowing. "I can pick up on things when we link, Jack Norman."

"I don't think I can do it," Jack said.

"If you cannot, then Earth is doomed no matter what we do," Neo said.

"How?"

"We Psyerrigen can feel dominant emotional traits when we connect. Your bravery was easy to detect when we linked. It's easy to detect even now. If you are not brave enough to face this, then your people surely will not be brave enough to face their new reality."

"New reality?" he asked.

Neo opened her arms and looked to the sky. "When Draconians and Ascendants battle above the land, Earth will be forever changed, no matter who wins or how many know."

"Captain Neo," Nelumbaum said, "we do not have any more time."

"What will it be, Jack Norman?" Neo asked one more time as her Correlative once more covered her face.

Jack closed his eyes and felt the Correlative try to pump his mind with artificial courage but he rejected it. No. His mind struggled against the urge that seemed to be coming both from within and without. *No. I don't need it,* he thought and the urge subsided. He looked at Neo. "I'll do it."

She nodded. "Follow me."

And the four Ascendants shot upwards as tiny sparks of red emerged from the rumbling black clouds.

The Draconians had arrived.

***

Though the people of Oakview had suffered strange occurrences over the last few days, they were unprepared for this. Seeing a lizard man was one thing, watching fires burst forth across highways and in remote farmhouses was another. Even witnessing their hospital eat itself and lick the remains clean with tongues of flame, was beyond unexpected. But this was something else entirely.

The ships, like rocky eggs of speckled brown and green, were graceful in their descent. Tornado strength winds were nothing against the hovering crafts. They appeared in the sky like suddenly realized holograms that hummed a deep and quivering sound. If it hadn't been so shocking to see, the sound might have been soothing. But the troopers shooting forth from various ports on the gargantuan things were held aloft by rocket propelled packs that sent them spinning like nightmares any and everywhere were madness to behold. Some crashed into brick buildings while others found footing on larger trees or in the middle of streets. It was engineered chaos and it was terrifying in its utter disregard of what should be. As the clouds swirled and the tornado neared, the Draconians landed in a fury and began to destroy.

Mike contacted Mary and Eugene who were, along with Ben, doing their best to calm the citizenry of Oakview.

"Hide," he said, "underground."

As they spun into action, buildings fell.

Streets burned.

A science-fiction war most of them never imagined possible ran rampant through the town. Rising winds and falling rain only added to the pandemonium as Draconians marched and killed as heedless as Mother Nature.

Mike was one of the first to fall as a Draconian found itself near the impromptu Nowhere Agency base and zeroed in on the only living thing within earshot. It was Mike's voice, a whining, keening thing screaming in Russian into a large phone.

He had no hope.

It was over before he could even process that it had begun.

From the phone came a frightened reply. Though it was in a language the Draconian could not understand, the tone was clear. It gave him pleasure, and he bounded out of the bubble-like structure and toward the collection of trailers and what he knew were very frightened lifeforms not far away.

***

Eugene found himself running through Oakview with Mary at his side. She used her lasgun to shoot as many falling Draconians as she could, but the sheer number made it look as though the sky was falling along with the rain.

The humming from the egg-shaped ships grew louder and louder.

"Mary!" he called, knowing she still had a lasgun. "We have to hide!"

"No!" she said. "I'm staying out here to kill as many of these fuckers as I can!"

"Mary, you—" Someone screamed and a swiftly approaching Draconian changed his course, heading toward a small child crying in the street.

"Dammit," Eugene said to himself as he charged toward it.

About to reach the monster and distract it, hopefully long enough so the kid could get away, Eugene wondered if he should have been praying. He wondered if he should have been praying his whole life. He wondered if his last moments alive would be spent attacking a monster he had no hope of defeating. Mostly he wondered if he had wasted his life, if he had been honest with himself, he had been too angry most of the time, but especially since all of his friends had gone mad or died in those test flights.

"Can't worry about that now," he whispered as he jumped, regretting everything and nothing at the same time. His hat flew from his head.

But before he could make contact, the Draconian's own head exploded in a sea of jagged black skull and chunky, wet flesh. As its body fell, he saw Mary standing over the girl.

"When these lasgun things are on target, they're amazing," Mary said.

He grinned and the night went on, filled with every atrocity the Draconian mind could imagine. Eugene and Mary fought them all.

***

As the panic became more than he could control, Ben wandered through the streets of Oakview, doing his best to rescue, to help people hide in basements, and to generally do his job. When, dashing through alleys and side roads had brought him to his house, he was not shocked to see that, like most of his neighborhood, it was burning. His wife was dead. He knew it. It was just something he could feel.

He thanked a god he was certain was a lie that his own sons had long since moved away from Oakview but wondered if that would only prolong the inevitable. It was with an odd mix of resignation and hope that he heard the puppy.

It had been his neighbors' puppy. Their house was all but gone and that little barking monster had been a nuisance since day one. But tonight, as the world crumbled and the sky rained alien lizard things, the puppy didn't bark. Instead, it yelped.

Ben knew what he had to do.

"Hey!" he called out at the Draconian that he could tell was teasing the poor animal. "Hey!" he repeated himself as the Draconian swiped at the shivering, yelping white dog.

It hadn't heard him. How could it have with the incessant humming booming forth from those damn egg ships and the howling wind and pounding rain? He pulled his pistol and shot.

That got then monster's attention.

The Draconian turned slowly and faced Ben.

"Why don't you pick on someone your own size?" Ben asked, knowing there was no one around who fit that description.

The Draconian's tongue fell from his mouth and he stepped toward Ben, growling something in a guttural language made of fear.

Ben shot again, thinking of his wife, thinking of his secretary, thinking of his officers who were scattered across the town, some dead, some dying. Mostly though, he thought of his boys.

He shot again.

The Draconian laughed.

The dog barked.

"What the?" He saw the puppy, no longer yelping, but somehow charged with bravery, shoot between the Draconian's disturbing digitigrade legs and toward him. The Draconian almost tripped as the dog zoomed around its feet.

"Dog! Get out of here!" Ben yelled.

The dog barked and headed toward him, running past in a speedy fury. Ben looked from it to the Draconian and decided to follow. Dogs, he thought, could probably hide with the best of them.

He watched the dog duck into a crumbled house of shattered windows and broken walls that he knew was once the home of some town government employee he had never really liked. Briefly he wondered what had happened to him. But he had no time to dwell on it, for a moment later, the Draconian reached out with claws like blades and cut through his shirt.

Batting at it and falling into the open door on the house, he heard the Draconian say something else and felt the ground shake below him.

Blackness took him and he felt around, unsure of what had happened. Before he had time to think though, he felt the puppy's tongue on his cheek. He touched its shaking head.

"What happened?" he asked.

His only answer was a muffled cry from above and what sounded like a wet explosion. He could not tell, buried as he was in the remains of a fallen home, but the Ascendancy had finally arrived in full force.

***

They flew through the night sky and ran over the burned and broken ground with single minded determination. Communicating through a Correlative connection, the Ascendants moved like water through the fire of Draconians. Jack, in the mix, remembering his time spent in the Vietnamese jungle, found that he was oddly in his element. When he swung the CorreAxe that had once been The Lonely One's, he commanded fear as much as he did the weapon. Though flight was not his strong suit, the Correlative took over for him as he soared through the sky and landed on burning ground, to battle wave after wave of

Draconian. His presence with the ax, in fact, was the first hole in the Draconian Reign's determined armor. For if he possessed it, then The Lonely One had lost it. If The Lonely One had lost it, then he was surely no more.

The second hole was ripped open when Draconian Diaspora ships appeared in the sky. The Draconians who emerged from their spacecraft, which had the same egg shape as the Reign's, were a bit more bedraggled, a bit more broken. But the Draconian who emerged from it fought with something their Reign counterparts could not. They fought with pride in who they were. They fought to rid themselves of the stain of the Draconian Reign.

The third and final hole for the Draconian Reign appeared when their numbers shone clearly as substantially smaller than that of their enemy's. Their arrogance and certainty in numbers, it seemed, had led to their ultimate downfall.

Together, the Ascendancy and the Diaspora forces were able to defeat the attacking army of Draconians.

And the second Draconian Reign ended before it had even begun in the skies above a small town in Nebraska, in that same town's streets, and all over the surrounding area.

The final battle was fought on a sprawling estate many miles to the north of Oakview. There were only two civilian casualties there, a man named Barry Breathwite and another named Ernest Clement.

When the dust settled on the battle, when the storm had passed, when all the fires had been put out, and the remaining Reign troopers captured, and all of the trapped Earthlings had been rescued, a bright and hopeful dawn shone over the destruction. Ascendant officers made their way through the rubble. Diaspora representatives spoke with them.

Those Earthlings who had survived the storm and the battle hid.

***

REBORN: HOW OAKVIEW NEBRASKA TURNED TRAGEDY INTO TRIUMPH

Nine months after a devastating storm, one small town is coming back Nebraska Strong.

By Charlie McKinstrey, Editor-in-Chief

Snow falls softly on the partially rebuilt town of Oakview, Nebraska. It is quiet, late, and peaceful in a way that only towns considered to be located "in the middle of nowhere" can be peaceful. There are no drunk drivers making their way through the slippery streets. The four police officers under the direction of the town's newest chief, Vietnam War Veteran Jackson Norman, are either sleeping in their warm beds, building their children's Christmas presents in quiet living rooms, or playing solitaire in a cruiser behind a brand new town sign on the northern city limits. On the sign, below the town's name and population, which was carved into the wood in an elegant approximation of an Old English font, there is a quote, "Home of the 1981 Great Spring Supercell."

Though Oakview lost a number of citizens when the supercell hit on March 25, including former "Oakview Courier" editor-in-chief Ernest Clement and several reporters, those who survived stayed and rebuilt. Chief Norman, along with his wife, May are among those who stayed. After all of the media coverage of the aftermath of the supercell, many in the wider world wondered why the survivors decided to stick around. It was, after all, the worst natural disaster the state of Nebraska had ever seen.

"I'm not sure why we stayed, really," Chief Norman said. "Other than the fact that this is our home, you know?"

His wife, who is thirty-eight weeks pregnant at the time of this interview, was equally enigmatic in her reasons.

"We just couldn't leave," May Norman said. "We just couldn't."

With additions that include a new hospital and memorial garden for those lost during the storm, a shining new Main Street complete with a series of buildings that might have been plucked from Andy Griffith's Mayberry, North Carolina, it does seem cozy in the new and improved Oakview. Former Mayor Greyson Rose, who died when City hall collapsed during the supercell had a plan in place to turn Oakview into a tourist attraction. Its inaugural activity was the Meteor Festival that was supposed to kick off a series of summer events. Unfortunately, due to the supercell, that never truly coalesced. However, Mayor Rose's tourist funds were shifted to a rebuilding account and anonymous donors added to it again and again and again. Somehow, the money came pouring in and the makeshift city council that has been in place for the nine months since the supercell used it to rebuild.

Unknowingly, they built an attraction.

"People love a good comeback story I guess," said lifelong Oakview resident Dora Langstrom. Formerly of the Oakview Police Department, Dora retired after the supercell and moved in with former Chief of Police Ben Wilton. "He wanted to leave but his boys insisted he stay and rebuild. I'm glad they did. I'm glad we did."

The Normans, Langstrom, and Wilton are only four of the over 5,000 citizens (of what used to be 10,000) who stayed and rebuilt. Now, something of a growing tourist attraction, Oakview, Neb. is ready to become a Midwestern hot spot in the summer of 1982. Though it has not lost any of its small-town flair. Along with a state-of-the-art hospital where Five Mile Field and Oakview Lanes used to be, there are cornfields bordering city limits, empty now, waiting for the spring. There is the aforementioned quaint Main Street. The football field outside of the newly built high school is state of the art and ready and waiting for next season's Friday Night Lights (this season all Oakview children were bussed to surrounding towns for the education). Right now, though, as the snow falls and each of the town's five churches ring their Christmas bells, Oakview takes a much deserved rest.

Throughout the town that appears to be steadily sinking beneath a slow barrage of snow, there are partially constructed buildings sprinkled between ones that survived the supercell with more than their fair share of bumps and bruises. And though it holds a somber appearance, the giant evergreen in front of the newly reconstructed city hall is strung with simple sparkling white lights and topped with a glowing angel, offering comfort to all who pass.

Oakview is a town that has been through hell and not only survived but thrived. Most citizens who stayed and worked to right the wrongs of the worst natural disaster to hit this state, are ready for the future and hopeful that more people will find their way to their new home.

Or, as Ben Wilton put it, "This is Oakview, Neb. and we're happy to have ya."

Chapter 29
Birth

"I WILL BE DAMNED, Charlie," Jack said, looking up from the latest issue of *Oakview Courier.* "This is amazing."

"Thank you," Charlie said before taking a sip of coffee. "It's not the most journalistically sound thing I've ever written but it's my first story as official EiC." She shrugged. "How are you doing?"

Jack took a moment to answer her. "I'm okay," he finally said.

Over the last nine months his life had changed in more ways than he could have imagined. There had been the ordinary changes that came with being an ordinary man in an ordinary town. His wife had grown their baby inside her belly. He had found a new job. Together, they had found a new home, and made new friends while mourning the loss of old ones.

But that was where anything ordinary about the last nine months had ended. For he had also grown accustomed to living with a strange, tickling voice in the back of his head. He had grown accustomed to the Correlative's body encasing his own and offering him a strange approximation of a leg where the one he had lost used to be. He had helped rebuild a town that had been nearly destroyed by literal alien invaders, though, he had also learned, that was a loaded term. Citizens in the UCA preferred "invasive lifeform." He had been to another planet, spoken with lifeforms from all over the cosmos. On a cosmic level, he had helped change laws that he hadn't even known existed. Side by side with his wife, he had done things the greatest science fiction writers in history had only dreamed about.

"A little nervous, I imagine," Charlie said softly.

"About May?" Jack asked, surprise in his voice.

"Of course about May," Charlie laughed.

She admired this man and his wife. She admired the way they had taken everything in stride, the way they had climbed from the rubble of this town, of what had happened to them, and stood atop the destruction, looking around—it seemed to her anyway—to find ways to fix it. The shock appeared secondary to the Normans. While Ben, Jenny, Bucky and Charlie herself, the only other four residents of Oakview and the surrounding areas who had not had their minds wiped of any memories of aliens, had struggled with the revelation that everything they knew was so far from everything there was to know, the Normans had embraced it. She wondered if it had been Jack's time in Vietnam that had helped them. Combine that with May's almost profound calm, and you had a couple, she thought, that could do anything as long as they were together.

Yes, she was a little jealous. But who wouldn't be?

"I'm not worried about May," Jack said, staring out the window in his office. It looked out over the half constructed Oakview Main Street. Ben's snowplow had been by three times now. Even though he was retired, even though he complained about the cold, even though he swore he was going to move to Florida, the man couldn't leave. He couldn't even retire really. No longer the police chief, but still working for the city, Ben seemed to love fixing things. Maybe it was because he missed his wife. Jack thought he might get like that if May died. Though, he didn't think he'd be able to find a woman like Dora to help him get by or a dog like that on he found the night of the invasion, that dog that Jack thought hadn't left Ben's side since.

"You're not worried about May?" Charlie's question pulled him from his thoughts.

"I'm worried about what Mary and Eugene are digging out of that weird lab below Broyles' place."

"Yeah well," Charlie shrugged, "I'm worried about that too. But May is more pressing."

Jack swiveled his chair so that he faced Charlie once again. "She's literally been checked over by some of the best doctors in the universe—"

"Cosmos," Charlie corrected.

Jack rolled his eyes. "Cosmos."

"But she's due today, isn't she?"

"As if you didn't know," Jack said.

"It's kind of funny, this kid being born on Christmas Day, isn't it?"

"Are we going to have this discussion again?" Jack replied playfully. "Shouldn't you be up in Omaha with your own family?"

"Family," Charlie released a bitter laugh. Ernest had been her family. Since she had found his journals in his office days after everything had gone down with the Draconians, she had come to realize that more than ever. In many ways, Ernest had known what it was like to be her. Hell, even Barry had. Her parents had never even tried to know her, who she truly was. They were none too fond of her lifestyle "choices," let alone her career. She knew now that was partly why she had looked up to her EiC so much. She also knew it was partly why her relationship with her publisher had been so strained.

Even though she had been connected to both of them, she hadn't known who they truly were and how they dealt with that. Now, after they had both died, she did know. Her body betrayed the emotions that these thoughts brought with them.

"Sorry," Jack said, noticing Charlie squirm, suppressing tears. "I didn't mean—"

"It's okay. I've never really told you about them."

"Are they not cool with your . . . um . . ."

"Sexuality Jack—don't be a prude—and no, they're not cool with that. But they're also not cool with my line of work."

"They don't like reporters?" Jack asked, shocked. "What are they, famous?"

"No," she said, smiling, "they're idiots who think reporting is just gossip." If they only knew that she was doing the exact opposite of what a reporter was supposed to be doing when it came to Oakview, the Draconians, the UCA, and everything, maybe they would've been proud of her. It stung to keep this secret from the world at large. But she understood. The SPJ Code of Ethics clearly stated, "Balance the public's need for information against potential harm or discomfort." That's what she was doing by keeping this secret. At least for now.

"Fair enough," Jack said, tapping his knuckles softly on the desk between them. "You're welcome at the Norman house for Christmas Dinner tonight. I invited Ben, but he'll probably stay home. He said something about his boys coming into town, but who knows if that's true. Neo will be there to try to convince me Friend and I should become full time soldiers in the Ascendancy."

"Friend?"

He shrugged. "I named him."

"Who?"

"My Correlative!"

Charlie blinked. "You know there is only one recorded case of an Ascendant naming their—"

"Jenny and Bucky are coming too," Jack said over her.

"All the way from Annam?" Charlie returned, taking the hint.

"They want to see the memorial garden again. I think Bucky will really like Linc's statue in particular."

"How is Jenny?" Charlie said, remembering the quiet calm woman who had lost everything before everyone else in this town had.

Jack shrugged. "She has good days and bad days. Bucky is good for her."

Charlie smiled. "I can't believe you convinced the Nowhere Agency to pay for a life-size statue of Linc and his damn golf cart."

"That was all Mary," Jack said. "I'm pretty sure he saved her life."

"Mary and Eugene." She rolled her eyes.

"Cut them some slack, Charlie. It was a rough few days for everyone."

"Yeah well," she said dismissively. "I wish we could tell everyone."

"Soon enough. The UCA and the Nowhere Agency outdid itself by keeping all of this quiet.

Charlie shook her head. "It just seems so wrong, especially since Ock and Aurora are part of why this is so secret."

"Come on Charlie, it's more than that. You've been to Annam. You've seen the scope of this. Our leaders can't handle this shit. Most people can't. Not yet."

"But sooner now, thanks to all of this."

"I don't know. I think—"

The phone on Jack's desk rang.

He yanked the receiver from its cradle. "May?" he said quickly.

***

The Sims Family Memorial Hospital stood on a wide expanse on the southern edge of Oakview that had once been known as Five Mile Field. Though it seemed nothing more than an afterthought of concrete tucked away in a field, it was growing larger by the day and the scaffolding and iron bones of medical promise sprawled that concrete. In the slowly falling snow, it almost looked like a work of art itself.

Sirens blaring, Jack's official police vehicle, a green Mitsubishi Montero with wood paneling that Ben gave him hell about regularly, screeched to a halt in front of the emergency room pull up. He jumped out, all of his cool, calm demeanor little more than the memory of a dream. Eyes wide and muscles tight, he ran into the hospital and screamed at the first nurse he saw, a woman with white hair and a tight face.

"Mr. Norman," she said. "I remember you."

"I don't—wait," he realized. "I'm sorry," he said quickly. "That was a strange night for me."

"I'm just happy you survived," she said. "You know, the only reason I did was because I was so angry at you that I stepped out to have a cigarette in my car and—"

"That's nice!" he interrupted. "I'm here about my wife though!"

"Your wife?"

"She's giving birth!" he screamed.

The nurse harrumphed and typed away at her computer, soft eyes going hard. "Third floor," she said without looking back at him. "Take the elevator."

"You know, I had to park that beast you drive," Charlie said, coming into the hospital and shaking off the cold.

"Never mind that now," Jack said and took her hand. "Come on."

He led her to the elevator where he hit the "3" button with a manic intensity Charlie had never seen in him. She almost laughed as the door shut and Jack tapped it with agitated fingers until it slid open a few moments later and he sprung out like a jack rabbit.

Then she heard the screaming.

It was definitely May and she was definitely in pain. Following Jack's lead, Charlie ran. Their footfalls echoed through the mostly empty floor until they came to a waiting room where Ock stood alone, staring at a television hanging from the wall. The final scene of *It's a Wonderful Life* played on its screen

"What the hell are you doing here?" Charlie asked.

Ock faced them, eyes filled with tears. "I'm sorry," he said in a weak approximation of English. "I just . . . er . . . uh . . ."

"You just what?"

"This story," he motioned toward the television, "it is . . . er . . . uh . . . beautiful, is it not?"

"Answer the question." Charlie crossed her arms before her chest. "Why are you here?"

Ock cleared his throat and wiped his eyes. "I have . . . just . . . er . . . uh . . . just as much a right . . . to . . . er . . . be here as you. It is . . . er . . . . uh . . . a legal requirement from the Cosmic Tribunal itself!"

"You do not have the same rights as him!" Charlie shouted, pointing a thumb at Jack. "How were you even able to get in? This is ridiculous! I'm contacting the Ascendancy now!"

"This is all . . . above board . . . er . . . um . . . I assure you. I . . . have . . . . er . . . a . . . holographic display to make . . . make me look Earthling to . . . others. It is part of my . . . er . . . agreement with the—"

"You can't be serious!" Charlie huffed. "This is what you've been doing these last nine months keeping your client's trial from the masses? Waiting for the birth! Aurora Vega tried to commit genocide against Earthlings, you have no right to be here representing her! None!"

"It . . . er . . . was part of the . . . er . . . agreement after . . . the Draconians—"

"Fuck your agreement! Your client is a monster! She invaded this planet, forced a Helix Needle on May! You can't—"

"That is . . . precisely why I . . . er . . . uh . . . can! I have to . . . er . . . um . . . see what happens with the . . . birth." His head swiveled as his eyes spun with indignation. "I'm . . . er . . . just happy Annam Standard . . . is . . . uh . . . almost identical to Earth time . . . or . . . I might have missed this. The coincidence is . . . um . . . shocking."

"You don't have to be here while it is actually fucking happening!" Charlie bellowed now, standing as tall as she could and approaching the Vastaloose with anger etched across her face and body. In her puffy winter coat, she almost looked comical, but neither 0ck nor Jack were laughing.

"Stop!" Jack said. "It's fine. Neither of you can come in the room though," he added, leaving them alone to head toward the sound of his screaming wife.

As he approached, he was perplexed at how much of a maze this small place was and how he kept feeling like he was lost only to be found only to be lost again. All the while, the sound of his wife's screams of pain led him on and, though they grew quieter, he felt them on a level he couldn't quite understand.

Thanks Friend, he thought as he came to a door behind which he knew was May. Now arrived, there was no sound.

He opened the door and saw her lying in bed holding a baby with thick black hair and the bluest eyes he had ever seen.

"This is Nat," May said quietly, "Nat Norman."

The doctor and nurses congratulated Jack and May and left the room, telling them that they would be back momentarily.

"Would you like to meet your son?" May asked.

Jack nodded and reached out for Nat. As he did so, May leaned away and reached for the purse beside her bed. "Put this in his hand," she said, handing the DieCyclo to Jack.

"I don't—" Jack began.

"We've talked about this, Jack."

He sighed and did as asked.

The DieCyclo looked huge in Nat's tiny hand. Before May or Jack had time to process that, it came to life, a bright light emerging from all of the dots on its many sides. When the light faded, a blue hued holographic man with platinum eyes stood before the three of them. He was clad in what both May and Jack now knew to be traditional Essan garb: a flowing white jacket and loose-fitting pants, no shoes.

"Hello," he said with a voice that sounded somehow liquid and mechanical, "my name is DC and we have much to discuss about your first born."

Acknowledgements

THIS BOOK WOULD NOT exist without the help of many. Always first amongst these great folk is my wife, Kim, who understands and tolerates my manic bouts of writing. Following her, of course, are my children, Quintin and Addisyn, who inspire and amaze me on the daily. But these ethereal supports are only part of the journey. To create art, one must also consult other artists. For that, I seek out those I know and trust whose work I find impeccable. Lou Wilham and Elle Beaumont and everyone at Midnight Tide Publishing come first. They have my eternal thanks for taking a chance on a weird little horror/sci-fi/comic book inspired epic. My great friend and colleague Julie Rowse deserves more praise than I have the words to give, mostly because I am speechless when thinking of her skill. With a sensible eye and a serious candor, she provides an enviable stoicism to her edits that only serve to make any writing she studies better. Naturally, my sister, Kitty Bardot, always has something to say to improve my work. Her insights are invaluable. I also must thank my editor, Lindsay Shane Oliver. Her words of wisdom, her questions, and her stealthy process are the best in the business. If you're looking for an editor, seek her out. You will not be sorry. For the amazing design and formatting skills, I offer this shout out to Vanae Uteros. There are many more though. There is Dottie Bossman, whose conversational skills are only matched by her writing skills.

There are Tim Benson and Carl Smith, my constant collaborators. There is Jeremy Morong, who read through one of the earliest drafts of this novel and helped me mold it into what you just read. There is Bryce Wetzler, whose photo of me taken in the fall of 2019 is my go-to author shot and probably will be until I've gone completely gray. There is ELA teacher Caleb Narva, who provided my first "early praise" quote. It is a long list and I am sure there are many more I missed, but above them all, I must acknowledge Jerry Siegel, Joe Shuster, Stan Lee, Jack Kirby, Max and William Gaines, Al Feldstein, Todd McFarlane, David Michelinie, Roy Thomas, Mike Zeck, Bill Finger, Gil Kane, Martin Nodell, John Broome, Ursula K. Le Guin, Octavia Butler, Margaret Atwood, Whitely Strieber, Stephen King, Gary Gygax, Dave Arneson, John Carpenter, George Lucas, Dave Filoni, and Chris Carter (and certainly a few more I'm forgetting). Their work inspires.

And finally and most importantly, you, Dear Reader.

Always.

About the author

AE Stueve teaches writing, journalism, photography, filmmaking, and design at Bellevue West High and the University of Nebraska at Omaha. His novels, short stories, poems, journalism, and essays can be found online, on podcasts, and in print. To learn more about him, check out https://linktr.ee/stueveae or follow him on various socials @aestueve.

Also by the Author

The ABCs of Dinkology
The ABCs of Dinkology: Life
The ABCs of Dinkology: Time In-Between
The ABCs of Dinkology: Death
Former
Deicide

More MTP Novels